Check it out!

FIONA ZIPPAN ★ DOUG ATKINSON

Check it out!

The Essential, Indispensable
GUIDE TO
CHILDREN'S VIDEO

Scholastic Canada Ltd.

Note to Teachers: The videos listed in this book are designated for home viewing. Please be aware that the showing of videos in classrooms is considered "public performance" under section 42(2) of the Canadian *Copyright Act*. If you wish to show videos in the classroom, you should contact your school board to determine whether a license has been or can be granted. Further information can be obtained from the Film and Video Security Office of the Canadian Motion Picture Distributors Association at 1-800-363-9166.

Cartoons by Ted Michener
Cover design by Yüksel Hassan, Terence Kanhai
Desktop publishing by Andrea Casault

Canadian Cataloguing in Publication data

Zippan, Fiona
 Check it out! : the essential, indispensable
guide to children's video

ISBN 0-590-74577-8

1. Children's films - Reviews. 2. Video
recordings - Reviews. I. Atkinson, Doug.
II. Title.

PN1992.945.Z45 1993   791.43'75   C93-093320-6

6 5 4 3 2 1   Printed in Canada   3 4 5 6 /9

Acknowledgements

A number of people's efforts helped to make this book possible. First and foremost, we need to recognize the dedication and commitment of Penny Fine, who nurtured the project to publication. Her heartfelt love for the project and her contribution to the initial stages of the text provided us with the means to synthesize our ideas. To her, we are indebted.

Thanks especially to Denise Bolton, Chris Darroch and Natasha Zippan for their efforts beyond the call of duty in checking the reviews and lists, which were enriched by their knowledge and expertise. And to the rest of the dedicated staff of The Original Kids Video Store who have been with us since the beginning and who "held the fort" while we spent months with the VCR and the computer — Elsa Denzey, Nancy and Tanya Varley and Mike Darroch.

Thanks to Stan Zippan whose computer expertise proved invaluable.

To David Collard and Lisa Bodnarchuk of Fieldview Telepictures Ltd., for their contribution to the glossary.

To Donald J. Flowers, Vice Chairman of the Ontario Film Review Board, for his help with the chapter on ratings and for the information provided.

To all the studios and reps for their co-operation in providing material.

To Denise Cherrington for believing in us, and Danielle for starting it all.

And to Don Sedgwick, designer Andrea Casault, and our miraculous editors Allison Gertridge and Diane Kerner at Scholastic Canada for their encouragement, positivity, and patience on this mammoth project.

And finally, to the parents, librarians and teachers whose loyal support over the years made this book possible.

Table of Contents

Chapter 1

ABOUT THIS BOOK

In an ideal world, parents would be able to prescreen every film their child was about to see. But with films running anywhere between half an hour and two hours, it's simply impossible; no one has the time to do it. Except us. We're professional movie watchers — that's all we do. And with this book we are, effectively, going to enable you to watch a two hour movie in about one minute. That said, it bears mentioning that in many cases we give away the ending — *if* we feel that the ending is a source of concern. (We've heard of parents renting a film like *Old Yeller*, because they heard it was "a nice dog story," to cheer up a child who has lost a pet.)

Understand that, although we ourselves are oriented towards presenting the finest in children's visual entertainment, this is *not* exclusively a book of recommended films. We have included summaries of certain popular movies which children commonly see (or commonly ask to see), which may contain violence, coarse language and/or sexual situations. In these (and, ideally, in all) cases we believe that the onus is on the parent or supervising adult to use discretion when renting. And we have tried to provide the information necessary for making those choices in this book.

How it all began

In 1988 we started a video store specifically for children. The store was based on a perceived need — a need which was brought to our attention by a dramatic incident in our own lives.

One day, Fiona picked up her ten-year-old daughter Danielle from school. The child's face was deathly white and she was obviously distracted. Concerned by the change in her otherwise cheerful child, Fiona asked what was wrong and after some prodding the answer came, "I'm trying to get those awful pictures out of my head."

The awful pictures, it turned out, were from the horror movie she'd seen at school. During a teachers' strike, one of the interim guardians, in response to the children's request for a "scary movie," had gone to the local video store and rented one. It turned out that the "scary movie" was a horror movie which included a repeated scene of a father drowning his child — and upon further investigation it was revealed that other children in the class were equally or more traumatized by what they had seen.

Fiona decided then and there that something had to be done to help adults select movies for children. The result was a store that provided not only access to quality children's videos, but also complete information about those videos.

What this book doesn't include

There is such a vast number of videos being produced for children today that it's impractical to include them all, in detail or otherwise. To this end we have purposely omitted a number of categories.

We have left out the classic cartoons, which have retained their popularity with today's children, but which are already more or less familiar to parents. These include cartoons like Warner Brothers favourites *Bugs Bunny* and *Daffy Duck*, and others such as *Casper the Ghost, Beany and Cecil, Asterix* and *Lucky Luke, The Flintstones* and so on.

We have not given space to the recycled television

shows of the '50s and '60s such as *The Mickey Mouse Club*, Disney's *Zorro*, *Tarzan*, *Lassie*, *Rin Tin Tin*, *The Three Stooges*, *I Love Lucy*, etc. Although they may be enjoyable for children, they are, for the most part, in black and white and have a style and a tempo which are very different from current creations.

We have not included videos known as teacher's aids in this book as we are mainly concerned with video product which is easily available to the home viewer.

We have purposely omitted almost all PG films that we feel have few redeeming features, in that the incidents of violence, sexual suggestion or representation, or derogatory representations of women and minorities negate any features which might otherwise appeal to children and young people. (Though, again, we have included a few which have had such a high profile that many young children expect to see them.)

We have also omitted many PG films with adult storylines, because many PG films are not necessarily made with children in mind.

We have included very few AA-rated films, as these represent a conflict between what is viable and useful for children and what begins to touch on strictly adult themes such as serious illness, realistic human evil and sexual awakening.

And omitted for obvious reasons are R-rated films. (At least, the reasons are obvious to us!)

Finally, just because an F or PG film isn't included doesn't necessarily mean that it's not a decent children's film. We just didn't have space for everything in this edition — we'll catch the others the next time around.

What this book does include

In the chapters that follow, we've divided the book into the following sections:

- Ages up to 3
- Ages 3 to 6 (pre-K to grade 1)
- Ages 6 to 10 (grade 1 to grade 5)
- Ages 10 to 13 (grade 5 to grade 8)

Each chapter begins with some practical pointers on characteristics of and problems associated with each age group. Summaries of individual videos and series of videos suitable for children within that age category follow.

We tend to err on the conservative side, usually placing a title in a higher age category if there is any doubt about its suitability. This is not to say, however, that all films in the 3 to 6 category, for instance, are unsuitable for children renting from the up to 3 category, or that some films in the 3 to 6 category won't delight your twelve-year-old. There are grey areas, and you will have to use your own discretion based on our reviews to make the final decision about any one film's suitablity.

You will also find the reviews in this book helpful when you are renting for a number of children, all of them of different ages and with different interests. You should be able to find a number of films that fit the bill for the group. The lists in chapter 10 are a good place to start.

How to use our system

Every video summary consists of a brief story synopsis which usually describes events in chronological order. This is followed by brief descriptions of potential points of concern and of the strengths of the film. Our concerns (if any) are listed in two categories: **STOP** and **CAUTION**.

STOP denotes a serious consideration and is indicated not only by a **STOP** description, but also by an **✗** character beside the title. **CAUTION** denotes a less serious consideration.

Strengths are described in our **GO** section and include such things as awards information, notable performances and sometimes even the comments of children who frequent our store.

Following the review you may also notice one or more of the following information bullets:

● — out-of-print
■ — based on a book
▲ — also available in French

A typical review might go as follows:

The title

✗BABAR: THE MOVIE

The studio that distributes the video

The year the film or video was made

The director of the film or video

The actors appearing or providing voices:

Synopsis

Astral
1989
77 minutes
Directed by: Alan Bunce
Starring the voices of:
  Elizabeth Hanna, Gavin McGrath,
  Gordon Pinsett, Sarah Polley

When the film opens, a mature King Babar is telling his children a bedtime story. In the story, a young Babar receives word from Celeste that the rhinos are attacking villages and snatching elephants. Impatient with the bureaucracy involved in organizing an army, Babar and Celeste set out alone. They learn that the rhinos are forcing the kidnapped elephants to labour on a colossal building project and after a couple of daring escapes, Babar and Celeste participate in a final confrontation with the rhino horde.

✗**STOP:** A rhino raiding party attacks an elephant village, torching the houses and carrying the adult elephants away. Celeste's mother is bound, painfully, and Celeste is thrown into a well.

CAUTION: This is a film about war and viewers can expect to see a great deal of violence.

GO: The film is entertaining, but because of the violence it may frighten children.

▲

note: also available in French.

STOP

CAUTION

GO

Got it? Now, on with the show...

Chapter 2

SELECTING A VIDEO FOR YOUR CHILD

Where are all the children's videos?

Even in large cities, with a video store seemingly on every corner, you may have trouble locating a good source of children's videos. Even stores with sizeable children's sections are organized in such a way that making the right choice is often very difficult. The situation is similar in small towns. But you do have options.

More and more libraries are adding video departments. If your library doesn't have a children's video section, tell the librarian that you would be interested in one, especially one with high quality videos. Librarians are interested in the needs of children, and they have better access to quality children's product than most retail stores.

Another alternative would be to ask your retailer for more or better children's material. A customer request carries a lot of weight because video retailers know that for every customer that asks for a title, there are at least ten others who will also be interested.

Be specific. Don't just ask your retailer or librarian to get better children's titles (their definition of better may differ significantly from yours); name the titles you're interested in and try to provide the name of the studio as well.

You may also consider ordering videos through the mail or through TV offers and video clubs.

Narrowing down the options

Ask yourself questions

Ask yourself: Who is this film for? The answer may seem obvious, but it can radically affect your choice. Is the film for the children to watch by themselves or will you be watching it with them?

- If the children are going to be by themselves, what is the age range of the viewers?
- Are there both boys and girls? Are there more girls than boys, or vice versa?
- Is the oldest a boy or girl? (This will make a big difference in the way the film is received.)
- Is the film intended for everyone to watch together or will it be primarily for the adults in the room, with the children present?

If you can think ahead of time about questions like these, they will help both you and your video retailer to zero in on the perfect movie.

Ask your video dealer questions

The question that most perplexes video dealers is: Is this a good movie? What could "good" possibly mean? By asking vague questions like this you are likely to end up with a film that you and your child are unhappy with. The moral: ask specific questions and provide the dealer with as much information about your child's interests as possible. You would probably do well to share the following information (even if it seems obvious):

- your child's age and sex
- your child's interests (animals, hobbies, etc.)
- your child's preferred genres (adventure, mystery, how-to, etc.)
- your requirements regarding coarse language, violence, mature content, etc.

preference, and say you're looking for something like them.

Then, after you have chosen a title, take your selection to the clerk and ask even more questions — questions like:

- ❿ Are there any really scary scenes in this movie?
- ❿ Do any of the characters die?
- ❿ Is this film violent? How?

Ask about anything that you think might upset your child or that might not meet with your standards.

Never take the description on the box as indicative of content. It's best to ask someone who has seen the film about their impression of it. It's best if this is soneone you know well, whose standards and opinions are familiar to you, but even the stranger standing next to you can be of help.

Ask your friends questions

Compile a list of your family's Top Ten favourite films, and have a friend's family do the same thing. Then exchange the lists. Even if you only find one new title to try, the exercise will have been worth it.

You might want to do the same thing with a Caution list as well, naming films you wished you hadn't seen — whether on video or in the theatre — and describing exactly why it was that you and your family were disappointed.

Alternative titles

Invariably it happens: you walk into the video store, having done all of your homework, and not one title on your list is available. Then it's time for some lateral thinking. Here are some alternatives you might want to consider.

Many children and teens are truly interested in the art of film-making. And aside from being an excellent choice when nothing else can be found, a "Making-of" film video can:

- ▶ Cure the "seen-it" syndrome by encouraging viewers to re-screen the original film.
- ▶ Satisfy a little one's curiosity about an unsuitable film. (One child we know believed he had seen a whole feature film after seeing an in-depth video describing how that feature was made.)
- ▶ Demystify — "that's not a real monster, it's just a clever combination of great animation and inventive special effects."
- ▶ Unglamourize, removing the unhealthy fixation some children develop with negative screen characters (eg. thinking "Freddy" from *Nightmare on Elm Street* is "cool.")
- ▶ Show children that a variety of fascinating skills are required to make films; this may interest them in new fields of study.

Documentaries

Be very careful when renting or buying documentaries for a child, as many contain potentially disturbing scenes. For instance, friendly looking videos about dolphins, pandas or rhinos (particularly those that deal with the destruction or preservation of a species) may contain some traumatizing footage.

That said, there are all kinds of documentaries that *are* suitable for young viewers. Begin your search by looking for one that is somehow connected to your child's hobbies or interests. (See our helpful lists for ideas.)

Biographies

Some children are very interested in the lives of famous people, and for them a biography or a film based on a real event may be just the thing. Check the ratings before you rent, though, as some real-life stories are hard to take.

Musicals

If your child has an interest in singing, dancing or musical theatre there are a number of great feature film videos on the market. (See chapter 10 for some ideas.) There are also compilation tapes of old musicals (eg. *That's Entertainment*) which are sometimes more engaging for children than a musical with a story running through it.

How-to

For the child who is interested in doing and making things, there are countless how-to videos on such topics as: art, magic, dance, animal care, cooking, horseback riding, hockey and even moving house!

Black-and-white movies

How about trying classic black-and-white movies? The children may groan at first, but they'll probably settle down and watch eventually, especially if you make a family event out of watching it, to add to the enthusism. Try making popcorn or inviting guests. Or try a colourized version of an old classic.

Remakes of classics

Don't confuse remakes of classics with movies that are restored, re-released or re-mastered. Remakes are updated versions, often set in the present day, that may include intense action scenes or explicit sexual situations that did not appear in the original.

After watching thousands of films, we've noticed that certain "destructive elements" occur over and over. The "constructive elements" we have listed below are things we look for in movies to counter-balance any destructive elements which appear. Note that all of these things commonly appear in PG-rated films!

Destructive elements

▶ There is gratuitous (unnecessary) violence.
▶ There is violent aggression (including destruction of possessions or property).
▶ Violence is used in a ritual or quasi-religious context.
▶ Brutalization of a weaker party by a stronger party is shown.
▶ Blood-letting (including graphic depiction of wounds) is shown.
▶ There are graphic depictions of death (eyes open, bleeding from the mouth, choking, etc.).
▶ The movie shows the death or inhumane treatment of animals.
▶ A parent or grandparent, sibling or close friend dies.
▶ Traumatic post-death experiences (damnation, deterioration of the body) are depicted.
▶ Destructive natural phenomena (earthquakes, floods, storms) are shown.
▶ Women or minorities are portrayed poorly.
▶ Stereotypes are reinforced.
▶ Family angst is featured, and relationships remain unresolved.
▶ Families experience divorce and/or difficulty dealing with separation.
▶ There is family violence.
▶ Authority figures are cruel or evil.

- There is a sense of tension or anxiety throughout.
- The film is aurally intense, with a relentless tempo or sound.
- The movie shows tasteless, gross or demeaning behaviour.
- Coarse language is used.
- There is a pervasive sense of hopelessness (especially in "visions-of-the-future" films.
- Sex is treated with ridicule.

Constructive elements

- A strong positive role model is present.
- An underdog wins.
- The protagonist overcomes significant odds.
- Characters experience inner discovery and growth, or affirmation of self.
- Positive images of women (independent, intelligent, capable) are present.
- Positive working relationships are shown.
- Characters overcome racial/national prejudice and/or stereotypes.
- Magical or spiritual power is used in a positive way.
- The film promotes education or revelation (seeing things in a new way).
- The film generates questions or interest in ideas or concepts.

It may be helpful to keep these questions in mind: Is the film useful for my child in any way? If it's just being chosen for entertainment purposes, then are the negative events outweighed by the positive? Is the overall effect at least balanced?

The bottom line is that every film makes an impression on children, whether dramatically or subtly. The above criteria, and your own personal ones, can help you choose films that have a positive effect on your children and avoid films that may be damaging to them.

Chapter 3

RATINGS: A WEALTH OF INFORMATION IN ONE OR TWO LETTERS

Who gives the movies their ratings?

In the United States the movie rating system is sponsored by The Motion Picture Association of America (MPAA) and The National Association of Theatre Owners, to provide parents with advance information on films. Films are voluntarily submitted by the filmmaker for a rating. In Canada, provincial film review boards such as the Ontario Film Review Board (OFRB) are responsible for placing films in certain classifications.

In both countries, boards are comprised of volunteers from all walks of life who, after watching a film in its entirety, make an educated estimate as to which rating most parents would consider appropriate.

When you are making a selection, it is important to understand that the ratings that appear on the back of most video boxes in stores are from the MPAA, and are based on criteria developed in the United States. There are equivalent ratings in Canada, but these rarely appear on video boxes.

MPAA and OFRB ratings differ slightly because the two countries have slightly different tolerances. In Canada we are less concerned with objectionable language, so a film rated R in the United States, mainly for language, might receive an AA rating in Canada. Conversely, Americans seem much less concerned by violence in films, and one will often find, in these cases, that the higher rating is from the OFRB.

We show both MPAA and OFRB ratings wherever

possible. (We do not rate films for children under 6; you may assume that these films are all G- or F-rated.) A listing of "Not rated" indicates that the film was not submitted to the rating boards. "No rating listed" means that we were unable to find a rating for the film.

MPAA ratings

G — general; suitable for viewers of all ages

PG — parental guidance is suggested as some material may not be suitable for children

PG-13 — parents are strongly cautioned as some material may be inappropriate for children under 13

R — restricted; anyone under 17 must be accompanied by a parent or adult guardian. (Age varies in some jurisdictions.)

NC-17 — no children under 17 are admitted. (Age varies in some jurisdictions.)

OFRB ratings

F — family; appropriate for family viewing

PG — parental guidance is required

AA — restricted to persons 14 years of age or older or to persons younger than 14 years of age who are accompanied by an adult (someone over 18)

R — restricted to persons 18 or older

In Canada, in addition to these ratings, information pieces are also used. These words or phrases are added to the symbol to give even more specific indications of the content. They are: Violence, Brutal Violence, Torture, Terror, Sexual Violence, Sexual Content, Nudity, Not Recommended for Children, May Offend Some, Martial Arts Violence, Mature Treatment, Mature Theme, Language May Offend, Horror, Frightening Scenes, Coarse Language, Brutal Violence, Alcohol and Drug Use, Adult Sex Film.

In our STOP-CAUTION-GO sections we try to be direct about a film's content. We use a variety of phrases to define problematic material for parents. They are:

▶ Coarse language: words such as son-of-a-bitch, asshole, jerk-off, prick, bitch.

▶ Gross behaviour: urinating, flatulence, burping, vomiting, nose-picking.

▶ Mature theme: terminal illness, mental illness, pregnant teens, abortion, divorce, family violence, etc.

▶ Mature treatment: scenes too intense or difficult to understand, eg. a realistic death-bed scene.

▶ Sexual innuendo: scenes that suggest sexual activity.

▶ Swearing: either obscenity (four-letter words like shit, fuck and so on) or profanity (Jesus Christ! God damn you! etc.).

What the letters can tell you: the criteria behind the ratings

Rated G (Rated F in Canada)

In a G-rated film there should be nothing that the majority of parents would consider offensive for even little ones to see or hear. There is no nudity, and there are no sex scenes or scenes of drug use; violence is minimal; some dialogue may go beyond polite conversation, but it will not go beyond common usage of words.

In Canada the equivalent rating is F. Language in an F-rated film might include darn, damn or hell. The violence should be restrained, with non-graphic portrayals of armed combat. Natural disasters would be shown in a restrained way, as would accidents, hand-to-hand combat and blood-letting. There can be nudity, but it should be casual and non-sexual with no close-ups. The sexual involvement is limited to kissing in a loving context and limited embracing. In Canadian F films there should be no horror and no glorification of anti-family and anti-social values.

Rated PG (Rated PG in Canada)

Because some of the material is for mature viewers, it is recommended that a parent examine or inquire about PG-rated films before allowing children to see them. There will be no explicit sex scenes and no scenes of drug use. If there is nudity it will be brief, and horror and violence do not exceed moderate levels. (Personally, we are not quite sure what "moderate levels" might mean, but to be sure, what may or may not be considered moderate is definitely changing — as a society we are becoming more tolerant.)

The PG rating in Canada permits occasional use of mild expletives such as: God, bastard, shit, piss and, interestingly, fuck. Violence must be restrained to portrayals of non-graphic violence, and may include limited blood-letting which is integral to the plot, providing it is not prolonged or shown in any close-ups. Brief nudity is allowed in a non-sexual context, with non-exploitive close-ups. Sexual involvement is limited to kissing in a loving context and limited embracing. In Canadian PG films there can be horror, but only comic horror (whatever *that* means; it sure sounds like a contradiction in terms to us) and the subject matter should not be promoting anti-family or anti-social values. PG films can also contain scenes of gross or unbecoming behavior.

Rated PG-13 (Most similar to AA in Canada)

Parents should be especially careful about letting their younger children attend AA-rated films. There is no rough or persistent violence and theoretically no sexually-oriented nudity (though we can give many examples to the contrary); there also can be much use of some of the harsher sexually-derived words.

In Canada there is no PG-13 rating. The closest Canadian rating is AA. When films that receive a PG-13 rating in the U.S. are rated in Canada, they are usually "raised" to AA, but occasionally they are "lowered" to PG.

A film with an AA rating can contain coarse language (sometimes an information piece is added to give further indication); violent prolonged combat resulting in tissue damage; violent sports; blood-letting; murder in non-graphic detail. There can be full nudity, albeit distance shots with no close-ups. Shots should be non-detailed, brief and casual. Sexual activity can include kissing, petting, fondling and implied sexual activity. Horror should be brief and not prolonged. Nor should the film encourage or glamourize drug use or violence. A film with a subject matter of an extreme nature with social or documentary significance could be considered for inclusion in this classification.

For our purposes here it is not necessary to mention the criteria for R-rated or Restricted films. Suffice it to say there are very few restrictions as to what is allowed in this category. Almost anything goes.

A WARNING BEYOND THE RATINGS: WHAT THE BOX DOESN'T TELL YOU

Aside from the ratings, there are other things that should influence your decision when selecting a video for children.

Misleading descriptions

Don't fall for the hype on the box; after all, they want you to rent the movie. Be careful of phrases like "intimate relationship" and "compelling story"; they may lead you astray. A good example of this is the box cover for the film *The Dollmaker*, starring Jane Fonda. The title sounds pleasant enough, and the description on the box says "it's a deeply moving story . . . that will charm and captivate your entire family." However, this film contains scenes of intense duress: in one, a young girl's legs are severed by a train as she sit on the tracks; in another, the mother must perform a tracheotomy on her child with a pen-knife. Although this is an excellent film, it is certainly not a charming film for the entire family. And to add to the confusion, there is no indication of rating on the box. This should be a clue. If you cannot find the rating on the box, don't show the film to a child without previewing it first. (Naturally, this isn't necessary if a film is obviously for a child, or if it's a classic which came out before the present rating system was developed.)

Don't assume that a movie is benign because it's "based on a true story"; horrific murders are a fact of life in our world, and so are countless other dreadful things you don't want your child to see. And you might also want to watch for "heartwarming story," which often involves the death of a loved one, and "coming of age," which is sometimes used to allude to a first romantic encounter, or the loss of virginity.

You may be wondering what in the world you can rent if you have to watch out for "heartwarming stories." We are not suggesting that you should steer clear of films with these descriptions, but want you to understand that movies described in this way are not necessarily free of anything that would upset your child.

Unrepresentative box art

Don't judge a video by its cover art. Great art on the box doesn't mean there's a wonderful movie inside and, conversely, bad cover art can hide a great film. Too, some cover art may be misleading in that the depicted scene doesn't even appear in the film, or worse, it may give the impression that a film is animated when in fact it is live-action. Try not to choose a film solely for the cover art, but for a combination of reasons such as its description, rating, stars and recommendations.

Misleading titles

Misleading titles can cause you to pass over some good family films. They can also cause you to rent inappropriate ones, so be careful to read more than the title when you rent.

Fully-animated vs partly-animated

If you're looking for an animated film, then look for the phrase "fully-animated" on the box. If you can't find it described in exactly this way, the video may not be animated at all; rather, it might feature still pictures with narration, or be only partly-animated. Not that this is necessarily bad; some of the most wonderful children's videos are iconographic.

Same title/wrong movie

Watch out! There are X-rated versions of *Cinderella* and *Snow White* available. And you can't simply rely on the studio labels to make your selection, because the studio that released these films may also make children's product. There is a chance that an inattentive clerk may give you or your child a nasty surprise, so always check your movies before leaving the store.

Same company/different styles

There are studio names that are no longer associated solely with children's entertainment. Disney now has an affiliated studio called Touchstone, and a film with the Touchstone label isn't necessarily a family film.

The ending

The text on the back of the box isn't going to give you

the ending of the film, for obvious reasons. But sometimes this information is very important when you are making a choice for your child. Ask someone who has seen the film about the ending, or pre-screen the film yourself. Or, if you're really stuck for time, run through the tape in fast-forward, scanning for suspicious-looking events. This could determine whether or not you show the video to your child.

Watch out!

Just because a child actor stars in a film doesn't mean that the film is suitable for children. Children appear in retrospectives of adult lives, as well as in horror movies, where filmmakers use the concept of the child in peril to intensify the worry level for an adult audience.

Trailers for restricted movies can appear at the beginning or the end of PG and AA rated films. And although the trailer will be approved for viewing by all audiences (trailers are subject to the ratings systems, too), they may interest a child in an unsuitable film.

Incidentally, we have heard of one occasion where the appearance of such a trailer had positive results. A young child we know once proclaimed that he had seen *Raiders of the Lost Ark*. And when his astonished mother asked him how this could be possible, he insisted that he had seen it on TV. After further questioning she realized that what he had seen was an advertisement in the form of a very long trailer. To him that was enough. As far as he was concerned he had seen *Raiders* and felt just as grown-up as his siblings.

Prevention strategies for little eyes

There are devices available for locking both the VCR and the tape itself. Inquire at your local video store for these, and look for a new device that enables you to program a specific amount of viewing time for each child in your family.

Chapter 4

COMMON QUESTIONS

I often see tapes on sale at super-low prices. Is this a bargain, or am I missing something?

Generally, the rule is: the more you pay for a videotape, the higher the quality will be. This is because picture quality is directly proportional to the speed at which the tape runs over the play-back heads of your VCR. In other words, high quality equals more tape. And cheap videos use very little tape.

Sometimes when I order a tape it seems to take forever to arrive. Why?

The order in which a studio schedules videos to be printed is almost completely according to perceived demand. For example, if a studio is printing copies of *Little Fluffy the Cat*, and suddenly acquires the box-office smash that needs to be released before Christmas, you can be sure that *Fluffy* will get bounced off the duplicating line and the box-office extravanganza will take its place. *Fluffy* will not return to the duplicating line until the furor is over. And even then, it won't go out to the distributors until enough copies have been ordered to justify the printing.

So if a retailer tells you that you may have to wait a while (like six months), he's not giving you a line; it's true. He is at the mercy of the production houses and the studios.

In some drastic cases, you may not be able to get a particular video anywhere because the video didn't sell enough copies or the studio carrying it has gone out of business or changed ownership, or the copyright is in the process of changing ownership. In these cases, all you can do is hope that the material will resurface and be re-released.

I want to buy a copy of The Little Mermaid, *but my local store told me it's no longer available for purchase. Why?*

Some studios, like Disney, put their titles on moratorium. That means that after they have printed a specific number of copies, the masters of that film are put back in the vault and not reproduced again until, sometimes, as many as seven or eight years later.

This is a way of building up customer demand for the product. The studio doesn't feel it can justify continually printing small runs of many films; it's more economical and profitable to concentrate on printing big runs of one film, one title at a time. So, if you plan to purchase a particular film for your child (to watch this year or years down the line), it's important that you do so when it is released because you may not get a second chance.

Why is it that I can't get all of the tapes in a particular series?

Like books, the material on video cassettes is subject to copyright laws. The producer of a series may hold the copyright to all of the films in the series. And foreign subsidiaries or purchasers may choose to buy the rights to only those films that they see as having large sales potential in their country. Over time, if the chosen films perform well, the purchaser may buy the rights to other titles in the series and release them.

If you visit another country, you may find titles that you cannot find at home. But before you purchase them, be sure to check that the tapes are compatible with the North American television system. (Read on for more information about machine compatibility.)

When I sent a video to my cousin in England, it wouldn't play on her VCR, even though our machines are both VHS format. Why?

A video cassette purchased in Canada or the United States will not play on a machine in Europe, Africa or Asia, regardless of the format of tape (VHS, Beta or Super 8). This is because the television systems used in these countries are completely different. In the Western Hemisphere and in Japan, the system used is called NTSC, while Europe, Africa and Asia use (depending on the country) one of many different systems including PAL, N-Pal, M-Pal, SECAM, MESECAM and 3.58 NTSC.

There are new multi-system VCRs available which are able to switch between systems,.

Can I buy a film and have it copied into a format that will work on a VCR in a different country?

You *cannot* buy a copyrighted film and have a transfer company make a copy for you to send away to another country. This is in violation of copyright laws.

It is, however, possible to have your home videos transferred. Consult the phone book or your video retailer for information about conversion or transfer houses.

Chapter 5

VIDEOS FOR AGES UP TO THREE

As extraordinary as it may seem, there are videos that are specifically designed for babies. These videos are not particularly common, but they do exist, and they are for the most part designed to be, in effect, moving mobiles, very often consisting of computer-generated images accompanied by synthesized music. The theory appears to be that, since mobiles work for babies, it should be possible to create successful mobiles on the television screen. However, in our experience, based on parental feedback from hundreds of rentals of such videos, they just don't seem to work.

Other videos for babies employ gentle voices, images of animals, babies or toddlers at play, animation or puppets. Jim Henson, one of the premiere children's entertainers in visual media history, tried something like this for very young children entitled *Peek-A-Boo*. But whether *Peek-A-Boo* or any other such efforts actually fulfil their objectives remains to be seen.

Song videos

Videos that work well with children under three are broadly categorized as song videos. There are two main types: concert videos and those that are set in specific locations or based on certain themes. The success of a particular concert video depends, of course, on the appeal that the performers hold for their young audiences, while the second group must usually possess one of the following features to achieve success:

▶ slightly older children engaged in activities like playing games, sight-seeing, singing and dancing
▶ a theme popular with most little ones, such as animals, vehicles, clowns and magical events
▶ minimal dialogue and rapid transition between songs
▶ rapid editing, often with visual images changing every few seconds, usually to the rhythm of the music, without lingering on any particular shot
▶ large, bright images, with an emphasis on close-ups

Because the song videos we have included are for the most part excellent, featuring tried-and-true children's entertainers or popular enjoyable themes, the reviews are minimal. We have discovered that most parents, children and grandparents just want to know exactly which songs are on which videos. And because the video box doesn't always list every title, we have tried to include them all in our reviews.

Quality storybook videos

There is an entire genre of video which is perceived by the public as being for babies or toddlers. These are most often nursery rhyme or story videos, and are fully- or partly-animated. Some feature well-known entertainers as singers or narrators, and all, despite the aforementioned perception, tend to be very appealing to adults, often winning awards as quality videos (which they absolutely are).

The effect of a storybook video is similar to that of having someone read your child a story. However, these videos generally seem to move too slowly to capture the interest of very young children. Most find it much more captivating to actually have a real live person read a story (thank goodness). Some of these videos have story lines that are too advanced for children under three, and ironically, when children are a bit older and have the attention span to follow these tapes, they would just as soon read the stories themselves.

Little kids and big movies

It's a fact that toddlers with older siblings are likely to watch more advanced television shows at a far younger age than their predecessors did.

In our store, we were suprised when the parents of a two-and-a-half-year-old came to the counter with *Superman.* His mother explained that the toddler watched everything that his revered older brother saw, and since the older boy, now six, watched *Superman* three times a week, so did his little brother. Of course, the older boy had never seen *Superman* even once when *he* was two-and-a-half.

It's not just younger siblings who are being exposed to films that are meant for older children. In general, more and more children under the age of three are watching full-length movies which were created for much older viewers. One of our customers, a first child, was obsessed with dolphins at the age of two-and-a-half. He would sit entranced through *Flipper* and *Tadpole and the Whale,* so focused on the object of his passion that the long and relatively sophisticated stories didn't deter him at all.

This viewer dedication is not unusual with young viewers. Many a small child has suffered through watching the evil tyranosaur Sharptooth in *The Land Before Time* simply because the film also features the dinosaurs they love. Other favourites with young viewers are dragons, dogs, animals, vehicles (particularly trains and fire engines) and, interestingly enough, Bad Guys.

Children seem to feel a peculiar mixture of terror and fascination toward representations of evil. At the store we've heard more times than we can count that little so-and-so loves to be scared. All well and good, but be careful; this *can* go too far.

One well-meaning parent of our aquaintance, knowing how much his young son loved scary movies, brought home a copy of *The Great Mouse Detective* as a treat. But it was too much. At bedtime that night, the child could not sleep until his father literally took the video out of the house.

Another risk of showing your toddler a movie when he or she is too young to appreciate it is that it may turn the child off the film for years. One of the great delights of childhood is looking forward to things such as an exciting holiday or a birthday; add to that list "movies I can watch when I get older."

THE ANIMAL ALPHABET

Scholastic-Lorimar Home Video
1985
30 minutes
Directed by: Geoffrey Drummond

Created to help kids learn about the alphabet, this video features National Geographic footage of animals in the wild. Pictures are accompanied by twenty-seven original songs by Broadway composer/lyricist Elizabeth Swados.

CAUTION: Some families have complained about the insensitivity of the song for the letter B in which a bear is told to go on a diet.

GO: The songs emulate the rhythmic movements of each featured animal.

ANIMAL BABIES IN THE WILD

Karl-Lorimar HomeVideo
1987
30 minutes
Directed by: Nancy Lebrun

Original stories and songs are narrated and accompanied by live footage of animal babies in the wild.

Stories featured are:
The Beaversons
Calhoun the Racoon
Sara and the Lion Club
The Tuxedo Junction

Songs featured are:
Animal Friends Theme Song
Bears Will Be Bears
Elephants of My Dreams
Let's Do the Hop
Monkey See
Splashin' around in the Water

GO: The live, sometimes humorous, footage shows animals in their natural habitats.

BABY ANIMALS JUST WANT TO HAVE FUN

Karl-Lorimar Home Video
1987
30 minutes
Directed by: Amy Jo Divine,
    Geoffrey Drummond

Original stories and songs accompany charming live-action footage of baby barnyard animals and animals in their natural habitats.

Stories featured are:
A Fawn in the Forest
Hortense Fuzzwuffle:
    The Curious Rabbit
Peter Puppy's Perfect Present
Raindance: The Shy Little Pony
The Skunk Children Find a Home

Songs featured are:
Baby Animals Just Wanna Have Fun
Kittens' Admittins
My Little Chickadee
Scholastic's Animal Friends Theme Song

CAUTION: Raindance the pony is stolen in the night.

GO: The songs are sung by children and the stories are told by adults. The animals are not manipulated into acting out the story; instead, stories are made up according to the footage.

BABY'S FIRST WORKOUT

HPG Home Video
1989
60 minutes
Directed by: Vicki L. Metz
Starring: Patti Gerard Hanna

Based on Patti Gerard Hanna's book *Teaching Your Child Basic Body Confidence*, this video demonstrates thirty-eight exercises designed to help babies with their motor skill development. The program requires no special equipment and takes only a few minutes a day.

GO: Patti Gerard Hanna demonstrates the exercises with a number of babies. All of the information is thorough and well-presented.

■

BABYSONGS COLLECTION

This collection includes song videos primarily, and is highly successful with children under five. Each features babies, toddlers, children, animals and adults acting out the lyrics. Excellent claymation, animation and video effects are used to introduce the songs, but most of the footage is live-action. Original songs are by Hap Palmer and, in the case of *John Lithgow's Kid-size Concert*, by John Lithgow. A songbook is included with each video.

Baby Rock

Hi-Tops Home Video/ HGV
1990
30 minutes
Directed by: Nate Bashor,
  Keith Fialcowitz, Lynn Hamrick,
  Allan Kartun, Lynda Taylor

Children dance and play with costumed characters to popular rock songs performed by the original artists. This video has appeal for children as old as eight.

Songs featured are:
Blue Suede Shoes (Carl Perkins)
Come On, Let's Go (Ritchie Valens)
Come Saturday Morning
  (The Sandpipers)
I'm So Excited (The Pointer Sisters)
I'm Walkin' (Fats Domino)
The Loco-Motion (Little Eva)
Pajamas (Livingston Taylor)
Twist and Shout (The Isley Brothers)
Woolly Bully
  (Sam the Sham and the Pharaohs)
You Baby (The Turtles)

Babysongs

Hi-Tops Home Video/ HGV
1987
30 minutes
Directed by: Dorian Walker

This live-action video features babies and children involved in daily activities.

Songs featured are:
Baby's Good Doggy
I Sleep 'til Morning
My Mommy Comes Back
Piggy Toes
Rolling
Rub a Dub
Security
Share
Shout and Whisper
Today I Took My Diapers Off

Babysongs Christmas

Golden Book Video
1991
30 minutes
Directed by: Nathan Bashor, Keith
  Fialcowitz, Rich Kinney,
  Lynda Taylor
Starring: Lori Lieberman

Children on horseback and horses pulling old-fashioned sleighs make this a truly special holiday video.

Songs featured are:
Deck the Halls
It Came upon a Midnight Clear
Jingle Bell Rock
Peace on Earth
Sleigh Ride
The Twelve Days of Christmas
Up on the Rooftop
The Wassail Song
We Wish You a Merry Christmas
We're Cooking Supper for Santa

Babysongs Presents: Follow-Along Songs

Golden Book Video
1990
30 minutes
Directed by: Lynn Hamrick,
  Chris Willoughby, Amy Weintraub

In short, live-action segments, children aged three to six use home-made instruments to accompany the songs. Instructions for making a bean bag are featured (adult supervision is recommended).

Songs featured are:
Bean Bag Alphabet Rag
Bean Bag Shake
Homemade Band
Just Fun
Let's All Clap Our Hands Together
The Mice Go Marching
Parade of Colors
Tap Your Sticks
Weekly Rap

Babysongs Presents: John Lithgow's Kid-size Concert

Hi-Tops Home Video and HGV
1990
32 minutes
Directed by: Greg Gold
Starring: John Lithgow

John Lithgow accompanies himself on guitar and performs both traditional and original songs.

Songs featured are:
Big Kids Scare the Heck out of Me
The Garden Song
  (Inch by inch, row by row...)
I Had a Rooster
Mommy, Daddy
Mr. McCloud
The Runaway Pancake
She'll Be Coming 'round the Mountain

Babysongs Presents: Turn on the Music

Hi-Tops Home Video and HGV
1988
30 minutes
Directed by: Lynda Taylor,
  Nate Bashor, Neal Brown,
  Barbara Dourmashkin

This music video features more sophisticated concepts than the other titles in the series. Recommended for children aged three to seven.

Songs featured are:
Amanda Schlupp
Backwards Land
Chomping Gum
Francie Had a Football
Hurry up Blues
If I Had Wings
Teddy Bear Ball
When Daddy Was a Little Boy
When Things Don't Go Your Way
You Can Do It

Even More Babysongs

Hi-Tops Home Video and HGV
1990
30 minutes
Directed by: Nate Bashor, Barbara
 Dourmashkin, Lynn Hamrick,
 C. D. Taylor, Lynda Taylor

Toddlers and parents are shown
involved in everyday activities
(eating, dressing and playing),
accompanied by up-tempo songs
with imaginative lyrics.

Songs featured are:
Baby's First
Finger Foods
Getting Up Time
Goodnight Story Time
I Can Put My Clothes on by Myself
Peek-A-Boo
Raggedy Rag Doll Friend
Teddy Bear
Wash Rag Blues
What a Miracle

More Babysongs

Hi-Tops Home Video and HGV
1987
30 minutes
Directed by: Nate Bashor, Lynda
 Taylor, Dorian Walker

Toddlers and their parents are
shown venturing out into the world.

Songs featured are:
Crazy Monster
Daddy Be a Horsie
Family Harmony
The Hammer Song
My Baby
Sittin' in a High Chair
Tickly Toddle
Walking
Watch a Witchie Whiz
Wild and Woolly

CAUTION: Because most of the songs in
this series will be new to children, young
viewers may not be able to sing along right

away. The sound track is over-dubbed
which is a particular shame on the
Babysongs Christmas tape, where it would
have been delightful to hear the horses
and the sleigh bells.

GO: This series is extremely popular with
young children. The families shown seem
like real families and a variety of ethnic
backgrounds are represented. There are
definite breaks between each song, giving
parents the opportunity to stop the tape if
necessary. The songs are excellent and a
songbook is packaged with each tape.

BABYVISION

J2
1987
90 minutes
Directed by: Barron Christian

A kind of video mobile, this film was
created to entertain and stimulate
children aged nine months to three
years. Children, animals, colours,

shapes, plants and toys appear and are identified by a disembodied voice. Synthesized music by Barron Christian is played throughout. Filmed in New Zealand. Music by Barron Christian.

CAUTION: All of the music is over-dubbed and there are no lyrics.

GO: This is a gentle, calming video. Different ethnic groups are represented.

BARNEY AND THE BACKYARD GANG COLLECTION

This collection combines live-action, animation and music to tell the adventures of Barney, a six-foot purple dinosaur who magically comes to life and visits the children in his neighborhood. Some videos in the series also star Sandy Duncan as Mom, who in true make-believe fashion can't see Barney.
Traditional tunes with new lyrics and original songs are included in every video. Songs and rhymes by Sheryl Leach and Kathy Parker, both M.A.s in early childhood education.

A Day at the Beach

Kids Edutainment Video
1989
45 minutes
Directed by: John Grable

One hot day, Barney transports the kids in The Backyard Gang from their crowded wading pool to the beach. Winner of a 1989 Parents' Choice Award and a Film Advisory Board Inc. Award of Excellence.

Songs featured are:
Are You Hungry? (Frère Jacques)
Barney Is Our Dinosaur (The Muffin Man)
I Love You
The More We Get Together
Peanut Butter
Row, Row, Row Your Boat
Sea, Sea, Sea
She Waded in the Water
Swimming, Swimming
There's a Hole in the Bottom of the Sea
This Is the Way We Leave the Beach
This Is the Way We Walk the Beach
Three Little Speckled Frogs

The Backyard Show

Kids Edutainment Video
1988
45 minutes
Directed by: John Grable

Barney and The Backyard Gang plan a show to surprise Dad on his birthday.

Songs featured are:
Baby Bumble Bee
For He's a Jolly Good Fellow
Heads and Shoulders (Instrumental)
Hello, Hello, Hello
The Hokey Pokey
Hey, Hey the Gang's All Here
Hickory Dickory Dock
Humpty Dumpty
I Love You
If You're Happy and You Know It
I've Been Working on the Railroad
Little Bunny Foo Foo
Six Little Ducks
Someone's in the Kitchen with Dinah
This Little Piggy
This Old Man (instrumental)
Up and Down in My Little Red Wagon

Barney Goes to School

Kids Edutainment Video
1990
40 minutes
Directed by: Gary Potts

Tina is sad because there is no school on Saturdays, until Barney transports her to school where the Backyard Gang is waiting to play.

Songs include:
ABC Song/Alphabet Chant
Alligator Pie
The Fishing Song
Goodbye Song
Hug a Color
I Love You
I Wish There Was School Every Day
If All the Raindrops Were Lemon Drops
The Shape Song
There Are 7 Days in a Week
The Three Bears Rap
The Weather Riddle Song
The Welcome Song
What I Want to Be
You're a Grand Old Flag

Barney in Concert

> The Lyons Group
> 1991
> 55 minutes
> Directed by: Jim Rowley

This live concert from the Majestic Theatre in Dallas features Barney, The Backyard Gang and a host of costumed characters, including Barney's dino-pal Baby Bop.

Songs featured are:
ABC's
Baby Bop's Song
Baby Bop's Street Dance
Backyard Gang Rap
The Barney Theme
Bubble Bubble Bath
Down on Grandpa's Farm
Everyone Is Special
French ABC's
Grand Ole Flag
Hebrew ABC's
Hurry, Hurry, Drive the Firetruck
I Love You
Itsy Bitsy Spider
Mr. Knickerbocker
The Noble Duke of York
Pop Goes the Weasel
Pufferbellies

Sally the Camel
We Are Barney and The Backyard Gang
Where is Thumbkin

Barney's Birthday

> The Lyons Group
> 1991
> 30 minutes
> Directed by: Jim Rowley

Barney turns two dinosaur years old and gets to wear the birthday crown. The Gang makes decorations and comes up with the perfect present for Barney. This episode features Baby Bop.

Songs featured are:
The Barney Theme Song
Everyone Is Special
Frosting the Cake
Growing
Happy Birthday (Filipino version)
Hey, Hey, Our Friends Are Here
I Love You
Las Mananitas
She'll Be Comin' 'round the Mountain
There Are 7 Days

Barney's Campfire Sing-Along

> The Lyons Group
> 1992
> 46 minutes
> Directed by: Dwin Tavell

When her mother reads her a bedtime story about camping, Tina dreams that she and The Gang camp out.

Songs featured are:
A-Camping We Will Go
The Ants Go Marching
Are You Sleeping?
Clean Up, Clean Up
The Frog on a Log
The Happy Wanderer

I Love You
  (English and Spanish versions)
I'm Being Eaten by a
  Tyrannosaurus Rex
Kookaburra
Little Cabin in the Forest Green
The Other Day I Met A Bear
Sarasponda
S'Mores
Tell Me Why
There Was a Little Turtle

Barney's Magical Musical Adventure

The Lyons Group
1992
40 minutes
Directed by: Jim Rowley

Barney and The Gang use their imaginations to go to a magical forest. There they meet an elf named Twinkle who escorts them to a castle where they fill in for the king while he goes fishing. This video features Baby Bop.

Songs featured are:
The Barney Theme Song
Castles So High
Go Round and Round the Village
I Am a Fine Musician
I Love You
If I Had One Wish
It's Good to Be Home
Looby-Loo
The Noble Duke of York
Old King Cole
Silly Sounds
Tea Party Medley (Polly Put the Kettle On, Little Jack Horner, The Muffin Man, Pat-A-Cake, Pease Porridge Hot, Sing a Song of Sixpence)

Rock with Barney

The Lyons Group
1991
30 minutes
Directed by: Jim Rowley

Adam's mom takes The Backyard Gang to visit the film studio where she works. Barney goes too and brings along his shy dinosaur friend, Baby Bop.

Songs featured are:
Apples and Bananas
Barney Theme Song
Boom, Boom Ain't It Great to Be Crazy
Down by the Bay
Frog on a Log
I Can Laugh
I Love You
Manners
Me and My Teddy
Protect Our Earth
Six Little Ducks
There Are 50 Stars on Our Flag
Tingalayo
We Are Barney and The Backyard Gang
The Yankee Doodle Boy

Three Wishes

Kids Edutainment Video
1988
39 minutes
Directed by: John Grable

When The Backyard Gang is bored, Barney appears and grants them three wishes. After some deliberation they decide to go to a fun park, a farm and the moon.

Songs featured are:
Barney and The Backyard Gang Theme
Do Your Ears Hang Low?
Friends Are Forever
I Love You
I See the Moon
Jack Be Nimble
London Bridge
London Town
Mr. Knickerbocker
Old MacDonald
Pat-a-Cake
Ring around the Rosies
The Rocket Song
Take Me Out to the Ballgame
Teddy Bear, Teddy Bear

Waiting for Santa

The Lyons Group
1990
30 minutes
Directed by: Dwin Towell

Derek, the new boy in the neighbourhood, is afraid that Santa won't be able to find him at his new address. So, with Derek in tow, Barney whisks The Backyard Gang to Santa's Workshop where Mrs. Claus assures Derek that he is on Santa's list. Then it's home again to see Santa delivering their presents.

Songs and stories featured are:
Deck the Halls
The Elves' Rap
Jingle Bells
Jolly Old St. Nicholas
I Love You, You Love Me
Let's All Do a Little Tapping
S.A.N.T.A.
Skating, Skating
'Twas the Night before Christmas
Up on the Housetop
Waiting for Santa
We Wish You a Merry Christmas
When Santa Comes to Town

CAUTION: Children may be frustrated when they recognize the tunes, but not the changed lyrics of many of the songs.

GO: The series features children from a number of different ethnic backgrounds, stresses positive values and inspires creative expression through dramatic, imaginative play. Most videos are winners of the Film Advisory Board's Award of Excellence, American Film & Video Association Honorable Mention and the California Children's Video Award. The series is one of the top ten picks for children in *TV Guide*, *Redbook* and *USA Today*.

CHARLOTTE DIAMOND:DIAMONDS AND DRAGONS

1990
30 minutes
Directed by: Tony Wade
Starring: Charlotte Diamond, The Hug Bug Band, Jackson Davies

Multi-talented entertainer Charlotte Diamond discovers all kinds of interesting things in Grannie's attic. Charlotte changes costumes, personas and musical styles throughout.

Songs featured are:
Animals Have Personalities
Competition
Dickie, Dickie Dinosaur
A Happy Street
Hug Bug
La Bamba
La Bastrange
The Laundry Monster
Slimy, the Bug
The Unicorn

GO: This well-paced video is a treat for little ones.

CHRISTMAS EVE ON SESAME STREET

Random House Home Video
1978
60 minutes
Directed by: Jon Stone
Starring: The Muppets, the Sesame Street cast, Holiday on Ice

In this Sesame Street holiday celebration, a little girl helps Big Bird learn to skate; Cookie, the Count, Ernie and Bert barrel jump on skates; Oscar is thrown off the ice in a game of crack-the-whip; Big Bird, Grover and Kermit try to find out how Santa gets down the chimney and Ernie and Bert do some unlucky gift-buying. Skating sequences are performed on the ice rink at Rockefeller Center.

Songs featured are:
Have Yourself a Merry Little Christmas
I Hate Christmas
Keep Christmas with You (sign language)
True Blue Miracle

CAUTION: This video doesn't move as quickly as the television show and only briefly mentions Hanukkah. Cookie Monster burps at the end of the video.

DISNEY'S SING-ALONG SONGS

Disneyland Fun

Walt Disney Home Video
1990
29 minutes
Directed by: Bruce Healy, Paul Hoen

In this live-action video, Mickey, Minnie, Goofy, Pluto, Donald, Chip 'n Dale, Roger Rabbit and Alice in Wonderland lead kids and grown-ups in a happy sing-along through the Magic Kingdom. The lyrics for the songs run along the bottom of the screen. See ages three to six for more in this series.

Songs featured are:
The Character Parade

Disneyland Is a Magical Place
Following the Leader
The Great Outdoors
Grim Grinning Ghosts
I'm Walkin' Right down the Middle of Main Street, USA
It's a Small World
Making Memories
Rumbly in My Tumbly
Step in Time
When You Wish upon a Star
Whistle While You Work
You Know It's a Thrill
Zip-A-Dee-Doo-Dah

CAUTION: There is no animation in this video; all of the Disney characters featured are people in costumes. Many parents consider the video to be a half-hour advertisement for the Disney theme parks.

GO: Live characters are a big favourite with young children. The pace is peppy and the atmosphere, happy.

FIREMAN SAM...THE HERO NEXT DOOR

f.h.e./MCA
1987
30 minutes
Directed by: John Walker
Starring the voice of: John Alderton

Brave and friendly, Fireman Sam spends his days helping the people in his community. He does everything from clearing away hazardous fallen telegraph poles to rescuing wayward kites.

GO: The pixilation is extremely well done. This video is a big hit with young boys.

FRED PENNER: A CIRCLE OF SONGS

Oak Street Music/Sony
1991
40 minutes
Directed by: Tony Dean
Starring: Fred Penner, Len Udow

Singer/banjo player Fred Penner and his piano-playing accompanist, Len Udow, perform an intimate concert for an audience of about thirty children.

Songs featured are:
The Bump
The Cat Came Back
Grandma's Glasses
Hush Little Baby
I Had a Rooster
John Russell Watkins
Land of the Silver Birch
Poco
Rock a Little Baby
Sandwiches

GO: Fred Penner is one of the most popular and talented children's entertainers today. He's very comfortable with his audiences and his performances have a spontaneous quality that most artists never achieve.

FRED PENNER: THE CAT CAME BACK

Oak Street Music
1990
45 minutes
Directed by: Tony Dean
Starring: Fred Penner

Singer/banjo player Fred Penner performs with The Cat's Meow Band for a large crowd.

Songs featured are:
The Cat Came Back
Collections
Holiday
A House Is a House for Me
I Am the Wind
Otto the Hippo
Sandwiches
We're Gonna Shine
You Are My Sunshine
You Can Do It If You Try

INFANTASTIC LULLABYES ON VIDEO (Vol. 1)

View Video
1989
25 minutes
Directed by: Dick Feldman

Synthesized music accompanies computer animation in this video mobile for children aged three months to two years. Music written and arranged by Lou Garisto.

Songs featured are:
The Alphabet Song
Brahms' Lullaby
Count to 10
Hush Little Baby
Pop Goes the Weasel
This Old Man
Three Blind Mice
Twinkle, Twinkle Little Star
Yankee Doodle

CAUTION: Although the pictures do move, the computer animation in this video doesn't come close to the quality of true animation. There are no lyrics to the music.

JIM HENSON PLAY-ALONG VIDEO

Mother Goose Stories

Lorimar Home Video
1988
30 minutes
Directed by: Brian Henson
Starring: Laura Goodwin,
 Ilan Ostrove, Anthony Walters

A beautiful puppet, Mother Goose, tells her goslings the stories behind the nursery rhymes Little Miss Muffet, Little Boy Blue and Sing a Song of Sixpence. Each story has a moral and young viewers are invited to join in as each nursery rhyme is recited.

CAUTION: With the exception of the goslings' rendition of "Happy Birthday," there are no songs in this video.

GO: This video employs the same video effects combining puppets and real children that were later developed and used for Jim Henson's *Storyteller* series.

Peek-A-Boo

Lorimar Home Video
1988
30 minutes
Directed by: David Gumpel

In this video designed for children up to three years old, gentle sequences of babies, toddlers, puppets and animals appearing and disappearing are combined with a track of synthesized music to become sort of a video version of the Peek-A-Boo game.

CAUTION: Except for the opening and closing songs, the synthesized music is without lyrics.

GO: This is a gentle, friendly tape featuring the age old game of Peek-A-Boo.

KIDSONGS MUSIC VIDEO STORIES

Viewmaster Video
1985-1992
25-30 minutes (each volume)
Directed by: Bruce Gowers

The *Kidsongs Music Video Stories* collection features children and adults singing and dancing to popular, upbeat songs. The music is over-dubbed with no breaks between songs. Each fast-paced video is based on a particular theme and a lyric card is included with every tape.

A Day at Camp

The Kidsongs Kids spend the day at camp, fishing, hiking and singing.

Songs featured are:
The Animal Fair
The Ants Go Marching In
Baa Baa Black Sheep
Boom, Boom, Ain't It Great to Be Crazy?
The Caissons Go Rolling Along
Fishin' Blues
Found A Peanut
The Hokey Pokey
I Had A Rooster
Little Bunny Foo Foo
The More We Get Together
Ninety-Nine Bottles of Pop on the Wall
The Old Grey Mare
On Top of Spaghetti
Pop Goes the Weasel
Pussy Cat, Pussy Cat

When the Saints Go Marching In
Whistle While You Work

A Day at the Circus

The Kidsongs Kids see a circus tent go up, watch circus acts rehearsing and take part in an old-fashioned circus parade.

Songs featured are:
The Circus Is Coming to Town
Entry of the Gladiators
If You're Happy and You Know It
The Lion Tamer
The Man on the Flying Trapeze
Polly Wolly Doodle
Put on a Happy Face
The Ringmaster Song
The Sabre Dance
Strolling through the Park

A Day at Old Macdonald's Farm

The Kidsongs Kids take a trip to the farm. Close-ups of live farm animals are featured. Winner of The Video Review Award in 1987.

Songs featured are:
Here We Go 'round the Mulberry Bush
John Jacob Jingleheimer Schmidt
Mary Had a Little Lamb
Old Macdonald Had a Farm
She'll Be Coming 'round the Mountain
Shortenin' Bread
Skip to My Lou
Take Me Out to the Ball Game
This Old Man
Twinkle, Twinkle Little Star

A Day with the Animals

The Kidsongs Kids visit a zoo where they see chimps, dolphins, whales, cats and dogs.

Songs featured are:
BINGO
Do Your Ears Hang Low?
Harmony
Hickory Dickory Dock
How Much Is That Doggie in the Window?
Itsy Bitsy Spider
Little Bo Peep
Little Duckie Duddle
Rockin' Robin
The Wanderer
Water World
Why Don't You Write Me ?

Cars, Boats, Trains and Planes

Mike the dog leads the kids on a merry chase as he rides a number of vehicles in a theme park.

Songs featured are:
The Bus Song
Car, Car Song
Daylight Train
I Got Wheels
I Like Trucks
Round and Round
Up and Down, Round and Round
Up, Up and Away
Where, Oh Where, Has My Little Dog Gone?
Wild Blue Yonder

Good Night, Sleep Tight

Two sandmen listen in on parents as they "sing" their children to sleep.

Songs featured are:
All the Pretty Little Horses
Good Night
Hush Little Baby
Let Us Dance, Let Us Play
Our House
Ring around the Rosy
A Tisket, a Tasket
Tomorrow Is a Dream Away
The Unicorn

Home on the Range

Uncle Sam invites the Kidsongs Kids to see a Fourth of July parade that takes them on a trip through American history.

Songs featured are:
America's Heroes
Deep in the Heart of Texas
Home on the Range
If I Had a Hammer
I've Been Working on the Railroad
Living in the U.S.A.
Oh Susanna
There's a Hole in My Bucket
Turkey in the Straw
Yankee Doodle Boy
You're a Grand Old Flag

I'd Like to Teach the World to Sing

The Kidsongs Kids travel around the world, learning songs.

Songs featured are:
Day-O
Did You Ever See a Lassie?
Frère Jacques
Funiculi, Funicula
I'd Like to Teach the World to Sing
Kumbaya
London Bridge
Los Pollitos
Sakura, Sakura
Waltzing Matilda

Let's Play Ball

The Kidsongs Kids join children as they play basketball, race cars, lead cheers, do gymnastics, ride horses and sail.

Songs featured are:
Bend Me, Shape Me
Catch a Wave
Centerfield
Footloose

I Get Around
It's Not If You Win or Lose
Practice Makes Perfect
Rah, Rah, Sis, Boom, Bah
You Know that You Can Do It

Ride the Roller Coaster

The Kidsongs Kids spend the day at an amusement park.

Songs featured are:
The 1812 Overture
A Pirate's Life
Anything You Can Do
Fast Food
Here We Go Loopty Loo
Let's Twist Again
Little Deuce Coupe
Splish Splash
We're Gonna Get Wet
Whole Lotta Shakin' Going On

Very Silly Songs

The Kidsongs Kids sing practically every silly song ever made when they visit Silly Dilly Ville.

Songs featured are:
Do the Silly Willy
Down by the Bay
Fiddle-I-Dee
Jim along Josie
Mail Myself to You
Michael Finnegan
The Name Game
Purple People Eater
Rig-A-Jig-Jig
The Thing

We Wish You a Merry Christmas

Frosty the Snowman comes alive and joins the Kidsongs Kids on a holiday adventure to visit Santa at the North Pole.

Songs featured are:
All I Want for Christmas Is My Two Front
  Teeth
Deck the Halls
Frosty the Snowman
Jingle Bells
Santa, Please Don't Forget Me
The Pony Song
Rudolph the Red-Nosed Reindeer
Santa Claus Is Coming to Town
The Twelve Days of Christmas
We Wish You a Merry Christmas

CAUTION: These videos contain popular songs and rock songs from the '60s that many children may not be familiar with. The sound is over-dubbed and songs are performed without breaks.

GO: These videos are positive and non-threatening and deal with themes of interest to children. The singing and dancing is high-quality, showing talented, capable children. They are for the most part non-gender specific and non-racist. Excellent for children under four.

LADY AND THE TRAMP

Walt Disney Home Video
1955
75 minutes
Directed by: Hamilton Luske,
  Clyde Geronimi, Wilfred Jackson
Starring the voices of: Peggy Lee,
  Stan Freberg

Lady, a gentle cocker spaniel, leads a pampered life until a new baby is born, and Aunt Polly and her two troublesome siamese cats come to help out. The trouble begins when Lady is wrongly suspected of mischief and is subsequently taken to be fitted for a muzzle. Escaping in terror she meets Tramp, a street-wise mongrel from the wrong side of the tracks. A romance is

kindled, but fades when Tramp involves Lady in a chicken-chasing incident and she's caught by dogcatchers. The dogs eventually manage to make their way back to the house where Tramp wins back Lady's affection by killing a vicious rat that's threatening the baby. And in the end, Lady is vindicated and Tramp is adopted into the household, where he and Lady raise a family of their own. Based on a story by Ward Greene.

Songs featured are:
Bella Notte
He's a Tramp
We Are Siamese

CAUTION: The animal parodies can be stereotypical (the Scottish terrier as miserly, for example). Small children may be disturbed by scenes of the baby in jeopardy and by the vicious dog-fights.

GO: The animation is of the highest quality and the songs are some of Disney's best. The relationships are warm and positive.

■

THE MOTHER GOOSE VIDEO TREASURY

J2 Communications
1987
30 minutes (each volume)
Starring: Cheryl Rhoads,
  Serafin Rocha, Will Ryan

In each of these enchanting live-action productions, Mother Goose and her pet goose, Bertram, are joined by a host of beautifully costumed nursery rhyme characters. Featured are the same advanced puppetronics first used by the Disney Channel. All of the songs are fully orchestrated and performed by talented singer/dancers. Each video box features a pop-up cover.

■

London Bridge/Little Miss Muffet (Vol. 2)

Songs and nursery rhymes featured are:
A, B, C, D
Betty Botter
I See the Moon
Little Miss Muffet
London Bridge
Mary Mary
Pease Porridge Hot
Simple Simon
Where Oh Where Has My Little Dog Gone?

Old King Cole/ Humpty Dumpty
(Vol. 1)

Songs and nursery rhymes featured are:
Humpty Dumpty
Jack Be Nimble
Mary Had a Little Lamb
Old King Cole
Old Woman Tossed in a Basket
Peter Piper
Ring Around the Rosy
There Was a Crooked Man
Tom Thumb
Twinkle, Twinkle Little Star

Old Mother Hubbard/Jack and Jill
(Vol.4)

Songs and nursery rhymes featured are:
Gregory Griggs
Handy Spandy
It's Raining, It's Pouring
Itsy, Bitsy Spider
Jack and Jill

Jumping Joan
Old Mother Hubbard
One, Two, Buckle My Shoe
Tom He Was a Piper's Son
Twinkle, Twinkle Little Star
Wee Willie Winkie

One, Two, Buckle My Shoe/Little Bo-Peep
(Vol. 3)

Songs and nursery rhymes featured are:
A Was an Archer
Here We Go 'Round the Mulberry Bush
I Knew a Little Person
I Would If I Could
Little Bo-Peep
One, Two, Buckle My Shoe
The Queen of Hearts
Star Light Star Bright
There Was an Old Woman Who Lived in a Shoe
This Is the House That Jack Built

GO: Each title in the series is non-threatening, charming and well-paced. A refreshing alternative to the high-power continuous song videos.

POLKA DOT DOOR: DINOSAURS

Golden Book Home Video
1983
Directed by: David Moore
Starring: Cindy Cook,
    Denis Simpson

Dinosaurs is the theme of this episode from the popular television series. Denis and Cindy sing about different species of dinosaurs and help the toys build a dinosaur landscape in the sandbox. Hedy Hoberlin, a visiting geologist, talks about fossils and bones; Polkaroo visits a dinosaur theme park and Denis reads Bernard Most's book *If Dinosaurs Came Back*.

GO: This program has a simple, gentle quality that appeals to children under five. It's entertaining and full of information.

GO: Although some adults find Raffi to be bland and his sound, monotonous, children adore him. His humour is genuine; he's never condescending; and he works at a pace well-suited to his young audiences. The audience participation in this tape is great.

RAFFI: A YOUNG PEOPLE'S CONCERT

A & M Video
1984
45 minutes
Directed by: David Devine
Starring: Raffi

Raffi performs to a sold-out crowd at a concert filmed in Toronto. Teacher/parent notes and song lyrics are included with the tape.

Songs featured are:
Baa, Baa Black Sheep
Baby Beluga
Brush Your Teeth
Bumpin' up and Down
Cluck, Cluck Red Hen
The Corner Grocery Store
Down by the Bay
He's Got the Whole World in His Hands
I've Been Workin' on the Railroad
The More We Get Together
Mr. Sun
Peanut Butter Sandwich
Shake My Sillies Out
The Shoe Song
Six Little Ducks
Something in My Shoe
Sur le pont d'avignon
Thanks a Lot
Y a un rat
You Gotta Sing When the Spirit Says Sing
The Wheels on the Bus

CAUTION: This is a concert tape. There is no story woven between the songs.

RAFFI IN CONCERT WITH THE RISE AND SHINE BAND

A & M Video
1988
50 minutes
Directed by: David Devine
Starring: Raffi, Deenis Pendrith, Nancy Walker, Mitch Lewis, Bucky Berger

Favourite Canadian performer Raffi sings his best-loved songs to a lively and attentive audience. Backed by his four-person band, Raffi accompanies himself on an acoustic guitar.

Songs featured are:
All I Really Need
Apples and Bananas
Baa, Baa Black Sheep
Baby Beluga
Bathtime
Day-O
De Colores
Everything Grows
Five Little Ducks
Go to Sleep (Fait dort dort)
He's Got the Whole World in His Hands
I Gotta Shake My Sillies Out
If You're Happy and You Know It
Itsy Bitsy Spider
Knees up Mother Brown
Like Me and You
The More We Get Together
One Light, One Sun
Rise and Shine
This Little Light of Mine
Time to Sing
Tingalayo
Twinkle, Twinkle Little Star

CAUTION: This is a concert tape. There is no story woven between the songs.

GO: Raffi is a genuine favourite with young children.

GO: *Follow that Bird* is one of the few full-length films that very young children will sit and watch. It's full of great songs and classic cameo performances and it even teaches a wonderful lesson on racism.

SESAME STREET PRESENTS: FOLLOW THAT BIRD

Warner Home Video
1985
92 minutes
Directed by: Ken Kwapis
Starring: Carroll Spinney,
   Joe Flaherty, Dave Thomas,
   Chevy Chase, John Candy,
   Sandra Bernhard

When the children's aid society decides that Big Bird needs a better home environment, he's taken to live with a foster family in Illinois. But when his new parents forbid him to make friends with anyone other than birds, Big Bird decides to leave his foster family and go back to Sesame Street. As soon as it's discovered that he's run away, the whole Sesame Street gang goes looking for him, and comic incidents abound. The Sleaze Brothers plan to kidnap Big Bird, paint him blue and make a fortune by displaying him as the Blue Bird of Happiness; Bert and Ernie take a harrowing ride in a biplane in a hilarious send-up of the classic scene from Hitchcock's North By Northwest, and the Sesame Street gang samples the not-so-delicious offerings at the Grouch Restaurant. Only the timely intervention of a motorcycle policeman saves Big Bird from a fate worse than having to eat spinach for breakfast.

SESAME STREET VIDEOS

Random House Home Video
1987-1992
30 minutes (each volume)
Directed by: Jon Stone and others

What we find most people ask about when it comes to the Sesame Street series is if a particular favourite segment, either animated or live-action, is on a particular video since individual segments are not described on the boxes. Some favourites are Ernie singing Rubber Duckie, that little red ball that rolls down a roller coaster apparatus counting off 1-2-3, Kermit reporting for Sesame Street news, and What's the Name of That Song? Lyric song posters or activity books are included.

Count It Higher: Great Music Videos from Sesame Street

Hip video jockey Count Von Count hosts this tape of eight songs between which he counts the number of things in the video. Ernie, Kermit, The Count, Oscar and Big Bird all make appearances.

Songs featured are:
Count It Higher
   (by Chris and the Alphabeats)

Counting to 10
   (to the tune of "Twist and Shout")
Do De Rubber Duck (a reggae tune)
Doo Wop Hop
   (a Doobie Brothers style song)
Letter B (by the Beetles)
Honk around the Clock (by the Honkers)
The Ten Commandments of Health (by
   Dr. Thad and the Medications)
Wet Paint (featuring the group How Now
   Brown Cow)
ZZ Blues (by Over the Top)

CAUTION: The video is a parody of adult
music and MTV music videos.

Dance Along!

This tape, presented in the style of
American TV dance shows, features
the Sesame Street kids,
demonstration dancers Gina and
Mike, Big Bird and the Count all
dancing to rock music. Some of the
dances are performed in a studio,
some on the Sesame Street set,
and some are from old Sesame
Street clips interspersed with shots
of the children in the studio dancing
along.

Dances featured are:
ABC Disco
Any Way You Feel Dance
The Batty Bat
The Birdcall Boogie
The Birdland Jump
Doin' the Pigeon
A New Way to Walk
Stop Dancing
A Very Simple Dance to Do

Elmo's Sing-Along Guessing Game

Elmo hosts a TV game show in
which contestants must listen to a
song, bounce on a trampoline, ring
a bell and shout out answers. It
might be easy if Elmo didn't keep
enthusiastically shouting out the

answers. Featuring Kermit, Ernie,
Elmo, The Alligator King, Big Bird,
Snuffy, Gordon, Olivia, Oscar and
The Count.

Songs featured are:
Eight Balls of Fur
Elmo's Song
Get Along
I Love My Elbows
I Love Trash
The Lambaba!
My Best Friend
One Fine Face

Monster Hits

Herry Monster hosts The Fuzzy
Awards in which the monster song
hit of the year receives the Fuzzy
Award. Elmo holds the envelope
with the winner's name. Herry is
kept busy trying to stop him from
opening it before all the songs have
been played and before Cookie can
eat the envelope. Herry's mother
receives a Lifetime Achievement
Award.

Songs featured are:
C is For Cookie
Comb Your Face
Frazzle
Fur
Fuzzy and Blue
Healthy Food
Herry's Family Song
That Furry Blue Mommy of Mine
Two Heads Are Better Than One
We Are All Monsters
What Do I Do When I'm Alone

Sesame Songs: Rock and Roll

Deejay Jackman Wolf answers
phone requests from Chrissy (a high
energy real life teen), Bert, The
Count, Officer Little Red Riding
Hood, Maria, Gina and Grover.

Animation and live-action footage are included. Other Sesame Street characters featured are Ernie and Bert, Oscar, The Cobble Stones, Jerry and the Monotones and Chrissy and the Alphabeats.

Songs featured are:
Count up to Nine
Forty Blocks from My Home
(I Can't Get No) Cooperation
Hand Talk
It's Hip to Be a Square
Monster in the Mirror
Rock 'n' Roll Readers
Telephone Rock
The Word Is No
You're Alive!

Sing, Hoot and Howl with the Sesame Street Animals

The Sing, Hoot and Howl Club is where Big Bird and the Sesame Street animals gather to sing their favourite animal songs. Some of the songs are sung by Sesame Street characters and some are dubbed over live-action footage of real animals. The menagerie includes a horse, a lion, an elephant, a cow, a wolf, a lamb, a pig and a goldfish.

Songs featured are:
Baa Baa Bamba
Hard Working Dog
I Love Being a Pig
I'm an Aardvark
I'm Proud to Be a Cow
The Insects in Your Neighbourhood
Laying Eggs around the Clock
Old MacDonald Had a Farm
Starfish
We Are All Earthlings
Which Came First, the Chicken or the Egg?

SingYourself Silly

Big Bird, the Count, Ernie and Kermit introduce some really silly songs performed by characters from the Sesame Street programs. "Put Down the Duckie" features cameos by Jeremy Irons, Madeline Kahn, Ladysmith Black Mombazo, Itzak Perlman, Paul Simon, Danny DeVito, Pete Seeger and Pee-Wee Herman.

Songs featured are:
Calcutta Joe
The Everything in the Wrong Place Ball
The Honker Duckie Dinger Jamboree
Jellyman Kelly
I'm Wavin Goodbye to You with My Heart
The Ladybug Picnic
Old MacDonald Cantata
One Banana
Mary Had a Bicycle
Put Down the Duckie
Ten Turtles

Singalong

Bob, Maria, David, Luis, Big Bird, Olivia, Linda and a group of kids move a piano up to the apartment building roof to sing songs together. They are joined by Sully and Biff, the construction workers. Some of the songs are performed by the group and some are clips from other Sesame Street programs.

Songs featured are:
The Alphabet Song
Cheer Up
Doin' the Pigeon
John Jacob Jingleheimer Schmidt
Old MacDonald
Rubber Duckie
Sing a Song
  (Olivia and Linda sign this one)
Sing after Me
Stand Up and Pinch Your Nose
We All Sing with the Same Voice
What's the Name of That Song

GO: The songs on this tape are some of the most popular ever performed on Sesame Street.

SHARON, LOIS AND BRAM SERIES

These videos are episodes of the highly successful television program, *Sharon, Lois and Bram's Elephant Show*. Each video contains two episodes; some have guest stars and they all have songs.

Animal Pals (Vol. 8)

C/FP Video
1987
60 minutes
Directed by: Wayne Moss
  (episode 1), Michael McNamara
  (episode 2)
Starring: Murray McLaughlin
  (episode 1), Max the Dog
  (episode 2)

Urban Cowboy Sharon, Lois and Bram and friends head out to Farmer John's for the weekend for a taste of life on the farm. They do chores, go for a hayride and, of course, sing songs.

Songs featured are:
Ferdinand
Goin' to the Country
Have a Banana, Hanna
Little Boy, Little Girl
The Muffin Man
Straw Hat and Old Dirty Hankies
Uncle Joe
When Other Friendships Be Forgot
  (Friendship)

Pet Fair Sharon, Lois and Bram decide to have a pet fair and everyone enters in hopes of winning big prizes. Elephant doesn't enter the contest until she finds a pet of her own — a friendly stray dog in the park. She's quickly introduced to the responsibility of pet ownership. In the end, everyone wins a prize, even Bram, whose pet rock garners the best-behaved pet award.

Songs featured are:
A Happy Disposition
The Animal Fair
I Had a Pet and My Pet Pleased Me
I Have a Dog and His Name Is Rags
Hercules, King of the Fleas
The Little Green Frog
Rock around the Clock
Three Little Fishes
Twinkle, Twinkle Little Star

Fairy Tales (Vol. 2)

MCA Home Video
1987
60 minutes
Directed by Wayne Moss
  (episode 1), Stan Swan
  (episode 2)
Starring: Terrence McDiddler
  (episode 1), Jayne Eastwood
  (episode 2)

Mother Goose An outing in the park turns into high adventure when a friend leads Sharon, Lois and Bram to an enchanted land. There they meet Rip Van Winkle, Celtic fiddle great Terrence McDiddler and a king and a queen. They help

47

prepare the legendary four-and-twenty blackbird pie, and are returned home in a flash by a bit of Van Winkle's magic.

Songs featured are:
Bye Bye Blackbird
Circle of the Sun
It's Raining, It's Pouring
Lavender's Blue
Oh! What a Merry Land Is England!
Rubber Blubber Whale
Sing a Song of Sixpence
Something in My Shoe
This Old Man

Snow White Elephant Sharon, Lois and Bram and friends plan their own production of Snow White called "Snow White Elephant." To ensure the success of the production, they recruit big star Miss Galore to play the Evil Queen. But when Miss Galore makes a few changes to the script, things get totally out of hand.

Songs featured are:
Another Opening of Another Show
Hi, My Name Is Joe
Mr. Gloom Be On
Pizza Is Our Business
Snow White Rap
There Was a Princess Long Ago
You Might Have Been a Beautiful Baby
Your Way
Walk Right In, Sit Right Down

Magic (Vol. 4)

MCA Home Video
1988
60 minutes
Directed by: Stan Swan (episode 1),
  Allan Z. Novak (episode 2)
Starring: Rick Green (episode 1),
  Barbara Hamilton (episode 2)

Elephant's Lamp One day Elephant produces a magic lamp. Everyone tries rubbing the thing, but in the end it's only Elephant who can get the magic genie to appear. When the group learns that this is

only a one-wish genie, Sharon, Lois and Bram fantasize about the perfect wish. In the end, Elephant's generous wish is that her three friends have their own wishes fulfilled.

Songs featured are:
Have You Had a Hug Today?
If I Knew You Were Comin'
Mexican Birthday Song
Three Wishes
Tutti Frutti

Curio Shoppe Sharon, Lois and Bram and friends discover a strange shop which has apparently materialized out of nowhere. Thanks to the magical powers of the shop's unusual owner, everyone experiences a particular special fantasy.

Songs featured are:
Bye, Bye Blackbird
Curio Shoppe Song
Hands, Knees, and Bumpsy-Daisy
The Rock Island Line
Simple Gifts
There's an Old-Fashioned Car
Winken, Blinken and Nod

Making News (Vol. 6)

C/FP Video
1991
60 minutes
Directed by: Eleanor Lindo
  (episode 1), Richard Mortimer
  (episode 2)
Starring: The Beirdo Brothers and
  Sister Sheila (episode 1),
  Ron Rubin (episode 2)

Newspaper Sharon, Lois and Bram read the newspaper and decide to create a neighbourhood paper of their own called *Elephant News*. But they soon discover that the newspaper business is more complicated than they'd expected. Elephant takes terrible pictures, and

Bram is the butt of a series of practical jokes.

Songs featured are:
Bizet's Toreador Song
Dear Eric, Dear Eric
Reporting's Lots of Fun
Shoo-fly Pie
The Wheels on the Bus
When Are We Gonna Be Married?
Who Are the People in Your Neighbourhood?
The Wee Cock Sparrow

Radio Show When the television blows up, Bram gets out the old-fashioned radio and he and the gang are whisked back to 1947 where they hear the old radio shows, *Jimmy Rock, Private Eye* and the zany *Theatre of the Imagination.*

Songs featured are:
Don't Poke Your Finger in Your Eye, Tommy Thumb
Fifteen Years on the Erie Canal
Samba Lalay
A Tisket a Tasket

Mysteries (Vol. 1)

MCA
1986
60 minutes
Directed by: George Bloomfield
Starring: Bob Berkey

Who Stole the Cookies? When Lois discovers that someone has taken all but one of her newly baked homemade cookies, she systematically eliminates suspects until no one is left. Meanwhile everyone ignores the multitude of clues that Elephant is discovering, and the mysterious thief manages to snatch away the last cookie.

Songs featured are:
All around the Kitchen
Apple Picker's Reel
Eric's Sewerphone Song

Grocery Shopping Song
I Had a Little Rooster
Picking Up the Paw Paws
Who Did Steal the Cookies?
Who Stole the Cookies from the Cookie Jar?

Treasure Island Sharon, Lois and Bram and friends discover a treasure map when they're cleaning out the hall closet. Determined to find the treasure, they put on pirate outfits and set sail for the island pictured on the map. There they discover a tree marked X, but are unable to find the treasure, even when Pirate Eric shows up with a back-hoe. They then realize that hundreds of other trees on the island are similarly marked.

Songs featured are:
Chant
Digging Chant
Fooba Wooba
Going on a Treasure Hunt
The Lion Sleeps Tonight
Medley: Dance, Boatman, Dance and Going over the Sea
Time to Go Adventuring
Walking Along Song
Way under the Ground

Out and About (Vol. 9)

C/FP Video
1986
60 minutes
Directed by: Stan Swan
Starring: The Inter-Community Group (episode 1),
The Leahy Family (episode 2)

Kensington Market Sharon, Lois and Bram and friends go to Kensington market for lunch, where they experience the rich diversity of a multicultural market.

Songs featured are:
Ché Ché
Five Brown Buns
Here We Go Cheerio

How Could Anything Be Wrong With
  Being Different
My Mother Did-A-Tell-Me (Mango Walk)
Portugese Dance Song
She'll be Coming 'Round the Mountain
Sitting Around Playing the Spoons
There Once was a Woman Who
  Gobbled Swiss Cheese
There Was a Little Man
There's a Brown Girl in the Ring

Pioneer Village Sharon, Lois and
Bram go to Black Creek Pioneer
Village during the apple harvest and
learn how pioneers baked, made
brooms and used a printing press.
Elephant makes an apple cake and
Eric eats "eleventy-seven" apples.

Songs featured are:
"A" You're Adorable
ABCDEFG
Hey, Ho, Makes You Feel So Fine
Hop Along Peter Where You Goin'?
Horsey, Horsey, on Your Way
Little Liza Jane
Six Men Went to Mow
Step-dancing by the Leahy Family
There Was an Old Woman
There's a Little Wheel A-turning in My
  Heart
Weevily Wheat

Sports Days (Vol. 3)

MCA Home Video
1986
60 minutes
Directed by: Stan Swan
Starring: John Pattison and Garlou
  (episode 1), Denis Simpson
  (episode 2)

Funny Field Day Sharon, Lois and
Bram host the first annual Funny
Field Day where contestants must,
among other things, compete to ride
a bicycle as slowly as possible.
Elephant is discouraged because
she can't seem to win in any event
until the big baseball game when
she hits a home run.

Songs featured are:
Ally O
I Have a Little Friendship Pin
I Know an Old Lady Who Swallowed a
  Fly
I Pass the Orange
Never Never in My Long-legged Life
Rig-a-dee Jig and Away We Go
Slow Down
Take Me Out to the Ball Game

Marathon Sharon, Lois and Bram
organize a run-a-thon to raise
money to buy musical instruments
for the community centre. Elephant
trains like a pachyderm possessed.

Songs featured are:
Blue Bird, Blue Bird
Dancin' in the Streets
Down in the Valley Two by Two
Eric's Banjo Instrumental
Father Abraham
Heidi Heidi Heidi Ho
O Lee O Lee, O Lay O Lay
Such a Gettin' Upstairs I Never Did See
Tony Chestnut
We Have a Band
When the Spirit Moves You

Summer Fun (Vol. 7)

C/FP Video
1984
60 minutes
Directed by: Stan Swan
Starring: Denis Simpson (episode 1),
  Susan Mendelson (episode 2)

Amusement Park Sharon, Lois and
Bram go to the amusement park
and goof around with their pal,
Denis. Elephant drives a a train, an
antique car and a swan paddle boat.

Songs featured are:
We Have a Band
The Darby Ram
Hi Ho, Come to the Fair
It's a Small World
Oh, Dear, What Can the Matter Be
Well, Once I Saw Three Goats
When I See an Elephant Fly
Where's Thumbkin

Camp Sharon, Lois and Bram visit Camp Elephant Walk where they hike, sing songs and experiment with different rhythms. Ms Mendelson makes pita pocket sandwiches for lunch and Eric demonstrates some interesting homemade instruments by the campfire.

Songs featured are:
Do Si Do Means Dough
Flea Fly Mosquito
Frère Jacques (and R2D2)
Here We Go Looby-Loo
Home On the Range
I'm Going to Leave Ol' Texas Now
John Jacob Jingleheimer Schmidt
One More Hour
Piccolo Mine
Row, Row, Row Your Boat
Three Chants from Ghana, the West Indies and Mexico

Trunk Troubles
(Vol. 5)

MCA
1986
60 minutes
Directed by: George Bloomfield
Starring: Maury Chaykin, Ron Rubine

Soap Box Derby Sharon, Lois and Bram help the kids build a soap-box racer while Eric works on a rival vehicle of top-secret design. In the end, Sharon, Lois and Bram allow Eric to join their team when his car falls apart during the test-run. Elephant isn't allowed to race because she doesn't come in under the weight limit.

Songs featured are:
A, You're Adorable
All over This Land
Debra's Car is Painted Green
   (Ah Ha Me Riddle I Day)
Going to Kentucky
I'm a Little Piece of Tin

This Old Car
We Wanted a Place for Our Car in the Race

There's an Elephant in That Tree
Sharon, Lois and Bram are hanging around in a park when for no apparent reason, Elephant climbs a tree and won't come down. Eric climbs the tree and shows Elephant how to make a whistle out of bark while Bram and a young friend leave to enlist the fire department's help. When the firemen arrive, they rescue Elephant, but almost forget Eric. It later turns out that Elephant was frightened into the tree by a mechanical mouse.

Songs featured are:
I Met a Little Elephant
If You Could Play a Ukulele
Move Over
One Elephant
Peanut Butter
There's a Big Green Monster under My Bed
We're All Together Again
Wither Shall I Follow Thee

GO: Sharon, Lois and Bram provide non-threatening, gentle, fun entertainment. There is often child participation.

SHARON, LOIS AND BRAM SING A TO Z

Elephant Records
1992
50 minutes
Directed by: Don Allan

In this live concert, Sharon, Lois and Bram and Elephant sing a song for every letter of the alphabet.

Songs featured include:
ABCDEFG
B-I-N-G-O

51

C-H-I-C-K-E-N
Come Ride with Me
Down in the Valley
Five Little Fishes
Grampa's Farm
Ham and Eggs
Hush Little Baby
Ice Cream
In the Land of the Pale Blue Snow
Jelly Man Kelly
Junior Birdsmen
Kitty Come Kimo
Little Sir Echo
The Lollipop Song
Mares Eat Oats (Mairzy Doats)
The Name Game
The Play Song
Skinamarink
S-M-I-L-E
There's a New World Coming
Tongue-Twisters
Tzena, Tzena
Up in the Air
W-a-l-k in the P-a-r-k

SHARON, LOIS AND BRAM'S ELEPHANT SHOW CONCERT PLUS ERIC NAGLER

MCA Home Video
1989 (episode 1), 1986 (episode 2)
60 minutes
Directed by: Stan Swan
Starring: Eric Nagler

Live in Your Living Room This video features concert footage of Sharon, Lois and Bram performing some of their best-loved selections.

Canadian Jig Medley (Lots of Fish, Sur le Pont D'Avignon, Danse Danse)
Eensy Weensy Spider
Five Little Monkeys
Little Peter Rabbit
Little Rabbit Foo Foo
Once I Saw Three Goats
One Elephant, Deux Elephants
Peanut Butter
Pufferbellies

Tingalayo

Making Music with Eric Selected cuts from *The Elephant Show* feature Eric Nagler on the set, on stage and live on location.

Songs featured are:
Barlow Knife
Come On In
Cornstalk Fiddle
Frère Jacques
Juba
Mama Don't Allow
My Aunt Came Back
My Dog Treed a Rabbit
The Old Bell Cow

STORIES TO REMEMBER COLLECTION

This set of videotapes is an elaborately produced, award-winning collection of animated children's stories. Rich voice talent and continuous music accompany a variety of animation styles. Other titles in the series include: *Beauty and the Beast*, *Merlin and the Dragons*, *Noah's Ark* and *Pegasus*. See Ages 3-6 for more information.

Baby's Bedtime

Hi-Tops
1989
26 minutes
Directed by: Daniel Ivanick
Starring the voice of: Judy Collins

Adapted from *The Baby's Bedtime Book* by Kay Chorao into a fully-animated video, this tape has original songs by Ernest Troost and lullabies sung by Judy Collins. Winner of a Cine Golden Eagle Award for Outstanding Children's Films.

Songs and rhymes set to music are:
Hush Little Baby (Mockingbird)
The Land of Nod
Lullaby and Good Night

Baby's Morningtime

Hi-Tops
1989
30 minutes
Directed by: Daniel Ivanick
Starring the voice of: Judy Collins

This fully-animated video, based on Kay Chorao's best-selling book *The Baby's Good Morning Book*, features Judy Collins singing and reciting the poems of Robert Browning, Emily Dickinson and Gertrude Stein. All designed to help parents and children greet the day. Set to music by award-winning composer Ernest Troost.

Baby's Storytime

Hi-Tops
1989
26 minutes
Directed by: Michael Sporn
Starring the voice of: Arlo Guthrie

Based on Kay Choao's book *The Baby's Story Book*, this animated video features the voice and storytelling of singer/songwriter Arlo Guthrie. Winner of a Cine Golden Eagle Award for Outstanding Children's Films.

Stories featured are:
The Ginger Bread Boy
The Hare and the Turtle
Henny Penny

The History of the Apple Pie
The Lion and the Mouse
The Little Red Hen
Little Red Riding Hood
The Princess and the Pea
The Three Billy Goats Gruff
The Three Little Pigs
The Wind and the Sun

CAUTION: All of the videos in the Stories to Remember collection are animated; there is no live action. Waltzes and folk-style tunes are used, making the videos low key and less stimulating than other videos at this level.

GO: These gentle videos are well-done and are edited to the rhythm of the music. ∎

THE THOMAS THE TANK ENGINE AND FRIENDS COLLECTION

Britt Allcroft's production of *Thomas the Tank Engine and Friends* is based on The Reverend W. Awdry's books, *The Railway Series*. Each multi-episode video combines working model electric trains with still models to tell the stories produced for the popular PBS TV series, *Shining Time Station*. Each video contains about seven short stories about the Island of Sodor where station master Sir Topham-Hatt, runs an efficient railway system with the mischievous engine, Thomas, and his friends. Because people frequently order these videos by the colour of the box, we have included this information for each title.

James Learns a Lesson and Other Stories (red)

STRAND V.C.I. Entertainment
1985
40 minutes
Directed by: David Mitton

James Learns a Lesson James, a cocky special mixed traffic engine, talks back to Sir Topham-Hatt and gets into trouble.

Foolish Freight Cars After completing an extremely difficult trip, Sir Topham-Hatt congratulates James on his perseverance.

A Proud Day for James Gordon, an old double engine, teases James about his mishaps until the day Gordon is unable to pull the express and James is asked to fill in.

Thomas and the Conductor Thomas is impatient with Henry, the conductor, and leaves him behind. To make up for lost time Thomas runs the route faster than ever before.

Thomas Goes Fishing When the water station closes down, Thomas is filled with river water and his boiler almost bursts because it's full of fish.

Terence the Tractor When Terence helps Thomas out of a snow bank, Thomas is thankful for Terence's unique ability.

Thomas and Bertie's Great Race Thomas races Bertie the Bus.

Better Late Than Never and Other Stories (purple)

STRAND V.C.I. Entertainment
1986
40 minutes
Directed by: David Mitton

Better Late Than Never Bertie is angry with Thomas for always being late, but when Bertie breaks down, it's Thomas who arrives to take Bertie's passengers home.

Pop Goes the Weasel A boastful new diesel comes to work and causes a great deal of damage when he ignores instructions and tries to move the wrong cars.

Diesel's Devious Deed Diesel tells the cars nasty stories about Gordon, Henry and Thomas and says that Duck made them up. Furious, the engines send Duck away.

A Close Shave for Duck Mischievous cars try to run Duck off the rails, but he bravely manages to stop them from causing a serious accident.

Gordon Takes a Dip When Gordon is asked to pull a special train, he considers the job to be beneath him and in trying to jam the turntable gets himself stuck in a ditch.

Down the Mine Thomas gets stuck in the mine and Gordon must pull him out.

The Runaway When his newly repaired brake is not applied, Thomas slides away without a driver and must be rescued by Harold the Helicopter and the Inspector.

Thomas Gets Tricked and Other Stories (blue)

STRAND V.C.I. Entertainment
1986
40 minutes
Directed by: David Mitton

Thomas Gets Tricked Tired of hearing Thomas call him lazy, Gordon tricks Thomas into pulling his express route. In the end, an exhausted Thomas realizes that Gordon isn't lazy at all.

Edward Helps Out Rarely removed from the shed, Edward is excited when he's finally taken out to do some work. The other engines jealously belittle his contributions until Gordon gets stuck and Edward saves the day.

Come Out, Henry! Henry refuses to work in the rain for fear of spoiling his beautiful paint and takes refuge in a tunnel. In the end, the soot and dirt from the tunnel spoil his paint.

Henry to the Rescue Sir Topham-Hatt coaxes Henry out of the tunnel to help Edward pull Gordon's load to the end of the line.

A Big Day for Thomas When Henry is ill, Thomas is asked to pull the passenger cars. He's so excited he starts off before the coaches are hooked up, feeling very important and looking very silly.

Trouble for Thomas When he swaps jobs with Edward, the cars Thomas is pulling cause him to go so fast that he nearly crashes.

Thomas Saves the Day James is forced into an accident and Thomas helps to clean up the mess. Sir Topham-Hatt rewards Thomas by giving him his own branch line.

Tenders and Turntables and Other Stories (yellow)

STRAND V.C.I. Entertainment
1989
40 minutes
Directed by: David Mitton

Tenders and Turntables While Thomas is running his own branch line, the important tender engines are angered by the increased workload and decide to go on strike.

Trouble in the Shed Sir Topham-Hatt temporarily replaces the striking tender engines with Edward, Thomas and a new tank engine named Percy.

Percy Runs Away Percy is so frightened after Gordon almost runs into him that he runs away. He's finally stopped by a clever signal box operator.

Thomas Comes to Breakfast Thomas foolishly decides to run the line without his driver. The next morning when a careless cleaner fiddles with his controls, Thomas runs into the side of the Stationmaster's house and sees the value of having someone at the controls.

Henry's Special Coal It is discovered that Henry needs special coal because his firebox is too small to process regular coal properly.

The Flying Kipper Henry runs into another freight train during a blizzard.

Toby the Tram Sir Topham-Hatt has to shut Toby's line down because fewer people are buying tickets and trucks are taking over the shipping industry. This story continues in the *Thomas Breaks the Rules* video

Thomas Breaks the Rules and Other Stories (green)

STRAND V.C.I. Entertainment
1989
40 minutes
Directed by: David Mitton

Thomas Breaks the Rules A policeman stops Thomas for not having a cow-catcher or wheel-covers.

A Cow on the Line Gordon and Henry boast that cows on the tracks would never stop them, until some do.

Old Iron Edward proves he's useful when he saves a runaway James.

Double Trouble Thomas and Percy make up after an argument.

James in a Mess James crashes into a tar wagon after making fun of Toby and Henrietta.

Duck Takes Charge A new engine named Duck stands up for Edward.

Percy Proves A Point Percy proves that he's not slow and out-of-date.

Thomas Gets Bumped and Other Stories (white)

STRAND V.C.I. Entertainment
1991
37 minutes
Directed by: David Mitton

Thomas Gets Bumped Bertie the Bus helps Thomas out with his passengers and returns a favour.

Edward, Trevor and the Really Useful Party Trevor the traction engine is the star of the vicar's garden party fund-raiser.

Diesel Does It Again When Percy and Duck are forced to work with the oily Diesel, they go on strike.

Gordon and the Famous Visitor A famous engine comes to visit Sodor. Pompous Gordon gets jealous and tries to match the famous engine's record but only succeeds in blowing his dome.

Donald's Duck Duck works hard and earns his own branch line. Donald gives him a hard time until Duck plays a joke on Donald, putting a duck in his water tank. Donald gets him back in fine fashion.

Percy and the Signal Percy loves playing jokes until Gordon and James pay him back with a joke of their own.

Thomas, Percy and the Mail Train Because mail service by rail permits delivery in all kinds of weather, plans to replace it with air mail service are abandoned.

Thomas, Percy and the Dragon and Other Stories (silver)

STRAND Home Video
1991
37 minutes
Directed by: David Mitton

Thomas, Percy and the Dragon Sometimes Percy teases Thomas about being frightened, but the tables are turned when Percy thinks he sees a dragon.

Donald and Douglas Twin engines from Scotland cause confusion. When a brake van takes a dislike to Douglas and Donald is involved in an accident, Douglas is left to push.

The Deputation Donald and Douglas, afraid Sir Topham-Hatt will send one of them back to Scotland, prove how valuable they are.

Time for Trouble James does Gordon's job and when Toby is stranded on the mainline James must push Toby.

A Scarf for Percy One cold winter Percy wants a scarf for his funnel. Instead he has a pair of trousers twisted around his funnel after an accident in which he gets covered with ham.

The Diesel Bill and Ben are twin tank engine diesels who pull cars at the harbour.

Edward's Exploits When old Edward struggles to move a heavy train, he is derided by Gordon and James. Later, he breaks a crank pin, but still manages to get back to the station, battered but unbeaten.

Trust Thomas and Other Stories (orange)

STRAND Home Video
1985
40 minutes
Directed by: David Mitton

Trust Thomas Thomas recovers a missing load of tar to repair Bertie's rough road.

Mavis Mavis ignores Toby's advice and gets stuck crossing an icy portion of the line. Toby agrees to help only because Mavis was doing a job that he was supposed to do.

Toby's Tightrope When the bridge is falling apart, lazy Mavis redeems herself by preventing certain disaster.

No Joke for James To prove to Gordon that Sir Topham-Hatt has great plans for him, James takes

Gordon's passenger coaches and leaves Gordon with the freight cars.

Percy's Promise Even when bad weather floods the tracks, Percy and Harold manage to pull two coaches full of children home.

Henry's Forest When a strong wind destroys the trees in Henry's favourite forest, Toby helps him transport new trees to plant.

The Trouble with Mud When Gordon refuses to be cleaned, James is asked to pull the express instead.

CAUTION: The characters in the series are often jealous and insulting (often telling each other to shut up) and not every argument is completely resolved. At times, Ringo Starr's accent is difficult to understand and he frequently uses British words and expressions not familiar to North American audiences. There are only three female characters in the series. Although the creators of these videos recommend them for children ages two to seven, we recommend them only for children under five.

GO: Cleverly produced and gentle in tone, the stories move quickly, but without the manic tempo of some programs, and most are complete in themselves so it's easy to stop the video and save the rest for another time. *Shining Time Station* is probably the only train series available for young children and has won an Emmy, an Action for Children's Television award and a Parents' Choice award.

WEE SING COLLECTION

The Wee Sing videos are based on the highly successful book and audio series created by mothers Susan Hagen Nipp and Pamela

Conn Beall. They feature children and adults singing and dancing to up-tempo versions of favourite songs. Each tape has a simple story-line of songs interspersed with dialogue and includes finger-plays, fanciful creature costumes and puppets. Music arranged by Cal Scott. A song book is included with each tape.

The Best Christmas Ever

Price Stern Sloan Video
1990
60 minutes
Directed by: Claudia Sloan
Starring: Melanie Chang, R. Dee,
  Sam Howard, Vic McGraw,
  Robert Milam, Sarah Werle

Susie, Johnny, Nellie and Will go Santa's workshop where they solve a problem for the elves.

Rhymes and finger plays featured are:
The Chimney
Chubby Little Snowman
Down through the Chimney
Here Are Mother's Knives and Forks
Star Light Star Bright
Tapping, Tapping Little Elf
'Twas the Night before Christmas
Two Little Christmas Trees
When Santa Comes

Songs featured are:
Angel Band
Christmas Is Coming
Christmas Wrap
Deck the Halls, Christmas Day
Gusty the Elf
Here We Come A-Caroling
Jolly Old St. Nicholas
Little Bells of Christmas
Oh Christmas Tree
Santa Claus Is Coming
Up on the Housetop
We Wish You a Merry Christmas

Grandpa's Magical Toys

Price Stern Sloan Video
1988
60 minutes
Directed by: Susan Shadbourne
Starring: Kevin Hageman, Sharene
  Mackall, Francisco Reynders,
  Daniel Straugh

Peter, David and Sarah visit Grandpa's toy-making workshop where they shrink down to the size of toys and play singing and clapping games and jump rope.

Songs featured are:
A Sailor Went to Sea
Did You Ever See a Lassie?
The Farmer in the Dell
Hambone
The Hokey-Pokey
I Love Coffee
Long-Legged Sailor
Mabel, Mabel
The Merry-Go-Round
Miss, Miss
The Muffin Man
One Potato
One, Two, Buckle My Shoe
One, Two, Three A-Twirlsy
One, Two, Three O'Leary
Playmate
Pretty Little Dutch Girl
Punchinello
Roll That Red Ball
Who Stole the Cookies from the Cookie
  Jar?

In the Big Rock Candy Mountains

Price Stern Sloan Video
1991
60 minutes
Directed by: David Poulshock
Starring: Renee Davis, Lisa White

Lisa takes the Snoodle-Doodles (stuffed bears that come alive) to the magical land of the Big Rock Candy Mountains for a picnic where they sing, tell stories and play games.

Songs featured are:
Baby Bird
The Big Rock Candy Mountains
The Fly Has Married the Bumble Bee
Follow Me
For He's a Jolly Good Fellow
The Hammer Song
Howdy-Ho-Hiya
Jimmy Crack Corn
Little Bunny Foo Foo
Nobody Knows the Trouble I've Seen
Nobody Loves Me, Everybody Hates Me
Rillaby Rill
Ring Around the Rosey
Row, Row, Row Your Boat
S.M.I.L.E.
This Is the Way We Wash Our Hands
The Upward Trail

King Cole's Party:
A Merry Musical
Celebration

Price Stern Sloan Video.
1987
60 minutes
Directed by: Susan Shadburne
Starring: Gary Basey, Zina Moreno,
  Joshua Taylor, Wendy
  Westerwelle

Everyone is invited to King Cole's castle to celebrate 100 years of peace. Jack and Jill, Mary and her lamb, Little Boy Blue, Humpty Dumpty and King Cole himself are all in attendance.

Nursery rhymes featured are:
Betty Botter
Humpty Dumpty Sat on a Wall
Jack and Jill
Jack, Be Nimble
Jack Sprat
Little Bo-Peep
Little Boy Blue
Little Jack Horner
Little Miss Muffet
Little Tommy Tucker
Mary Had a Little Lamb

Old King Cole
Pat-A-Cake
Pease Porridge Hot
Peter Piper
Polly Put the Kettle On
Rub-a-Dub-Dub
See-Saw Sac-Ra-Down
Sing a Song of Sixpence
Six Little Ducks
There Was a Crooked Man
This Old Man
Walking Chant
Wibbleton to Wobbleton

Wee Sing in Sillyville

Price Stern Sloan Video
1989
60 minutes
Directed by: David Poulshock
Starring: Joy Anderson,
  Renee Margolin, Ryan Willard

When no one is getting along in the colouring book land of Sillyville, Barney the basset hound and his owners, Laurie and Scott, magically pay a visit and help Sillywhim bring peace.

Songs featured are:
A Cold upon His Chest
An Austrian Went Yodelling
Boom, Boom, Ain't It Great to Be Crazy?
Do Your Ears Hang Low?
Down by the Bay
Fish and Chips and Vinegar
I'm A Nut
John Jacob Jingleheimer Schmidt
The Little Green Frog
Make New Friends
Michael Finnegan
Rillaby, Rallaby, Mauw, Mauw, Mauw
Roll Over
Sing Together a Joyous Song
We're Here Because We're Here

Wee Sing Together

Price Stern Sloan Video
1985
60 minutes
Directed by: John W. Mincey Jr.
Starring: Aaron Cooley,
  Marky Mason, Hollie Weikel

On the night of her sixth birthday, Sally's toys Melody Mouse and Hum Bear come to life and take her and her brother, Jonathan, to Wee Sing Park where they celebrate with Wee Rabbit Peter III and a real dog named Bingo.

Songs featured are:

The Alphabet Song
Bingo
The Finger Band
Head and Shoulders
Here We Go Looby Loo
I'm a Little Tea Pot
If You're Happy and You Know It Clap
  Your Hands
The Itsy Bitsy Spider
Knees and Toes
Little Peter Rabbit Had a Fly upon His
  Ear
Old MacDonald Had a Farm
Rain, Rain Go Away
Rickety Tickety Look at Me
Sally's Wearing a Red Dress
Skidamirink
Teddy Bear
Twinkle Twinkle Little Star
Walking, Running, Now Let's Stop

Wee Sing in the Marvelous Musical Mansion

Price Stern Sloan Video
1992
minutes
Directed by: David Poulshock

Alex, Benji, Kelly and Auntie Annabella visit Great Uncle Rubato and his cat Cadenza in the Marvelous Musical Mansion.

Songs featured are:

The Ballerina's Waltz
Clap Your Hands
The Doodle-Det Quintet!
Hey Diddle Diddle
Hickory Dickory Dock
How Do You Do, My Friends
The Magic of Music
The Marching Song
The Melody Song
My Aunt Came Back
My Hat It Has Three Corners
Oh, When the Saints Go Marching In
Oh Where, Oh Where Has the Little
  Gong Gone
The Orchestra Game Song
Round the Clock
Rueben and Rachel
She'll Be Coming 'Round the Mountain
Tap-A-Capella
Vive La Compagnie

CAUTION: The sound track is over-dubbed and most of the music is synthesized. The producers recommend the series for children ages two to eight, but because the stories tend to be babyish, we recommend it only for children under five years of age.

GO: The Wee Sing videos have simple story lines and contain no violence, sarcasm or conflict; they have positive themes and demonstrate good relationships. This is a good series for young children who are just beginning to watch complete story videos.

WINNIE-THE-POOH CLASSICS SERIES

The following films are based on the characters and stories from the books by A. A. Milne, but include dialogue contributed by other writers.

Winnie-the-Pooh and a Day for Eeyore

Walt Disney Home Video
1983
25 minutes
Directed by: Rick Reinert
Starring the voice of: Paul Winchell

Pooh, Piglet, Rabbit and Roo are playing Pooh Sticks when they see Eeyore floating down the river on his back. After a daring rescue, Eeyore explains that Tigger had bounced him into the river (the latter claims that it was only a joke) and goes on to complain about the fact that no one has remembered his birthday. Christopher Robin saves the day when he throws Eeyore a party with cake and presents and everyone goes to play Pooh Sticks together.

■

Winnie-the-Pooh and the Blustery Day

Walt Disney Home Video
1968
25 minutes
Directed by: Wolfgang Reitherman
Starring the voices of:
  Sebastian Cabot,
  Sterling Holloway, Paul Winchell

On a windy day, Pooh visits Owl whose whole tree has been blown over by the gale. That night the wind rages on and Pooh hears strange sounds. It is Tigger (introduced in this story) who bounces in and out singing. Later Pooh falls asleep and dreams of strange elephant and weasel-like creatures he calls heffalumps and woozles. When he awakes, the Hundred Acre Wood is flooded and Piglet must send a message in a bottle. However, when everyone is rescued they have a Hero Party and Eeyore finds a new house for Owl. Songs are interspersed throughout the story.

Songs featured are:
Happy Windsday
Heffalumps and Woozles
The Wonderful Thing about Tiggers

CAUTION: Some children may be frightened by the storm and the dream-sequence in which plaid creatures continuously change shapes.

■ ▲

Winnie-the-Pooh and the Honey Tree

Walt Disney Home Video
1965
25 minutes
Directed by: Wolfgang Reitherman
Starring the voices of:
  Sterling Holloway, Howard Morris,
  Sebastian Cabot

After a failed attempt at disguising himself as a little black rain cloud to steal honey from the bees, Winnie-the-Pooh raids Rabbit's honey pantry instead. He eats so much honey and becomes so big that he gets stuck in the doorway when he tries to leave. Unable to remove the pudgy bear, Christopher Robin, Rabbit, Gopher and Owl decide to postpone their efforts for a few days until Pooh becomes thin again.

Songs featured are:
I'm Just a Little Black Rain Cloud
There's a Rumbly in My Tumbly

CAUTION: Some children may be frightened by the stinging bees.

■ ▲

Winnie-the-Pooh and Tigger Too

Walt Disney Home Video
1974
25 minutes
Directed by: John Lounsbery
Starring the voices of:
Sterling Holloway, Sebastian Cabot,
Paul Winchell

Rabbit is so bothered by Tigger's bouncing that he convinces the gang to help him with a plan to "take the bounce out of [Tigger]." One cold misty morning they all go for a walk and "lose" Tigger, but their plan backfires when Pooh, Piglet and Rabbit are the ones who really get lost. Tigger does learn to control his bouncing, however, when after one

tremendous bounce he finds himself stuck in a tree. This tape also contains the sequence in which Pooh tracks a mysterious creature around a tree.

CAUTION: Very little ones are sometimes wound up or frightened by the high energy of Tigger's bounciness. Too, the thought of getting lost in the woods may frighten some children.

GO: At around twenty-five minutes each, the animated tapes in the Winnie-the-Pooh series are good first animated films for young viewers. True to the original stories, Christopher Robin has an English accent. For more Pooh stories see also *The New Adventures of Winnie-the-Pooh*.

■ ▲

VIDEOS FOR AGES THREE TO SIX

At a certain stage in any child's life, the stories he or she is told, reads or sees on the screen are going to become more sophisticated. With that increase in sophistication will come an increase in the intensity of the situations in which the story's characters find themselves. Where only a short time ago your child was watching the musical antics of the Sillyville characters and learning how to count with Richard Scarry's Busytown gang, he or she is now approaching the cannibal witch's house with Hansel and Gretel. And things just might get a tad unpleasant.

True, if your child were reading the story *Hansel and Gretel*, the experience probably wouldn't be very traumatic. But when the drama is acted out on the television screen, there is a quantum jump in the intensity of the experience. Your child no longer has the power to control the images that tell the story (with a book, a child can create a monster only as scary as his or her imagination will allow); adults have harnessed artistic talent and technology to create what is, for a child, the unimaginable.

But instead of simply saying book equals good, video equals bad, and putting the VCR in the yard sale, let's look at a few ways you can make video-watching a positive experience, by teaching your child to use the same control they use when reading a book. Video watching needn't be a passive experience.

When reading, children can:

▶ imagine the detail for themselves
▶ control the pace (reading as fast or as slowly as they want)
▶ pause to think about scenes they have not understood
▶ skim scary content, and linger on the rest
▶ skip graphic descriptions.

The same control is available when you and your child are watching a video. You can:

▶ Stop the action to discuss with your child how an image may have been created, stressing the fact that one doesn't have to accept the filmmaker's version of, for instance, the witch. (My witches' faces are always blue, but the filmmaker's are green. What colour are your witches' faces?) This will help to demystify a character and possibly reduce a child's fear.
▶ Fast-forward over scary parts.
▶ Turn the sound down (or even off) to reduce the intensity of the experience, to reinforce pleasant images.
▶ Rewind and review parts your child likes.
▶ Freeze-frame or play in slow-motion parts your child likes, for extra fun.
▶ Demonstrate that it is your child who has control over the evil or frightening images on a video, and not the other way around.

One parent we know was watching *The Wizard of Oz* with his four-year-old daughter. When the Wicked Witch appeared, his child, like so many others, was terrified. But then he had a brilliant idea. He handed her the remote control, pointed out the Pause button and said: Make the witch stop.

When the child pressed the button indicated, the witch magically froze.

The child was amazed. And when she learned how to use the Fast-forward and Rewind buttons to make the witch go away, it was a different ball game. Terror was a thing of the past, and *The Wizard of Oz* became her favourite movie.

Try to establish your child's control over frightening images early because he or she will be bothered by things you can't possibly anticipate. A video which thrills your neighbour's four-year-old may terrify yours — and vice versa. We have, for instance, heard of children who were afraid of:

- Puff the Magic Dragon . . . but only when he sang
- the balloon in the film *The Red Balloon*
- fireworks, after seeing the scene in *Mary Poppins* in which Admiral Boom shoots fireworks at the dancing chimney-sweeps
- Sesame Street's The Count
- Polkaroo (Who could be less scary than Polkaroo?)

Inevitably, after a certain period of time, characters and situations will lose their power to frighten your little viewers.

MOVING FROM LIVE-ACTION TO ANIMATION

We created the ages three to six category when we first began our business; however, experience has since taught us that this is a tremendously wide age range, which spans many developmental periods in the viewing preferences of children.

People often associate very young children with animation, and literally hundreds of times parents have come into our store believing that their three-year-old is abnormal because he or she shows no interest whatsoever in Bugs Bunny. But the fact of the matter is that for most children, live-action (or real people) is the preferred entertainment from babyhood right through to the age of four. These productions (which are usually concert or song videos) rarely exceed one hour in length, which seems to be the outer limit of the average three-year-old's attention span.

But around the age of four this preference changes, and suddenly children become interested in cartoon images. There are some four-year-olds who want nothing but animation, and whose entire perception of fairy tales, folklore and legends is learned through that medium.

One day, in the children's theatre in our store, we were showing the Errol Flynn version of *Robin Hood*. A four-year-old came in, plunked himself down, studied the morning's offering and asked: What's this?

When the answer came that it was Robin Hood, he gave us a sceptical look and said: That's not Robin Hood; Robin Hood's a fox!

(Incidentally, if you want to use videos to introduce your child to fairy tales in their traditional form, be careful. Fairy tales and nursery rhymes are easy targets for updating or satirizing. Not everything on video with a fairy tale or nursery rhyme in the title will be the version you expect.)

Watch out!
Not all cartoons are made for children

Some animations are not created specifically for children and some are not for children's eyes at all. Older children may be able to watch some, though parental guidance (and maybe even pre-viewing) will be in order.

Specific examples of animations for mature viewers (some with adult themes and terrifying representations of evil) are:

- *The Point*, a morality tale about self-sufficiency and the absurdity of prejudice
- *Watership Down*, a social comment on ecology
- Ralph Bakshi's *Lord of the Rings*
- *Who Framed Roger Rabbit?*

Animations that are definitely *not* for children are:

- Ralph Bakshi's *Wizards*, *Fritz the Cat*, *Heavy Traffic* and *Cool World*
- *When the Wind Blows*, which is about the aftermath of a nuclear explosion
- *Animal Farm*, a political satire
- *Heavy Metal*, a sexy collection of stories originally featured in the illustrated French magazine *Metal Hurlant* and the American *Heavy Metal*.
- *Akira*, about government experiments on psychic children in a post-nuclear war Tokyo

Be careful. Often video personnel will put these films in the children's section simply because they believe that all animated films are for children. Read the box before you rent.

A wealth of animation choices

If you are looking for animations of high quality there are many on the market. Some are now out of print, but are still available for rental at some stores. Don't forget to read the box, because even though an animation can be of high quality, the story may not be to your taste.

Look for:

- the VidAmerica series called *Forever Fairy Tales*
- Michael Sporn's *Abel's Island*, *The Story of the Dancing Frog*, *The Marzipan Pig*, and *Nonsense and Lullabyes*, and Sony's *The Snowman*, *Granpa* and *The Angel and the Soldier Boy*
- the Children's Circle series, featuring animation styles derived from the illustrations of well-known

books such as *Dr. De Soto*, *Really Rosie* and *The Maurice Sendak Library*.

▶ the National Film Board's *Fables and Fantasy* and *The Magic of Discovery* (though be careful, not all NFB animations are suitable for children)

▶ Babar movies and the Care Bears movies by Nelvana Studios

▶ the MCA series featuring *The Little Mermaid*, *The Selfish Giant*, *The Remarkable Rocket* and *The Happy Prince*

▶ British animations such as *Jimbo and the Jet Set*, *Ivor the Engine* and *Rupert*

▶ pixilations such as *The Wombles* and *The Wind in the Willows*

▶ Will Vinton's claymation films *The Star Child*, *Martin the Cobbler*, *The Little Prince*, and *Rip Van Winkle*

▶ all of Jim Henson's work, particularly the Muppet movies (just be careful with *The Dark Crystal* and *Labyrinth*)

OTHER INFORMATION FOR PARENTS

Tie-in merchandise

The problem with tie-in merchandise (movie-related paraphernalia which saturates the market before, during and after the release of certain mega-hits) is that it often interests very young children in movies that are not made specifically for them. What child with *Jurassic Park* T-shirts, lunch-boxes and play figurines can possibly understand his parents' flat refusal to allow him to watch the movie that inspired it all?

What can a parent do? If your child is clamouring for a video featuring the latest object of fascination, look for tamer alternatives. Instead of Tim Burton's *Batman* or

Batman Returns, try renting *Batman: The Movie* (which was the pilot for the mild-mannered TV show starring Adam West), or a Batman animation, such as *Batman Superpowers*.

There are also animations available of *Beetlejuice*, *Robocop* and even *Rambo*, but these are still primarily about fighting and may only serve to sustain your child's fascination with the characters.

What is the appeal of these toys, anyway? In many cases, it's possible that these characters simply represent the power to directly resist violence. For a small child, bombarded with frightening images of violence, the concept of meeting fire with fire must be attractive. But there are other film heroes who have the same power, whose primary response to any crisis is not to instigate a full-scale massacre, and who are much more suitable role models for young children. Try sharing some of these heroes with your child:

- ◗ Sinbad
- ◗ Jason and the Argonauts
- ◗ the *Star Wars* good guys, Luke Skywalker, Obi Wan Kenobi, Yoda and Han Solo
- ◗ Superman
- ◗ Wonderwoman
- ◗ even Nancy Drew and the Hardy Boys qualify

There are also real live heroes to consider, such as explorers, inventors and ordinary people who respond heroically in crises.

Play it again

Try to remember that it's better for your child to watch an old favourite with benign images over and over again than to be pushed into something different because your own tolerance level is dropping fast. Children, especially those under ten, are repeat viewers.

They seem to want the same thing over and over again. (You have probably noticed the same phenomenon happening with favourite bedtime stories.)

One parent told us: I used to try to steer him toward new things in the hope of expanding his horizons, but I found that if I left him alone and just rented the same one again and again he was happy, and then one day, all of a sudden, he'd say he was finished with that one and wanted something new.

Our theory about all of this is that some children watch things over and over because movies are so loaded with content that they just can't take it all in in a single viewing — or even in several viewings. It's as if children have their own time frames. They move on to new material when they are good and ready.

✖ 101 DALMATIANS

Walt Disney Home Video
1961
79 minutes
Directed by: Clyde Geronimi,
    Hamilton S. Luske,
    Wolfgang Reitherman
Starring the voices of:
    Betty Lou Gerson, J. Pat
    O'Malley, Rod Taylor

When Dalmatians Pongo and Perdita are blessed with a litter of fifteen puppies, it doesn't take long for something to go wrong. The evil Cruella de Vil hears about the puppies, steals them away and adds them to her collection. (She and her henchmen have already collected eighty-four puppies which she intends to skin and make into a coat.) Pongo and Perdita use the night bark, a kind of dog telegraph, to call for help. And when Captain, Sergeant Tibbs and Colonel Tolboy (a horse, a cat and a sheepdog, respectively) hear the call, they begin an investigation that leads them right to the puppies. In the end, Pongo and Perdita rescue their children and then must escort all ninety-nine puppies back to safety. Based on a book by Dodie Smith.

✗STOP: Cruella de Vil is scary, vicious and unrepentant.

CAUTION: The climactic car chase and the puppies' long trudge through bitter winter winds may upset some children. One overweight puppy is chastised for impeding the progress of the group and another is thought to be stillborn. The animation is not as detailed as in some Disney films.

A CRICKET IN TIMES SQUARE

fhe
1973
30 minutes
Directed by: Chuck Jones
Starring the voice of: Mel Blanc

Chester, a little country cricket, hitches a ride in a picnic basket to a newsstand in Times Square. In New York City he meets Tucker the mouse and Harry the cat. As it turns out, Chester has an unusual talent: when he rubs his legs together he doesn't make ordinary chirping, he makes music that sounds like violins. And when the newsstand encounters financial problems, Chester helps out by bringing in crowds with his amazing music. Based on the book by George Selden.

GO: This fully-animated video is the winner of a Parents' Choice Award.
■

ADVENTURES IN WONDERLAND

Walt Disney Home Video
1992
57 minutes (each volume)
Directed by: Kam Anway, Annie
    Court
Starring: Elisabeth Harnois,
    Armelia McQueen

Music and video effects combining live-action and fantasy, tell the story of Alice (a contemporary little girl with a cat named Dinah) in Wonderland (a strange place full of fanciful characters where lessons are learned through misadventures).

Titles in the collection are:
Hare-Raising Magic (Vol. 1):
  Off the Cuffs; For Better or Verse
Helping Hands (Vol. 2):
  Pop Goes the Easel; Techno Bunny
The Missing Ring Mystery (Vol. 3):
  Pretzelmania; Noses Off

GO: This program is an Emmy Award Winner and was recommended by the National Education Association.

ALICE IN WONDERLAND

Walt Disney Home Video
1951
75 minutes
Directed by: Clyde Geronimi,
  Wilfred Jackson, Hamilton Luske
Starring the voices of: Kathryn
  Beaumont, Richard Haydn,
  Sterling Holloway, Ed Wynn

One afternoon during Alice's lesson in the meadow, a white rabbit dressed in a waistcoat speeds by. Imprudently, Alice follows the rabbit down a hole and finds herself in a strange land where animals talk. There she meets the Cheshire Cat and Tweedle Dum and Tweedle Dee; attends the Mad Hatter's Tea Party; encounters a philosophically inclined Caterpillar; plays flamingo-hedgehog croquet with the Queen of Hearts; and goes on trial for her very life.

Songs featured are:

All in the Golden Afternoon
The Caucus Race
I'm Late
In a World of My Own
The Unbirthday Song
The Walrus and the Carpenter
Very Good Advice
We're Painting the Roses Red

CAUTION: Some children may find the strange world of Wonderland disorienting and inaccessible. The Queen of Hearts is savage and leering.

GO: Superior effort has gone into this classic Disney animation, full of fanciful characters and songs. Alice is a self-assured and mostly undaunted heroine.
■ ▲

ALL DOGS GO TO HEAVEN

MGM/UA
1989
87 minutes
Directed by: Don Bluth
Starring the voices of:
  Loni Anderson, Dom DeLuise,
  Burt Reynolds

When his evil partner has him killed, German shepherd and gambler Charlie B. Barkin gets into heaven on a technicality. But he finds it boring, and even though he knows that once he leaves he can never return, Charlie conspires to escape back to Earth. There he uses Anne-Marie, an unwitting orphan who can communicate with animals, to set up a betting scam. But Charlie soon realizes the error of his ways, and when the chips are down he sacrifices himself for his devoted friend Anne-Marie.

CAUTION: Charlie dies twice in this film, and in one particularly frightening scene, dreams he goes to hell. The themes of damnation and redemption, and the big handkerchief ending, may be too much for young children.

GO: Former Disney animator Don Bluth did a superb job with the animation, voice-overs and characterization. This film is best suited to children over five.

ALLIGATOR PIE

CF/P
1991
47 minutes
Directed by: Christopher Sanderson
Starring: Alanna Budhoo,
   Heath Lamberts, Lance Paton,
   Kate Trotter

Unaware that he's being followed by Mr. Hoobody, a frightening character who lives in the furnace and whose job it is to spread temptation (when you've eaten too much candy, he always brings some more), Nicholas sets off for the park with his best friend, Egg. Nicholas's friends Bigfoot, Hanna and McGonigle see the danger at once and try to warn Nicholas, but Mr. Hoobody delays them, sets up an ambush and captures Egg. With nowhere to turn, Nicholas and his friends must overcome their fear of Mr. Hoobody to rescue Egg.

CAUTION: Mr. Hoobody is a bit scary, especially when he speaks from the furnace vents. There is a food-fight which might give your three-year-old some ideas.

GO: Based on the clever, quirky poems in Dennis Lee's books *Alligator Pie, Nicholas Knock* and *Garbage Delight*, this is a good video about kids overcoming their fears. The claymation interludes are excellent.

■

ALVIN AND THE CHIPMUNKS COLLECTION

Buena Vista Home Video
1990
25-30 minutes (each volume)
Directed by: Don Spencer

Alvin and the Chipmunks Sing-along

Talented chipmunks Alvin, Simon and Theodore are featured in this fully-animated song video. The words for the songs run along the bottom of the screen.

Songs featured are:
A Bicycle Built for Two
Alouette
Alvin's Harmonica
Alvin's Orchestra
Git Along Little Doggies
Old MacDonald
Polly Wolly Doodle
Ragtime Cowboy Joe
Where, Oh Where Has My Little Dog Gone?
While Strolling in the Park One Day
Witch Doctor

Other titles in the collection are:
A Chipmunk Christmas
Rockin' with the Chipmunks featuring Michael Jackson

ALVIN AND THE CHIPMUNKS GO TO THE MOVIES

Buena Vista Home Video
1990
25 minutes (each volume)
Directed by: Don Spencer

Alvin, Simon and Theodore are up to some new antics in this fully-animated series.

Titles in the series are:
Back to Alvin's Future
Batmunk
Funny, We Shrunk the Adults
Kong!

encounters a number of honest and dishonest street characters along the way. Throughout the film there's an ongoing struggle between the forces of justice (the mice) and the forces of evil (a group of cats led by Warren T. Rat, who just happens to be a cat in disguise).

Songs featured are:
Never Say Never
Somewhere Out There
There Are No Cats in America

CAUTION: A number of scenes may disturb young children, not the least of which is one in which cossack cats attack at the beginning of the film. As in most films produced by Steven Spielberg, the sound track is intense. This film is probably too complex for children under four, and may be too much for sensitive four-year-olds.

GO: This is an excellent animated film. The voice treatments are charming, and the songs are memorable.
▲

AN AMERICAN TAIL

MCA
1986
81 minutes
Directed by: Don Bluth
Starring the voices of: Dom DeLuise, Peter Falk, Madeline Kahn, Christopher Plummer

When they hear a rumour that there are no cats in America, Fievel Mousekewitz and his family decide to emigrate from Russia. During the voyage across the Atlantic, Fievel is swept overboard and instead of arriving with the rest of his family, reaches New York City in a bottle. He then spends the rest of the film searching for his family and

AN AMERICAN TAIL: FIEVEL GOES WEST

MCA
1991
75 minutes
Directed by: Phil Nibbelink, Simon Wells
Starring the voices of: John Cleese, Dom DeLuise, Amy Irving, James Stewart

Young Fievel's fantasy about living in the wild west promises to become a reality when he and his family happen upon a cowboy mouse handing out train tickets to the western town of Green River. But when he and his family are aboard the train, Fievel learns that the whole western trip is nothing more than an elaborate plot, devised by Cat R. Wall, leader of a dastardly gang of cats, to turn the mice into mouseburgers. Forced off the train before he can warn the others, Fievel must make the dangerous trip to Green River on foot. And when he arrives to discover that no one believes his story, Fievel turns to the legendary dog sheriff (now something of a laughing stock) Wiley Burp. In a dramatic showdown, with some help from Fievel's friend Tiger, Wiley saves the mice and the day.

CAUTION: The plot may be too complicated for very young children. Also, the bad-guy cats are pretty scary and in one scene Fievel encounters a terrifying scorpion in a dark hole.

▲

THE ANGEL AND THE SOLDIER BOY

BMG Video
1989
25 minutes
Directed by: Alison de Vere

For her birthday, a little girl gets a new coin and the miniature figurines of an angel girl and a soldier boy. That night when the girl is asleep, two pirates from a picture in a book come to life and steal the coin. The soldier boy wakes up and tries to stop them, but his sword is no match for the Pirate Captain's revolver and the two thieves take him away as their prisoner. Soon after, the angel awakes. Certain that something's wrong, she ventures downstairs, climbs into a model pirate ship and is whisked away into a picture of a roaring sea. There she finds and frees the soldier and

together they retrieve the coin and escape back to the little girl's room.

CAUTION: On her way downstairs, the angel has frightening encounters with a huge black spider and a cat. The pirates may be a bit threatening for some children. There is no dialogue in this video.

GO: This film is an exciting, exquisitely animated romp, perfect for small children. The musical score is by the popular Irish group Clannad.

✗ ANNIE

RCA/Columbia Pictures Home Video
1981
128 minutes
Directed by: John Huston
Starring: Carol Burnett,
    Albert Finney, Aileen Quinn,
    Ann Reinking
OFRB rating: PG
MPAA rating: PG

After living with orphan Annie for just one week, billionaire philanthropist Daddy Warbucks and his secretary Miss Farrell offer to adopt her. But Annie declines. Showing them half of a locket, she explains that one day her real parents will come to get her, bringing the other half of the locket with them. However, Miss Hannigan who runs the orphanage knows that Annie's parents are dead and has in her own possession the other half of the locket. And when Daddy Warbucks offers $50,000 as an incentive for Annie's parents to come forward, Miss Hannigan's con-artist brother Rooster and his girlfriend impersonate Annie's parents to claim the reward. After a dangerous chase, Annie is rescued and goes to live with Daddy Warbucks and Miss Farrell.

✗**STOP:** In the chase scene, Rooster punches Miss Hannigan in the face,. knocking her unconscious. Annie is forced to climb to the top of a high railway drawbridge.

CAUTION: Miss Hannigan is nasty to practically everyone and she drinks heavily.

GO: The dancing, singing and gymnastics are excellent. This film is extremely popular with girls ages four to eight. Featuring the hit song "Tomorrow."
▲

✗ BABAR: THE MOVIE

Astral
1989
77 minutes
Directed by: Alan Bunce
Starring the voices of:
    Elizabeth Hanna, Gavin McGrath,
    Gordon Pinsett, Sarah Polley

When the film opens, a mature King Babar is telling his children a bedtime story. In the story, a young Babar receives word from Celeste that the rhinos are attacking villages and snatching elephants. Impatient with the bureaucracy involved in organizing an army, Babar and Celeste set out alone. They learn that the rhinos are forcing the kidnapped elephants to labour on a colossal building project and after a couple of daring escapes, Babar and Celeste participate in a final confrontation with the rhino horde.

✗**STOP:** A rhino raiding party attacks an elephant village, torching the houses and carrying the adult elephants away.

Celeste's mother is bound, painfully, and Celeste is thrown into a well.

CAUTION: This is a film about war and viewers can expect to see a great deal of violence.

GO: Despite its violence, the film is entertaining.
▲

BABAR THE ELEPHANT COMES TO AMERICA

Vestron Video
1974
30 minutes
Directed by: Ed Levitt, Bill Melendez
Starring the voice of: Peter Ustinov

When Babar and his family are invited to tour America, he and Celeste decide to travel by balloon; they encounter rough weather and crash land on a beach. After an encounter with a friendly but forgetful whale, the ocean liner carrying Cornelius and Arthur happens by and rescues them, and all four arrive in New York City together. They tour New York, then move on to visit Washington, New Orleans and Chicago, and when they arrive in Hollywood, they all become big stars.

GO: The film's animation is similar to the illustrations in the book by Jean and Laurent de Brunhoff on which the film was based.

✗ BABAR'S FIRST STEP

```
f.h.e./Nelvana
1990
49 minutes
Directed by: Raymond Jafelice
Starring the voice of:
  Gordon Pinsent
```

Babar is born in the great forest, and immediately begins to display the courage and resourcefulness that will one day make him a good leader. When a strange monster with a voice like thunder (a hunter with a gun) comes to the forest, Babar's mother is killed and Babar must learn how to deal with his grief as well as with the terrible enemy.

✗**STOP:** There are frightening close-ups of the hunter's face and of an elephant gun being loaded. The sequence in which Babar's wounded mother charges the hunter to save the herd may disturb some children.

GO: This is an environmentalist's film, albeit heavy-handed.

BABES IN TOYLAND

```
Walt Disney Home Video
1961
105 minutes
Directed by: Jack Donohue
Starring: Ray Bolger,
  Annette Funicello, Tommy Kirk,
  Tommy Sands, Ed Wynn
```

Based on an operetta by Victor Herbert and Glen McDonough, the story begins when Mother Goose invites viewers to celebrate the wedding of Mary Contrary and Tom Piper in Toyland. Aware of the fact that Mary will inherit a great deal of money when she weds, the villainous Barnaby will stop at nothing to make her marry him instead of Tom. To this end, he instructs his thugs to drown the young man. But they are unable to follow through with the terrible deed and instead sell Tom to a band of gypsies. Unaware of the fact that her fiancé is still alive, Mary is inconsolable when, dressed as sailors, the thugs explain that Tom was lost at sea and that his dying wish was that she marry Barnaby (for her own good). She agrees to accept Barnaby's proposal, but before the marriage can take place an amazing army of toys led by Tom himself restores order in Toyland.

Songs featured are:
Castle in Spain
I Can't Do the Sum
Toyland, Toyland

CAUTION: Young children may be frightened by the Forest of No Return, where trees have faces and branches that move menacingly.

GO: Full of fantasy toys and effects, this was Disney's first live-action musical.

BAMBI

```
Walt Disney Home Video
1942
69 minutes
Directed by: David D. Hand
```

This film, based on the classic book by Felix Salten, tells the story of a faun named Bambi and his friends Flower the skunk and Thumper the rabbit. As Bambi grows, he experiences the wonders and hardships of life in the forest. (His mother is shot by hunters; he matures and experiences the first awakenings of love.) And in the powerful climax, careless hunters set the forest on fire, and Bambi is shot and wounded.

CAUTION: Bambi's mother is shot by hunters (not shown). When Bambi is grown he fights an intense battle with a rival deer and later he and his new mate, Faline, are pursued by a terrifying pack of wild dogs

GO: This film features superior animation. Older children will benefit from its message.
■▲

BEAUTY AND THE BEAST

Walt Disney Home Video
1992
84 minutes
Directed by: Gary Trousdale and
    Kirk Wise
Starring the voices of:
    Robby Benson, Angela Lansbury,
    Paige O'Hara, Jerry Orbach

Long ago, an enchantress disguised as a hag offers a spoiled young prince an enchanted rose in exchange for lodging. But the prince, repulsed by the hag, refuses and is subsequently turned into a hideous, buffalo-like beast. The only way he can break the spell is to earn the love of a young woman.

And as the years pass, he falls into despair, convinced that no one could love a beast. Enter Belle, the kind and bookish daughter of eccentric inventor Maurice. (Belle is being pursued by the handsome but arrogant Gaston, whose affections she absolutely rejects.) One day, when Maurice becomes lost in the woods, he tries to take refuge in the beast's castle and is thrown into the dungeon. Belle discovers her father's plight and agrees to change places with him and be the beast's captive forever. At first immovable, her heart softens as she grows to know the beast, and when he grants her request to go to her ailing father, she realizes that the beast loves her. But Gaston and his henchmen then learn of the beast's existence and lay siege to the castle, setting up a dramatic final confrontation, after which Belle declares her love for the dying beast and releases him from his curse.

CAUTION: The forest outside the beast's castle is home to a pack of vicious wolves that attack anyone who passes. In their final confrontation, Gaston stabs the beast in the back and falls from the castle tower, shrieking as he disappears into the abyss.

GO: The combination of photo-realistic, computer-generated backgrounds and hand-drawn character cels is pure state-of-the-art. (The ballroom scene is particularly stunning.) This film was nominated for six Academy Awards including Best Picture. Three songs from the team of Howard Ashman and Alan Menken were also nominated for Academy Awards. Winner of the Golden Globe Award for best picture.
■▲

BEDKNOBS AND BROOMSTICKS

Walt Disney Home Video
1971
117 minutes
Directed by: Robert Stevenson
Starring: Angela Lansbury,
  Roddy McDowall,
  David Tomlinson

The film opens in England in 1940 in a children's evacuation centre, where Miss Eglantine Pryce, a motorcycle-riding apprentice witch (who has just received her first broom), is assigned the last three children: Carrie, Charles and Paul. She reluctantly agrees to take them in, on the understanding that they will stay with her only until a suitable home is found. But when the children accidentally witness her first solo flight, the jig is up and she's forced to take them into her confidence. In order to seal their pact, Miss Pryce gives the children a travelling spell which she conjures onto Paul's bedknob. When the war forces the closure of the college of witchcraft, Miss Pryce takes the children to London on the magic bed to get her final spell (which is used to give life to inanimate objects). But her professor turns out to be a huckster who got his spells

out of some old book, so the crew has no choice but to set off in search of the now missing book and the final spell. Meanwhile, the German army is massing on the beaches of France and Belgium in preparation for the invasion of England. And when a German raiding party arrives, the group is ready with the last spell. Based on the book by Mary Norton.

CAUTION: The Professor makes some disparaging remarks about women. The climax of the film features a battle between the Germans and an army of animated armour; there is a great deal of combat, though no one gets killed.

GO: The resemblance in style of *Bedknobs and Broomsticks* to the earlier *Mary Poppins* is unmistakable and children who enjoyed one will likely enjoy the other. Winner of the 1971 Academy Award for best visual effects.
■

BEN AND ME

Walt Disney Home Video
1953
25 minutes
Directed by: Hamilton Luske
Starring the voice of:
  Sterling Holloway

Based on Bill Peet's charming book, this film tells the story of Amos Mouse, Benjamin Franklin's best friend and the real brains behind the famous inventor's insights and contributions to civilization.

GO: Children will get a glimpse into the origins and workings of such things as printing presses, bifocals and electricity. The animation isn't Disney's best, but the quirky story is very engaging.
■

THE BERENSTAIN BEARS FIRST TIME VIDEO SERIES

Random House Home Video
1982-1990
30 minutes (each volume)
Directed by: Buzz Potamkin
Starring the voices of: Ruth Buzzi,
   Brian Cummings, Christina
   Lange, David Mendenhall,
   Frank Welker

Based on the books by Stan and Jan Berenstain, these fully-animated videos chronicle the experiences of Mama Bear, Papa Bear, Sister Bear and Brother Bear, a kind and loving family who live in a split-level treehouse in the friendly community of Beartown and who face the typical problems of people everywhere. As the children grow they constantly encounter new aspects of growing up. Mama and Papa Bear do their best to be good parents and in turn learn valuable life-lessons from the children.

Titles in the series are:
The Berenstain Bears and the Messy
   Room plus The Terrible Termite
The Berenstain Bears and the Truth plus
   Save the Bees
The Berenstain Bears Get in a Fight plus
   The Bigpaw Problem
The Berenstain Bears and the Trouble
   with Friends plus The Coughing Catfish
The Berenstain Bears and Too Much
   Birthday plus To the Rescue
The Berenstain Bears No Girls Allowed
   plus The Missing Dinosaur Bone
■

THE BERENSTAIN BEARS AND THE MISSING DINOSAUR BONE

Random House
1990
20 minutes
Directed by: Ray Messecar
Starring the voices of: Fran Brill,
   Michael Fass, Alison Hashmall,
   Ron Marshall, Brandon Pamy

This video is iconographic with voice-over narration.

Stories featured are:
The Berenstain Bears and the Missing
   Dinosaur Bone
Bears in the Night
The Bear Detectives
■

THE BERENSTAIN BEARS SERIES

HGV
1980-1983
30 minutes (each volume)
Directed by: Mordecai Gerstein,
   Al Kouzel
Starring: the voices of Gabriela
   Glatzer, Knowl Johnson,
   Pat Lysinger, Ron McLarty

Titles in this fully-animated series are:
The Berenstain Bears Meet Big Paw
The Berenstain Bears Play Ball
The Berenstain Bears and Cupid's
   Surprisen
■

BIG BIRD IN CHINA

Random House Home Video
1982
60 minutes
Directed by: Jon Stone
Starring: Brian Muehl,
    Quyang Lien-Tze, Caroll Spinney

Big Bird and Barkley the dog engage in a "treasure-hunt" to find the magical Phoenix and are helped in their search by the Monkey King. Actually filmed in China, this video introduces the Chinese culture through stories, language and songs. Shown are: the Great Wall of China, little girls performing the "duck dance," tai-chi in the park and children playing games in a schoolyard.

CAUTION: The Monkey King, although familiar to most Chinese children, may frighten some North American viewers.

GO: Featured are Oscar the Grouch, Ernie and Bert, Cookie Monster and Grover. This is a charming, albeit simplistic, look at Chinese life.

BIG BIRD IN JAPAN

Random House Home Video
1991
60 minutes
Directed by: Jon Stone
Starring: Maiko Dawakami,
    Brian Muehl, Caroll Spinney

Big Bird and his dog Barkley embark on a whirlwind tour of Japan, where they visit Tokyo, Mt. Fuji, Naguya and Kyoto. Predictably, Big Bird gets lost right away and ends up touring Tokyo alone, unable to understand a single word anyone says. Then a young English-speaking Japanese woman comes to his rescue and promises to help him link up with his tour. She teaches him about Japanese culture and as he gets to know her, the air of mystery around her deepens. And it's only when Big Bird sees a play called "The Bamboo Princess" about a princess from the palace of the moon that he realizes his mysterious friend is one and the same.

CAUTION: In one scene, Barkley goes into a temple and sees some very frightening gargoyle-type statues. Children who cannot yet read will miss the subtitled dialogue.

GO: A good way to introduce children to Japanese culture, this video is warm and friendly.

BONGO: A MUSICAL STORY ABOUT A BEAR

Walt Disney Home Video
1947
36 minutes
Directed by: Hamilton Luske
Narrated by: Cliff Edwards

Bongo is a multi-talented, world-famous circus bear, who, when he's before the crowds, performs amazing feats of strength and agility. But when he's out of the limelight, he's treated as a prisoner and more and more Bongo feels the call of the wild. One day, when the circus train is rumbling through some mountainous forestland, Bongo makes his escape. He immediately discovers the drawbacks of his decision, however (he can't find food and the night sounds keep him awake), and is beginning to regret his choice when he encounters a female bear named Lulubelle. It's love at first sight. Unfortunately, a huge and hostile bear named Lumpjaw also has his eye on Lulubelle. And to complicate matters, Bongo is unfamiliar with bear etiquette, so when Lulubelle reaches out to slap him (a bear custom, meaning she has chosen him), Bongo ducks and she accidentally smacks Lumpjaw instead. Believing himself to be chosen, the delighted Lumpjaw grabs Lullubelle. But when Bongo realizes what has happened, he uses his circus skills to take on Lumpjaw and rescue his true love. Based on the story by Sinclair Lewis.

CAUTION: The bears' method of communicating positive feelings is a little contrived and may confuse young viewers. The fight between Bongo and Lumpjaw is intense.

GO: This film is funny, charming and well-animated.

∎

CHILDREN'S CIRCLE VIDEO SERIES

CC Home Video
1960-1992
30-50 minutes (each volume)

Producer/filmmaker Mort Schindel created Weston Woods studio to bring faithful adaptations of critically acclaimed children's books to film. On the Children's Circle label, these videos are presented in a variety of styles, from fully-animated to iconographic, and have won over one hundred prestigious awards. Recommended for children ages three to nine.

The Amazing Bone and Other Stories

Stories featured are:
A Picture for Harold's Room
The Amazing Bone
John Brown, Rose and the Midnight Cat
The Trip

Animal Stories

Stories featured are:
Andy and the Lion
Petunia
Why Mosquitoes Buzz in People's Ears

Christmas Stories

Stories featured are:
The Clown of God
The Little Drummer Boy
Morris's Disappearing Bag
The Twelve Days of Christmas

Corduroy and Other Bear Stories

Stories featured are:
Blueberries for Sal
Corduroy
Panama

Danny and the Dinosaur and Other Stories

Stories featured are:
The Camel Who Took a Walk
Danny and the Dinosaur
The Happy Lion
The Island of the Skog

Doctor Desoto and Other Stories

Stories featured are:
Curious George Rides a Bike
Doctor Desoto
The Hat
Patrick

The Emperor's New Clothes and Other Folktales

Stories featured are:
The Emperor's New Clothes
Suho and the White Horse
Why Mosquitoes Buzz in People's Ears

The Ezra Jack Keats Library

Stories featured are:
A Letter to Amy
Getting to Know Ezra Jack Keats
   (documentary)
Pet Show
Peter's Chair
The Snowy Day
The Trip
Whistle for Willie

Five Stories for the Very Young

Stories featured are:
Caps for Sale
Changes, Changes
Drummer Hoff
Harold's Fairy Tale
Whistle for Willie

Happy Birthday, Moon and Other Stories

Stories featured are:
Happy Birthday, Moon
The Napping House
The Owl and the Pussy-Cat
Peter's Chair
The Three Little Pigs

Homer Price Stories

Live-action stories featured are:
The Case of the Cosmic Comic
The Doughnuts

Joey Runs Away and Other Stories

Stories featured are:
The Bear and the Fly
The Cow Who Fell in the Canal
Joey Runs Away
The Most Wonderful Egg in the World

Madeline's Rescue and Other Stories About Madeline

Stories featured are:
Madeline and the Bad Hat
Madeline and the Gypsies
Madeline's Rescue

The Maurice Sendak Library

Stories featured are:
Getting to Know Maurice Sendak
   (documentary)
In the Night Kitchen
The Nutshell Kids
Where the Wild Things Are

Maurice Sendak's Really Rosie

Stories featured are:
Alligators All Around
Chicken Soup with Rice
One Was Johnny
Pierre

Mike Mulligan and His Steam Shovel and Other Stories

Stories featured are:
Burt Dow: Deep-Water Man
Mike Mulligan and His Steam Shovel
Moon Man

More Stories for the Very Young

Stories featured are:
The Little Red Hen
Max's Christmas
The Napping House
Not So Fast, Songololo
Petunia

The Mysterious Tadpole and Other Stories

Stories featured are:
The Five Chinese Brothers
Jonah and the Great Fish
The Mysterious Tadpole
The Wizard

Norman the Doorman and Other Stories

Stories featured are:
Brave Irene
Lentil
Norman the Doorman

Owl Moon and Other Stories

Stories featured are:
The Caterpillar and the Polliwog
Hot Hippo
Owl Moon
Time of Wonder

The Pig's Wedding and Other Stories

Stories featured are:
The Happy Owls
A Letter to Amy
The Owl and the Pussy-Cat
The Selkie Girl

Raymond Briggs' The Snowman

The Robert McCloskey Library

Stories featured are:
Lentil
Make Way for Ducklings
Blueberries for Sal
Time of Wonder
Burt Dow: Deep-Water Man
Getting to Know Robert McCloskey
  (documentary)

Rosie's Walk and Other Stories

Stories featured are:
Rosie's Walk
Charlie Needs a Cloak
The Story about Ping
The Beast of Monsieur Racine

Smile for Auntie and Other Stories

Stories featured are:
Make Way for Ducklings
Smile for Auntie
The Snowy Day
Wynken, Blinken and Nod

Stories from the Black Tradition

Stories featured are:
A Story, A Story
Goggles!
Mufaro's Beautiful Daughters
The Village of Round and Square Houses
Why Mosquitoes Buzz in Peoples Ears

Strega Nona and Other Stories

Stories featured are:
Strega Nona
Tikki Tikki Tembo
The Foolish Frog
A Story, A Story

Teeny-tiny and the Witch Woman and Other Scary Stories

Stories featured are:
A Dark, Dark Tale
King of the Cats
The Rainbow Serpent
Teeny-tiny and the Witch Woman

The Three Robbers and Other Stories

Stories featured are:
Fourteen Rats and a Rat-Catcher

The Island of the Scog
Leopold and the See-Through Crumbpicker
The Three Robbers

The Ugly Duckling and Other Classic Fairy Tales

Stories featured are:
The Ugly Duckling
The Stonecutter
The Swineherd

What's under My Bed and Other Creepy Stories

Stories featured are:
Georgie
Teeny-Tiny and the Witch-Woman
The Three Robbers

CINDERELLA

Walt Disney Home Video
1950
76 minutes
Directed by: Clyde Geronimi, Wilfred Jackson, Hamilton Luske

This beloved Disney classic is an expanded version of the famous fairy tale in which Cinderella, slave to her horrible stepmother and stepsisters, dreams of the day when a prince will come to take her away from her misery. That day's arrival is facilitated by the appearance of Cinderella's kindly fairy godmother who, with the help of a little magic, sends her off to the ball. There, Cinderella enchants the prince and, in her haste to be home before the magic wears off, loses a slipper. The king's servants try the slipper on every woman in the kingdom until they discover Cinderella. Then she and the prince are reunited and are married.

Songs featured are:
Bibbidi-Bobbidi-Boo
Cinderelly
The Work Song

CAUTION: The direct correlation of evil with unattractiveness may concern some parents.

GO: Cinderella is accompanied by a host of singing mice and birds, the antics of which make the story more accessible to young children. The songs are terrific.

CINDERELLA

Playhouse Home Video
1964
84 minutes
Directed by: Charles S. Dukin
Starring: Stuart Damon,
    Walter Pidgeon, Ginger Rogers,
    Lesley Ann Warren

Although produced for television some thirty years ago, this traditional telling of the classic fairy tale still works today.

Some of Rodgers and Hammerstein's songs are:
Do I Love You Because You're Beautiful?
In My Own Little Corner
Impossible

GO: Lesley Ann Warren has an average singing voice, but she portrays Cinderella sweetly.

CLASSIC FAIRY TALES

f.h.e./MCA
1982
62 minutes
Narrated by: George Cole,
    Sheila Hancock

Six well-known fairy tales are told via narration and illustrations.

Stories featured are:
The Emperor's New Clothes
The Four Magicians (The Bremen Town Musicians)
The Princess and the Pea
Puss in Boots
Rapunzel
The Ugly Duckling

CAUTION: The music doesn't vary very much and, despite what the box says, the stories are *not* animated. Some children may snicker to see the Emperor in *The Emperor's New Clothes*, who is shown totally nude.

GO: Often humorous, the traditional stories are faithfully and simply told. Don't be put off by the fact that this tape is not animated; there is plenty of movement and visual appeal to make it a superior fairy tale video.

CURIOUS GEORGE

SVS
1983
83 minutes
Directed by: Alan J. Shalleck

Curious George, the mischievous little monkey, has been a popular literary character for over forty years. No matter what trouble he gets into, it always seems to work out in the end.

This tape is very simply animated with single moving elements in each scene. Sometimes the effect of animation is achieved by zooming in on a picture or by the rapid editing of still pictures. The stories are narrated and the music and sound effects are subtle. Based on the books by Margaret and H.A. Rey.

Stories featured are:
Curious George and the Dump Truck
Curious George and the Lost Letter
Curious George at the Greenhouse
Curious George at the Pet Shop
Curious George Gets a Pizza
Curious George Gets an X-Ray
Curious George Goes Hiking
Curious George Goes to a Wedding
Curious George Goes to the Amusement Park
Curious George Goes to an Ice Cream Shop
Curious George Goes to the Library
Curious George Meets the Balloon Man
Curious George Meets the Painter
Curious George Paints a Billboard
Curious George Rings the Bell
Curious George Takes a Ferry
Curious George Visits a Catsup Factory
Curious George Visits a Hotel
■

CURIOUS GEORGE COLLECTION

SONY
1983
30 minutes
Directed by: Alan J. Shallock

Curious George
(Vol. 1)

Stories featured are:
Curious George at the Ballet
Curious George Goes Sledding
Curious George Goes to an Art Show
Curious George Goes to the Aquarium
Curious George Plays Basketball
Curious George Walks the Pets

Curious George
(Vol. 2)

Stories featured are:
Curious George Goes to a Flower Show
Curious George Goes to a TV Station
Curious George Goes to the Circus
Curious George Goes to the Library
Curious George Visits the Railroad Station
Curious George Goes to the Tailor Shop

Curious George
(Vol. 3)

Stories featured are:
Curious George and the Costume Party
Curious George Goes Fishing
Curious George Goes Skiing
Curious George Goes to a Bowling Alley
Curious George Goes to a Restaurant
Curious George Goes to the Zoo

CAUTION: In every episode George disobeys an adult's instructions. Then, just as he is about to suffer punishment for his disobedience it's discovered that some inadvertent good has resulted and George is forgiven.

GO: These videos, despite their simple animation, still keep the attention of very young children.

■

DANCE! WORKOUT WITH BARBIE

Buena Vista Home Video
1991
30 minutes

Exercise with Barbie and a group of nine energetic pre-teen girls. Computer animation brings Barbie to life in this well-produced, well-choreographed tape. Great exercises with lots of variety teach rhythm and co-ordination in a fun way. Approved by the Aerobics and Fitness Association of America. Songs performed by Love Hewitt.

GO: Wonderfully put together, this video features routines that are more fun and choreographically complex than some tapes for adults. Moms may want to work out with their daughters after seeing this video!

DARKWING DUCK — HIS FAVORITE ADVENTURES COLLECTION

Walt Disney Home Video
1991
48 minutes (each volume)
Starring the voices of: Christine
    Cavanaugh, JimCummings,
    Terry McGovern

In the crime-plagued metropolis of St. Canard, the intrepid and flamboyant Darkwing Duck battles evil-doers, aided by his adopted daughter Goslyn and his sidekick Launchpad McQuack.

Titles in this fully-animated collection are:
Birth of Negaduck (Vol. 4)
Comic Book Capers (Vol. 3)
Darkly Dawns the Duck (Vol. 1)
Justice Ducks Unite (Vol. 2)

DENVER THE DINOSAUR COLLECTION

Fries Home Video
1988-90
23-60 minutes (each volume)
Directed by: Tom Burton

The series begins when California teens Mario, Jeremy, Shades and Wally visit an abandoned construction site near the tar pit exhibit of the local museum. There, they happen upon a huge fossilized egg out of which pops Denver, a friendly dinosaur who understands everything they say. The kids try to conceal him from an exploitive world, but unscrupulous rock promoter Morton Fizzback and evil paleontologist Dr. Funt have other plans.

Titles in the collection are:
Big-Top Denver
Chips 'n' Robbers
Denver and the Cornstalk
Denver and the Time Machine
Denver, the Last Dinosaur (first episode)
Dino-Star
Holiday on Skis
Hooray For Denver
Lions, Tigers & Dinos Oh Boy
Monster Maze and School Days
Ride 'Em Denver!
Rock 'n' Roll Denver

CAUTION: The boys make a few disparaging remarks about girls and the teens have some run-ins with a gang of bullies. This series is standard Saturday morning fare; the animation and voice-overs are average and the music is uninspiring.

DISNEY'S SING-ALONG SONGS SERIES

Walt Disney Home Video
1987-92
30 minutes (each volume)

This series has been extremely successful, particularly with children who are just becoming interested in animation. The lyrics run across the bottom of the screen and a bouncing ball indicates the words as they are sung. (This is especially useful when Donald Duck sings!) Each tape, with the exception of *Disneyland Fun*, features a collection of songs taken from a variety of Disney full-length features. The tapes in this series include songs from films that have gone into moratorium and songs from films which have not yet been (and may never be) released on video.

The Bare Necessities
(Vol. 4)

Songs featured are:
The Bare Necessities
Cinderella Work Song
Everybody Wants to Be a Cat
Figaro and Cleo
I Wanna Be Like You
Look out for Mr. Stork
Old Yeller
The Ugly Bug Ball

Winnie-the-Pooh
You Are a Human Animal

Be Our Guest
(Vol. 10)

Songs featured are:
Be Our Guest
Beauty and the Beast
Bella Notte
Heffalumps and Woozles
Little Wooden Head
Spoonful of Sugar
The World's Greatest Criminal Mind

Fun With Music
(Vol. 5)

Songs featured are:
All in the Golden Afternoon
Blue Danube Waltz
Boo Boo Boo
Fun with Music
Good Company
Green with Envy Blues
Let's All Sing Like the Birdies Sing
Old MacDonald Had a Farm
Scales and Arpeggios
While Strolling through the Park
Why Should I Worry?
With a Smile and a Song

Heigh-Ho
(Vol. 1)

Songs featured are:
A Cowboy Needs a Horse
The Dwarf's Yodel Song
Heigh-Ho
Hi Diddle Dee Dee
Let's Go Fly a Kite
The Siamese Cat Song
Theme From Zorro
The Three Caballeros
Up, Down and Touch the Ground
Yo-Ho

I Love to Laugh
(Vol. 9)

Songs featured are:
Bluddle-Uddle-Um-Dum
Everbody Has a Laughing Place
I Love to Laugh
Jolly Holidays
Oo-De-Lally
Pink Elephants on Parade
Quack, Quack, Quack Donald Duck
Supercalifragilisticexpialidocious
Who's Afraid of the Big Bad Wolf?
The Wonderful Thing about Tiggers

Under the Sea (Vol. 6)

Songs featured are:
At the Codfish Ball
By the Beautiful Sea
Kiss the Girl
Never Smile at a Crocodile
Sailing, Sailing
Sailor's Hornpipe
Someone's Waiting for You
That's What Makes the World Go Round
Under the Sea
A Whale of a Tale

Very Merry Christmas Songs (Vol. 8)

Featured are vintage Disney cartoons and the Disneyland Santa Claus Parade.

Songs featured are:
Deck the Halls
From All of Us to All of You
Here Comes Santa Claus
Jingle Bells
Joy to the World
Let It Snow! Let It Snow! Let It Snow!
Parade of the Wooden Soldiers
Rudolph, the Red-Nosed Reindeer
Silent Night
Sleigh Ride
Up on the Housetop
We Wish You a Merry Christmas
Winter Wonderland

You Can Fly!
(Vol. 3)

Songs featured are:
The Beautiful Briny
Colonel Hathis March
He's a Tramp
I've Got No Strings
Little Black Rain Cloud
The Merrily Song
Step in Time
When I See an Elephant Fly
You Can Fly

Zip-A-Dee-Doo-Dah
(Vol. 2)

Songs featured are:
The Ballad of Davy Crockett
Bibbidi-Bobbidi-Boo
Casey Junior
Following the Leader
Give a Little Whistle
It's a Small World
The Mickey Mouse Club March
The Unbirthday Song
Whistle While You Work
Zip-A-Dee-Doo-Dah

DON'T EAT THE PICTURES: SESAME STREET AT THE METROPOLITAN MUSEUM OF ART

Random House Home Video
1987
60 minutes
Directed by: Jon Stone
Starring: Linda Bove, Paul Dooley,
    Bob McGrath, James Mason,
    Caroll Spinney, Fritz Weaver

At closing time on a visit to The Metropolitan Museum of Art, Big Bird and friends go looking for

Snuffy and everyone is accidentally locked in overnight. This gives the whole gang a chance to learn an awful lot about art from different cultures. Cookie Monster drools over the beautiful still lifes of food and is constrained only by an official looking sign which reads: Please Don't Eat the Pictures. Oscar is really in his element in the Greek and Roman galleries where he discovers broken statues. Meanwhile, Big Bird finds Snuffy and together they meet Sahu, the son of an Egyptian God. Sahu is under a spell and cannot depart this earth until he answers the riddle: Where does today meet yesterday? (which is posed by a demon who comes every night at midnight). In the end, Sahu answers the question correctly, and the love of his new friends sees him through the final trial.

CAUTION: Very young children may find the demon and Sahu's plight a little scary.

GO: This is a terrific way to introduce very young children to the art of the ages. (And the songs are there, just in case.)

THE DRAGON THAT WASN'T (OR WAS HE?)

MCA
1983
83 minutes
Directed by: Bjorn Frank Jensen,
   Bob Maxfield, Ben Van Voorn

In this animated film produced in the Netherlands, baby dragon Dexter mistakenly thinks that Ollie the bear is his father. Which is fine, until Ollie finds that whenever anything upsets

Dexter, he grows to gigantic proportions, often larger than the house. Ollie knows that it's best to take Dexter to the Dragon Realm beyond the Misty Mountains where he can live with others of his own kind. And after harrowing experiences with a couple of thieves and an unjust internment in jail, Ollie finally returns Dexter to the Dragon Realm.

CAUTION: This film has an overly complex plot and some children will be quite upset when Dexter leaves his adopted bear father.

DUCKTALES: THE MOVIE — TREASURE OF THE LOST LAMP

Walt Disney Home Video
1990
74 minutes
Directed by: Bob Hathcock
Starring the voices of:
   Terence McGovern, Russi Taylor,
   Alan Young

While exploring a pyramid on an archaeological expedition, Uncle Scrooge and friends find a lamp. They take it home and polish it up, and when a genie appears, promptly squander their first two wishes by wishing for an elephant, then wishing the elephant would go away. Meanwhile, the evil magician Merlock wants the lamp for himself, and Scrooge is only narrowly saved from the villain when the genie pulls him into the safety of the lamp. Then, as an appreciative Scrooge prepares to return the lamp to the pyramid, Merlock's sinister accomplice Dijon takes the lamp and wishes to be the rightful owner of Scrooge's fortune. And at the film's climax, Merlock returns, takes control and prepares to return to his desert home as ruler of the world.

CAUTION: There is a recurring theme of violence in the film. In one scene, Merlock changes himself into a frightening ferocious ape, and in another, huge crabs climb up onto a sinking platform and threaten the escaping ducks. One of Merlock's toadies is an unfortunate caricature of an Indo-Aryan.

GO: This fully-animated movie will not disappoint fans of the popular television series.

▲

DUCKTALES SERIES

Walt Disney Home Video
1987
45 minutes
   (each two-episode volume)
Directed by: various
Starring the voices of: June Foray,
   Joan Gerber, Terry McGovern,
   Russi Taylor, Alan Young

Huey, Dewey and Louie live in a huge mansion with their Uncle Scrooge McDuck, a Scottish skinflint billionaire. In this fully-animated series the McDucks's good friends Gearloose and Launchpad McQuack help them thwart the evil villains Magica de Spell and the Beagle Boys. Most of the titles in this series are also available in French.

Titles in the series are:
Accidental Adventurers:
   Jungle Duck; Maid of the Myth
Daredevil Ducks:
   Home Sweet Homer; The Money
   Vanishes

Duck to the Future:
   Duck to the Future; Sir Gyro de
   Gearloose
Fearless Fortune Hunter:
   Earth-Quack!; Masters of the Djinni
High-Flying Hero:
   Hero for Hire; Launchpads Civil War
Lost World Wanderers:
   The Curse of Castle McDuck; Dinosaur
   Ducks
Masked Marauders:
   Send in the Clones; The Time-Teasers
Raiders of the Lost Harp:
   The Pearl of Wisdom; Raiders of the
   Lost Harp
Seafaring Sailors:
   All Ducks on Deck; Sphinx for the
   Memories
Space Invaders:
   Micro Ducks from Outer Space; Where
   No Duck Has Gone Before

GO: With lots of action-adventure, these stories are lively and adequately animated.

▲

DUMBO

Walt Disney Home Video
1940
63 minutes
Directed by: Ben Sharpstein

A stork brings a baby elephant to the circus — a baby elephant with huge, outlandish ears who promptly gets the cruel nickname Dumbo. Enraged when nasty kids tease her son, Dumbo's mother is moved to physically defend him. Unjustly accused of dementia, she is carted off and put in solitary confinement, leaving baby Dumbo alone. His only friend is a tiny mouse named Timothy who tries everything in his power to find Dumbo a place in the circus. When the pair awake one morning in a tree, Timothy puts two and two together and realizes that

Dumbo must have flown in his sleep. The nervous Dumbo refuses to try flying while he's awake until Timothy presents him with a "magic feather." But when Dumbo loses the feather in a high diving act, he realizes that his flying abilities depend on his skills alone.

CAUTION: The idea of being forcibly separated from one's mother can be very upsetting for young children. Also potentially frightening is the "Elephants on Parade" sequence. The black crows are unpleasant caricatures of Black Americans.

GO: The song "When I See an Elephant Fly" is a favourite with children.

FAERIE TALE THEATRE

Playhouse Home Video/Fox
1982-1984
54-60 minutes (each volume)
OFRB rating: PG

This series of twenty-six live-action films produced by actress Shelley Duvall were directed by a host of accomplished directors and feature well-known film stars in the lead roles. Some stories are played more or less traditionally, while others are tongue-in-cheek portrayals with satirical elements, sexual innuendo and humour.

Films in this group are, for the most part, traditionally played:
Aladdin and His Wonderful Lamp
Beauty and the Beast
The Boy Who Left Home to Learn about the Shivers
Cinderella
The Dancing Princesses
The Emperor's New Clothes

Goldilocks and the Three Bears
Hansel and Gretel *
Jack and the Beanstalk *
The Little Mermaid
The Nightingale *
The Pied Piper of Hamelin
Pinocchio
Puss in Boots
Rapunzel
Rip Van Winkle *
Rumpelstiltskin *
The Snow Queen
Snow White and the Seven Dwarfs *
Thumbelina
(*contains frightening scenes)

Films in this group include sexual innuendo, coarse language and satire:
Little Red Riding Hood
The Princess and the Pea
The Princess Who Had Never Laughed
The Sleeping Beauty
The Tale of the Frog Prince
The Three Little Pigs

✗ FERNGULLY: THE LAST RAINFOREST

20th Century Fox
1992
76 minutes
Directed by: Bill Kroyer
Starring the voices of: Tim Curry, Samantha Mathis, Christian Slater, Robin Williams

The film begins in the ancient past when Hexxus, the spirit of pure destruction, escapes during a volcanic eruption. He causes havoc around the world until he is finally imprisoned in a tree by Magi, the leader of the Faeries. All humans are believed to have perished in the calamity. The story then returns to the present, where Magi is giving her young apprentice Crysta a history lesson. But Crysta is a reluctant pupil, and as soon as her lesson is over she sets out to investigate rumours that the humans have returned. Before long she comes across some humans herself, busy levelling the forest with an enormous tree-cutting machine. Believing that the machine is a monster, Crysta saves a young man named Zak from a falling tree by shrinking him to her own size. And while Zak comes to understand the beauty and sanctity of the forest, his friends inadvertently liberate the evil spirit Hexxus from his prision. Hexxus promptly possesses the levelling machine and prepares to exact his gruesome revenge on Ferngully, and only the combined efforts of every fairy in the forest can defeat the evil spirit and the humans. In the end, Zak is returned to his normal size and leaves the forest sadder and wiser. Based on the Ferngully stories by Diana Young.

✗**STOP:** Hexxus is a pretty scary character, especially when he transforms from his smoky form into a horrible skeletal figure.

CAUTION: The film's environmentalist message is timely, but clouded by the participation of the evil spirit in the destruction of the forest; the humans would have

AGES 3 TO 6

destroyed the forest all by themselves had Hexxus not appeared.

GO: Despite certain flaws this is an entertaining animation, featuring high production values and excellent voice-overs. All of the plants featured in the film are botanically correct (the animators actually spent time in the rain forest) and the music is by world-renowned musicians Johnny Clegg, The Bulgarian Women's Choir and L.L. Cool J.
■ ▲

THE FROG PRINCE: A CANNON MOVIETALE

Warner Home Video/
  Cannon Home Video
1988
86 minutes
Directed by: Jackson Hunsicker
Starring: Helen Hunt, John
  Paragon, Aileen Quinn

When the king announces that the throne will go only to the true princess, Princess Zora worries that she isn't one. After all, she doesn't have long hair, grace and a beautiful face like her sister. (Zora is a tomboy who likes to play ball and whose hair never seems to grow.) Then one day, when she drops a ball into a well, a frog retrieves it and makes her promise to be his friend. She honours her promise even when doing so jeopardizes her chance for the throne. And it's through that commitment that Zora learns she is indeed a true princess; and that her friend the frog is a handsome prince.

CAUTION: This film is not for fairy tale purists.

GO: Elaborate sets and costumes, a non-threatening plot and no sexual overtones make this film suitable for young children. Actress Aileen Quinn performs a number of songs.

●

FUNHOUSE FITNESS: THE SWAMP STOMP WITH J.D. ROTH

Warner Home Video
1991
40 minutes
Directed by: Anita Mann
Starring: Jane Fonda, J.D. Roth

J.D. Roth and costumed animal characters lead a group of girls and boys in simple, silly dance routines called "The Penguin Waddle," "The Spider Crawl" and "The Swamp Stomp." Recommended for children ages three to seven.

GO: *Funhouse Fitness* is a high-quality production designed to help children develop balance, co-ordination, agility, endurance and strength.

GOOF TROOP COLLECTION

Walt Disney Home Video
1992
47 minutes
Starring the voices of: Jim
    Cummings, Bill Farmer, Dana Hill,
    Rob Paulsen

Disney's legendary character Goofy is cast as the father of a very hip eleven-year-old named Max. Max's best friend is P.J., whose father is Pete (often cast as a Disney villain),

and together they share some slapstick adventures.

Titles in the fully-animated collection are:

Banding Together (Vol. 3.):
    Shake, Rattle and Goof; Close
    Encounters of the Weird Mime
Goin' Fishin' (Vol. 1):
    Slightly Dinghy; Wrecks, Lies and
    Videotape
The Race Is On! (Vol. 2):
    Meanwhile, Back at the Ramp; Tub Be
    or Not Tub Be

GRANPA

Sony Video
1992
30 minutes
Directed by: Dianne Jackson
Starring the voice of: Peter Ustinov

This film tells the story of a young girl named Emily and her beloved grandfather who empowers her imagination every time he visits. When they're out skipping, he whisks her back to the days of his own youth; when it rains, it becomes the Great Flood of Noah and all the animal pairs swim aboard the house; when Granpa plays the piano, the dolls and the teddy bears come alive and sing along; a simple donkey ride at the beach turns into an elaborate parade; and a roller-coaster ride becomes high-speed maneuvering in a WWII Spitfire. Their days of imagining together end when Granpa passes away.

CAUTION: Granpa's death is tastefully handled; he falls asleep in his chair and when his granddaughter returns from playing outside his chair is empty. She is very sad, until the spirit of her grandfather in his youth, surrounded by the spirits of his childhood playmates, reaches out to take her hand.

GO: Description hardly does justice to this splendid effort. John Burningham's book is a testament to the human imagination and the film has captured it expertly. A marvelous musical score is featured.

■

AGES 3 TO 6

✘ THE GREAT MOUSE DETECTIVE

Walt Disney Home Video
1986
74 minutes
Directed by: Ron Clements,
    Burny Mattinson, Dave Michener,
    John Musker
Starring the voices of: Val Bettin,
    Barrie Ingham, Vincent Price,
    Alan Young

The Great Mouse Detective opens in London in 1897. When a toy shop owner is kidnapped by a fierce, peg-legged bat, his daughter manages to escape into the rain-drenched streets. There she meets Dr. Dawson, a military surgeon who has just returned from India, and explains her plight. The pair seek out the famous detective Basil of Baker Street, who takes on the case. Basil soon determines that the toy shop owner is the prisoner of the evil criminal genius Professor Ratigan, who has forced the toy shop owner to create a mechanical duplicate of the mouse Queen of England; Ratigan plans to replace the real queen with his wind-up robot and thus gain control of the whole country. High adventure ensues as Basil thwarts the evil Ratigan's designs.

✘STOP: This film is too violent and too scary for most children under the age of five; it's replete with images of snarling faces illuminated by lightning flashes and saliva dripping from bared fangs. Of special concern may be the scenes in which one of the evil villain's incompetent henchmen is fed to a huge cat.

CAUTION: There is a real Saturday morning cartoon flavour to this film and the final chase scene goes on and on.

GO: Kids who like this film, *really* like it.

✘ THE HAPPY PRINCE

Random House Home Video
1987
30 minutes
Directed by: Michael Mills
Starring the voices of: Glynis Johns,
    Christopher Plummer

After his untimely death, the spirit of a happy young prince inhabits a beautiful, gold-plated statue, where he is forced to oversee the misery of his poverty-stricken city. Helped by a courageous young swallow, the Happy Prince distributes pieces of his gold covering throughout the city to alleviate the suffering of the masses. Based on the story by Oscar Wilde.

✘STOP: The swallow dies.

CAUTION: The story's ancient themes of enlightenment, suffering, repentance and redemption may be inaccessible to younger children and its tragic ending, upsetting for older ones.

■

HORTON HEARS A WHO!

```
MGM/UA
1970
26 minutes
Directed by: Chuck Jones
Narrated by: Hans Conreid
```

In the Jungle of Nool, Horton is taking refuge from the noon heat in a refreshing pool, when his super-acute hearing alerts him to the presence of a microscopic world called Whoville on a speck of dust on a poppy. No one else can hear the Whos, so not a soul believes him. Instead they ridicule him and, seeking to destroy the source of his madness, decide to boil Whoville, dust mote, poppy and all. Horton implores the Whos to make as much noise as they possibly can in order to prove that they really do exist. So every Who responds by whacking pots and blowing a horns, but it isn't until the last and tiniest Who makes his contribution to the din that Horton's fellow jungle-dwellers hear the Whos. And Horton helps them recognize the maxim: A person's a person, no matter how small. Based on the book by Dr. Seuss.

CAUTION: The original text guides this fully-animated production, but some small additions and changes have been made to the story. Songs were added, the lyrics for which were written by Dr. Seuss.

GO: The story makes it clear that everyone's contribution is important in a group effort, and that size is not an indicator of worth.

IT'S THE MUPPETS COLLECTION

```
Buena Vista Home Video
1993
35 minutes (each volume)
Directed by: Jim Henson
```

Both videos are compilations of *Muppet Show* highlights and have been put together in the same format as the original shows.

Titles in the collection are:
Meet the Muppets (Vol. 1)
More Muppets, Please! (Vol. 2)

IVOR THE ENGINE

```
BFS Video
1991
60 minutes (each volume)
Starring the voices of:Olwen Griffiths,
   Antony Jackson, Oliver Postgate
```

Together, a steam engine named Ivor and his driver, Jones, run a Welsh railway line. Ivor is a very human character; he communicates with Jones the Steam by blowing his horn, and even sings bass in the local choir. Created, written and produced by Oliver Postgate.

Ivor the Engine and the Dragons

When Ivor and Jones the Steam encounter Adrius the Dragon and his family, they discover that Welsh dragons are hardly the bold, ferocious monsters of classical mythology. On the contrary, they are small and mischievous and enjoy flitting around. Their only problem is that they require intense heat to survive, which Ivor's fire temporarily provides. But problems arise when the dragons make a nuisance of themselves and steps must be taken to find them a permanent home before the authoritarian Antiquarian Society locks them away.

Ivor the Engine and the Elephants

Ivor, Jones the Steam and choir director Eben Evans are riding the line when they discover an elephant sleeping on the tracks. After she's awake, they discover that the elephant has a nasty cut on her foot. They give her a ride, and while Jones the Steam gets the vet, discover both the elephant's name (Alice) and her owner (Banger's Famous Circus).

CAUTION: The heavily-accented narration of the films in this series is bound to cause some difficulties for North American viewers. The animation is limited and the stories are rather complex. In *Ivor the Engine and the Elephants* the depiction of a South Asian may offend some viewers.

GO: The *Ivor the Engine* films are charming and gentle.

JACK THE GIANT KILLER

MGM/UA
1962
95 minutes
Directed by: Nathan Juran
Starring: Kerwin Matthews,
   Torin Thatcher, Judi Meredith
OFRB rating: PG

The story takes place a thousand years ago, when Pendragon, master of all witches, giants and hobgoblins, lives in exile, dreaming of the day he can return to power in Cornwall. When Princess Elaine is declared heir to the throne of Cornwall, Pendragon makes an appearance disguised as a foreign prince and gives her the gift of a tiny dancing homunculus. That night, he goes to the princess's bedchamber and turns the homunculus into a monstrous giant who kidnaps her. The giant smashes his way out of the castle and strides across the countryside, only to be stopped and defeated by a local young farmer named Jack. The overjoyed king promptly makes Jack a knight of the realm and, needless to say, Pendragon isn't pleased; he vows to destroy Jack using all the powers at his command, and the king decides that the best defence is secrecy. He plans to send the princess to a convent in Normandy and Jack is ordered to accompany her. But spies are everywhere, and the fiendish Pendragon arranges an ambush and carries Elaine off. As Pendragon attempts to force the King to abdicate the throne, Jack manages to rescue the princess.

CAUTION: Pendragon's demonic servants, glowing, skull-faced apparitions, will frighten most little ones. The giants, too, are quite fierce in appearance. The captain of the ship is killed in one attack, and his son Peter, a young boy, is shown grieving over his father's body.

GO: This is a spirited live-action adventure with lots of Ray Harryhausen's patented mythologicals.

JIMBO AND THE JET SET

BFS Video
1987
50 minutes (Vol. 1), 54 minutes (Vol. 2)
Directed by: Keith Learner
Starring the voices of:
  Peter Hawkins, Susan Sheridan

When one of the designers at the aircraft factory mistakes inches for centimetres, a small new jumbo jet is built. And when the Chief Controller of London Airport sees the unusual little plane and exclaims that he ordered a Jumbo, not a Jimbo, Jimbo gets his name. Both volumes describe the misadventures of this endearing character and his friends, Tommy Towtruck, Amanda Baggage and Chrissy the Catering Truck.

Jimbo and the Jet Set
(Vol. 1)

Stories featured are:
April Fool's Day
The Chief Gets a Rocket
Chinese Pandemonium
First Time Flyers
Jimbo and the Whale
Jimbo Down Under
Jinglebells Jimbo
Jungle Jimbo
The Little Big Problem
The Old Timer
Quiet Please
Trouble at Sea

Jimbo and the Jet Set
(Vol. 2)

Stories featured are:
Bermuda Triangle
The Computer Clanger
The Controller's Apprentice
Every Silver Lining Has a Cloud
The Great Air Race
Holiday Weather
Jet Lag
Jimbo and the Astronaut
The Little Red Devil
The Royal Visitors
The Penn and Inca Story
The UFO
Winter Wonderland

CAUTION: In the story *The UFO*, the Chief is beamed up by a friendly alien whose skeletal face may frighten very young children. There are a few simplistic representations of a number of cultures that may be considered offensive.

GO: Although somewhat stilted, these simple animated stories are ideal for young vehicle fans.

THE JUNGLE BOOK

Walt Disney Home Video
1967
78 minutes
Directed by: Wolfgang Reitherman
Starring the voices of:
  Sebastian Cabot, Phil Harris,
  George Sanders

This fully-animated film opens in the middle of the Indian Jungle where Bagheera, a black panther, has just discovered a basket containing an abandoned newborn. Realizing that the child will die before he can get it back to the "man-village," he elects to take it to a family of wolves that has just had a litter of cubs. Luckily, the child is accepted by the mother and raised with the other cubs. And he lives in this way for ten years, unaware of the civilized world. Then, in the tenth year, news spreads through the jungle that the great tiger Shere Khan has returned. Shere Khan hates all humans and Bagheera and the wolves know that the tiger will kill Mowgli as soon as he finds him. So they decide to return Mowgli to his own kind. But the journey to the "man-village" is a perilous trip of many days, which is complicated by Mowgli's unwillingness to go. On the way, they encounter the boa constrictor Kaa, a free-spirited bear named Baloo, a monkey named King Louie and finally the ferocious Bengal tiger, Shere Khan himself. In the end, Mowgli is saved by Baloo and a quartet of vultures (a hilarious

send-up of the early Beatles), and eventually makes it to the "man-village."

Songs featured are:
The Bare Necessities
Colonel Hathi's March
I Wanna Be Like You

GO: There's little to worry about here. Even Shere Khan is so dignified that he's only marginally scary, and very young children routinely enjoy this film.

■

✗ THE LAND BEFORE TIME

MCA Home Video
1989
69 minutes
Directed by: Don Bluth
Starring the voices of: Judith Barsi,
   Burke Byrnes, Gabriel Damon,
   Pat Hingle, Candy Hutson,
   Helen Shaver

An earthquake separates four little dinosaurs from their families. Pursued by predators, they are forced to journey without their parents through fire and famine to the Great Valley, where happiness awaits.

✗**STOP:** Littlefoot's mother is killed. (Her death is tempered slightly by her appearance as a guiding force, and by the viewer's knowledge that Littlefoot also has grandparents.)

CAUTION: This is a visually beautiful, but often intense, full-length animation. After a great earthquake the four toddler dinosaurs are separated from their families and left to find their way alone and as they travel they encounter volcanoes and terrifying predators. (Some children we have talked to worry: Will we have an earthquake here?)

GO: The underdogs win, overcoming significant odds, and the film does show the benefits of positive working relationships, and of overcoming stereotyping. Breathtaking animation, adorable characterizations and an inspirational story make this film a classic.

▲

THE LION, THE WITCH AND THE WARDROBE

Vestron Home Video
1979
95 minutes
Directed by: Bill Melendez
Starring the voices of: Beth Porter, Stephen Thorne, Rachel Warren

When English children Lucy, Peter, Edmund and Susan discover that another world can be reached through the back of an old wardrobe in their guardian's house, their adventures in the land of Narnia begin. There, they learn that the evil White Witch keeps Narnia in an eternal winter and agree to help the magical lion Aslan restore spring to the land. But Edmund has become a traitor and informs the Witch of their plans. Aslan is forced to give himself to the Witch in exchange for the boy's freedom. (In Narnia, the law dictates that traitors belong to the Witch.) Aslan is killed, but in the end is restored to life by virtue of a higher law, and returns to conquer the Witch. Lucy, Peter, Edmund and Susan are made the rulers of Narnia where they live for a long time, eventually returning to England to discover that no time has passed. This is a fully-animated version of the first book of seven in the Chronicles of Narnia by C.S. Lewis.

CAUTION: The animation is very simple and seems to lack the depth necessary to sustain the scenes of long and faithful dialogue. Although the children are supposed to be English, their accents are American (or inconsistently English, or Australian) and the White Witch screams her lines throughout the film. The story's language may be too sophisticated for little ones and at ninety-five minutes is very long. The White Witch tries to kill Edmund and does kill Aslan with a sharp dagger; the battle is quite scary.

GO: Recommended by the National Education Association and funded by the Episcopal Radio/TV Foundation, the story is often considered to have religious overtones.

● ■ ▲

THE LITTLE CROOKED CHRISTMAS TREE

Cineglobe Video Inc.
1990
24 minutes
Directed by: Ron Broda, Michael Cutting
Starring the voices of: the Appleby College Choir, Christopher Plummer

When a dove lays her eggs in its branches, a little tree on Brown's Christmas Tree Farm protects the chicks by leaning into the sun. In so doing, he becomes crooked and learns that he is no longer desirable as a Christmas tree. Unsure about what this means, the little tree asks: What is Christmas and what is a Christmas tree? The dove tells him that Christmas is the celebration of the birth of Jesus Christ and the coming together of family. She also tells him that he has been spared the fate of being decorated for a day and then discarded after the celebrations. But after all of his friends are taken to be decorated, the tree becomes lonely. Then in the summer Farmer Brown transplants the tree to a garden where the following Christmas he is decorated so beautifully that people come from miles around to see him. Based on the book by Michael Cutting and Ron Broda.

CAUTION: This video is not fully-animated; the camera pans over the beautiful paper sculpture illustrations, zooming in and out on elements of the picture.

GO: A charming but somewhat melancholy story about sacrifice. A portion of the purchase price of this video is donated to the Hospital For Sick Children and to your local children's hospital.

THE LITTLE FOX

Celebrity Home Entertainment
1987
80 minutes
Directed by: Attila Dargay
Starring the voices of: John Bellucci, Anne Costelloe, Maia Danziger

A young fox named Vic isn't content to stay at home with the rest of the family when his father goes hunting, and sets out to help. His father sends him back, but Vic becomes lost, and that night a farmer (Chester) tracks his father back to the den and discovers the whole family. When Vic finally returns to the den hours later, his family is gone and his Uncle Karak is waiting. Karak explains that his family will not be returning and proceeds to teach Vic the essentials of being a

fox. Seasons pass and Vic grows big and strong and very clever. And when Chester launchs an all-out foxhunt and Karak is forced to give his life to save Vic and his new mate Foxy, Vic vows revenge and steals all of Chester's chickens, roosters and geese.

CAUTION: Death is a relentless feature of this story. Though none of the deaths are graphic, characters are obviously killed. One young viewer we know told us she thought that the story was a bit depressing.

GO: Despite the stiff animation and the not-so-great score, this film does give viewers a glimpse at the life of a wild creature living on the fringe of human civilization.

THE LITTLE MATCH GIRL

f.h.e.
1990
30 minutes
Directed by: Michael Sporn
Starring the voice of:
F. Murray Abraham

The story takes place in New York City in the year 1999, where the city's poor find homes wherever they can. Angela's family lives in the 18th Street subway station where Angela sells matches to subsidize her family's income. On New Year's Eve, a cold and snowy night, Angela goes into an alley and finally strikes a match to try to get warm. It doesn't work. Instead though, an apparition of Angela's favourite aunt appears. Together they fly over the rooftops to the Botanical Gardens New Year's Eve Benefit for the Homeless, where she meets the Monkey Puzzle Tree and other plants with whom she has a swinging time. Then suddenly, she is back out in the cold again. She lights another match and from the street hears the saxophone of Louis, her favourite street musician. They go ice-skating and see fireworks. Back in Times Square once more, Angela strikes a third match and this time flies with her grandmother to their old home, which has long since been torn down. The storm grows worse and when it breaks early the next morning, a crowd has gathered around a bluish little girl lying on the pavement. But she comes back to life when she hears the promises of people to help the homeless. This contemporary version of the popular Hans Christian Andersen fairy tale features jazz music by Caleb Sampson and hip-hop New York talk.

GO: In its updated version, this little moral tale has now become a tale of social conscience dealing with the homeless, the rainforest and urban expansion.

■

THE LITTLE MERMAID

Starmaker Video
1979
71 minutes
Directed by: Tim Reid
Starring the voices of: Kiersten
    Bishopric, Thor Bishopric,
    Ian Finley

When Marina, the youngest mermaid in the Royal Merman family, is old enough to go to the surface, she spies a prince on board a ship and immediately falls in love with him. But the wicked sea-witch sees an opportunity to make trouble and conjures up a terrible storm. The mermaid just manages to save the drowning prince and drag him to shore. When he finally comes to, people arrive to help and Marina is forced to return to the water to prevent them from seeing her. The prince thinks that the young girl who is tending to him is the one who rescued him and Marina is understandably distraught. She goes to the sea-witch and asks for legs, knowing that to assume human form is the only way that she can be with the prince. The witch agrees on two conditions: Marina must give up her voice, and she can never see her family again. And if the prince marries another, Marina will be doomed to become foam on the waves of the sea. Marina agrees, and when she washes up naked on the beach the prince takes her into his care. They become friends, despite her muteness, but his parents order him to marry the princess of another land. When he discovers that that princess is also the girl he believes saved his life, he instantly marries her. Marina, broken-hearted, is preparing to die when her sisters arrive with news. They have sold their hair to the sea-witch in exchange for a magic knife which, if plunged into the prince's heart, will allow Marina to regain her mermaid form and her old life. Marina refuses, giving up her own life instead, and her soul goes to heaven.

CAUTION: The trip into the sea-witch's domain is terrifying, and she herself is frightening, with fangs and red eyes. In one scene wolves with red eyes and huge teeth attack Marina, and the prince's arrows pierce their bodies and blood spurts everywhere. The mermaids are shown with naked, child-like breasts.

■

THE LITTLE MERMAID

Random House Home Video
1986
26 minutes
Directed by: Peter Sander
Starring the voice of:
    Richard Chamberlain

This story is similar to the 1979 version, but when the little mermaid refuses to kill the prince and save her own life, she floats up into the skies and becomes a Daughter of the Air. We are told that if she strives for 300 years to help the children of the earth, she will receive a soul. (When a child is bad, a day is added to her sentence; when one is good, a year is removed.) The time passes quickly and the mermaid earns everlasting happiness.

CAUTION: This is a bizarre and depressing tale, and there are many references to death and life after death. The Enchantress is frightening.

GO: The animation and production are good and the narration is excellent.

■

THE LITTLE MERMAID

Walt Disney Home Video
1989
83 minutes
Directed by: Ron Clements,
    John Musker
Starring the voices of: Rene Auberjonois, Pat Carroll, Buddy Hackett

Concerned by his youngest daughter Ariel's fascination with all things human, King Triton assigns Sebastian (a crab and the royal court composer) the job of watching over her. Sure enough, Ariel goes to the surface where she sees Eric, a handsome prince. When a sudden storm causes a fire and explosion which sinks his ship, Ariel drags him safely to land. The prince awakens just in time to catch a glimpse of Ariel and hear her lovely voice before she disappears back into the water. When Sebastian informs Triton of Ariel's latest escapade, Triton is livid. He angrily destroys Ariel's prize possession (a statue of Eric she retrieved from the ship's wreckage), and in an act of defiance Ariel vows to find a way of being with the prince. She makes a deal with the sea-witch Ursula: Ariel will receive a human form, in return for her voice. And if the prince doesn't kiss her within three days, Ariel will be Ursula's forever. On the surface, Ariel and Eric get along splendidly, but the sea-witch puts a stop to that; using Ariel's stolen voice, she bewitches Eric and arranges to be married to him. Ariel and her friends do manage to stop the wedding and break the enchantment, but it's too late for Ariel. The sun has gone down on the third day and she now belongs to Ursula. Then the sea-witch's true plans are revealed. With Ariel as a hostage, Ursula blackmails Triton and replaces him as ruler of the oceans. But at the last minute, Eric steers the bowsprit of an old wreck through the witch's heart and the next morning Triton himself returns Ariel to human form.

CAUTION: A great many small children have been scared by Ursula who, when she grows huge at the end of the film, is a fairly terrifying figure.

GO: With splendid animation, lively characters and an engaging tale, this feature contains some of the best Disney songs ever, including "Under the Sea" and "Kiss the Girl."

▲

THE LITTLE MERMAID: ARIEL'S UNDERSEA ADVENTURES

Walt Disney Home Video
1992
44 minutes (each volume)
Directed by: Jamie Mitchell
Starring: Jodie Benson, Jim
   Cummings, Sam Wright

The adventures of Ariel, Flounder and Sebastian continue in the undersea realm of Atlantica. (Ariel is in mermaid form throughout.) Ariel sings songs, outwits villains and has fun with her friends, some familiar and some new.

Titles in the collection are:
Double Bubble (Vol. 3):
   Double Bubble; Message in a Bottle
Stormy, the Wild Seahorse (Vol. 2):
   Stormy, the Wild Seahorse; The Great
   Sebastian
Whale of a Tale (Vol. 1):
   Whale of a Tale; Urchin

LYRIC LANGUAGE FRENCH/ENGLISH SERIES 1

Penton Overseas Video Inc.
1992
35 minutes
Directed by: Mike Sarain,
   Terramar Video

Close-up, fast-moving footage of animals and children involved in appealing activities in a variety of locations is dubbed over with children's voices singing catchy songs in English and French. Words are subtitled in white at the bottom of the screen in both languages. Original music is by Bobby Crew with lyrics by Rick Knowles and Kitty Morse.

Songs featured are:
The Alphabet
At the Zoo
The Beach
Days of the Week
Happy Birthday to You
I Wish I Could Fly
Jump Rope
The Night
The Rain
The Seasons
The Supermarket

CAUTION: The songs are sung by children who don't possess highly trained voices; this may make the video more accessible to children, but it can be hard on a viewer with a good ear.

GO: The production is excellent and has enough variety to be viewed numerous times (which will be necessary in order to become familiar with the languages).

▲

MADELINE'S CHRISTMAS

Golden Book Video
1990
24 minutes
Directed by: Stephan Matiniere
Starring the voice of:
   Christopher Plummer

This is the story of the twelve little girls in two straight lines who live at a boarding school in France. When they visit their friend Madame Maria they tell her of their plans to go home for the Christmas holidays to be with their families. They wrap presents and bake goodies, but on the night before Christmas everyone except Madeline, comes down with a cold. Madeline busies herself with nursing them all. But the girls are worried about not being able to get their gifts home to their families, and when Madame Maria is unable to travel because of a bad storm and seeks refuge at the school, she makes a special porridge that cures everyone. Then all of the girls' families come to the school and while they are having the best Christmas ever, Madame Maria disappears. Based on the book by Ludwig Bemelmans.

GO: Animated to resemble the book illustrations, this is a non-threatening story with plenty of charming songs.

◼

The Official Mermaid Bathtub

MARY POPPINS

Walt Disney Home Video
1964
139 minutes
Directed by: Robert Stevenson
Starring: Julie Andrews,
   Karen Dotrice, Matthew Garber,
   Glynis Johns, David Tomlinson,
   Dick Van Dyke, Ed Wynn

When George and Winifred Banks put out an ad for a new nanny (none of them ever lasts long), their children, Jane and Michael, prepare an ad describing their own requirements, which George promptly tears up. The next morning, a grim crew of nannies assembles outside of the house, only to be blown away by a mysterious magical wind. A single young woman floats calmly to earth (by virtue of her unusual umbrella) and presents George with the children's note, mysteriously reconstituted. Before the dumbfounded George knows what has happened he hires Mary Poppins, and for the children, the most amazing adventures are about to begin. Under Mary's direction the nursery cleans itself, so there's plenty of time to explore the magical world in a sidewalk chalk illustration and to visit Uncle Albert who floats in the air when he laughs. When George tries to fire Mary for her unorthodox methods, he finds himself instead taking the children to his stodgy bank where he tells Michael to open an account. Michael, however, wants to use his money to feed the birds and screams to get it back, causing mass panic and a run on the bank. The children flee the scene and are rescued by Bert, the chimney sweep who, along with Mary Poppins, takes them up to the smoky roof tops of London for a dazzling song-and-dance. George, meanwhile, is summoned to the bank to be reprimanded, but during the process experiences a transformation, thumbs his nose at his superiors and returns home in good spirits to enjoy the company of his children. Her work done, Mary opens her umbrella and drifts back up into the sky. Based on the *Mary Poppins* books by P.L. Travers, the story is set in Victorian London and combines live-action with animation.

AGES 3 TO 6

Songs featured are:
Chim, Chim Cher-ee
Feed the Birds
Let's Go Fly a Kite
Step in Time
Supercalifragilisticexpialidocious

CAUTION: Very young children may find the dancing chimney sweeps and the fireworks which drive them away scary. The acerbic Mary Poppins as portrayed in the books is changed instead into saccharine sweetness in the film.

GO: The film won five Academy Awards (best actress, editing, song, musical score and visual effects).
■▲

THE MARZIPAN PIG

f.h.e.
1990
minutes
Directed by: Michael Sporn
Narrated by: Tim Curry

Based on the story by Russell Hoban, this is the tale of a little candy pig that falls behind the sofa and is forgotten. One day he hears a mouse and hopes that he will be saved, but is instead eaten by the hungry mouse who all the while marvels at his sweetness. The mouse, intoxicated by the sweetness, becomes enamored of a grandfather clock. And when one day the clock stops ticking the mouse is heartbroken and runs out into the street where she is eaten by an owl, who is also touched by the sweetness. "The sweetness" is then transferred from creature to creature in this beautiful but almost incomprehensible story which has something to do with the spreading of love and the unsuspected connections between apparently unrelated things.

CAUTION: As you may guess from our outline, this is a bizarre story.

GO: Beautifully animated by Tissa David and marvellously narrated by Tim Curry, this is certainly a quality animation. Recommended for children ages five and up.
∎

MICKEY AND THE BEANSTALK

Walt Disney Home Video
1967
29 minutes
Directed by: Hamilton S. Luske

Professor Ludwig Von Drake tells his own version of *Jack and the Beanstalk* in which idyllic Happy Valley is kept prosperous by the presence of a singing harp. When a giant comes and steals the harp,

Happy Valley is devastated, and three young peasants (Mickey, Donald and Goofy) find themselves on the brink of starvation. To make matters worse, Mickey trades their cow for a couple of magic beans which an enraged Donald throws away. That very night, a magic beanstalk grows and takes the trio (and their house) up into the clouds where they find the giant's castle and the harp. And after a number of exciting Disney chases and escapes, everyone lives happily ever after.

CAUTION: At first, some children may be frightened of the giant, although he is soon revealed to be more of a simple-minded stumblebum than a ferocious monster.

GO: This short features some of the finest animation on record.

MILO AND OTIS

Columbia Home Video
1989
76 minutes
Directed by: Masanori Hata
Starring the voice of: Dudley Moore

When a farm kitten named Milo meets a pug-nosed puppy named Otis, the two are best friends right from the start. One day disaster strikes when, during a game of hide-and-seek, the crate in which Milo is hiding falls into the water and is swept downstream. Otis tries to save his friend, but when a bear cub threatens to interfere, Otis gives up the rescue in order to lead the bear away. Now separated and far from home, the two are caught up in a series of exciting adventures as they search for food, warmth and each other. In their travels they encounter a fox, a faun, screech owls, racoons, ducks, pigs, seagulls, snakes and finally, when Milo falls into a pit, each other. But on their way home they are separated again when Milo meets and runs off with Joyce, a female cat. Otis soon finds a mate of his own in a pug-nosed pup named Sandra. And that winter, after Joyce and Sandra both have litters, Milo and Otis agree to meet again in the spring and travel back to the farm with their families.

CAUTION: In one scene, an owl pounces on a mouse and carries it away. There are close-ups of Joyce having kittens and of Sandra having puppies.

GO: Gentle, non-threatening and funny, this is a good film for viewers of all ages.

MOUSERCISE

Walt Disney Home Video
1985
55 minutes
Directed by: Chris Christian
Starring: Kellyn Plasschaert

In this video designed to improve stamina, rhythm and co-ordination, Mickey Mouse and Donald Duck join in high energy exercises with children and pre-teens. Aerobics, dance steps and tough floor exercises are demonstrated by a peppy female instructor and a group of girls and boys aged ten to fourteen. There is also a section devoted to general health and nutrition and the importance of a positive mental attitude. Mickey and Donald are not animated, but are people in costumes.

GO: The program was developed with the assistance of consultants from the Children's Hospital of Los Angeles.

THE MUPPET BABIES SERIES

Jim Henson Video
1989
48 minutes
   (each two-episode volume)
Directed by: various

The videos in this series are fully-animated and sometimes include segments of live black-and-white footage.

Titles in the series are:
Explore with Us (Vol. 2):
   The New Adventures of Kermit Polo;
   Transcontinental Whoo-Whoo
Let's Build (Vol. 1):
   Eight Flags over the Nursery; Six to Eight Weeks
Time to Play (Vol. 3):
   Muppet Babies: The Next Generation;
   Beauty and the Schnoz

THE MUPPETS TAKE MANHATTAN

CBS Fox Home Video
1984
94 minutes
Directed by: Frank Oz
Starring: Art Carney, James Coco, Dabney Coleman, Joan Rivers

After performing their variety show *Manhattan Melodies* to a cheering audience at Danhurst College, the Muppets are so encouraged they decide to take their show on Broadway. In New York, they approach countless Broadway producers, but are completely unsuccessful. Finally, out of money, they decide to go their separate ways, find work and reunite when Kermit is able to sell the show. Kermit devises some pretty elaborate plans to get his scripts read and eventually sells the show. But Kermit's excitement is short-lived when he is promptly hit by a car and hospitalized with amnesia. And when the gang gathers in New York with opening day only two weeks away, they're forced to go into rehearsals without him. It isn't until opening night that his friends finally find Kermit, and after a sock to the head from Miss Piggy, he regains his memory just in time for the opening number.

GO: The film is another great in the Muppet tradition, full of funny sketches, catchy songs and cameos by notables.

THE MUSICAL LYLE, LYLE CROCODILE: THE HOUSE ON EAST 88TH STREET

Hi-Tops Video/HBO/Astral Video
1987
25 minutes
Directed by: Michael Sporn
Starring the voices of: Liz Callaway,
  Tony Randall, Arnold Stang

When the Primms move into a house on East 88th Street they are amazed to find a crocodile in the bathtub. They are even more surprised to learn that the crocodile (whose name is Lyle) eats only Turkish cavier and is an artist and a performer who wouldn't hurt a flea. The Primms come to see that Lyle is a dream come true — he cooks and helps their son Joshua with his homework — and they soon can't remember how they ever did without a crocodile. Then one day a brass band parades past the house and Lyle joins in, marching and twirling a baton. He becomes famous and receives great numbers of letters from his fans. He also, however, receives a letter from his former owner, Hecta P. Valenti, who plans to fetch him. When Hecta comes, Lyle hides. The Primms ask Hecta why he left Lyle behind in the first place and when Hecta explains that he couldn't afford the caviar any more, but that this has changed since Lyle has become famous, it's a tearful parting for everyone. Hecta, it turns out, has big plans for Lyle; they perform all over the world and stay in many hotels, but in the end the crocodile is not happy and returns to live with the Primms. The songs are by Charles Strouse. Based on Bernard Waber's book *The House On East 88th Street*.

GO: Up-tempo songs and unusual animation make this video a charmer for any age.
∎

MY SESAME STREET HOME VIDEOS

Random House Home Video
1986-1988
30 minutes (each volume)

These videos, compiled from the *Sesame Street* progams aired by The Children's Television Workshop, are not song videos — although each does contain a couple of songs. Each video also comes with an activity book.

The Alphabet Game

Play "The Alphabet Treasure Hunt" with host Sunny Friendly. When the alphabet flashes on the board contestants have 30 seconds to find and bring back something that begins with that letter. Also on this tape are songs and animated segments featuring the letters D, H, J, Q and S.

Bedtime Stories and Songs

The Sesame Street characters prepare for bed in a series of segments (some sketches, some songs) devoted to: getting comfortable at bedtime, counting sheep, lullabies, sleep-overs and overcoming a fear of monsters and shadows.

Songs featured are:
Everybody Sleeps
Snuffleullaby

The Best of Ernie and Bert

Ernestine the baby looks at a photo album of Ernie and Bert and asks about the pictures. "Best-of" vignettes include those in which: a lady with a tall hat sits in front of Ernie at the movies; Bert tries to sleep on a camping trip, while Ernie

identifies night sounds; a doctor visits Ernie but can't find anything wrong with him; Ernie and Bert visit the pyramids of Giza where a statue talks to Ernie; the friends go to a meeting of the National Association of W Lovers; and Bert teaches Bernice (a live pigeon) to play chess.

Songs featured are:
I'd Like to Visit the Moon
That's What Friends Are For

Big Bird's Favourite Party Games

Songs and games featured are:
The Clap Your Hands Game
Head, Shoulders, Knees and Toes
I Have a Furry Shadow
In a Cabin in a Wood
Oscar (Simon) Says
The Remembering Game
The Stop Game
Wheels on the Bus

Big Bird's Storytime

Big Bird and Snuffy want Maria to read them stories, but they don't have a book. Then Gilbert and Sullivan sing to Oscar about the different kinds of books in the library with help from Maria, Olivia, Linda, Gordon, Bob, Luis and David dressed in fanciful costumes.

Stories featured or retold are:
Goldilocks and the Three Bears
Humpty Dumpty (Kermit reports)
Rapunzel (Kermit reports)
Snow White (Kermit reports)
The Three Little Pigs (Kermit reports)

Getting Ready for School

Big Bird admits that on the first day of school he was scared. But after he saw the alphabet on the wall he felt better (even though he did think it was all one word). Combinations of live-action and animation allay children's fears about what to expect at school. Featuring the Count counting to twenty, Snuffy, real children forming huge letters and David singing about how to tie your shoes.

Songs featured are:
Big Bird's Alphabet Song
Everyone Makes Mistakes
Raise your Hand

Getting Ready to Read

Animation segments and Muppet sketches demonstrate how words are formed. Suggestion for rhyming words, creating poems and sounding words out are included.

Songs featured are:
A Fat Cat Sat on a Mat, a Small Ball on a Tall Wall, See a Red Head Being Fed Bread on His Sled
Take an H That's ... and an O P Op, Put 'Em All Together and They Spell Hop

I'm Glad I'm Me

Maria reads the story *I'm Glad I'm Me* while the Sesame Street Muppets act it out. Also featured are segments in which: Maria identifies Big Bird's eyes, ears, beak etc; an animated mountain climber climbs up a real boy identifying parts as he goes; Kermit talks about hands; four scarecrows (David, Maria, Luis and Bob) sing a song about the ankle, shoulder and knee; Kermit shows what is inside Herry Monster and Princess Grouchy talks about the other things inside people, like feelings and imaginings.

Songs and stories featured are:
It's Not Easy Being Green (Kermit)
Let's Make a Face (pictures of eyes, ears and noses are used to compose a picture of a face)
Me Got to Be Blue (Cookie Monster)

Learning about Letters

The Sesame Street characters perform in sequences (some songs, some sketches) about the letters B and M. There is one animated sequence about the villain in the Panama hat and another of the alphabet which is accompanied by Elizabethan music.

Songs and stories featured are:
The Alphabet Song (Lena Horne)
C is for Cookie (Cookie Monster)
The King Banishes the Letter P
La, La, La ,La, Lightbulb (Ernie and Bert)

Learning about Numbers

Big Bird and The Count introduce short segments (some animated) about numbers. Featured are: Chip and Dip meowing about the number two; animated chickens who dance 1-2-3; and The Count counting rings of the phone, honks of The Honkers and floors on a ride in the elevator; Grover counting to ten with John-John.

Songs featured are:
I Just Adore Four (Big Bird)
The Tucan Two-Step

Learning to Add and Subtract

Big Bird promises to teach Elmo how to add and subtract, only he doesn't know how himself. He asks Maria to help and, using animated segments and Sesame Street live segments, Big Bird adds cookies, crayons, spoons and his fingers. Other animated segments feature Cookie Monster subtracting cupcakes from Ernie's plate and an animated King Minus touching his princess with disastrous results.

Songs featured are:
Six Cookies (Cookie Monster)

Play Along Games and Songs

This is a collection of eleven games and songs in which children are invited to play along. Featured are segments in which: Herry Monster puts objects into a child's hand while his eyes are closed and asks him to identify them; a con man sells Ernie a picture that he says has four elephants in it, but only Bert can find them; Grover sings a song around a door, demonstrating the concepts around, under, through, near and far. At the end, Big Bird makes Forgetful Jones try to remember all the games they have seen in sixty seconds.

Songs and games featured are:
Beat the Time (Guy Smiley)
Follow That Penguin (an animated penguin makes rhythmic sounds and participants must repeat it)
One of These Things Is Not Like the Others
The Rhyme Game

THE NEW ADVENTURES OF PIPPI LONGSTOCKING

RCA/Col
1988
100 minutes
Directed by: Ken Annakin
Starring: Eileen Brennan, Dennis Dugan, Tami Erin, Dianne Hull

Pippi Longstocking and her father, a fierce but kindly pirate captain, are sailing to see the Kuri islanders (whose specialty is Little Girl Stew) when a storm blows Pippi out of the crow's nest and into the sea. The currents carry her away and wash her up near a small town where her father owns a house. There she lives with a talking horse named Alphonso and a monkey named Mr. Nielsen and without any grown-ups. She befriends her next door neighbour's children, Annika and Timmy, who soon discover that Pippi's life is a kid's fantasy. When the floor needs cleaning, she straps brushes to her feet and skates around in a house full of soap bubbles. When she needs money she finds more than she needs in her father's treasure hoards which are buried in the basement. She doesn't see the purpose of going to school, so she doesn't go. And villainous treasure-hunters and child welfare workers hold no terror for Pippi. In one scene Pippi even walks a high-wire to rescue her friends from a flame-wrapped building. When adventure after adventure is complete, and even though Pippi's father comes back for her, Pippi decides to give up life at sea to attend school and to be with her friends. Available in French as *Fifi Brin D'Acier.*

CAUTION: The storm and the fire may frighten some children.

GO: Fearless Pippi is a good female role model and splendid fun for the young crowd (we even know a few boys in their early teens who like her). The film contains some songs. This is an American film company's version of the previously produced Swedish films of Astrid Lindgren's books.
■▲

THE NEW ADVENTURES OF WINNIE-THE-POOH SERIES

Walt Disney Home Video
1988-
45 minutes
  (each multi-episode volume)
Directed by: Karl Geurs
Starring the voices of:
  Jim Cummings, John Fiedler,
  Tim Hoskins, Ken Sanson,
  Hal Smith, Paul Winchell

Titles in this series feature the characters from the original series in new situations. Many are also available in French.

Titles in this fully-animated series are:

All's Well that Ends Well! (Vol. 6):
  All's Well that Ends Wishing Well!;
  Bubble Trouble; Where Oh Where Has
  My Piglet Gone?
Everything's Coming up Roses (Vol. 9):
  Eeyi, Eeyi, Eeyore; My Hero; Honey for
  a Bunny; Owl Feathers
The Great Honey Pot Robbery (Vol. 1):
  Stripes; Monkey See, Monkey Do Better

King of the Beasties (Vol. 7):
  King of the Beasties; Tigger's Shoes;
  Up, up and Awry; Luck Amok
Newfound Friends (Vol. 3):
  Find Her, Keep Her; Donkey for a Day;
  Friend in Deed
Pooh to the Rescue (Vol. 10):
  Oh Bottle; The Old Switcheroo; The
  "New" Eeyore; Goodbye, Mr. Pooh
The Sky's the Limit (Vol. 8):
  Pooh Skies!; Rabbit Takes a Holiday;
  Owl in the Family
There's No Camp Like Home (Vol. 4):
  There's No Camp Like Home;
  Balloonomatics; Paw and Order
Wind Some, Lose Some (Vol. 5):
  Gone with the Wind; How Much Is That
  Rabbit in the Window?; Nothing But the
  Tooth
The Wishing Bear (Vol. 2)
  The Piglet Who Would Be King; The
  Wishing Bear

CAUTION: Fans of the classic A.A. Milne stories, as presented in the original four Winnie-the-Pooh episodes, should be warned that these new episodes are not based on Milne stories.

GO: The stories aren't bad (just irritating to purists). Your little ones will love "The Bear of Very Little Brain."
▲

NONSENSE AND LULLABIES COLLECTION

f.h.e./MCA
1991-1992
30 minutes (each volume)
Directed by: Michael Sporn
Starring the voices of: Karen Allen,
  Giana Cherkas, Linda Hunt,
  Grace Johnston, Donny Jones,
  Randy Kaplan, Sue Perrotto,
  Phillip Schopper, Heidi Stallings,
  Jessie Suma-Kusiak,
  Courtney Vance, Eli Wallach

Nursery Rhymes

The following fully-animated rhymes are told by a variety of people. Caleb Simpson provides the music and songs. The changing channels of a television set are used as a bridge between stories.

Stories featured are:

A Young Lady of Linn
Animal Fair
The Boy and the Wolf (The Boy Who Cried Wolf)
The Chivalrous Shark
The Crooked Man
Did You Ever Go Fishing?
Hey Diddle Diddle
The House That Jack Built
I See the Moon
Little Miss Muffet
Little Robin Red Breast
The Queen of Hearts
See a Pin and Pick It Up
Solomon Grundy
Star Light, Star Bright
Toot Toot (Peanut Butter)
Turtle Soup
Twinkle Twinkle Little Star
Wynken, Blinken and Nod

Poems for Children

This is a collection of fifteen poems, some fully-animated, some stills. Musical accompaniment and songs are featured throughout and the changing channels of a car radio are used as a bridge between stories.

Stories featured are:

Autumn Fires
The Bogeyman
Bugs in the Night
Creature in the Classroom
The Duel
Homework
Jigsaw Puzzle
Matilda
Mr. Nobody
The Owl and the Pussycat
The Story of Augustus Who Would Not Eat His Soup
The Tin Frog
Windy Nights
Wrimples

CAUTION: In *The Story of Augustus Who Would Not Eat His Soup*, Augustus dies of starvation. In *Matilda*, the fireman won't save her from a fire. *The Bogeyman* is about scary things in the basement.

GO: The complete *Nonsense and Lullabies* collection is suitable for viewers of all ages, although it may not engage the very young.

THE NUTCRACKER PRINCE

MCA
1991
72 minutes
Directed by: Paul Schibli
Starring the voices of:
  Megan Follows, Peter O'Toole, Kiefer Sutherland

When Clara finds a nutcracker shaped like a toy soldier under the Christmas tree, Uncle Drosselmeier, the toymaker, tells her a story about the King's birthday, when mice got at the King's favourite blue cheese cake. In the story, the King orders the Mouse Queen executed, but she and her muscular son cannot be caught. And when the Queen's son scares the beautiful young princess so badly that she becomes hideous, the King learns that there is only one way to throw off the spell: a young man with certain characteristics (Hans) must crack a certain nut. This done, the enraged Mouse Queen turns Hans into a nutcracker, and when a pillar falls over and kills the Mouse Queen, her son becomes king. And so ends the tale. But that night, Clara can't sleep and when she goes downstairs and introduces her nutcracker to her dolls, an apparition of Drosselmeier appears and throws magic dust over everything. A fierce battle is suddenly engaged between the Mouse King and the dolls, during which Clara falls and knocks herself unconscious. She wakes up Christmas day with her head bandaged and that night, the Mouse King returns and demands the Nutcracker, only to be beaten by him again. The dolls then shrink Clara to their size and take her to the land of the dolls. And although Clara would like to stay with the romantic Nutcracker Prince, her own world is where she belongs, and she decides to return. The Mouse King returns too, staggering back to kill Clara. But he expires after a tense chase and Clara springs out of bed and rushes to see the toymaker, demanding to know the truth. He has a nephew, Hans.

CAUTION: There is a lot of fairly intense fighting in this movie, and the Mouse King is evil, rude and frightening.

GO: This is a convoluted tale, but the voice-overs are great.

Young Pete escapes from a nasty family of unkempt hillbillies with the help of his dragon, Elliott (a large green cartoon who can disappear at will). The two make their way to the small coastal town of Passamaquitty where Elliott, though invisible, wreaks havoc. Pete is blamed. He's driven out of town and takes refuge in a cave on the seashore. There he is discovered and taken in by a lonely lighthouse keeper named Nora, who sings a *lot* of songs. Meanwhile Doc, a con man, and his accomplice arrive in Passamaquitty and, learning of the existence of the dragon, devise an evil plan to kidnap Pete and use Elliott to make a lot of money. This film combines live-action and animation.

✗STOP: After clamping a patient's mouth to a device that looks as if it came out of a medieval torture chamber, Doc abandons his victim, telling him to keep his foot on a certain pedal or the weight will rip his lips off and break his jaw. Viewers are left with a close-up of the poor wretch, his mouth painfully stretched open and his eyes wide with horror.

CAUTION: The film takes an unbelievably long time to tell its story and many young viewers may lose interest.

GO: This is a generally friendly, happy film with a warm message about love, friendship and the joys of belonging.

▲

✗ PETE'S DRAGON

Walt Disney Home Video
1977
128 minutes
Directed by: Don Chaffey
Starring: Helen Reddy,
    Mickey Rooney, Shelley Winters

PETER PAN

Walt Disney Home Video
1952
76 minutes
Directed by:
Starring: Clyde Geronimi,
    Wilfred Jackson, Hamilton Luske

On a quiet street in Bloomsbury, George and Mary Darling prepare for a night out, while their children, Peter, Michael and Wendy, get ready for bed. Concerned that Wendy is stuffing the boys' heads full of nonsense about Peter Pan, George informs her that this is her last night in the nursery. Children are people, he says, and sooner or later, people have to grow up. (So is established the central theme of *Peter Pan*.) And on that last, very important night, Peter returns to the Darling household to retrieve his shadow (lost on a previous visit) and transports the children through faith, trust, and pixie dust, of course, to Neverland. There they meet Tinkerbell, Captain Hook and his sidekick Mister Smee, The Lost Boys, the Indian braves and the famous alarm-clock crocodile. After fantastic adventures, the children leave the land where no one grows up and return to their nursery. Based on the book by J.M. Barrie.

Songs featured are:
Following the Leader
You Can Fly

CAUTION: The portrayal of the Indians in this film has caused some controversy and the crocodile may be too scary for some children. Slitting throats is mentioned twice.

GO: Considering the date of its production, this film is remarkable; particularly striking are the scenes in London, the natural look of the flying sequences and the terrific songs and score.

■▲

PETER PAN

HGV
1960
90 minutes
Directed by: Vincent J. Donehue
Starring: Margalo Gillmore, Sondra Lee, Mary Martin, Cyril Ritchard

Wendy, Michael and John are put to bed in the nursery as their parents prepare to go out. When they leave, Tinkerbell heralds the arrival of Pan who is looking for his shadow. When the shadow refuses to stick, Peter begins to weep, awakening Wendy who then utters the famous line: Boy, why are you crying? Peter tells Wendy all about his life in a kingdom far away (Never-Never Land) while Wendy sews his shadow back on. After some discussion and a sprinkling of fairy dust it's agreed that Wendy and her brothers will accompany Peter back to Never-Never Land. There they meet The Lost Boys, Captain Hook and Mr. Smee, the alarm-clock crocodile, and Tiger Lily and the Indians. After a number of adventures, the pirates are defeated and the children bring the Lost Boys home, where their parents adopt everyone. Only careless Peter comes back to Earth decades later when Wendy is married and grown with a child of her own.

GO: This Broadway musical version of the play by Sir James M. Barrie is filmed entirely on stage, and represents an opportunity for young viewers to experience the theatre. The songs are engaging and the production still entertains in spite of its age.

■

PINOCCHIO

Walt Disney Home Video
1940
87 minutes
Directed by: Hamilton Luske,
    Ben Sharpsteen

When a kindly toymaker named Geppetto wishes for a son, he fashions one out of wood and calls him Pinocchio. That night the Blue Fairy grants his wish and brings the marionette to life. Life is not that easy for Pinocchio who is so trusting that he finds himself in many dangerous predicaments. One day unsavoury con men convince him to come with them to meet Stromboli where fame on the stage of his travelling sideshow is assured. But Stromboli keeps Pinocchio locked in a cage and the Blue Fairy must come to his rescue. She warns him that from now on every time he tells a lie his nose will grow (which it does — to ridiculous proportions). He runs home only to meet the two con men again and this time they convince him that he's ill and needs a vacation on Pleasure Island. They even give him a ticket to get there. On the island, Pinocchio finds himself in a boys' fantasy land where he can do whatever he wants (smoke, drink, fight or play pool). But it's a trap. That night the boys turn into donkeys and are taken away to be sold to the salt mines. Pinocchio witnesses the terrifying transformation of one of the boys, and manages to escape having only acquired donkey ears and a tail. He

returns home to learn that Geppetto has gone looking for him and has been swallowed by a whale. So Pinocchio ties a rock to his body (the only way a wooden boy can sink) and throws himself into the sea where he is eventually swallowed by the same whale. Reunited with Geppetto, the two build a fire inside the whale. The whale expels them and Pinocchio (who floats) saves Geppetto from drowning, but doesn't recover himself until the Blue Fairy turns him into a real boy.

✗STOP: The boys' unnerving transformation into donkeys may frighten some children. The donkeys are threatened with a whip until the transformation is complete. Other things to watch out for include Pinocchio's captivity with the travelling sideshow and the black shadowy demons with burning white eyes who are Stromboli's servants. Too, the idea of being swallowed by a whale has given many a little one nightmares.

GO: This is an 1882 Italian story by Carlo Collodi, unusual in its creativity. A classic. And every child should know the origin of the saying "tell a lie and your nose will grow." Winner of two Academy Awards: Best Original Score and Best Song for "When You Wish Upon A Star." Also includes the terrific song "There Are No Strings on Me."

■

THE PIRATES OF DARK WATER

Hanna Barbera
1991
90 minutes
Directed by: Don Lusk
Starring the voices of: Jodi Benson,
    Barry Denmen, Frank Welker

"The alien world of Mir is being devoured by Dark Water. Only Ren, a young prince, can stop it by finding the lost treasures of Rule. At his side is an unlikely but loyal crew of misfits. At his back, the evil pirate Lord Bloth, who will stop at nothing to get the treasures for himself."

The preceding introduction pretty well tells it all, and if you can steer your way through the host of Tolkienesque names (Octopon, Lord Bloth, Alamar, King Primus, the Abbey of Guldobar, etc.) and hang in there through ninety minutes of non-stop wisecracks, sword-fights and boat chases, you'll end up discovering that this is only the introduction to a continuing swashbucklerama.

CAUTION: If your child tends to behave aggressively after watching videos that feature combat, you'll probably want to avoid this video as it's pretty much nothing but fighting and posturing from start to finish; also, be warned, unlike a lot of efforts in this vein, people die.

THE RELUCTANT DRAGON PLUS MORRIS THE MIDGET MOOSE

Walt Disney Home Video
1946 (episode 1), 1950 (episode 2)
28 minutes
Directed by: Hamilton Luske (episode 1), Charles Nichols (episode 2)

The Reluctant Dragon A young shepherd-boy's conceptions about dragons are altered when he meets a nonviolent dragon who recites poems and coaches the local birds in singing. So when Sir Giles, the famous dragon-slayer, arrives in town to take on the beast, the young shepherd explains that the dragon is a poet and he, Sir Giles and the beast devise a ruse. They stage a mock fight in which the dragon pretends to be defeated and reformed, after which he is accepted into the village society.

Morris the Midget Moose "...Morris was four years old, and should have been full grown, but no matter how hard he tried, he couldn't grow an inch..." So begins the story of Morris, a small moose with big antlers and a host of problems, not the least of which is putting up with the way the other moose tease him. Then comes the big day when all of the bulls challenge an enormous moose named Thunderclap for the leadership of the group. Morris teams up with Balsam, a huge moose with tiny antlers, and together they take on the big boss and win.

CAUTION: There is some fighting.

GO: These are great stories about two friends who work together to overcome their difficulties.

THE REMARKABLE ROCKET

Random House Home Video
1986
26 minutes
Directed by: Gerald Potterton
Starring the voice of: David Niven

When the king's son marries a Russian princess, the delighted kingdom celebrates wildly. The last item on the wedding program is a grand display of fireworks, to be let off at midnight. The fireworks are set up on a great stand at the end of the royal gardens, and (excited themselves about the festivities) begin to converse. Each of the fireworks represents a certain sort of person, the most notable being the conceited title character, the infinitely self-important Rocket, who thinks the entire world revolves around him. He doesn't hesitate to let the others know just how absolutely superior he is, over and over again, until he drives himself into fits of affected weeping. But when midnight arrives, the rocket is so wet with his own tears that he can't go off. So he stands alone until the next morning. When the workmen come to tidy up, one of them contemptuously throws him over the wall into the moat. That doesn't stop the Rocket, however, who continues pontificating about his own glory, until two small peasant boys find him and stick him on top of their campfire. Eventually the Rocket dries out and goes off, but no one sees or hears him, not even the two small boys; they are asleep. Based on the story by Oscar Wilde.

CAUTION: During one of the Rocket's meandering soliloquies, he imagines that the prince's future son falls off a cliff into the river and drowns. Also, we question the back of the jacket which describes this video as a story in which ". . . a conceited rocket learns an important lesson about humility." But in fact, he doesn't, and that's the whole point.

GO: Good animation, terrific music and superb voice-overs highlight this strong effort.
∎

RESCUE RANGERS SERIES

> Walt Disney Home Video
> 1989
> 44 minutes
>   (each two-episode volume)
> Directed by: Alan Zaslove

Classic Disney trouble-makers Chip 'n' Dale are involved in a series of new adventures with their friends Gadget, a girl chipmunk; Zip, a superpowerful fly; and Monty, a large mustachioed English-type mouse.

Titles in the series are:
Crimebusters:
  Catteries Not Included; Pirates under the Sea
Danger Rangers:
  Kiwi's Big Adventure; Bearing up Baby
Double Trouble:
  Dale beside Himself; Flash, the Wonder Dog
Super Sleuths:
  The Pound of the Baskervilles; Out to Launch
Undercover Critters:
  Adventures in Squirrel-sitting; Three Men and a Booby

CAUTION: Those who remember the classic cartoons with Chip 'n' Dale vs Donald Duck should be sure not to confuse them with the *Rescue Rangers*.

GO: The stories are lively and the animation is adequate, but the effort is very definitely of the Saturday morning variety.

THE RESCUERS

Walt Disney Home Video
1977
76 minutes
Directed by: John Lounsbery,
    Wolfgang Reitherman,
    Art Stevens
Starring the voices of: Eva Gabor,
    Bob Newhart, Geraldine Page

Penny, a ragamuffin orphan, sends out a distress note in a bottle. It is found by the animals of the Rescue Aid Society. Penny is being held captive in an old river boat in Devil's Bayou by the mean Medusa, who needs a small child to go down a narrow shaft in the ground and retrieve the largest diamond in the world. Brave little mice Bernard and Bianca join forces with Evinrude the dragonfly and Orville the Albatross to rescue Penny.

CAUTION: Medusa's two huge crocodiles carry out her evil wishes and there are three near-drownings (which young children find particularly scary). Alcohol is used to revive both Evenrude and Bernard, and the scene in which Penny is lowered into the shaft may be upsetting for some. Penny is told that she won't be adopted because she is too plain.

GO: Penny is a brave little girl who gets parents at the end of the film.

▲

✗ THE RESCUERS DOWN UNDER

Walt Disney Home Video
1991
77 minutes
Directed by: Hendel Butou,
    Mike Gabriel
Starring the voices of: John Candy,
    Eva Gabor, Bob Newhart,
    George C. Scott

Cody is on an expedition through the Australian Outback when he learns that the giant golden eagle Marahuté is caught in a poacher's trap. To release her, he must scale a sheer cliff. After the daring rescue, Marahuté offers her thanks in the gift of a feather, and sets Cody down on solid ground. But Cody becomes caught in another of the traps, where he's found by McLeach, the vile poacher himself. McLeach notices the feather in Cody's pack and, determined to find the location of Marahuté's nest, abducts him. Then it's up to the Rescue Aid Society to speed to Cody's rescue and stop McLeach from getting Marahuté.

✗STOP: Many children are frightened by McLeach, a sinister and threatening character.

CAUTION: Cody is in peril throughout this film. He plunges from a precipice (and is saved by the eagle) and, when McLeach tries to make him reveal the location of Marahuté's nest, he is suspended over a river full of crocodiles and even has knives thrown at him.

GO: This is a brilliant state-of-the-art animation and the sequel to *The Rescuers*.

▲

ROBIN HOOD

This animation masterwork, featuring a star-studded voice-over cast, is a reasonably faithful retelling of the classic tale — only in this version the characters are animals. Robin and Marion are a pair of charming foxes, Prince John is a lion, Little John is a bear and Friar Tuck is a badger. Original songs are by Roger Miller.

GO: This cartoon (like *Lady and the Tramp*) is one of the few Disney features that is suitable for the very young. There is a decided absence of frightening characters and what little violence there is, is harmless. (Swords don't cut and arrows always miss.)

▲

✗ ROCK-A-DOODLE

In the animated introduction, an old dog named Patou tells the story of Chanticleer, an Elvis-like rooster who believes that his crowing raises the sun each morning. Then one dawn, an evil owl called the Grand Duke sends a hired thug to prevent Chanticleer from performing his morning ritual, and when the sun rises anyway, Chanticleer leaves in shame. Then comes perpetual darkness and rain, and the Grand Duke and his band of owl henchmen terrorize the farm. The film then becomes live-action where Edmond's mother is reading him a bed-time story about Chanticleer. But the story is interrupted when torrential rains threaten to flood the farm. And when Edmund goes to the window to summon Chanticleer and end the storm, a lightning bolt promptly blasts him into the world of the story, and into an instant confrontation with the Grand Duke. In order to make Edmund more digestible, the owl turns him into a kitten, but Patou arrives just in time to save Edmund, who then assembles a band of adventurers. Leaving the rest of the farm animals behind and armed only with a failing flashlight to ward off the owls, they set out for the big city to find Chanticleer. But when they finally arrive in the city, Chanticleer has become such a big star that his former friends can't get near him, and to complicate matters, Chanticleer's millionaire manager is actually in cahoots with the Duke, and takes every opportunity to thwart their attempts to contact the rooster. High comedy/adventure then ensues, climaxing in a long chase scene which brings everyone back to the farm for a final confrontation.

✗STOP: Some scenes may be too frightening for young children. The Grand Duke's first confrontation with Edmund, the owls that come to eat the farm animals, and the Grand Duke's metamorphosis into an enormous creature are probably the ones of greatest concern.

CAUTION: The plot is meandering and convoluted. Violent scenes and images abound, and are magnified in power by Bluth's masterful animation.

GO: The animation, voice-overs and breath-taking mattes (background paintings) are first rate, and rock-and-roll fans will enjoy the songs.

SEBASTIAN'S CARIBBEAN JAMBOREE

Walt Disney Home Video
1991
30 minutes
Directed by: Steve Purcell
Starring Sam Wright

Animated Sebastian the crab and live-action singer Sam Wright perform with a group of children at Walt Disney World.

Songs featured are:
Arise
Day-O
Hot, Hot, Hot
Jamaica Farewell
Music Sweet
Three Little Birds
Under the Sea
You Can Get It If You Really Want

SEBASTIAN'S PARTY GRAS

Walt Disney Home Video
1991
30 minutes
Directed by: Steve Purcell
Starring Sam Wright

Sebastian the crab and entertainer Sam Wright perform live at Walt Disney World. A thread of a story is woven through these songs.

Songs featured are:
Carousel
Give a Little Love
Iko, Iko
In the Conga Line
Life Is a Magic Thing
Limbo Rock
Octopus's Garden
Sing Along
Twist and Shout

THE SELFISH GIANT

Random House Home Video
1986
26 minutes
Directed by: Peter Sander
Narrated by: Paul Hecht

Oscar Wilde's morality tale about the price of selfishness begins in a small town, where at three o'clock of every day, the children stream out of the local school to the abandoned giant's castle to play in his lovely garden. The giant is away, visiting his friend the Cornish Ogre. But after seven years — having said all that he had to say — the Selfish Giant returns to his own castle, scares the children away, and builds a great wall around the garden to keep everyone out. The seasons turn. But when spring comes, it does not come to the giant's garden. Spring has forgotten it. And so the castle and the grounds stay locked in ice, at the mercy of the cruel spirits Frost, Snow, North Wind and Hail. Then, one day, the children creep in through a hole in the wall, and the garden flowers again. The giant sees the error of his ways and is especially touched by one mysterious little boy. But the little boy is never seen again. Long years pass, and the giant grows old, then in the middle of one winter, the farthest tree in the garden flowers, and there stands the little boy. He has come back, to take the giant to paradise.

CAUTION: The conclusion of the tale has religious overtones that may leave some families uneasy.

SESAME STREET START-TO-READ VIDEOS

Random House Home Video
1987
30 minutes

These videos are iconographic (slides with words running along the bottom of the picture). The story is narrated as the words go by. The aim is to enable beginning readers to follow along with the story.

Titles in the series are:
Don't Cry, Big Bird and Other Stories
Ernie's Big Mess and Other Stories
Ernie's Little Lie and Other Stories
I Want to Go Home! and Other Stories

SESAME STREET VISITS THE HOSPITAL

Random House Home Video
1990
30 minutes
Directed by: Ted May
Starring: Sonia Manzano,
  Robert Klein,
  the Sesame Street cast

When Big Bird has a sore throat and a cough, Maria decides to take him to the hospital. There they take his blood pressure, listen to his heart, take blood (it pinches), give him an X-ray and put him on intravenous. Learning that he has to stay for a few days, Big Bird is afraid and wants to go home. But Hootz the Owl sings him to sleep when he is feeling alone in the middle of the night. And in the morning when friends begin to arrive with gifts and good wishes, Big Bird is no longer angry with Maria for bringing him to the hospital and thinks that his stay won't be so bad after all. Of course, just when he's all better and it's time to leave, Big Bird wants to stay.

Songs featured are:
Busy Getting Better
You've Got to Be Patient to Be a Patient

CAUTION: This is an instructional tape and not purely for entertainment.

GO: Up to the middle of the tape it doesn't seem like this video would alleviate any child's fear of the hospital, and your child may want to turn it off when Big Bird seems to be in distress, but try to stick it out because the ending resolves itself nicely.

●

SESAME STREET VISITS THE FIREHALL

Random House Home Video
1990
30 minutes
Directed by: Ted May
Starring: Bob Gunton,
   Roscoe Orman

Big Bird, Elmo, Lisette and Gordon call the fire department when they think there's a fire in Oscar's trash can. But when it turns out that Oscar is only barbecuing, they go back to the firehouse with the firemen. There they learn that firemen take their own air and water to a fire; they see how a hose works and how a ladder extends; and they

even get to try on fire-fighter's helmets, coats and boots. And when the bell rings they rush off to a real fire and watch as the fire department saves a gentle furry monster.

Songs featured are:
Waiting for the Bell to Ring

GO: This film is one of the very few available for young children about fire engines.

SHELLEY DUVALL'S BEDTIME STORIES

MCA
1992
25 minutes
Directed by: Arthur Leonardi,
   Jeff Stein
Narrated by: (see below for names
   of individual narrators)

These videos based on books are partly-animated.

Titles in the series are:
Blumpoe the Grumpoe Meets Arnold the Cat (John Candy); Millions of Cats (James Earl Jones)
Elbert's Bad Word (Ringo Starr); Weird Parents (Bette Midler)
Elizabeth and Larry (Jean Stapleton); Bill and Pete (Dudley Moore)
Little Toot and the Loch Ness Monster (Rick Moranis); Choo Choo: The Story of a Little Engine Who Ran Away (Bonnie Raitt)
Patrick's Dinosaurs; What's Happened to Patrick's Dinosaurs? (Martin Short)
There's a Nightmare in My Closet (Michael J. Fox); There's an Alligator under My Bed (Christian Slater); There's Something in My Attic (Sissy Spacek)

■

SHARI LEWIS PRESENTS 101 THINGS FOR KIDS TO DO

Random House Home Video
1987
60 minutes
Directed by: Jack Regas
Starring: Charlie Horse, Lamb
    Chop, Shari Lewis

Creative PBS star, well-known ventriloquist and Emmy Award winner Shari Lewis leads kids through one hundred and one really neat things to do. Activities require only household objects like paper clips, old rubber balls and pens and include: making simple puppets and masks, telling riddles and doing tongue twisters, performing magic tricks, and learning trick questions — just to name a few.

Also available from Shari Lewis are four 30 minute videos compiled from the PBS television series *Lamb Chop's Play Along* (A & M Video, 1992). These are interactive and theme-based and include:

Action Songs
Action Stories
Betchas, Tricks and Silly Stunts
Jokes, Riddles, Knock-Knocks and
Funny Poems

CAUTION: This video is too full of information to be used all at once. You'll probably want to remember the number of the stunt you finished with, then begin the tape there on another day.

GO: A number of things can be done by children as young as five and the video is still entertaining for kids as old as ten. Great for rainy days.

SIMPLY MAD ABOUT THE MOUSE

Buena Vista Home Video
1991
35 minutes
Directed by: Scot Garen
Starring: Michael Bolton,
    Harry Connick Jr.,
    The Gypsy Kings, Billy Joel,
    LL Cool J, Bobby McFerrin,
    Ric Ocasek, Soul II Soul

Eight contemporary artists perform Disney's classic songs in music-video style.

Songs featured are:
A Dream Is a Wish Your Heart Makes
The Bare Necessities
I've Got No Strings
Kiss the Girl
The Siamese Cat Song
When You Wish upon a Star
Who's Afraid of the Big Bad Wolf?
Zip-A-Dee-Doo-Dah

SLEEPING BEAUTY

Walt Disney Home Video
1959
75 minutes
Directed by: Clyde Geronimi
Starring: Eleanor Audley,
    Mary Costa, Taylor Holmes,
    Barbara Luddy

When Princess Aurora is born, King Stefan and his queen invite everyone to a great feast. The most prestigious guests are Stefan's lifelong friend Hubert and his young son Phillip, who is that day betrothed to the infant princess. Also in attendance are the three good fairies, Flora, Fauna and Merriweather. Flora and Fauna each give their gifts, but before Merriweather has a chance to present hers, there is a sudden interruption. The evil sorceress Maleficent (who was not invited to the celebration) makes a sudden and frightening appearance, and as everyone looks on in horror, presents her gift: a dreadful curse, which promises that before the sun sets on Aurora's sixteenth birthday, she will prick her finger on the spindle of a spinning wheel and die. But Merriweather still has her gift to give and although she cannot prevent the curse from coming true, she can soften it. The princess shall not die, but will merely sleep until the kiss of true love awakens her. Still, all of the spinning wheels in the kingdom are burned and Aurora is kept safely hidden in a secluded cabin until after her sixteenth birthday. But on that day, Aurora returns to the castle, where she is trapped by Maleficent, and the good fairies decide to put the whole place to sleep along with her. Meanwhile, Maleficent seizes Phillip, intending to keep him a prisoner until he is old and bent before releasing him to wake Aurora. But the three fairies rescue the prince, and he defeats Maleficent and awakens the slumbering castle.

CAUTION: Maleficent, who among other things turns into a fire-breathing dragon, has scared thousands of little kids. So be careful. If your little one is prone to being frightened, this film may *terrify*.

GO: Exquisite animation and wonderful songs make this a favourite Disney classic.

THE SNOWMAN

Sony and Children's Circle
1982
26 minutes
Directed by: Dianne Jackson

This is a charming story about a boy who spends a magical evening when the Snowman he builds somehow comes to life. The boy shows the Snowman the inside of his house where the Snowman tries on clothes and powders his cheeks. (His favourite place is the freezer.) Then the Snowman takes the boy on a breathtaking flight to the icelands where they meet the Snowman's friends and Santa Claus. After their return, however, the Snowman melts in the dawning sunrise and the boy is left with his memories. Based on the book by Raymond Briggs.

CAUTION: The Snowman melts (read: dies) at the end. There is no dialogue.

GO: This fully-animated film is a one-of-a-kind collector's item. Superbly animated in the same illustrative style as the book and without any dialogue (Briggs's books are known for not having text), it is accompanied only by an award-winning score.

SO DEAR TO MY HEART

Walt Disney Home Video
1948
84 minutes
Directed by: Harold Schuster
Starring: Beulah Bondi,
Bobby Driscoll, Burl Ives

"The greatest wealth a man may acquire is the wisdom he gains from living, and sometimes out of small beginnings come the forces that shape a whole life."

So begins the 1903 tale of young Jeremiah whose Granny allows him to keep a newborn black lamb. Jeremiah dreams of entering his lamb in the county fair even though it has no pedigree. And it's because he presents himself so earnestly that the judges are moved to award him (and his lamb) a special prize.

Songs featured are:
Lavender Blue (Dilly Dilly)

CAUTION: Jeremiah and his friend appear to have no parents, although they do receive guidance and effection from caring adults. In one scene, the lamb runs away and is lost in the woods on a stormy night.

GO: A gentle story full of love and lessons (Granny warns Jeremiah that he is thinking of things that are vain, and has forgotten about things of the spirit), the film contains a number of gentle songs performed by Burl Ives. Animated sequences are interspersed throughout and add to the overall charming effect of the film.

SPORT GOOFY
(Cartoon Classics, Vol. 4)

Walt Disney Home Video
1942-1947
43 minutes

In this cartoon compilation, Goofy participates in and demonstrates a number of different sports.

Stories featured are:
Footracing
Goofy Gymnastics
Hockey Homicide
How To Play Baseball
How to Play Golf
The Olympic Champ
Tennis Racquet
Track

GO: A cartoon compilation truly for all ages.

THE STORY OF BABAR THE LITTLE ELEPHANT

Vestron Video
1968
30 minutes
Directed by: Ed Levitt, Bill Melendez
Starring the voice of: Peter Ustinov

When his mother is killed by a hunter, Babar runs away to the city where he stays with a kindly old lady. Two years later his cousins, Arthur and Celeste, find Babar and take him back to the forest where he's promptly made king of the elephants. He begins his reign by building a city, thereby angering the rhinos who declare war on the elephants. Babar eventually defeats the rhinos, and the elephants rebuild their city and live happily ever after.

CAUTION: The story begins with the death of Babar's mother.

GO: This is a credible effort to bring the Babar books to life, with a few songs for the little folk.

■

THE SUPERPOWERS COLLECTION

Warner Home Video
1985
60 minutes (each multi-episode
 volume)

In each of these multi-episode volumes, superheroes go up against their perennial enemies to triumph in the end. *Batman* is by far the current favourite of *The Superpowers Collection*.

Titles in the collection are:
Aquaman
Batman
Superboy
Superman

CAUTION: The animation is simplistic and very stilted, although this is not necessarily a bad thing because it causes the violence (the odd punch or tackle) to lose its impact.

GO: Because this collection contains only minimal violence it's a great compromise for the parents of a young child with a Batman fixation (thanks to all of that dreaded tie-in merchandising).

THE SWORD IN THE STONE

Walt Disney Home Video
1968
79 minutes
Directed by: Wolfgang Reitherman
Starring the voices of:
 Sebastian Cabot, Rick Sorenson,
 Karl Swenson

Based on the first and best-known book of T.H. Whites four-book novel *The Once and Future King*, *The Sword in the Stone* chronicles the early life of young Arthur (Wart), who has been hidden away by concerned parties, and who, unbeknownst to himself and his guardian, is destined to become a great king. Wart, as he is known to Sir Ector, his guardian, is forced to perform the menial castle chores; that is, until a search for an errant arrow leads him to the forest home of Merlin the Magician, who takes young Wart in as his student. Magical adventures follow as Merlin instructs his young friend by turning him in turn into a fish, a squirrel and a bird. Wart's tutelage reaches a climax when he falls into the hands of Merlin's evil rival, the sinister Madame Mim, and Merlin is forced to fight a wizard's duel to save him. True to the book, the first part of Arthur's life comes to a close at a great tournament where, having left his knight's sword at the inn, Authur pulls Excalibur from the anvil and is chosen to be the next king. Available in French as *Merlin L'Enchanteur*.

CAUTION: Some little ones find Madame Mim's transformations pretty scary. Arthur is in peril in the animal scenes, particularly when, as a fish, he encounters a monster pike in the moat.

GO: A charming effort, featuring two of the most beloved characters in English literature. This is a good way to introduce young viewers to the Arthurian lore.

■ ▲

THE TALE OF THE BUNNY PICNIC

> Jim Henson Video/Buena Vista
>   Home Video
> 1986
> 51 minutes
> Directed by: Jim Henson and
>   David G. Hillier

When Lugsy and his sister Twitch are getting ready for the bunny picnic, their little brother Bean wants to help. When they send him away because he's too little, Bean goes for a walk through the farmer's lettuce patch. There he runs into a barking dog and when his siblings don't believe him (he's always playing pretend) the dog raids the picnic. (The mean farmer has ordered the dog to bring him rabbits for a stew.) Now aware that the dog exists, the bunnies are left to wait for the next attack. Bean suggests they give the dog a sleeping potion, but Lugsy gets caught. So the bunnies fashion a Trojan Horse-type rabbit and scare the dog into letting Lugsy go. Then, taking pity on the terrified dog, the bunnies use their knowledge of the farmer's allergy to rabbits to drive the farmer away.

CAUTION: Lugsy is nasty to Bean and is constantly making disparaging remarks; consequently Bean tells Lugsy he hates him. The farmer is ominous and his dog is afraid that the farmer will kill him when he sees that he didn't get any bunnies.

GO: This video contains songs and ingenious puppetry without anything really scary making it suitable for little ones. This is a Henson Associates Production in association with BBC-TV.

TALES OF BEATRIX POTTER

> Thorn EMI
> 1971
> 86 minutes
> Directed by: Reginald Mills
> Starring: The Royal Ballet

Set to the music of John Lanchbery and choreographed by Sir Fredrick Ashton, various Beatrix Potter tales are brought to life with a dazzling array of incredible sets, and splendid masks and costumes, all portrayed as if through the imagination of Beatrix Potter. Characters featured are: Mrs. Tiggywinkle, Peter Rabbit, Mrs. Tittlemouse, Johnny Townmouse, Jemimah Puddleduck, the Fox, Pigling Bland, Alexander, Mrs. Pettitoes, the Black Berkshire Pig, Jeremy Fisher, Tom Thumb, Hunca Munca, Squirrel Nutkin, Owl, Tabitha Twitchit.

CAUTION: The film may simply be too much, and too long, for very little children. There is no dialogue.

GO: The dexterity of the performers, considering the restraints imposed by their costumes, is astonishing (particularly wonderful is the dance of the frog, Mr. Jeremy Fisher), though those viewers who are looking for the acrobatics associated with some ballet may be disappointed. All in all, this is a terrific way to introduce young children to ballet, and will certainly be enjoyed by adult fans of the genre.

■

THE TALES OF BEATRIX POTTER

C V L
1986
43 minutes
Directed by: Brian McNamara
Starring the voice of:
    Sidney S. Walker

The illustrations in this video are from Potter's books and are accompanied by a musical score. The video also features rhymes by Cecily Parsley printed at the bottom of the screen.

Stories featured are:

The Story of Miss Moppet
The Tale of Benjamin Bunny
The Tale of Jeremy Fisher
The Tale of Peter Rabbit
The Tale of Tom Kitten
The Tale of Two Bad Mice

Rhymes featured are:

Cecily Parsley
Goosey, Goosey Gander
Little Garden
Ninny, Ninny Netticoat
Pussycat, Pussycat
Three Blind Mice
Three Little Pigs
Tom Tinker's Dog

CAUTION: This video is not animated; rather, it's similar to watching the pages of a book while the story is being read. There are some moving elements.

GO: These are gentle, classic stories.

■

TALESPIN SERIES

Walt Disney Home Video
1990
30-46 minutes
Directed by: Ed Ghertner,
    Larry Latham, Jamie Mitchell,
    Robert Taylor
Starring the voices of: Jim
    Cummings, Ed Gilbert, Sally
    Struthers

The Talespin Series features some characters who originally appeared in the feature film *The Jungle Book*. Baloo the bear flies a pontoon plane for his own transport business, Higher for Hire. Along with him are new creations, his bear friends Rebecca, Kit and Molly. The orangutan Louie is also back as a club owner on his own island, and Shere Khan the tiger owns a huge corporation, Khan Industries. There is also the sporadic menace of air-pirates, led by the swashbuckling Don Karnage. All the films in this series are available in French.

Titles in the series are:

Fearless Flyers (Vol. 4):
    Jumping the Guns; Mach One for the Gipper
Imagine That! (Vol. 6):
    Flight of the Snow Duck, Flight School Confidential
Jackpots and Crackpots (Vol. 3):
    A Touch of Class; Her Chance to Dream
Search for the Lost City (Vol. 8):
    For Whom the Bell Klangs
That's Show Biz! (Vol. 2):
    Stormy Weather; Mommy for a Day
Treasure Trap (Vol. 5):
    Idol Rich; Polly Wants a Treasure

True Blue Baloo (Vol. 1):
  From Here to Machinery; The Balooest
  of Blue Bloods
Wise Up! (Vol. 7):
  Molly Coddled; The Sound and the Furry

CAUTION: Don't be confused by the presence of the *Jungle Book* characters. These stories are only based on the characters and are in no other way connected to the original feature film.

GO: The plots are fast-moving and engaging and the animation is better than the average Saturday-morning fare.

▲

TEENAGE MUTANT NINJA TURTLES ANIMATIONS

fhe
1987-1991
47-72 minutes (each volume)

There are a number of Teenage Mutant Ninja Turtles animation series, but they all share the same basic points and so we have grouped them all here together. To understand the series you really need to know the characters. The Turtles are distinguishable by their coloured half-masks and by the weapons they use. Leonardo is the leader and is the most mature of the group; he is in blue and he carries two katanas (swords). Michelangelo is the most juvenile and he's always watching TV and reading comic books; he is in orange and uses the nuchakus. Donatello has a technical bent; he wears purple and uses the bo or staff. And finally, Raphael is the rebel and the agitator; he wears red and uses the sais (daggers). And there is Splinter, a huge rat who is the Turtles' spiritual mentor

and martial-arts master. The villains are Krang (a disembodied brain from Dimension X) and Shredder (a mysterious, masked martial-arts master who is constantly hatching plots to rule the world).

Titles in The Bad Guys (Sewer Heroes Series 2) series are:
Turtles vs The Fly
  Turtles vs The Fly; Shredderville
Turtles vs Leatherhead
  Turtles vs Leatherhead; Leatherhead
  Meets the Rat King
Turtles vs Rhinoman
  Turtles vs Rhinoman; Blast from the
  Past
Turtles vs The Turtle Terminator
  Turtles vs The Turtle Terminator; Turtles,
  Turtles Everywhere

Titles in the Bodaciously Big Adventures series are:
The Big Blow Out
The Big Cuff Link Caper
The Big Rip Off
The Big Zipp Attack

Titles in the Hollywood Dudes series are:
Four Turtles and a Baby
  Four Turtles and a Baby; Shredder's
  Mom
Planet of the Turtles
  Planet of the Turtles; Plan Six from
  Outer Space
Rebel Without a Fin
  Rebel without a Fin; Splinter Vanishes
Turtles of the Jungle
  Turtles of the Jungle; Turtlemaniac

Titles in The Sewer Hero series are:
Donatello's Degree
  Donatello's Degree; Donatello Makes
  Time
Leonardo Lightens Up
  Leonardo Lightens Up; Leonardo vs
  Tempestra
Michelangelo Meets Bugman
  Michelangelo Meets Bugman; What's
Michelangelo Good For?
  Raphael Meets His Match
  Raphael Meets His Match; Raphael
  Knocks 'Em Dead

Titles in the Teenage Mutant Ninja Turtles series are:
Attack of the Big Macc
Case of the Killer Pizzas
Cowabunga, Shredhead
The Epic Begins
Heroes in a Half Shell
Hot Rodding Teenagers
The Incredible Shrinking Turtles
Pizza by the Shred
The Shredder Is Splintered
Super Rocksteady and Mighty Beebop
Turtles at the Earth's Core
The Turtles' Awesome Easter
Turtles Soup

CAUTION: Though the violence in the *Teenage Mutant Ninja Turtles* animations is nowhere near as graphic as it is in the live-action Turtle movies, the Turtles do solve all of their problems with force. Granted, you don't discuss problems with supervillains, but it is possible that this distinction is lost on very young children. We have received feedback from many parents who have informed us that their young children become more agressive after exposure to the show.

TEX AVERY ANIMATIONS

MGM/UA
circa 1940-1955
44-60 minutes
Directed by: Tex Avery
Starring the voices of: Tex Avery

Tex Avery is one of the great pioneers of animation. His wild and zany adventures have captured the imaginations of generations of viewers (much of the animation in *Who Framed Roger Rabbit?* pays a heavy tribute to Tex). And his jokes come from an age when it was still funny to have a character get shot a hundred times, say "Ha! You missed me!" then have a drink of water and

have the water spurt out of all the holes. Depending on the period from which a particular cartoon comes, the animation can vary from classic Warner Bros. quality ('60s Bugs Bunny et al), to the "Saturday-morning" look. But no matter what the budget, Tex's genius shines through.

Titles in the collection are:
The Adventures of Droopy
Here Comes Droopy
Droopy and Company
Tex Avery's Screwball Classics (Vol. 1)
Tex Avery's Screwball Classics (Vol. 2)
Tex Avery's Screwball Classics (Vol. 3)
Tex Avery's Screwball Classics (Vol. 4)

CAUTION: Tex also made a few racier cartoons with some pretty sexy women in them, like *Swing-shift Cinderella* and *The Lady Who's Known as Lou*. Also, be aware that Tex's stuff is primarily adversarial; that is, good guys conking bad guys on the head.

GO: The jokes may be old to us, but remember that it's all new to your six-year-old, and when it comes to kids, Tex sure knows how to crack 'em up.

THE TIMELESS TALES SERIES

Hanna Barbera
1990, 1991
30 minutes (each episode)
Directed by: Don Lusk, Carl Urbano
Hosted by: Olivia Newton-John

Each 1990 episode begins with a short live-action introduction by Olivia Newton-John. Then the camera pans up to the attic, where a teddy bear comes alive and two children, Emily and Kevin, discover a fantastic book which opens and projects pictures right out of its pages. The animation is decent, and more importantly, the storylines more or less adhere to the classical versions of the fairy tales. There are also songs in the episodes, which may help keep the little ones interested. At the end of each of these episodes, Olivia Newton-John gives viewers some brief tips on how to help the environment.

Titles in the series are:
The Elves and the Shoemaker
The Emperor's New Clothes
Puss in Boots (not introduced by Olivia Newton-John)
Rapunzel
Rumpelstiltskin
The Steadfast Tin Soldier (not introduced by Olivia Newton-John)
Thumbelina
The Ugly Duckling

CAUTION: The two titles filmed in 1991, *Puss in Boots* and *The Steadfast Tin Soldier*, are not completely true to the classical versions; the ending of each has been softened, probably to make them more palatable for young viewers.

TINY TOON ADVENTURES: HOW I SPENT MY SUMMER VACATION

Warner Home Video
1991
80 minutes
Directed by: Rich Arons, Ken Boyer, Kent Butterworth, Barry Caldwell, Alfred Gimeno, Art Leonardi, Byron Vaughns
Starring the voices of: Edie McClurg, Jonathan Winters

Stephen Spielberg had a hand in this effort (as executive producer), which features junior versions of Bugs (Babs and Buster Bunny), Daffy (Plucky and Shirley), Porky (Hammy or Hampton), Sylvester, Pepe LePew, Wile E. Coyote, the Road Runner, the Tasmanian Devil (Dizzy), and totally original characters Elmira and Fowlmouth in musical adventures of their own. The film opens at ACME Looniversity, during the last minute of the last school-day before summer vacation. The kids get out, and Babs and Buster engage in the greatest water fight of all time, which ends up washing them through satires of *Deliverance*, *Superman*, and *The Little Mermaid*; meanwhile, Plucky contrives to be invited along with Hampton's family to Happy World Land (the ultimate new fun megalopolis on the other side of the country), and ends up on the cross-country ride from Hell. And young female skunk Fifi tries to get into a four-star hotel to see her idol, Johnny le Pew.

CAUTION: The kids in this film are rude and combative and may not provide the best behavioural role models for children too young to identify satire. Hampton's family (Uncle Stinky, in particular) is disgusting and on their trip to Happy World Land, Plucky must endure such things as car-sickness and saliva jokes. The Hamptons are also menaced by an insane axe-wielding mass-murderer who really is hideous.

GO: No one makes fun of the Californians like the Californians. This is a wild send-up of California culture and youth, with shots at such celebrities as Carson, Arsenio Hall, Roseanne Barr, and Letterman, and plenty of tongue-in-cheek humour. It really is designed more for adults than for children, but should provide an enjoyable viewing experience for the whole family. (See cautions!) Don't miss the credits at the end.

TOO SMART FOR STRANGERS WITH WINNIE-THE-POOH

Walt Disney Home Video
1985
40 minutes
Directed by: Philip F. Messina,
    Ron Underwood

Winnie-the-Pooh, Tigger, Piglet, Owl, Eeyore, Rabbit and Roo explain what a stranger is and give kids sound advice about avoiding unsafe places, answering the phone when you're home alone and knowing when to say no. They talk about the tricks strangers use (your mother asked me to pick you up) and urge kids to tell a grown-up about strangers they encounter and about upsetting experiences. Also included is a song about not letting people "touch you in your private parts" in which Pooh explains the difference between "OK touching" and "not OK touching." The characters sing songs to emphasize each lesson. This is a live-action video with people in costumes.

GO: This is one of the best tapes available for young children on this subject and its entertaining presentation makes it more watchable. Professionals from the Child Welfare League and others contributed to the preparation of this video for children ages three and up.

TRAIN MICE

Celebrities Just For Kids
1984
40 minutes
Directed by: Jürgen Egenolf
Starring the voice of: Rick Jones

A little mouse's dream of going to Switzerland (where he hears that mice drill the precision holes in Swiss cheese) is accidentally fulfilled when he sneaks onto a train and is locked in. But he soon finds out that he was misinformed about the cheese and continues on to Paris where life is easier for mice because the streets aren't so clean. But Paris proves to be too exciting for the mouse and he returns to Munich. Based on the book *Die Zugmaus* by Uwe Timm and Tatiana Haustmann

CAUTION: The animation quality is very uneven and the mice look more like small rats. Guards search a woman's suitcase for drugs and the mouse has a few scary run-ins with people and cats.

■

THE VELVETEEN RABBIT

f.h.e./MCA
1985
30 minutes
Directed by: Pino Van Lamsweerde
Starring the voice of:
    Christopher Plummer

Because he's just an ordinary stuffed animal, the toy soldiers want to send the rabbit away. But they cannot find his wind-up parts, so they banish him instead to the farthest part of the nursery. There a skin horse reassures him by telling him that the soldiers are nothing but wind-up, and that they will never be real. He goes on to explain that real isn't how you are made, but something that happens to you after you have been loved for a very long time. One night during a thunderstorm, the rabbit is taken to comfort the boy, and from then on they are inseparable. But after the boy recovers from a serious illness, the doctor orders that everything the boy touched be destroyed and, the rabbit is thrown out. As night falls a magical transformation takes place and a fairy turns the Velveteen Rabbit into a really real rabbit. Based on the book by Margery Williams.

GO: This fully-animated effort, due to its weighty theme, is more suited to children five and up.
∎

WALT DISNEY CARTOON CLASSICS COLLECTION

Walt Disney Home Video
1930s to 1950s
22-27 minutes (each volume)

This collection is made up of vintage cartoons and in some cases two or three short films are included on each video.

Titles in the collection are:
Halloween Haunts (Vol. 13)

Here's Donald (Vol. 2)
Here's Goofy (Vol. 3)
Here's Mickey (Vol. 1)
Here's Pluto (Vol. 5)
Mickey and the Gang (Vol. 11)
Nuts About Chip and Dale (Vol. 12)
Silly Symphonies (Vol. 4)
Starring Animals 2 X 2 (Vol. 8)
Starring Chip and Dale (Vol. 9)
Starring Donald and Daisy (Vol. 7)
Starring Mickey and Minnie (Vol. 6)
Starring Pluto and Fifi (Vol. 10)
▲

WALT DISNEY CARTOON CLASSICS SPECIAL EDITION

Walt Disney Home Video
1930s to 1950s
27-31 minutes (each volume)

Titles in the collection are:
Fun on the Job:
  Clock Cleaners; Baggage Buster;
  Mickey's Fire Brigade; The Big Wash
The Goofy World of Sports:
  Olympic Champ; Donald's Golf Game;
  The Art of Skiing; Aquamania
Happy Summer Days:
  Father's Lion; Tea for Two Hundred; The
  Simple Things; Two Weeks Vacation

WALT DISNEY MINI-CLASSICS: PETER AND THE WOLF PLUS TWO MORE CARTOONS

Walt Disney Home Video
1946
30 minutes
Directed by: Clyde Geronimi
Narrated by: Sterling Holloway

In this fairy tale, with music by Sergei Prokofieff, viewers are first introduced to the instruments of the orchestra as they will represent the characters in the story — Peter, by a string quartet; Sasha the bird, by a flute; Sonia the duck, by an oboe; Ivan the cat, by a clarinet; Grandpa, by a bassoon; the hunters, by the kettledrums, and of course the wolf, by the brass section.

One day, when his grandfather is asleep, Peter ventures out of his yard (with his popgun in hand) to catch the wolf. He is joined by Sasha, Sonia and Ivan. The wolf is soon upon tham and appears to swallow the duck, Sonia. Sasha goes after the wolf but to no avail. Just as he is going to be eaten too, Peter lowers a rope down from a tree and catches the wolf by his tail. The hunters happen along just in time to help Peter with the wolf and Sonia reappears from the tree, none the worse for wear.

CAUTION: The wolf has scary yellow eyes and huge teeth and a drooling mouth. There are frightening close-ups.

GO: This video is a palatable version of the famous Russian tale and also contains two shorts: *Music Land* and *Symphony Hour.*
∎

We have to mention the Warner Brothers animations. It seems evident that these cartoons have always been made more with adults in mind; it may even be that the people who enjoy these cartoons most are the people who made them. The cartoons themselves have come under some criticism in recent years for the level of inherent violence; however, when compared to today's fare, this is something of an open question. Certainly, many of the Warner Brothers cartoons (of the sixties especially) are masterpieces. The zany characters are blistering send-ups of different personality types, and each has a particular identity which the creators have rigidly maintained through the years. Bugs is the Bronx trickster; Yosemite Sam is always angry to the point of idiocy; both Sylvester's and Wile E. Coyote's complicated gadgets never work; Foghorn is a loudmouth; Daffy is an egocentric; and Porky usually ends up with the short end of the stick until the final scene. Tied in with it all is Mel Blanc's genius. He's one of the greatest comics of the age. May

WARNER BROTHERS ANIMATIONS

Warner Home Video
1950-1965
38-91 minutes (each volume)
Directed by: Chuck Jones,
  Fritz Freleng, and other notables
Starring the voices of: Mel Blanc

ROADRUNNER

kids and adults watch these characters forever.

Titles in the Warner Brothers collection are:

The Bugs Bunny Road Runner Movie
Bugs Bunny, Superstar
Bugs Bunny's Third Movie: 1001 Rabbit Tales
Bugs Bunny's Hare Raising Tales
Daffy Duck's Madcap Mania
Porky Pig Tales
Salute to Chuck Jones
Salute to Friz Freleng
Salute to Mel Blanc
Looney Tunes Video Show (Vol. 1)
Looney Tunes Video Show (Vol. 2)
Looney Tunes Video Show (Vol. 3)

Titles in the Warner Brothers Golden Jubilee collection are:

Bugs Bunny's Wacky Adventures
Daffy Duck: The Nutiness Continues
Elmer Fudd's Comedy Capers
Foghorn Leghorn's Fractured Funnies
Pepe LePew's Skunk Tales
Porky Pig's Screwball Comedies
Road Runner vs Wile E. Coyote
Speedy Gonzales Fast Funnies
Sylvester and Tweety's Crazy Capers

THE WHITE SEAL

f.h.e.
1975
30 minutes
Directed by: Chuck Jones
Starring the voice of:
  Roddy McDowell

Kotik the seal is in search of the perfect island where he can go during the hunting season to be safe and free. His search for refuge takes him to the Galapagos, Georgia and the Orkneys. He seeks out the Great Whale who takes him to the sea-cow (a creature that has found a haven from hunters). And so Kotik leads a great migration to the mystical island where all the seals find safety. Based on Rudyard Kipling's story.

CAUTION: The story is about a seal hunt and is not all pleasant. Commercial blacks interrupt the story.

GO: This fully-animated video is targeted to children aged three to eight; however, the film's tone and its conservationist message make it better-suited to older children.

■

THE WILL VINTON COLLECTION

Golden Book Video
1977-1989
30 minutes (each volume)
Directed by: Will Vinton

Will Vinton's remarkable talents are showcased in these four claymation films. His figures move with a life-like quality that is absolutely magical, and their faces are extraordinarily expressive. The casting and direction of voice-overs is superb.

Martin the Cobbler

(Features a brief introduction by Alexandra Tolstoy.) This is a fine telling of Leo Tolstoy's wonderful story of a bitter, lonely man who sees the face of God. Martin the cobbler has lived a hard life. His beloved wife and son died when he was still young, and he gave way to despair, blaming God for taking his family from him. He only wishes to die as well, and his days have passed practically unnoticed. Now he is old and bitter, and when his jolly friend Vladimir comes to ask him to help with a festival, Martin rudely refuses him. Then a holy man comes to ask him to rebind his holy book and that night, Martin begins to read it. He is particularly moved by a passage about a rich merchant who invites the Lord into his house, but does not welcome him. When Martin falls asleep, a mysterious voice says: Martin, tomorrow I will come. But the next day only a raggedy old street-sweeper, a desperately cold woman and her baby, a street urchin and an old apple-woman come to the house. Because Martin is waiting for God, he notices their troubles and helps them. And that night, God appears to him in a vision, taking on the forms of all the people Martin helped, and Martin realizes the truth. Full of new life, he rushes off to join his friend at the festival.

■

The Little Prince

In Antoine de St. Exupéry's magnificent, haunting tale, a pilot stranded in the desert a thousand miles from the nearest human habitation encounters an explorer, the beautiful, child-like ruler of a distant, alien world. With drinking water in short supply, and while he desperately effects repairs to his damaged aircraft, the true nature of his inquisitive companion is revealed. And as their relationship evolves, and the Little Prince relates his discoveries (both external and internal), the pilot, who had long turned his attention to matters of consequence, experiences a reawakening of the heart.

■

Rip Van Winkle

Washington Irving's classic story concerns the man who meets the ghost of Henry Hudson and his crew, and subsequently sleeps for twenty years.

Rip Van Winkle, the laughingstock of the village, is a good-hearted but shiftless dreamer who spends his time flying kites, telling stories and singing songs. One day, Rip does what he does best: he ducks his responsibilities and goes squirrel-hunting. But Fate has a surprise in store for Rip. He stops at a stream and as he bends to take a drink, his reflection becomes unfriendly. Rip runs away and stumbles upon Hudson and his boys, who are boozing it up and bowling (the source of thunder in New England). Rip has a drink and passes out, and when he wakes up he is an ancient, white-bearded man.

CAUTION: Rip has a psychedelic nightmare which contains a number of frightening images, and his return is fraught with anxiety and confusion.

■

The Star Child

Oscar Wilde's dark story of vanity, suffering and redemption is faithfully recreated. Two woodcutters out on a bitter winter's night witness a shooting star and run to its landing site. There they discover a beautiful boy-child — the Star Child. One of the woodcutters keeps the child and raises him as his own. But despite his foster father's kindness, the Star Child grows to be a spoiled and heartless boy, an expert with the slingshot who delights in tormenting others. Then one day, an ugly old beggar woman comes to the village. And when she tells him that she is his mother, the Star Child ridicules her. She then rises up and announces that, as she has been forced to travel the roads of the earth under an evil spell, so too shall he. He is then instantly transformed into a misshapen, rag-clad hunchback, which is how he remains until at last he finds the true meaning of beauty.

CAUTION: There are some intense moments in the scene where the young boy is transformed, and again when he is forced into the service of a hideous magician.

GO: An excellent effort. This film has great songs and a timeless message that we can all afford to hear again.

■

WILLY WONKA AND THE CHOCOLATE FACTORY

Warner Home Video
1971
100 minutes
Directed by: Mel Stuart
Starring: Jack Albertson,
   Peter Ostrum, Gene Wilder

Based on Roald Dahl's stories, this musical succeeds admirably in its own right. Charlie Bucket, a little boy from a destitute family, finds a Golden Ticket in a Willy Wonka chocolate bar, which entitles him and his grandfather to a lifetime supply of Willy Wonka's chocolate, and an invitation to a tour of the enigmatic and legendary Willy Wonka Chocolate Factory. Four other children (naughty, disrespectful, and spoiled) have found tickets as well, and are also along for the tour. Throughout the

tour, the spoiled children each receive their due through Willy's magic in a variety of humorous ways. And in the end, Charlie's qualities of fairness, kindness and honesty earn him the greatest reward of all: Willy Wonka's legacy, the Chocolate Factory.

Songs featured are:
Candy Man
Pure Imagination

CAUTION: The scenes in which the bad children receive their just desserts may worry young viewers (for example, a girl turns into a blueberry and appears as if she will explode); although it is, of course, explained later in the film that this is just a way of teaching them a lesson and that they will all be all right later. Also, a boat ride down the chocolate river complete with flashing images and psychedelic effects and a menacing song sung by Willy Wonka himself may disturb or confuse some young children.

GO: Charlie's relationship with his grandfather and his behaviour in general are exemplary. Kids are sure to recognize and enjoy Anthony Newley's songs.

■ ▲

THE WIZARD OF OZ

MGM/UA
1939
101 minutes
Directed by: Victor Fleming
Starring: Judy Garland,
   Margaret Hamilton, Bert Lahr,
   Frank Morgan

Dorothy is more or less content living with her aunt and uncle on their farm in Kansas, until a nasty neighbour, Miss Gulch, threatens to take away her beloved dog, Toto. Dorothy runs away with her pet, but she doesn't get very far. A kindly travelling magician, recognizing that she's a runaway, contrives to send her back. Even as she returns, a tornado strikes the farm and, after a board hits her on the head, Dorothy dreams that the house is whisked up into the air. The house lands in a strange place (Oz) directly on top of the Wicked Witch of the East, and Dorothy immediately finds herself on the bad side of the dead witch's sister (the Wicked Witch of the West, who bears a startling resemblence to Miss Gulch). But before tragedy strikes, Glinda the Good Witch of the North gives Dorothy the Witch of the East's ruby slippers, and frightens the Witch of the West away. She tells her that in order to get back to Kansas, she must find the Wizard of Oz by following the yellow-brick road. So, Dorothy sets off, and on the way she meets the Scarecrow, the Tin Woodsman and the Cowardly Lion. Together they travel through peril to the Emerald City, all the while threatened by the Wicked Witch of the West. And when they do finally meet the Wizard, he demands one token of them — the broomstick of the Wicked Witch of the West. After perilous adventures the quartet destroys the evil witch and returns to the Emerald City. But they soon discover that the wizard is a fraud who cannot help. Dorothy then discovers that the ruby slippers, coupled with her own desire to return home, are all she needs to get back to Kansas.

CAUTION: Dorothy is separated from her family during the tornado and as the house is flying, Miss Gulch appears on her bicycle outside of Dorothy's window where she turns into the Wicked Witch of the West, on a broom and cackling hideously. In Oz, the dead witch's feet are shown sticking out from under the house (most children are disturbed by this) and the Wicked Witch of the West appears suddenly, in a ball of fire, and threatens to kill Dorothy and Toto. The witch's henchmen are flying monkeys (winged creatures resembling bats) and they fill the whole screen in one scene. The witch throws fire onto the scarecrow and his arm burns before Dorothy can extinguish it.

GO: This film won an Oscar for the musical score and a special miniature Oscar went to Judy Garland for her performance. A family classic for the past fifty years.

■ ▲

Chapter 7

VIDEOS FOR AGES SIX TO TEN

Try to remember what you were like when you were six, or eight or ten years old. How did you perceive the world? What did you like and what kinds of things frightened you? Did particular situations, characters and monsters (not just in movies) cause you anxiety? Now add to that memory the high-powered impact and realism of the modern media (compare *Lost in Space* to *Star Wars*, or *Godzilla* to *Jurassic Park*), and this can help to give you a frame of reference for understanding what children are up against today.

In this introductory section we will look at two ways you can make your visits to the video store as positive as possible: by becoming knowledgeable about suitable films and by giving your child the power to say "no."

KNOW WHAT'S OUT THERE

Using the rating system

When a film receives a PG rating, this means that young viewers require some guidance from a responsible adult. To better prepare yourself to provide that guidance, you should know something more about the PG rating itself. (See chapter 3 for more on ratings.)

In modern PG films, coarse language has escalated to the point where it gets its own information piece (PG—Warning: Coarse Language or PG—Swearing), while sex is usually ridiculed, treated as a joke or loaded with a complex assortment of neuroses. Gender and racial stereotyping still abound, providing generally poor role models for young viewers. And there is more violence in PG films than ever before.

In fact, much of what we considered violent in even the recent past starts to seem pretty bland now. For example, *Star Wars* was rated PG—Violence when it was released in 1977. Compare that to the level of violence in the 1992 release of *The Last of the Mohicans*, which was rated PG—Brutal Violence. After sitting through scenes of intense violence which included scalpings, throat slitting, suicide, ritual burnings, knifings and a heart being carved out, one viewer commented: Well . . . so much for PG.

And to compound the problem, it is reaching the point where no self-respecting teen will see a "baby PG film." And the peer pressure is filtering all the way down to younger friends and siblings.

HELPING YOUR CHILD BECOME A RESPONSIBLE VIEWER

The demon: peer pressure

Right from their earliest social interactions, children have to cope with the pressure to belong. Today, belonging also means seeing the "coolest" movies — movies which are usually totally inappropriate for young children. But that doesn't prevent some children from seeing these films, and then putting pressure on others to do so as well.

The following examples of peer pressure at work have been overheard in our store.

▶ Why won't your mother let you watch this?
▶ How is she going to know if we watch it at my house?

- What can she do after you've already seen it?
- All the movies you want to see are stupid baby movies.
- I've seen everything you pick.
- If that's all you want then I don't want anything.
- You're such a suck.
- I've already seen it. There's no bad stuff in it. It's really good.

We even heard one weary seven-year-old sigh and mutter to himself: I guess I *should* see *Raiders of the Lost Ark* . . . I'm the only one in my class who hasn't; and a ten-year-old who was using most of the phrases above to convince his buddy to rent *The Hand that Rocks the Cradle.*

The situation quickly reaches a point where it must become the child's responsibility to resist the peer pressure and become a self-motivated viewer.

Becoming a self-moderating viewer

When Fiona's daughter Natasha was ten, she went to a birthday party where they showed the film *The Watcher in the Woods*. It's not *The Silence of the Lambs*, but it's scary enough, with lots of terrifying, supernatural imagery. And for Natasha, it was simply too much. Finally, she got up, said: I'm sorry, but this movie's too scary for me, and left the room. Before very long, one of the other girls joined her, and then another, and another, and so on, until fully half the party had walked out on the film. The girls later confessed to Natasha that they were glad that someone had been the first to leave.

It takes real self-assurance to risk the ridicule of peers by walking away from frightening, disturbing or disgusting films. We should do everything in our power to cultivate that self-assurance in our children.

Doug recalls an incident from his own childhood: "I

vividly remember watching a Bob Hope movie with my mother when I was eight. It was, of course, a comedy, but it had a supernatural element in it, and I can still feel the cold, electric dread I experienced when the ghost appeared. My mother noticed my obvious discomfort and quietly said: You know, you don't have to watch this if you don't want to. With relief, I replied that I'd rather not, and she turned the movie off."

What your child really thinks about a film

There will be times when your child will see a frightening film — with or without your permission. But because children often have trouble expressing complicated emotions, they will not be able to tell you how they feel.

They're scared all right, but they'll deny it under oath. And instead of admitting their true feelings, frightened children often say things like:

▶ That wasn't scary, that was stupid.
▶ It's just a movie.
▶ It doesn't scare *me*.
▶ It was really cool. (Remember: we're talking about things like torture, murder and extreme sadism here.)

Even before you rent, your child may give you clues that he or she is leery about seeing a particular film, by saying things like:

▶ That's too confusing.
▶ That's boring.
▶ It sounds stupid.
▶ I don't like it. (Even before your child has seen it.)

Some children will avert their eyes when the box is moved closer to them, while others know their own limits and will come right out and ask: Will this give me nightmares?

Altered states

Renting movies for children aged six to ten isn't all hard work, though. The reviews in the section that follows will get you off to a start, and we have included plenty of tips and suggestions in chapters 1 to 4 of this book to help you along. Beyond that you might want to try one of the following:

- Introduce your child to a number of more obscure feature films that his or her friends have probably never heard of, films that he will want to turn his friends on to, that still provide the excitement young viewers crave without containing negative images and nightmare-inducing elements. (This will help get past some of the peer pressure.)
- Try renting different types of films — branch out if you are stuck in action-adventure or comedy.
- Look for a theme that might pique your child's interest in a subject, inspiring him or her to explore the subject further. (These don't necessarily have to be educational films, but could be feature films or made-for-TV specials with subjects that can lead to more exploration.)
- Rent films that are based on books; you might even encourage reading in an otherwise reluctant reader.

Hosting a video party

If you're planning to show a film to a group of kids, there are some things you can do to empower your guests:

- Make other activities available simultaneously, and make it clear to your young guests that they do not have to watch the film if the don't want to.
- Select films according to tried-and-true criteria

(either your own criteria, built up through experience, or those we have suggested in this book).

▶ Keep in mind that you don't have to show a feature film. Why not try one of the following:
— a film that documents the making of a popular feature film
— cartoon compilations
— a documentary or how-to video that complements your party's theme.

3-2-1 CONTACT "EXTRA" SERIES

> Children's Television Workshop
> 1990-1991
> 30 minutes (each volume; *Bottom of the Barrel* is 60 minutes)
> Directed by: Ozzie Alfonso
> Starring: Stephanie Yu, Z Wright

Full of facts that will amaze even adults, this quality program (shown on PBS television) offers children information simply but without condescension.

Bottom of the Barrel

Stephanie Yu and Z Wright host this program which examines oil — where it comes from and how we drill for it, refine it and make use of it. Also included are animated illustrations, location visits and hands-on demonstrations.

CAUTION: There are shots of animals killed by oil spills.

Down the Drain

Engaging teen host Stephanie Yu investigates the water cycle — how we get water, how we clean it and how we save it — and makes viewers aware of the large role water plays in our lives.

The Rotten Truth

Viewers learn the rotten truth about garbage when Stephanie Yu visits a landfill mountain and a recycling facility. Amazing facts and colourful animation make this informative video fascinating.

You Can't Grow Home Again

Stephanie visits the Costa Rican rainforest to see the diversity of its wildlife, and to witness its destruction. Accompanied by a twenty-four page booklet, the video also talks about ways the rainforests can be saved.

GO: This is an educational series without the flavour of "those films you see in school."

THE 5,000 FINGERS OF DR. T.

> RCA/Columbia
> 1953
> 88 minutes
> Directed by: Roy Rowland
> Starring: Hans Conried, Peter Lind Hayes, Mary Healy, Tommy Rettig
> OFRB rating: F

This fantasy-musical, written and conceived by Dr. Seuss, concerns the adventures of one Bart Collins. Subjected to the regular torture of piano lessons under the tyrannical Dr. Terwilliker, Bart is convinced that Dr. Terwilliker has his mother hypnotized. While practicing, Bart drifts off into a nightmare in which he's seated at a stupendous piano in an imposing fortress called The Happy Fingers Insititute. There, Bart is preparing for Dr. Terwilliker's goal of a lifetime: the next day, five hundred little boys will begin practicing on the monster piano, twenty-four hours a day, three hundred and sixty-five days a year. In the dream, Bart's mother is Number Two, a co-conspirator in the Happy Fingers racket. Unable to leave the fortress, Bart instead gains access to Dr. Terwilliker's vault where he discovers all the money stolen from unsuspecting mothers. And in the film's climax, Bart and a helpful handyman foil the evil doctor's plans.

CAUTION: There are some strange fantasy scenes (it is, after all, a child's nightmare). Bart is imprisoned in a dungeon in a small cage; he is pursued by strange characters (Siamese twins connected by their beards); his mother is hypnotized and doesn't recognize him. This film may be too full of disturbing images for little ones and it doesn't move fast enough for today's older child. Also of concern may be the fact that Bart's father is dead.

GO: Lively songs and a zany plot make this film fun.

20,000 LEAGUES UNDER THE SEA

Walt Disney Home Video
1954
127 minutes
Directed by: Richard Fleischer
Starring: Kirk Douglas, Peter Lorre,
  Paul Lukas, James Mason
MPAA rating: G

Rumours of a terrible sea monster are sweeping the western coast of the United States to the point where it's almost impossible to collect a crew for a sailing vessel. There are,

however, a few brave souls: Ned Lands, sceptical of the rumours, signs on with a warship to harpoon the beast, and, hired by the U.S. government, a marine biologist named Professor Aronnax and his faithful apprentice, Conseille, also join the crew and the search. After a long voyage, the monster finally makes its appearance and sinks the ship. Only the Professor, Conseille and Ned survive the terrible collision, and in the mist they find that the monster is in fact a bizarre nuclear-powered submarine called The Nautilus. The ship seems abandoned at first, but the trio are soon captured by the twisted genius, Captain Nemo, and become witnesses to the most incredible marine adventure in human history. Based on the book by Jules Verne.

CAUTION: Nemo is initially cruel, and rough scenes include a fairly tough fistfight and a harrowing battle with a giant squid. At the climax of the film, Nemo is mortally wounded and dies.

GO: The cinematography is extraordinary. Winner of two Academy Awards (Best Special Effects and Best Art Direction/Set Decoration). Young viewers may be inspired to read the prophetic book.
■ ▲

A CHRISTMAS STORY

MGM/UA
1984
95 minutes
Directed by: Bob Clark
Starring: Peter Billingsley,
  Darren McGavin, Melinda Dillon
MPAA rating: PG

In Holman Indiana, in 1947, nine-year-old Ralphie Parker is

looking forward to Christmas. And there's only one thing on his mind: a Genuine Red Ryder Carbine Action Two Hundred Shot Lightning Loader Range Model Air Rifle (with a compass in the stock). But it isn't going to be easy to convince his mother of the worthiness of the gift. (Her automatic block is: You'll shoot your eye out.) So, Ralph conspires and schemes daily to embed the idea in his parents' subconcious. For school, he writes an impassioned theme on the virtues of owning a Red Ryder rifle and gets a C+ accompanied by the warning: You'll shoot your eye out; he goes before the grouchiest department-store Santa of all time, who warns him of the same and when finally the Big Day arrives (and it doesn't look good), we see that the excitement has only just begun. Based on the novel *In God We Trust: All Others Pay Cash* by Jean Shepherd.

GO: One of the greatest Christmas films of all time, *A Christmas Story* can be enjoyed by viewers of any age, anytime — even in July.

■

A SUMMER TO REMEMBER

MCA
1989
93 minutes
Directed by: Robert Lewis
Starring: James Farentino, Louise Fletcher, Sean Gerlis, Tess Harper, Burt Young
OFRB rating: PG

When a highly intelligent orangutan who understands sign language is being transferred back to her home facility, a mishap with a drunk driver causes a serious accident and the terrified creature flees the scene. Meanwhile, on a nearby farm, a deaf boy named Toby Wyler has completely withdrawn from the world — only his sister Jill can communicate with him through sign language. When Toby is the only one to see the orangutan, his parents don't believe him, since there has been no mention of its escape in the media (the authorities have suppressed all news reports to protect the ape from trigger-happy locals). But when the kids leave fruit out and it vanishes, they know that the ape exists and they camp out in their treehouse where they discover that the orangutan is living above them. And when the creature rescues Jill from a potentially nasty fall, not only do they realize that the ape is friendly, they also learn that she can sign! The children decide to keep the orangutan a secret; that is, until a circus moves into the area — a circus featuring a giant gorilla named Mighty Max. In the end, Toby finally speaks when he must call out to the orangutan to save her.

CAUTION: Some people may be a little concerned about the emphasis placed on the importance of Toby's speaking aloud. There is a scene in which some local children are cruel to both Toby and the orangutan.

THE ABSENT-MINDED PROFESSOR

Walt Disney Home Video
1961
96 minutes
Directed by: Robert Stevenson
Starring: Tommy Kirk, Fred
   MacMurray, Nancy Olson,
   Keenan Wynn
OFRB rating: F
MPAA rating: G

Ned Brainard, a chemistry professor at Medfield College of Technology, is so forgetful that he leaves himself reminder notes about his impending marriage. But even they don't help, since on the day of his third attempt to marry he invents a miraculous gravity nullifying substance, flubber (flying rubber), and again misses the big event. Meanwhile, tycoon Alonzo Hawke is angry with the college (and Brainard in particular) for flunking his lazy son Biff. He plans to pull the plug on the college, which owes him a great deal of money. As if that weren't enough, the big basketball game against rival Rutland College is scheduled for that night, and Biff had been Medfield's star player. After a dreadful first half they are behind 46-3, so Ned sneaks into the Medfield locker room and flubberizes the players' shoes; Medfield then annihilates Rutland. And after more exciting episodes (Alonzo tries to steal the flubber), Ned flies his flubberized Model T to Washington where he makes sure that the military gets his invention. Ned becomes a celebrity, and he and Betsy finally get married. Black and white. Based on the story by Samuel W. Taylor.

CAUTION: The film is dated where women are concerned. Betsy, a full-grown woman, is referred to as a girl, and her main aspiration is to get married.

GO: Despite its age, this film still stands up as a good fantasy film for kids under ten.
■

✘ ADVENTURES IN DINOSAUR CITY

Malofilm Video
1991
90 minutes
Directed by: Brett Thompson
Starring: Shawn Hoffman,
   Omri Katz, Tiffanie Poston
OFRB rating: PG

Timmy and his friends, Mick and Jamie, decide to watch a new dinosaur cartoon on the huge screen in his physicist parents' lab. Unaware that Timmy's parents have set up an experiment involving the transference of living beings in time and space, they inadvertently activate the device and are transferred into the fantasy world of their dinosaur video. There, they discover themselves in a place co-inhabited by dinosaurs and Cro-Magnons. The three are quickly drawn into an adventure in which they must enlist the aid of Rex, a tyrannosaur private-eye, and his styracosaur sidekick, Tops, to foil the plans of a nasty allosaur.

✘STOP: The movie is violent, full of martial arts and fist-fights, and probably isn't a great choice for children who are prone to emulating aggressive behaviour.

CAUTION: Rex's imprisoned father sacrifices himself. One of the Cro-Magnon women isn't exactly a positive female role model. This film isn't going to impress young viewers who are keen on scientific accuracy, since dinosaurs and humans did not really co-exist.

GO: Despite the low-budget effects, the film manages to be entertaining.

AMERICAN HEROES AND LEGENDS

Rabbit Ears Productions
1992
30 minutes (each volume)
Directed by: various

These quality efforts are iconographic; that is, they feature still pictures, moving mats, and lots of camera motion. The illustrations are uniformly excellent, as are the music and the narration.

Titles in the collection are:
Annie Oakley (told by Keith Carradine, music by Los Lobos)
Brer Rabbit and Boss Lion (told by Danny Glover, music by Dr. John)
Davy Crockett (told by Nicolas Cage, music by David Bromberg)
Follow the Drinking Gourd (told by Morgan Freeman, music by Taj Mahal)
John Henry (told by Denzel Washington, music by B.B. King)
Johnny Appleseed (told by Garrison Keillor, music by Mark O'Connor)
Princess Scargo and the Birthday Pumpkin (told by Geena Davis, music by Michael Hedges)
Rip Van Winkle (told by Anjelica Huston, music by Jay Ungar and Molly Mason)
The Song of Sacajawea (told by Laura Dern, music by David Lindley)
Squanto and the First Thanksgiving (told by Graham Greene, music by Paul McCandless)

Stormalong (told by John Candy, music by NRBQ)

AND YOU THOUGHT *YOUR* PARENTS WERE WEIRD!

Malofilm/Vidmark Entertainment
1991
92 minutes
Directed by: Tony Cookson
Starring: Edan Gross, Joshua Miller, John Quade, Marcia Strassman, Eric Walker
Starring the voice of: Alan Thicke
OFRB rating: F
MPAA rating: PG

Josh Carson and his younger brother Max are technical wizards, intent on designing and building a fully functional robot. The boys win the Junior Inventor Award with their prototype for a garbage removal robot and invest half their prize money in Newman, their most advanced effort. That same night, Josh goes to a Halloween party, and during some Ouija board fun, his dead father (whom Josh believes commited suicide) tries to contact him. Josh thinks the whole thing is a bad joke, until a mysterious entity flashes down from the heavens and enters Newman. Newman instantly begins to exhibit some very sophisticated behaviour and informs the boys that he is, in fact, their father, returned from heaven. Meanwhile, as Newman renews acquaintance with the boys' mother, a nosy reporter starts snooping around, and the evil Cottswinkles (the Carsons' arch-rivals) form a pact with a sinister industrialist to steal Josh's invention.

CAUTION: The villains are fat and ugly and it's a shame that fat equals bad. The film deals with the problems of grief, and may raise some questions about Ouija boards, the hereafter, and so on.

GO: At the climax of the film, the truth about Josh's father's death is revealed — his death was an accident, not a suicide — and Josh and his father are reconciled. This film won an Award of Excellence from Film Advisory Board, Inc.

AFRICAN STORY MAGIC

f.h.e.
1992
27 minutes
Directed by: Peter Thurling
Narrated by: Brock Peters
Starring: Ricky O'Shon Collins,
  Diane Ferlatte, Tejumola
  Ologboni
OFRB rating: no rating given

A young African-American boy named Kwaku lives in an unfriendly inner-city neighbourhood. One day, as he's searching for mirrors in abandoned buildings, he is visited by a round hovering light which introduces itself as Sam and tells him that it brings magic words from far away. But Kwaku doesn't want any stupid stories and Sam makes an equally mysterious exit. Then Kwaku becomes aware that he's being followed by a green man; he hides, and Sam reappears telling Kwaku to use the mirror he has found to enter the world of imagination. Kwaku (and the green man) pass through a magic door into the Africa of his ancestors, where they hear the stories of the magic story people. One storyteller tells about an eagle that thought he

was a chicken, while another uses sign language to tell about a mouse who saved a lion king. They learn why mosquitoes buzz in people's ears and how the lion got his roar. And, in the end, when the story people tell Kwaku to take courage from the drumming, he faces the green man and has a wonderful encounter. The stories are accompanied by African drumming, singing and dancing, and either tell life-lessons or encourage self-esteem.

CAUTION: The green man who stalks Kwaku is supposed to represent Kwaku's fear, and he is scary.

GO: This is an unusual but appealing sort of storytelling.

ALADDIN

Walt Disney Home Video
1992
90 minutes
Directed by: John Masker,
  Ron Clements
Starring the voices of:
  Robin Williams, Gilbert Gottfried
ORFB rating: F
MPAA rating: G

Hoping to steal the magic lamp, Jafar, advisor to the Sultan, summons the entrance to the legendary Cave of Wonders from the desert sands, only to learn that the only one who can set foot inside is a young street thief named Aladdin. Disguising himself as an old soothsayer, Jafar visits Aladdin and tells him about the cave of wonderous riches and about the lamp, which Jafar hopes to steal from Aladdin when he leaves the cave. Aladdin is warned not to touch anything except the lamp (those who do, forfeit their lives). Jafar then follows the boy out into the desert. Inside the cave, Aladdin finds the lamp, but when his pet monkey touches one of the jewels the cave immediately begins to collapse, and Aladdin is trapped inside with his monkey and their new-found friend, a courteous but mute flying carpet. Aladdin rubs the lamp while examining it, and out pops a genie, who releases them from the cave and transforms Aladdin into a prince in order that he may better woo the princess Jasmine. (The law decrees that Jasmine must marry a prince.) But not recognizing him in his princely disguise, and determined to marry the young thief she knows as Aladdin, Jasmine turns the "prince" away. It's only when Jafar tells Jasmine that Aladdin has been beheaded that she finally agrees to marry Jafar instead. In the end, Aladdin reveals himself and with the genie's help, tricks Jafar into imprisonment in the lamp; the Sultan changes the law so the lovers can marry and they live happily ever after.

CAUTION: The tempo of this film is intense (the genie's rapid-fire transformations, in particular) and may be too much for children under five. There are also some pretty tense moments when, in one scene, Jafar ties Aladdin to a ball and chain and throws him in the ocean, and in another, Jasmine is imprisoned in an hourglass with the sand running onto her. The climax includes a very scary Jafar transforming himself into increasingly threatening entities.

GO: Where the film really succeeds is in its animation. Robin Williams's wacky genie provided animators with virtually unlimited possibilities for creative invention. There are just enough songs to appeal to the little ones, but not too many to turn older ones off. And popular Disney characters like Pinocchio and Sebastian the crab turn up in the corners of the frame.

ANNE OF GREEN GABLES

Junior Home Video
1985
196 minutes
Directed by: Kevin Sullivan
Starring: Colleen Dewhurst, Richard Farnsworth, Megan Follows
OFRB rating: unrated

Elderly brother and sister Matthew and Marilla Cuthbert run a farm near the town of Avonlea on Prince Edward Island. Matthew is getting too old to do the heavy labour, so he and Marilla send for a boy from the orphanage to help out. But the orphanage makes a mistake and sends a girl instead, and Matthew, at a loss for what to do, takes her home. Marilla insists that the girl must go back, and plans are made to return her the next day. But Anne so bewitches the pair with her enthusiasm and charm that she ends up staying for a "try-out." That try-out turns into a permanent relationship, and Anne, brilliant, talented and wildly imaginative, turns the Cuthberts' staid life utterly upside down. Anne's escapades are outrageous: she gets her best friend Diana Barry drunk (by serving her what she thinks is raspberry cordial, but is in fact wine), and accidentally dyes her hair green (in an attempt to achieve an auburn tint). But her capers are counterbalanced by her love of life and learning. And as Anne grows up, the Cuthberts come to see her as their own child. Then Matthew dies suddenly; Anne's entire life is dramatically changed, and she discovers compassion and friendship from an unexpected source. Based on the book by Lucy Maud Montgomery.

CAUTION: Matthew dies of a heart attack.

GO: Absolutely terrific, this is a uniformly excellent production.

■

ANNE OF GREEN GABLES: THE SEQUEL

Junior Home Video
1987
232 minutes
Directed by: Kevin Sullivan
Starring Frank Converse,
   Jonathan Crombie,
   Colleen Dewhurst, Megan Follows
OFRB rating: no rating given

Anne, as romantic and dreamy as ever, is now a teacher, and an aspiring writer of romantic fiction. Her former arch-rival and now fast friend Gilbert Blythe is going to medical school and has fallen in love with her, but Anne rejects him — her own notions of romance are much more flowery. When Anne's former teacher Miss Stacy becomes head of the school board, she recommends Anne for a teaching job at an exclusive ladies' college in Kingsport. However, Kingsport is ruled by the snobbish Pringles, who aren't fond of Anne and do everything in their power to sabotage her career. But Anne prevails. She charms almost everyone she meets and even wins the admiration of the handsome Michael Harris. In the end, though, Anne discovers that despite his

charm, Michael is not for her, and when she returns to Green Gables and learns that Gilbert Blythe is very ill, Anne realizes the true depth of her feelings for her childhood friend. This sequel to *Anne of Green Gables* is based on Lucy Maud Montgomery's novels *Anne of Avonlea*, *Anne of the Island* and *Anne of Windy Poplars*.

GO: Warm-hearted and witty, this is a positive film about persistence and recognizing the worth of a true heart.

■ ▲

THE APPLE DUMPLING GANG

Walt Disney Home Video
1975
100 minutes
Directed by: Norman Tokar
Starring: Bill Bixby, Tim Conway,
   Don Knotts, Henry Morgan,
   Slim Pickens
MPAA rating: no rating given

When travelling gambler and conman Russel Donavan drifts into town, he makes a deal to pick up some valuables for an old acquaintance. Thinking he has made an easy score, Donavan meets the stage (driven by an attractive woman named Dusty) and discovers that the "valuables" are three children. With the kids in tow, Donavan tries to find a family in town that will take them; of course, no one will, and Donavan is stuck. The kids are no end of trouble, and they single-handedly annihilate the town, leaving Donavan stuck with the tab. But when the kids discover a huge gold nugget (worth $87,425), there is suddenly no shortage of people willing to take the children in.

Meanwhile, the villainous bank-robber Stillwell and his evil gang of desperados come to town and plot to rob the bank, while the kids form The Apple Dumpling Gang with stumblebums Theodore and Amos (who used to ride with the Stillwell Gang until Amos accidentally shot Stillwell in the leg). The climax of the film is a collection of shoot-outs and good old-fashioned chases, during the course of which the kids' gold nugget is destroyed. Then, once again, no one wants the kids — except Donavan and Dusty.

CAUTION: There is some comic violence in this film and, of course, some very physical slapstick involving Knotts and Conway.

GO: For young fans of action and comedy, this is the film.

BABES IN TOYLAND

Orion
1986
96 minutes
Directed by: Clive Donner
Starring: Drew Barrymore,
　Eileen Brennan, Googy Gress,
　Richard Mulligan, Keanu Reeves,
　Jill Schoelen
MPAA rating: G

On a stormy Christmas Eve in Cincinnati, Lisa Piper, her older sister Mary and their friends Jack and George quit their jobs working for obnoxious store owner Mr. Barney. While driving the others home through a blizzard, Jack swerves to avoid a falling tree and Lisa is thrown out of the jeep, hits her head and is promptly projected into Toyland, a magical kingdom surrounded by the Forest of the Night. There she discovers that the evil Barnaby Barnacle is forcing his nephew Jack Nimble's sweetheart, Mary Contrary, to marry him instead. Lisa arrives just in time to break up the wedding and learns the whole story. Jack was supposed to have become keeper of the cookie factory when his father died, but Barnaby had a law passed saying that Jack must be married by his twenty-first birthday before he can assume control. If he isn't married in time, then Barnaby gets the factory for life. But Barnaby's ambitions are even higher than that; he intends to unleash a dreadful army of forest trolls upon Toyland, and take over. And it's only Lisa's rekindled belief in toys that enables an army of toy soldiers to drive away the monsters.

CAUTION: Young children may be frightened by the army of spooky, misshapen trolls. There is a rough fist-fight between Jack and Barnaby at the climax of the film.

THE BABY-SITTERS CLUB SERIES

Goodtimes Video/HGV Video
1990-1991
30 minutes (each volume)
Directed by: Abbie H. Fink,
　Carol S. Fink, Lynn Hamrick
Starring: Meghan Andrews,
　Melissa Chase, Avriel Hillman,
　Meghan Lahey, Nicole Leach,
　Jessica Prunell, Jeni F. Winslow
OFRB rating: no rating given

Seven enterprising teenage girls form a club in order to deal with baby-sitting jobs. They earn money through fund-raisers to put together "kid kits" which they then use to occupy their young charges. The girls are Claudia, Stacey, Mary Anne, Kristy, Dawn, Mallory and Jessica. Based on Ann M. Martin's popular series of books.

The Baby-sitters Club Christmas Special (Vol. 5)

When Stacey's diabetes lands her in the hospital, Kristy finds the true spirit of Christmas and gives her hard-earned baseball glove to a boy convalescing there.

Claudia and the Missing Jewels (Vol. 6)

At a craft show, Claudia displays the jewelry she has made. And when a local merchant places an order everything seems great, until one pair of earrings mysteriously disappears.

Dawn and the Dream Boy (Vol.7)

Dawn loves Jamie Anderson, but a misunderstanding about him causes a rift between her and Mary Anne.

Dawn and the Haunted House (Vol. 2)

Dawn believes Mrs. Slade is a witch, and when she learns the truth she feels pretty silly.

Kristy and the Great Campaign (Vol. 4)

Kristy tries to help Courtney win the Grade Three student council election, but soon realizes that she is trying to live Courtney's life for her.

Mary Anne and the Brunettes (Vol. 1)

Marcey, the most popular girl in school, invites Logan, the boy Mary Anne likes, to a costume party. There is rivalry until Mary Anne works it out with Logan.

Stacey's Big Break (Vol. 3)

Stacey gets a chance to see what life is like for a fashion model, but prefers to spend her time baby-sitting.

CAUTION: The girls spend a great deal of time talking about boys, putting on make-up and shopping for clothes.

GO: The girls are responsible, innocent, loyal and caring.
∎

BATMAN: THE MOVIE

Playhouse
1966
104 minutes
Directed by: Leslie H. Martinson
Starring: Frank Gorshin,
    Burgess Meredith,
    Lee Meriwether, Cesar Romero,
    Burt Ward, Adam West
MPAA rating: no rating given

In this made-for-TV, tongue-in-cheek send-up of the Caped Crusader, all of Batman's supervillain foes (The Penguin, The Joker, The Riddler and Catwoman) team up against him. Sure that Batman will attempt to rescue a prominent citizen, the evil quartet plot to kidnap Bruce Wayne. Catwoman's alter-ego, a sophisticated Soviet reporter, lures Bruce to her pad where the rest of the gang arrive on giant flying umbrellas, knock him out and take him to their secret wharf-side hide-out. But Bruce makes a daring escape and returns as Batman, even as the Penguin is testing out a new weapon which will freeze-dry people, allowing him to reconstitute them at will. (He plans to ambush a conference of world leaders, freeze-dry them and hold the world hostage.) Only the Dynamic Duo can save the day, which they do in a final punch-out. And when Catwoman trips and her mask falls off to reveal herself as Batman's sweetheart, Robin sums up the whole film with the words: Holy heartbreak!

CAUTION: The violence is so utterly spoofed and comic that it should be of little concern; however, parents should know that fighting (wimpy fighting, but fighting nonetheless) is a central element of this film.

GO: If you have a little person who's Batman crazy, this film is the perfect solution. Like all great family films, this movie can be appreciated on two levels: as an action film for little kids and as a zany send-up of the Dark Knight.

BEETHOVEN

MCA
1991
87 minutes
Directed by: Brian Levant
Starring: Charles Grodin, Bonny Hunt, Dean Jones, Alice Newton
OFRB rating: F
MPAA rating: PG

Beethoven is an adorable St. Bernard puppy, but he's already big, and he's having trouble getting himself sold to the right family for just that reason. Then, to complicate his young life even further, he's kidnapped by the henchman of an evil vet who uses dogs to test ammunition. But, thanks to a resourceful little terrier, Beethoven makes his escape, and the next morning sneaks into the family home of uptight businessman and dog-hater George Newton. When he is discovered in the bed of George's youngest daughter, George's wife quickly points out that you can't just show a child a puppy and then take it away, so George is stuck with a lovable monster who tears up his home and drools on everything in sight. But Beethoven isn't just your average slobbering St. Bernard; he's a very special dog who helps the family in some extraordinary ways. Still, George is determined to get rid of the mess-maker, until the evil vet Dr. Yarnick kidnaps Beethoven for a particularly gruesome test. Only then does George understand how much he's come to love the big dog, and sets out to rescue him.

CAUTION: For young dog-lovers, a number of scenes may be a bit intense. For instance, it is revealed in dialogue that the evil vet is using dogs for ammunition testing, and needs Beethoven because he requires a full-sized skull for a particularly powerful type of bullet. Also, in one scene the evil vet strikes Beethoven repeatedly.

GO: Grodin is wonderful as the finicky, harried father, Dean Jones is perfect as the sinister veterinarian and the canine lead is the best of all. This is a great film for the family.

BEETHOVEN LIVES UPSTAIRS

The Children's Group Video Release
1991
60 minutes
Directed By: David Devine
Starring: Sheila McCarthy,
  Neil Munro, Fiona Reid,
  Illya Woloshyn
MPAA rating: no rating given

In Vienna, 1827, nine-year-old Christoph is shattered by the unexpected death of his father. The family is now in dire straits, and Christoph's mother is forced to rent out the upper room to a lodger, who turns out to be none other than the great composer Ludwig van Beethoven. Beethoven promptly terrorizes the poor family with his eccentricities and tyrannical behavior, and Christoph instantly loathes him, cheered only by the knowledge that the mad genius is famous for never staying in one place for very long. But as time passes, Christoph comes to appreciate the great heart which lies beneath the composer's rough exterior, and the tremendous will with which Beethoven battles his

failing hearing. As he himself says: Great men like Beethoven don't conform to other people's standards, they make their own. Based on the story by Barbara Nichol.

CAUTION: Although related to the highly successful audio-cassette of the same name, this is a feature film set in period costume and may not be engaging enough for children who enjoyed the audio-cassete.

GO: This is a refreshing film, beautifully filmed in both Port Hope and Prague. The score comprises well-known selections of Beethoven's music, which is bound to attract the interest of many a budding musician.

■

✗ BENJI THE HUNTED

Walt Disney Home Video
1987
89 minutes
Directed by: Joe Camp
Starring: Benji
MPAA rating: G

While filming in Oregon, Benji and his trainer are out in a small, open fishing boat, when the boat capsizes. His trainer is rescued, but Benji is stranded in the coastal forestlands of Oregon, and is forced to fend for himself. To complicate matters, he witnesses the shooting of a cougar, and foregoes rescue to stay and care for the cougar's orphaned kittens. Benji tries his best to feed his charges, but he doesn't have the heart to kill anything for them. Then he discovers a woodsman's cabin and steals one of the dead birds the woodsman has left out to cure. The kittens get their meal, but when Benji goes back to the cabin the next day, the woodsman captures him and ties him up. Benji manages to escape and returns to take care of the kittens, but it's an uphill battle as he's forced to face the threatening advances of a wolf, a bear, a fox and a hawk. In the climax, Benji lures the wolf to its death, and when another cougar appears and is willing to assume responsibility for the kittens, Benji is free to be rescued.

✗STOP: The female cougar is shot dead near the beginning of the film and later, a hawk swoops down and carries one of the kittens away — the kitten doesn't come back. Benji tricks the wolf into leaping to its death.

CAUTION: Benji and the kittens are in peril right from the start, and the relentless tension, combined with the animal casualties, may be too much for some young viewers.

GO: Spectacular scenery, great editing and solid animal training highlight this faced-paced animal adventure.

▲

BIG TOP PEE-WEE

Paramount Home Video
1988
86 minutes
Directed by: Randal Kleiser
Starring: Valeria Golina,
    Kris Kristofferson,
    Penelope Anne Miller,
    Paul Reubens
OFRB rating: F
MPAA rating: PG

Pee-Wee runs an unusual farm where, with the help of his friend Vance the Pig, he makes

concoctions to stimulate the growth of vegetables. When a terrible storm blows the Cabrini Circus onto his farm, Pee-Wee suggests they stay and have a vacation. But the crabby townspeople reject the circus, and the disheartened ring master, Mace, decides that he needs a new theme to liven up the show. Pee-Wee tries to find an act for himself and falls for a trapeze artist named Gina Piccolapupola. And when Pee-Wee's fiancée Winnie catches them together she breaks off the engagement and joins the Piccolapupola brothers' act. Even when the circus performers are ready to do their show, the townsfolk still won't have anything to do with it. But Pee-Wee has a great idea: he uses one of his experiments gone wrong to turn the crabby old townspeople into children, who are only too delighted to attend. So the circus has an audience, Mace has his barnyard theme, and Pee-Wee and Gina, Winnie and the Piccolapupola Brothers are together for good.

CAUTION: There is some sexual parody in this film and Winnie's comment after catching Pee-Wee and Gina together (I'm not surprised, you're a man, she's Italian) may be offensive to some.

160

GO: *Big Top Pee-Wee* is a fun, silly film for the kids and a plethora of parody for adults. This film features the longest screen kiss in history.

THE BLACK STALLION

MGM/UA
1979
117 minutes
Directed by: Carroll Ballard
Starring: Hoyt Axton, Teri Garr,
    Kelly Reno, Mickey Rooney
OFRB rating: F
MPAA rating: G

In 1946, on a voyage with his father, Alec Ramsey sees a group of Arab trainers struggling to control a wild Arabian stallion. He tries to befriend the horse, but is sent away by the horse's handlers. Then one night, a fierce storm rises and the ship begins to sink. Alec and his father are separated and the boy follows the black stallion overboard. The pair save each other and the next morning Alec finds himself washed up on an unknown shore. He finds the stallion, completely tangled in ropes, and cuts it free. The stallion runs off, but later saves Alec from a cobra and eventually lets the boy ride him. Then fishermen arrive, and the two are saved. At home, Alec is hailed as a boy celebrity, but his happiness is short-lived when the black stallion escapes. Alec finds him in the care of a horse-trainer named Henry Dailey and together they decide to run the stallion in a head-to-head competition against the two greatest horses in America. (Alec will ride.) And at the film's climax, viewers are treated to one great horse race. Based on the novel by Walter Farley.

CAUTION: During the panic aboard the sinking ship, a frightened adult tries to cut Alec's life-jacket off to use it himself; Alec's father and the man vanish, struggling into the chaos. The horse, panic-stricken, is pulled underwater. Alec shows an eerie lack of emotion over his father's death.

GO: This classic adventure story is renowned for its breathtaking images.
■

THE BLACK STALLION RETURNS

CBS/Fox
1983
103 minutes
Directed by: Robert Dalva
Starring: Teri Garr, Alan Goorwitz,
    Ferdinand Mayne, Kelly Reno,
    Vincent Spano
OFRB rating: PG—Intense Scenes
MPAA rating: PG

One year after their victory, Alec Ramsey and the Black Stallion are living an idyllic existence together. However, two Arabic factions are conspiring to take the stallion back to the Sahara — the first, the stallion's original owners, hope to retrieve property they feel is rightly theirs; the second, the evil Kurr, leader of the Uruk, hope simply to stop the stallion from taking part in the great race in the Sahara. When Berbers from the first faction take the horse back, Alec hides in the trailer and rides undiscovered as far as the seaport. There the Berbers find Alec, tie him up and leave him behind to watch as they load the black stallion onto a ship bound for the Sahara. Undaunted, Alec escapes and stows away on an airplane bound for Casablanca.

There, Alec soon becomes embroiled in the tribal politics which are gripping the region, all the while guided by the unshaken belief that the horse belongs with him. He locates the stallion, and it becomes apparent to everyone that no one can ride the great horse but Alec. The day of the great race arrives, pitting the rival horsemen against each other. Alec wins, but in the end comes to realize that the great horse is where he belongs. This film is the sequel to *The Black Stallion*.

CAUTION: Alec bids a tearful farewell to his horse at the end of the film.

GO: *The Black Stallion Returns* is a delightful, basically non-violent adventure about persistence and love.

AGES 6 TO 10

BLACKBEARD'S GHOST

Walt Disney Home Video
1968
107 minutes
Directed by: Robert Stevenson
Starring: Dean Jones,
    Suzanne Pleshette, Peter Ustinov
MPAA rating: G

When coach Steve Walker arrives in the small New England town of Godolphin to help the track and field team, he encounters a number of problems: the team is utterly and completely hopeless; Blackbeard's Inn, where he's staying, is about to be repossessed by local gangster-cum-businessman Silky Seymour, and on his first night there he accidentally resurrects the ghost of Blackbeard. And the only person who can see or hear Blackbeard is Steve, so everyone thinks he's

crazy. Comic adventures ensue as Steve's invisible companion raises heck, helps him win the track and field meet, saves the inn and defeats the evil Seymour.

CAUTION: There is some comic violence, and a scene in front of the old a-kiss-for-a-dollar booth could be considered sexist. When Blackbeard's ghost is summoned, it is mildly spooky.

GO: One of Disney's best, this film can be appreciated by the whole family.

CANDLESHOE

Walt Disney Home Video
1977
101 minutes
Directed by: Norman Tokar
Starring: Jodie Foster, Helen Hayes,
    David Niven
MPAA rating: G

Casey Brown, an orphan and a perennial escapee from Juvenile Hall, is selected by master con artist Harry Bundage for the ultimate scam. Casey happens to bear an uncanny resemblance to the long-lost granddaughter of Lady St. Edmond, the aged mistress of Candleshoe Manor. And as it is rumoured that pirate-captain Joshua St. Edmond hid his vast treasure somewhere in the manor, Harry intends to insert Casey into the family as the miraculously found granddaughter so that she can search for the lost loot. But in the course of her stay, Casey swiftly grows to appreciate the family, especially the wonderful butler, who impersonates other servants in order to hide the truth about the family's plummeting fortunes from Lady St. Edmond. In the end, Casey must chose between gaining wealth and protecting those she has come to love.

CAUTION: There is a little slapstick violence in the finale, but no one is seriously injured.

GO: This is a wonderful film with a positive message.

✗ THE CANTERVILLE GHOST

Columbia
1986
96 minutes
Directed by: Paul Bogart
Starring: Sir John Gielgud,
   Alyssa Milano
MPAA rating: no rating given

When Harry Canterville loses his job, he decides to move with his second wife Lucy and his daughter Jennifer to the English castle he stands to inherit. To gain ownership of the property, the family must occupy Canterville Castle for three months. But no one has ever stayed even three weeks in the spooky place, which is rumoured to be haunted by the ghost of Sir Simon de Canterville. Sure enough, on the very first night, the chain-wrapped spirit appears; however, Harry and Lucy are unimpressed, suspecting that the ghost is really the result of special effects created by someone who is trying to frighten them away. Their lack of terror leaves the ghost powerless. Meanwhile, Jennifer, who intensely dislikes her stepmother, tries to strike a deal with the ghost to scare Lucy off. In

the course of negotiations, the two become friends and Jennifer learns about the ghost's plight. (He murdered his wife in 1635 and is now forced to walk the earth in perpetuity.) Life begins to run smoothly for all of the Cantervilles; that is until the ghost learns that they plan to sell the castle to a hotel chain. Then his antics get so outrageous that Harry brings in a paranormal specialist. But when the doctor's equipment succeeds in briefly bringing back the spirit of Sir Simon's wife, the ghost falls into a depression. Only Jennifer can save the day by appealing to the Angel of Death to give Sir Simon rest. Based on a story by Oscar Wilde.

✗STOP: Look out! There are plenty of scares in this one, including a scene in which Lucy looks into the mirror and sees her own reflection, hideously aged.

CAUTION: The ghost is scary, and his wife-killing past is grim. The final scene in which Jennifer prays to the Angel of Death is full of spooky atmospherics and ghostly light.

GO: This is a good ghost story with enough frights to keep kids interested. If they like this one, your gang may even want to see Margaret O'Brien's black and white version, filmed in 1944.

■

THE CAT FROM OUTER SPACE

Walt Disney Home Video
1978
103 minutes
Directed by: Norman Tokar
Starring: Ken Berry, Sandy Duncan,
   Roddy McDowall, Harry Morgan,
   McLean Stevenson
MPAA rating: G

A UFO in trouble goes down in rural America. The pilot is an alien cat named Zoonar J5/9 Doric47, who manipulates his environment with his superpowered collar. The alien cat bails out, but the army witnesses the crash and General Stilton has the craft brought to the military base where he assembles a top IQ staff (including gambling addict Dr. Link, Dr. Liz Bartlett, industrial agent Stallwood and flaky genius Dr. Frank Wilson) to examine it. Soon though, Frank's unorthodox observations get him booted out, and he ends up back in his office with the cat, which he names Jake. Amazed, Frank discovers that Jake is able to communicate with him through thought transference, and agrees to help repair its spacecraft. The problem is that Jake has only thirty-six hours to rendezvous with the mother ship, or he's stranded permanently on Earth. So the unlikely pair break back into the base and after analysing the problem, determine that they need $120,000 worth of gold. They evade the army, return to the apartment and fill Link in on the situation. He uses his gambling expertise (and Jake's telekinetic powers) to win the money they need. Then, to

complicate things even further, Stallwood's sinister boss kidnaps Liz to force Jake and the IQ staff to give up the collar. Only Jake's superpowers can save her and in the final chase scene, Liz is rescued. But Jake misses his chance to rejoin the mother ship and instead stays to become an American citizen.

GO: This is a fine film, cast in the mold of *The Absent-Minded Professor* etc.

THE CHALLENGERS

Astral Home Video
1991
97 minutes
Directed by: Eric Till
Starring: Eric Christmas,
    Gwynyth Walsh,
    Gema Zambrogna
OFRB rating: PG

The story opens on the stage of a local public school, where ten-year-old Mackie Daniels receives the news that her father has suddenly died. After the funeral, for economic reasons, Mackie and her mom are forced to move to a small town. There, Mackie finds the going rough as she struggles to adapt to life in her new environment, and deal with the grief of having lost a parent. Another frustration for Mackie is the fact that the only junior-age rock group in town has been formed by the Challengers, a rough-tough boys' club with the credo: No Girls Allowed. But Mackie, with an intense love of music, overcomes the obstacle with an ingenious plan: she adopts an alter-ego, Mac, with the judicious use of a baseball hat to conceal her long hair. She impresses the Challengers with her bicycle derring-do and keyboard playing, and is promptly admitted into the gang as her own twin brother. There she experiences a slice of boy-life (fishing and trouble-making) and whips the band into shape, all the while changing back and forth from Mac to Mackie as circumstances dictate. The whole charade eventually falls apart, allowing Mackie to resolve her struggle with grief, and forcing the Challengers to face the fact that girls are "okay."

CAUTION: Any child who has recently lost a parent may be upset by the depiction of Mackie's grief; although the subject is handled sensitively, it may hit too close to home.

GO: The film is a compilation of many components familiar to kids' movies: the weird old person who turns out to be nice, the awful kids who turn out to be nice, but it's fun, well-written and well-acted. Winner of the 1991 Children's Broadcast Institute Award of Excellence and of five International film awards.

CHARLOTTE'S WEB

Paramount Home Video
1972
85 minutes
Directed by: Charles A. Nichols,
    Iwao Takamoto
Starring the voices of: Henry
    Gibson, Paul Lynde, Debbie
    Reynolds
OFRB rating: F
MPAA rating: G

Wilbur, the runt of a litter of pigs, is saved from certain death by the farmer's daughter, Fern, who takes him in as a pet. Wilbur grows up strong and healthy and pampered and, after six weeks, Fern's father decides it's time Wilbur stopped being a pet and started being a pig. So Wilbur is moved down the road to Fern's uncle's farm where he soon learns he will be slaughtered when the weather gets cold. Understandably distraught, Wilbur finds consolation from a literate spider named Charlotte, who assures him that she will take care of him when the time comes. Sure enough, when the snow falls, Charlotte does indeed save Wilbur from the chopping block. She writes "Some Pig" in her web above Wilbur's pen. People come from miles around to see the amazing pig and Charlotte spins new messages in her webs again and again until Wilbur becomes a star attraction. All the while, Charlotte is teaching Wilbur all about the cycles of life and death and about the coming and going of the seasons. The following year, Wilbur is taken to the county fair as a show pig where he wins a special award. His safe future assured, the film ends as Charlotte dies. But she leaves behind an egg-sack which releases hundreds and hundreds of children, three of which stay with Wilbur. This animated musical version of E.B. White's famous children's book is a perennial favourite of both children and adults.

CAUTION: Charlotte dies. Questions may arise about the mechanics of farm life and animal husbandry in general. (Why does Fern's daddy want to kill the runt?)

GO: The animation isn't the greatest and the musical interludes seem imposed, but the story is so strong that it doesn't matter. This is a solid film and a good way to introduce kids to the book.

■

CONDORMAN

Walt Disney Home Video
1981
90 minutes
Directed by: Charles Jarrott
Starring: Barbara Carrera,
    Michael Crawford,
    James Hampton,
    Jean-Pierre Kalfon, Oliver Reed
MPAA rating: PG

Woody, cartoonist of the superhero Condorman, is so dedicated he won't have his hero do anything that isn't possible in real life. So when, in his latest episode, Condorman is sent to help the French government, the obsessive Woody goes and stays in Paris with his friend Harry, who also happens to be a CIA agent. There, the CIA is involved in an exchange of secrets with Russians in Istanbul, and they want a civilian to do the job. Woody is signed up and arrives at the drop-off point where he meets a gorgeous Russian agent named Natalia. Woody tries to impress her by introducing himself as Condorman, but her reception is cool; that is, until a group of thugs show up and Woody defeats them through a series of comical blunders. Natalia decides to defect, but wants only Condorman to handle the exchange. Woody agrees to do it, and, with a great deal of luck, succeeds again. Enraged, Natalia's sinister boss, Krokov, catches on and reads Zowie comics to predict Woody's next move. Natalia is captured. And in the end, Woody puts on his Condorman outfit, flies Natalia out of Krokov's

Mediterranean fortress and, after a hairy boat chase, escapes with Natalia and Harry to the United States.

CAUTION: There is a certain amount of comic violence: shots are fired, rockets go off, and the occasional car or boat blows up.

GO: This film would never have been rated PG in 1992. It's fun and funny — the perfect secret agent spoof for younger kids.

✗ CRYSTALSTONE

MCA
1987
90 minutes
Directed by: Antonio Pelaez
Starring: Laura Jane Goodwin,
    Frank Grimes, Kamlesh Gupta,
    Edward Kelsey
OFRB rating: PG

It is 1908. Deserted by their father and orphaned by their mother, Pablo and Maria avoid being separated by their mean-spirited aunt by running away and jumping a train, where they meet a mysterious white-bearded man. He tells them the story of Alonzo d'Alba, a sixteenth century caballero, who came into the possession of the Aztecs' sacred gem, the Crystalstone. The story goes that Alonzo set sail for Spain, but was shipwrecked near an ancient monastery and ended his days in a French prison. The only clue as to the location of the Crystalstone is to be found when three wooden crosses are reunited. After the story, the three go to sleep, and when the children awake in the morning, the old man is gone, and in his place they find the first wooden cross. Pablo and Maria then leave the train. The next day, while walking through a village, they witness a one-armed man murdering another man, whom they quickly realize is wearing the second wooden cross around his neck. (Only the chance passing of a drunken Captain saves them from a similar fate.) Pablo and Maria begin their search in earnest. They discover d'Alba's diary in an antique shop, and after narrowly escaping the one-armed man (who falls into the sea) and rescuing the Captain (who has taken the rap for the murder) the three sail to d'Alba's monastery where they discover vital clues in its dusty, abandoned library. That night, the Captain puts the children to bed, then begins to play the flute. Pablo realizes that the Captain is their father and, after a stormy argument, runs away. The Captain goes after him and when Pablo slips and falls over a waterfall, he discovers a secret subterranean chamber containing the gem.

✘STOP: There is a very scary scene in which Pablo and Maria dig up a grave and are terrified by a close-up of a dead man's maggot-ridden face.

CAUTION: The children see the silhouette of a murder taking place as a hook rises and falls and a man screams in pain. The one-armed man who pursues the children is scary.

GO: This is an exciting mystery, probably most suitable for children over nine, with stirring themes of physical and spiritual rehabilitation.

✘ DARBY O'GILL AND THE LITTLE PEOPLE

Walt Disney Home Video
1959
90 minutes
Directed by: Robert Stevenson
Starring: Sean Connery,
   Janet Munro, Jimmy O'Dea
MPAA rating: G

The film takes place in turn-of-the-century Ireland, where Katie O'Gill and her father Darby run the manor house for Lord Fitzpatrick. Katie works hard, but her shiftless father has been distracted for years — ever since he caught the leprechaun king and was tricked out of his three wishes. So, when Lord Fitzpatrick hires a new groundskeeper, and a crestfallen Darby is retired on half-pay, Darby doesn't dare tell Katie. Meanwhile, to complicate matters, Darby falls into the leprechaun kingdom, where they plan to keep him forever. But the sly Darby has his own agenda. He makes his escape and recaptures the leprechaun king. And this time, he won't be outwitted.

✘STOP: At one point, when Katie is on her deathbed, Darby hears a mournful wailing outside. He goes to the door and encounters the truly terrifying apparition of Death. Darby takes his daughter's place in the Death Coach and viewers see things from his point-of-view as he is carried away. (You may want to fast-forward over this.)

CAUTION: Darby "bends the truth" every now and again and there is one fairly intense fist-fight.

GO: Decent special effects (for the time) and fine performances mark this fanciful tale of a man who sacrifices everything for those he loves.

DIGBY, THE BIGGEST DOG IN THE WORLD

Prism
1974
88 minutes
Directed by: Joseph McGrath
Starring: Richard Bealmont,
  Jim Dale, Angela Douglas,
  Spike Milligan
MPAA rating: G

AGES 6 TO 10

When Billy brings home a sheepdog named Digby and is told he can't keep it, he takes the dog to stay with Jeff Eldon, an accident-prone animal psychologist who works for the government. Unfortunately, Jeff is testing a growth compound on his garden and when things get mixed up and Digby gets a taste of Project X, the sheepdog gets very, very big. Jeff's efforts to conceal the dreadful truth from an unsuspecting world result in further hilarity. He tries to spirit Digby out of the city in a horse-trailer, but loses the dog when crooks switch trailers and take Digby — twenty-five feet tall and still growing — on an exhibition tour with a local circus. It isn't long before Digby manages to escape, though, and he causes havoc across the country. Jeff, meanwhile, struggles to break into the army base to get an untested antidote he has developed, and somehow succeeds in getting it into Digby. At first it looks like the antidote will kill the giant dog before it returns him to his normal size; that is, if the air force

doesn't kill him first. In the end, though, everything works out, with one final surprise for viewers.

CAUTION: In one tense scene, Jeff is momentarily trapped in the giant dog's mouth and in another, the air force launches a strike on Digby, and it looks like he's a goner for sure.

DINOSAURS SERIES

Walt Disney Home Video
1991
47 minutes (each volume)
Directed by: Brian Henson and
  others
MPAA rating: no rating given

The made-for-TV *Dinosaurs* series is set in 60,000,000 B.C., where dinosaurs Earl and Fran Sinclair live in a house in a city suburb. They have three children, teenagers Robby and Charlene, and a baby named Baby. And they share their house with Fran's wheelchair-bound mother Ethyl. In a way similar to *The Flintstones*, this live-action series is about the day-to-day living of a middle class family.

Dinosaurs (Vol. 5)

When Food Goes Bad Earl and Fran go out for dinner, and leave Baby with Robby and Charlene. But the two teenagers are so wrapped up in their own plans they don't even notice that Baby has been kidnapped by crazed left-overs.

Fran Live When Fran calls up the TV show *Just Listening* and suggests that the host do more than just listen, the show's producers take her up on her idea and give her the show. She becomes an instant success and Earl's initial misgivings about his wife working are swept away when he sees her first paycheck. But Fran's long hours and Earl's cooking begin to wear a little thin.

Endangered Species
(Vol. 3)

High Noon A huge Tyrannosaurus Rex named Gary meets Fran and wants to take her as his mate. According to dinosaur law, he is legally entitled to do so if he defeats Earl in mortal combat, so Earl prepares to meet his maker.

Endangered Species Delicious grapdelites are almost extinct, and when Earl scores a pair at a local market, it turns out that they are, in fact, the last two. Earl's boss makes him a big cash offer for the grapdelites, which Earl, under pressure from his conscience, reluctantly turns down. Mr. Richfield then tricks Earl into leaving them in his care, and promptly eats them. But there is still hope . . .

The Mating Dance (Vol. 2)

The Howling The Howling is a once-a-month ritual in which every male dinosaur of age goes to the top of the highest mountain and howls to prevent the dark spirit from turning dinosaur against dinosaur. Robby, who's scheduled for his first howling, considers it mere superstition and refuses to participate. But when dinosaurs turn against each other, Robbie has a change of heart.

The Mating Dance When Fran feels unappreciated, Earl decides to take the kids away for a weekend. But the problem isn't the kids, it's her life with Earl. So Earl takes lessons at Mel Luster's Mating Dance Academy.

Mighty Megalosaurus
(Vol. 1)

Mighty Megalosaurus Earl describes to Baby the events which preceded his birth, when Earl asked for a raise and got fired, and his Fran presented him with the egg from which Baby would come.

Hurling Day According to ancient tradition, when old dinosaurs reach the age of seventy-two, they are to be hurled into a tarpit, and sons are appointed to toss their mothers-in-law; however, Earl's family is outraged that he is clinging to the ancient tradition, to the point where Robby kidnaps Ethyl and runs away with her.

Other titles in the series are:
Dinosaurs, Volume 4:
   The Golden Child; The Last Temptation of Ethyl
Dinosaurs, Volume 6:
   Power Erupts; A New Leaf
Don't Cross the Boss:
   And the Winner Is...; Wesayso Knows Best
I'm the Baby
   Switched at Birth; Nature Calls

CAUTION: The *Dinosaurs* shows satirize modern life on a fairly sophisticated level. Underlying topics include: the extinction of a species, the unwanted elderly, boredom with one's spouse and so on. A lot of the humour is black.

GO: The series features incredible sets, special effects and Muppets. Perfect for the older crowd, this series is a 1991 Parents' Choice Award winner.

AGES 6 TO 10

THE DIRT BIKE KID

Charter Entertainment
1985
91 minutes
Directed by: Hoite C. Gaston
Starring: Peter Billingsley,
    Anne Bloom, Patrick Collins,
    Stuart Pankin
MPAA rating: PG

When Jack's mother Janet finally gets a job interview, she gives him her last fifty dollars to buy groceries. On his way, Jack stops at the track to watch his friend Max in a dirt bike race. During the race, Max's bike starts doing strange things, and an elderly man turns to Jack and says that Max doesn't deserve the bike. When Jack looks around again, the old man is gone, and a disgusted Max agrees to sell the dirt bike to his friend . . . for fifty dollars. Jack's mom is in no way thrilled. He is exiled to his room, but manages to sneak away to try his bike out. Well, it's soon obvious to Jack that this is no ordinary bike; it proves to be supernaturally fast *and* it can fly. It even seems to have a kind of personality, which becomes evident the next day when Jack's mother tries to take it out and sell it, and it refuses to go with her. Meanwhile, Mike, manager of the local favourite burger and fries hang-out, is up against the sinister Mr. Hodgkins of Hodgkins bank, which has selected Mike's restaurant as the perfect location for its next bank site. The magic bike takes Jack right into the bank just as Hodgkins is making a sleazy come-on to Janet (her interview was for a position with the bank) and Jack is able to get Hodgkins's assurance that he won't appropriate Mike's restaurant. But when Hodgkins immediately goes back on his word and forecloses, Jack and his bike must take on the bank any way they can.

CAUTION: One of Jack's friends leers at a well-endowed young woman, and remarks, " . . . more bounce to the ounce." Hodgkins's attitude towards women is despicable; he even uses a guard dog to keep them in the house while he's making his sleazy come-ons.

GO: *The Dirt Bike Kid* is a fun, inoffensive fantasy.

DIVORCE CAN HAPPEN TO THE NICEST PEOPLE

LCA
1987
30 minutes
Directed by: Andrea Bresciani

This fully-animated video answers questions children have about divorce, explaining such things as how nice people like mom and dad can fall into and out of love, and what might be involved when a new parent comes into the picture. Based on the book by Peter Mayle and Arthur Robins.

GO: Humorous yet informative, this video is caring and honest.

■

AGES 6 TO 10

✗ E.T.: THE EXTRA-TERRESTRIAL

MCA
1982
115 minutes
Directed by: Steven Spielberg
Starring: Drew Barrymore,
    Peter Coyote, Henry Thomas
MPAA rating: PG

While on a sample-gathering expedition, an explorer from another solar system is stranded when his ship is forced to take off without him to avoid detection by the "natives." The "natives" are a group of human scientists, intent on obtaining clear-cut evidence of extra-terrestrials. The little alien evades them and finds refuge in a suburban backyard. There, he is discovered by a young boy named Elliott who lures the alien into the open with candy. Soon Elliott and the extra-terrestrial (which he names E.T.) become fast friends. They form a deep telepathic bond, which plays havoc with Elliott's classroom life, and E.T. has an opportunity to learn more about how humans live in North America. But the conditions on Earth are not good for E.T., who is slowly dying, and he builds a device from every-day implements with which to "phone home." And as E.T. grows weaker and weaker, an army of scientists descends on Elliott's house, placing the neighbourhood under quarantine and encasing the whole house in a huge plastic bubble. Nothing seems able to save E.T., but just as he seems to have died, E.T.'s distress call is answered. The alien miraculously revives and Elliott, his brother and his friends help E.T. return to his ship and to safety.

✗**STOP:** Certain images in this film have terrified children too young to understand that the alien, despite his bizarre appearance, is kind and friendly. This is an emotionally intense film especially during the scene in which doctors try to "jump start" E.T.'s heart, and at the end when E.T. leaves and Elliott must stay.

CAUTION: Many young children are frightened when, at their first meeting, Elliott and E.T. scream; the scene in which scientists take over Elliott's house may be upsetting, too. There is some coarse language in this film and at nearly two hours it may be too long and too much for young viewers.

GO: A heart-warming story full of magic, *E.T.* is one of the biggest box-office hits ever.

✗ THE ELECTRIC GRANDMOTHER

LCA
1981
50 minutes
Directed by: Noel Black
Starring: Charlie Fields,
    Edward Hermann, Tara Kennedy,
    Robert MacNaughton,
    Maureen Stapleton
MPAA rating: no rating given

After the premature death of his wife, Henry and his three children, Tom, Timothy and Agatha, visit the Fantoccini Company, which specializes in made-to-order robotic humans. There, they choose the characteristics they would most like to have in a caregiver and, in a short time, receive a wonderful electric grandmother. She is a marvel. She makes their favourite meals, pours drinks from her index finger and runs the household splendidly, retreating to her basement rocker at night to recharge her batteries. There's only one problem. Agatha has still not recovered from the death of her mother, and she utterly rejects the grandmother, until the grandmother can prove to her that she will never leave. The grandmother proves that she cannot die when she pushes Agatha out of the way of an oncoming car and is struck herself, but remains unharmed. She stays until the children go off to college, then returns to care for them in their old age. Based on Ray Bradbury's story "I Sing the Body Electric."

✗STOP: The film opens immediately after the death of the children's mother. Any child who has suffered a recent loss should not see this film.

CAUTION: The Fantoccini Company is dark and scary and the car accident scene is very traumatic. Viewers may find the whole concept of the film a little bizarre.

GO: Despite its melancholy feeling, has heartfelt sentiments.

■

EMIL AND THE DETECTIVES

Walt Disney Home Video
1964
92 minutes
Directed by: Peter Tewkesbury
Starring: Roger Mobley,
    Bryan Russell, Walter Slezak
MPAA rating: no rating given

Ten-year-old Emil Tischbein boards the morning bus in Neustadt for post-World War II Berlin, carrying a large sum of money for his grandmother. Little does he know that The Mole, a small-time crook, spotted the money changing hands and has arranged to sit beside Emil on the bus. Hypnotizing Emil with a pocket-watch, The Mole lifts the money and makes off with it. Emil dashes off the bus and into the street, but when the police ignore him, Emil is alone and penniless in the shattered city. Soon though, a multi-talented street-urchin named Gustav Fleischman and his comrades, The Detectives, come to his aid. The crew fans out through the streets of Berlin and in so doing, stumble upon a greater crime than just petty theft. A conspiracy to rob a major bank is afoot and someone plans to tunnel into the vault from the ruins down the street. But as The Detectives uncover more evidence, they have more trouble convincing the police to do anything about it. There's another problem, too. The time is near when Emil will have to confront his grandmother and admit that he doesn't have the money. On Emil's last night in Berlin, the boys stake out the ruins and sure enough, the conspirators arrive. But when Emil is captured, things get tense, especially when the crooks force him to help them finish the tunnel, then leave him and The Mole to be blown up by a bomb. In the end, it's up to Gustav and The Detectives to rescue Emil before it's too late. Based on the novel by Erich Kastner.

CAUTION: During the climax, as The Mole and Emil are frantically trying to dig their way out, The Mole's claustrophobic panic is evident.

GO: For young mystery fans, this is the movie. It's also a great film about kids making a difference.

■

AGES 6 TO 10

✗ THE EMPIRE STRIKES BACK

CBS/Fox
1980
124 minutes
Directed by: Irvin Kershner
Starring: Carrie Fisher,
    Harrison Ford, Mark Hamill,
    Billy Dee Williams
MPAA rating: PG

Despite their success in destroying the Death Star, the rebels have fallen on dark times and they are hidden in a secret base on an ice-world in the Hoth system. Vader has been searching the galaxy for them, and as the film opens Imperial probes have landed on the planet and identified the rebel base. Sure enough, the Empire launches a massive assault, but an incompetent Imperial admiral brings the huge armada out of warp too close to the system, and the element of surprise is lost. As the rebels get set to flee, Vader orders another sinister general to prepare his troops for a surface assault. The Imperial forces must attack on the ground to knock out the force field generators which protect the rebel base. This sets the stage for one of the most memorable battle scenes in sci-fi history, as the Imperial troops advance in giant elephantine walking machines. A handful of rebels escape — Han Solo and Princess Leia in the Millenium Falcon and Luke Skywalker in a single-seat fighter. As Han and Leia run from the agents of the Empire, Luke travels to the Dagobah system to study under the ultimate Jedi master, the eight-hundred-year old

Yoda. But before Luke's training is complete, Vader captures Han and Leia and sets a fiendish trap, luring Luke into a duel he does not yet have the strength to fight. At the height of the confrontation, Vader reveals the awful truth about his identity. This film is the second in the Star Wars trilogy; the first is *Star Wars* and the third is *Return of the Jedi*.

✗**STOP:** Vader absently dispatches an incompetent subordinate who gargles and chokes before falling dead. The duel between Luke and Vader is extremely intense and Vader cuts off Luke's hand. Han Solo is lowered into a huge machine and carbon-frozen, a look of anguish on his face.

CAUTION: The films is replete with combat and frightening images. If comparisons are to be made, this is probably the darkest film of the trilogy.

GO: Cautions aside, this is also the most exciting film in the trilogy.

ENCINO MAN

Hollywood Pictures Home Video
1992
98 minutes
Directed by: Les Mayfield
Starring: Sean Astin,
    Brendan Fraser,
    Marriette Hartley, Pauly Shore,
    Megan Ward
OFRB rating: PG
MPAA rating: PG

When Dave Morgan is digging a swimming pool by hand in his backyard, an earthquake reveals an underground glacier in which a Cro-Magnon man is frozen. Dave and his friend Stoney decide to thaw the iceman out, thereby gaining fame, fortune and popularity. They clean him up and introduce him to Dave's parents as Linkavitch Chomofsky, an exchange student who has come to help dig the pool. The next day they take "Link" to school where the girls begin to vie for his attention and where, during a class trip to the museum, Link realizes the truth of his dilemma. He is understandably upset but, after a series of crazy incidents, finds his place in high school society, and when Link's true identity is finally revealed to the other students, no one minds a bit.

CAUTION: Despite the coarse language and sexual gestures this is a funny, innocent film.

GO: *Encino Man* is a fun, if completely improbable, yarn. At the end of the film it is suggested viewers read *Encino High: Stoney's Notebook.*

ENCYCLOPEDIA BROWN: MYSTERY OF THE MISSING TIME CAPSULE

Hi-Tops Video
1989
55 minutes
Directed by: Savage Steve Holland
Starring: Scott Bremner,
 Laura Bridge, Bruno Marcotulli,
 Tiana Pierce, Dion Zamora
OFRB rating: PG

When boy detective Leroy "Encyclopedia" Brown proves that Bugs Meany swindled one of his friends with a bogus Civil War sword, Bugs vows revenge. And revenge comes just days before Idaville's one hundredth birthday, when a time capsule from the year 1889 is to be opened. The time capsule is stolen and somebody leaves one of Encyclopedia Brown's cards at the scene. Encyclopedia easily detects the thief (Bugs), but when Bugs confesses and hands over the capsule, it turns out to be a Tupperware container (Bugs didn't know that Tupperware hadn't been invented in 1889) containing a ransom note from the real thief which reads: five hundred Gs by Saturday, or the capsule will be destroyed. Encyclopedia Brown and his partner Sally take the case and things get complicated fast. But his clear, logical mind enables the boy detective to solve the case. Characters and stories are based on the books by Donald J. Sobol.

Other Encyclopedia Brown titles to try are:
Encyclopedia Brown, the Boy Detective

in the Case of the Amazing Race Car Encyclopedia Brown, the Boy Detective
in the Case of the Ghostly Rider Encyclopedia Brown, the Boy Detective: One Minute Mysteries

CAUTION: Sally, Encyclopedia's lightning-fisted partner, really beats the stuffing out of Bugs.

GO: For young mystery fans, this is the perfect choice. Sally and Encyclopedia Brown represent an interesting and healthy role reversal — he is the brains and she is the brawn. Kids who like this film will probably enjoy the others in the series.

■

force, and it's up to Ernest and his young charges to stand up to Sherman's thugs.

✗**STOP:** There is one particularly violent fight, after which Ernest is kicked while lying on the ground bleeding.

CAUTION: A lot of the humour is violent. At the climax of the film, Krader fires a rifle at an unarmed Ernest, clearly attempting to kill him in cold blood.

GO: If you like slapstick comedy, this is the film for you. The kitchen features such delicacies as eggs erroneous and Varney's Ernest is the classic stumblebum.

✗ ERNEST GOES TO CAMP

Touchstone Home Video
1987
92 minutes
Directed by: John R. Cherry
Starring: Victoria Racimo,
  Jim Varney, John Vernon
MPAA rating: PG

At Camp Kikakee, blundering camp handyman Ernest P. Worrell dreams of one day becoming a camp counsellor. He eventually gets his wish, when the Governor (as part of a state program) delivers a group of disadvantaged youngsters to the camp and a full-scale war errupts. The "second-chancers" dispose of their regular counsellor in short order, and are handed over to Ernest. Meanwhile, Krader Industries, run by ruthless mining executive Sherman Krader, has targeted Camp Kikakee as the site of a huge deposit of the mineral petricide and is trying to get the owners, Miss St. Cloud and her grandfather, to sell. When this fails, Sherman resorts to trickery and

✗ ERNEST GOES TO JAIL

Touchstone Home Video
1990
81 minutes
Directed by: John R. Cherry
Starring: Barbara Rush,
  Gailard Sartain, Jim Varney
OFRB rating: PG
MPAA rating: PG

Know-it-all Ernest P. Worrell (now a night cleaner at a bank) is a dead ringer for Felix Nash, a notorious crime czar who rules Dracop Prison from the inside. And when Ernest is assigned to jury duty, and the defendant is one of Nash's fellow-prisoners, the cons arrange a switch and Ernest is incarcerated. Felix then takes over Ernest's bank job and his life, changing his gadget-filled house into a tacky seduction parlor and completely alienating his prospective girlfriend. Meanwhile, Ernest is forced to impersonate the crime czar in his daily prison routine. Unbeknownst to our mutton-headed hero, he is only days away from the electric chair, and as the days turn to hours Ernest must break out and foil Nash's plans to rob the bank.

✘STOP: One scene involves the electric chair, so be prepared to answer your child's questions about capital punishment.

CAUTION: Ernest is electrocuted three times in the film, once in the electric chair. As in other Ernest films, a lot of the humour revolves around violent slapstick comedy, with a great deal of punching.

GO: For older kids and adults — particularly fans of slapstick — Ernest is hilarious. The disaster sequences always have a cartoon flavour to them.

vagrancy, and it isn't until Ernest happens to glance in the sack and realizes, "He's him," that Santa manages to get out of jail. Together they find Joe, and try to convince him to carry on the tradition. Still unconvinced (Santa's bag has been stolen and there is no other tangible proof of his identity), Joe sets off to pursue a movie career instead. It's up to Ernest to save the day, driving Santa's sled across town from the airport, just in time to pick up Joe, who has come to realize that he is, indeed, the "new him."

GO: Jim Varney does his Ernest shtick, the usual gallery of funny impersonations.

ERNEST SAVES CHRISTMAS

Touchstone
1988
91 minutes
Directed by: John Cherry
Starring: Oliver Clark, Noelle Parker, Jim Varney
OFRB rating: F

Stumblebum cab driver Ernest P. Worrell drops an elderly white-bearded man at the Children's Museum to meet with Joe Carruthers, a man who has dedicated his life to entertaining children. Although Joe doesn't know it yet, the elderly man is the current incarnation of Santa Claus, who is about to retire and who has chosen Joe as his replacement. But things begin to go wrong. Ernest leaves with Santa's sack still in his cab and Joe thinks that Santa's merely a confused, ordinary elderly man. Santa ends up being arrested for

ESCAPE TO WITCH MOUNTAIN

Walt Disney Home Video
1975
94 minutes
Directed by: John Hough
Starring: Eddie Albert, Ike Eisenmann, Ray Milland, Donald Pleasance, Kim Richards
MPAA rating: G

Orphans eleven-year-old Tony and his nine-year-old sister Tia are psychics, capable of telekinesis, telepathy and clairvoyance. One day, Tia uses her powers to save the life of a man named Lucas Deranian, a sinister servant of the unscrupulous billionaire Aristotle Bolt. After hearing about the gifted children and seeing the opportunity for increased wealth, Bolt adopts Tony and Tia under false pretenses and brings them to his coastal mansion. There, he lavishes gifts upon the children, but they soon see through him, and telepathically overhear his plans to ship them to an inaccessible island. That night the children escape, sneaking into the back of tourist Jason O'Day's camper. The bitter and reclusive Jason grudgingly helps the children, and as they drive towards Witch Mountain, Tia and Tony begin to remember their origins. They belong to a race of aliens from a dying world who migrated to earth, and who have been living secretly and peacefully among humans. But when their particular starship arrived, it crashed in the ocean and Tony and Tia are afraid that they may be the only survivors. Meanwhile, Bolt and Deranian are in hot pursuit and the children narrowly escape capture, time after time. They follow a mysterious voice and the directions on a map (which they've always had, but which only now begins to make sense) and reach Witch Mountain, where they are greeted by their guardian Bené. Bené informs Jason that there are many others like Tony and Tia lost in the world, and Jason vows to help them get to Witch Mountain as well.

GO: This is an entertaining effort without violence, but sophisticated enough for the older crowd.

EXPLORERS

Paramount Home Video
1985
107 minutes
Directed by: Joe Dante
Starring: Ethan Hawke, River Phoenix, Mary Kay Place, Jason Presson
OFRB rating: F
MPAA rating: PG

Explorers concerns the adventures of three boys: Ben, a visionary; Wolfgang, a scientific prodigy; and Darren, a social rebel whose father owns a junkyard. Ben has been having strange dreams in which he feels he is being "called" (he hopes by some alien force, so he can learn from them the secrets of the universe). He draws sketches of machinery from the dreams and Wolfgang enters them as three-dimensional drawings into his computer. Then, quite unexpectedly, Wolfgang hits upon a spherical object called an "electrically generated point of force" which escapes from the computer and actually comes to exist. They find that this sphere can travel at unimaginable speeds with no inertia or resistance; so, using Darren's father's junkyard for parts, they fabricate a vehicle to fit inside it and christen this space ship the Thunder Road. Then they launch themselves into space and are beamed aboard an alien ship, where they encounter two friendly, insect-like creatures who know all about Earth's civilizations from television programs. Ben is disappointed that they cannot tell him the secrets of the universe, but after a crash landing in which the Thunder Road is destroyed, the boys learn that things are not always as they seem and that dreams and aspirations can sometimes be of real value.

CAUTION: The boys are trapped inside the spacecraft and are chased by a huge iron insect-like creature. Later they are photographed, smelled, frisked and inspected by the creature. The aliens project a blue beam of light into Darren's head. He is unperturbed, saying "they put pictures into your head." The aliens show the boys — via old movies — that earthlings kill aliens, and there is a bit of swearing, but usually in the context of exclamations.

GO: Light, humorous and (by today's standards) non-violent, this is a film for the whole family. Parents, in particular, will appreciate parodies the aliens make on television shows of the '50s and '60s.

FANTASIA

Walt Disney Home Video
1940
120 minutes
Directed by: Walt Disney
MPAA rating: G

Arguably the most famous assembly of animation in the history of film, *Fantasia*'s timeless appeal has enthralled generation after generation of film-goers. Working in conjunction with the composer Leopold Stokowski and the Philadelphia Orchestra, Walt Disney and an imaginative group of artists took several favourite pieces of music and expressed their impressions of them in the form of brilliantly conceived fantasies. No words can do justice to the impact of this work.

Animated sequences were created for:

A jazzy musical interlude
A Night on Bald Mountain (Modeste Mussorgsky)
Ave Maria (Franz Schubert)
Dance of the Hours (Amicare Ponchielli)
The Nutcracker Suite (Tchaikovsky)
The Pastoral Symphony (Ludwig von Beethoven)
The Rite of Spring (Igor Stravinsky)
The Sorcerer's Apprentice (Paul Dukas)
Toccata and Fugue in D Minor (Johann Sebastian Bach)

CAUTION: There is a prevailing misconception that *Fantasia* is a children's film; it is not, although older children may indeed enjoy it. And there are some frightening images, particularly in *The Sorcerer's Apprentice* and *Night on Bald Mountain*.

GO: The plan for *Fantasia* is an interesting one. Following Disney's original concept that this film would be the first in a series, Disney studios will no longer release this version of *Fantasia* but will drop one of the sequences and add a new one, releasing the new combination as *Fantasia II*. The plan is to continue to drop and add sequences so each combination is unique. One of the great achievements in animation, this film has more than survived the test of time.
▲

FLIGHT OF THE NAVIGATOR

Walt Disney Home Video
1986
89 minutes
Directed by: Randal Kleiser
Starring: Mark Adler,
    Veronica Cartwright, Joey
    Cramer, Cliff de Young, Howard
    Hesseman, Sarah Jessica Parker
MPAA rating: PG

One night, twelve-year-old David Freeman falls into a ravine and is knocked unconscious. And when he awakes and struggles home, he find that his parents don't live there anymore — in fact, they haven't lived there for eight years. He himself has not changed, but his parents have aged, and his once "younger" brother is now twice his size. David's traumatic re-appearance is investigated, and it's discovered that an alien spacecraft crashed at the same time that David returned home. So, David is taken to a research centre for an examination, where the scientists find that his mind is absolutely full of star charts. They plan to keep him until the mystery is unravelled, but David sneaks out and is drawn psychically to the spacecraft. And when its previously impenetrable hull opens to admit David, the frantic security forces rush to prevent him from going aboard . . . too late. David finds that the spacecraft is intelligent, that it responds to his verbal commands and that he has already been the ship's navigator for an eight-year interstellar trip. Frightened by the commotion he has caused, and afraid that he's in trouble, David wishes out loud that he could get away, and the ship complies, taking him twenty miles straight up into the atmosphere. David shortly realizes that the ship will do anything he asks and when he also learns that the star charts were transferred to his mind as a means of safeguarding them in the landing accident, he transfers them back to the ship's memory banks. But in so doing he also transfers many of his human characteristics, and the ship begins talking suspiciously like Pee-Wee Herman and takes David on a wild joy-ride, during which the pair get lost. Then it's up to David to find his way back home, and eventually, to his own time eight years in the past.

CAUTION: Young ones may find the time paradox confusing and frightening. David is obviously alone and afraid, and finding his family again provides little initial comfort. In one scene, when they stop at a road-side filling station, the talking spaceship insults the overweight attendant.

GO: This film features brilliant special effects and an entertaining and non-violent plot.

FREAKY FRIDAY

Walt Disney Home Video
1977
95 minutes
Directed by: Gary Nelson
Starring: John Astin,
   Kaye Ballard,
   Ruth Buzzi, Jodie Foster,
   Barbara Harris
MPAA rating: G

On Friday the thirteenth, teenage baseball and field-hockey star Annabel fervently wishes for the easy life her mother enjoys; conversely, her mother Ellen longs for the bygone days of high school. And as their powerful wishes are made on this particularly spooky day, their consciousnesses switch bodies. Annabel must stay home and cook and clean (with disastrous results) while her mother goes back to school. In her mother's body, Annabel plays a mean baseball game and everyone is astounded to see "Ellen" whacking home runs, making diving catches and stealing home. Ellen is not so lucky as she encounters the usual teen traumas, making such gaffes as scoring on her own net in a critical field-hockey match. At the end of this slapstick farce, both individuals are relieved to return to their own lives. Based on the book by Mary Rogers.

CAUTION: The portrayal of the female situation is a little dated.

GO: The end degenerates into pure slapstick, but the film is loads of fun for kids under ten. Children who enjoy *Freaky Friday* may also enjoy films with similar situations, *Big* and *Vice Versa*. (Check the ratings to make sure that these films are suitable for your child before you rent.)

■

FROG

Orion
1988
55 minutes
Directed by: David Grossman
Starring: Shelley Duvall,
    Elliott Gould, Scott Grimes,
    Amy Lynne, Paul Williams
MPAA rating: no rating given

Arlo Anderson is a nerd who's fascinated with reptiles and amphibians. And when the latest addition to his collection, a huge bullfrog, suddenly starts talking to him, Arlo has trouble convincing himself that he hasn't lost his mind. The frog introduces himself as Italian prince Guiseppi Buono Duno, and goes on to explain that he is under a six-hundred-year-old curse that can only be broken if he is kissed by a pretty young woman. Arlo, now convinced that the frog really is talking to him, is at a loss as to how to help. None of the girls in his class will even talk to him, let alone kiss his hideous bullfrog. But then an attractive girl named Suzy cynically tries to raise her grades by becoming Arlo's partner in the science fair, and the strangest thing happens: Suzy gets to really like Arlo, enough even to kiss his frog or, as it turns out, a lot of frogs, because right at the critial moment Gus accidentally falls into a pool full of thousands of them. Still, Suzy gamely kisses away, frog after frog after frog, but nothing seems to happen, and although Arlo *does* win the respect of the scientific

community for his work on frog communication, he's upset that the prince's best chance to achieve human form seems to have been lost. As it turns out, though, all is well. And in an Italian restaurant, the prince — complete with polyester leisure suit — shows up to serenade his friends.

CAUTION: The prince sings "That's Amore" right at the end of the film, and it isn't pretty.

GO: At one hour in length, this is a great party video that will appeal to kids of all ages.

FUNHOUSE FITNESS: THE FUNHOUSE FUNK

Warner Home Video
1991
45 minutes
Directed by: Anita Mann
Starring: Jane Fonda, J.D. Roth

The MTV-style dancing and exercise routines in this video will help kids develop balance,

co-ordination, agility, endurance and strength. With a mixed group of boys and girls, J.D. Roth shows that boys can do aerobics too! Recommended for children aged seven and up.

CAUTION: Included are scenes from the show *Fun House* where kids get covered with paint and whipped cream.

GO: An effective aerobic video, Funhouse Fitness has great music and high energy.

GEORGE'S ISLAND

```
Astral
1991
90 minutes
Directed by: Paul Donovan
Starring: Ian Bannen,
    Maury Chaykin, Sheila McCarthy,
    Nathaniel Moreau, Gary Reineke,
    Vicki Ridler
OFRB rating: PG
MPAA rating: no rating given
```

Strict teacher Miss Cloitha Birdwood is making life miserable for George Waters, a young orphan who lives with his salty, wheelchair-bound grandfather. She sends Bonnie, a despised over-achieving classmate, to befriend George and spy on his home life, and once (what she believes is) sufficient damning evidence has been collected, Miss Birdwood goes to a deranged childcare worker named Mr. Droonfield and manages to have George removed from his grandfather's care and sent to live with evil foster parents Roger and Buelah Beane. But the Beanes keep George in a cell, and he makes a hasty escape (accompanied by

foster child number one who is, oddly enough, Bonnie). George's grandfather rescues the kids, and with Miss Birdwood and Mr. Droonfield in close pursuit, they race to George's Island (an island on which a treasure has been buried and which is guarded by the ghosts of Captain Kidd and an assortment of pirates). In the end, everyone ends up on George's Island where Kidd orders the ghosts to kill everyone. But after some discussion, the ghastly crew is persuaded to haunt the Beanes' residence, instead. George and his grandfather are reunited, and Bonnie is adopted by the newly married Droonfield and Birdwood.

CAUTION: At the beginning of the film, Kidd and his henchman kill the other members of the treasure-burying party, and heads literally roll (no blood, though). The pirate ghosts are scary, and one young Halloween prankster is shot in the behind with rock-salt. Some viewers — both children and adults — may find the treatment of George and his grandfather upsetting.

GO: Spooky, non-violent and packed with adventure, this excellent film is full of great performances.

GIRLS JUST WANT TO HAVE FUN

```
New World Video
1985
90 minutes
Directed by: Alan Metter
Starring: Helen Hunt,
    Lee Montgomery,
    Sarah Jessica Parker,
    Jonathan Silverman
MPAA rating: PG
```

Janey Glenn is a terrific dancer, and when a show called *Dance TV* holds auditions for two new dancers, she and her outrageous friend Lynne Stone enter the competition. Sure enough, the talented Janey makes the finals, but she is to be paired with a stranger, Jeff Malene, and in order to do their routines they need to practice. But there are three problems: first, Janey and Jeff just can't seem to get along (one of the promoters calls them *Rebel Without a Cause* meets *The Sound of Music*); second, Janey's hopelessly spoiled rival Natalie Sands schemes constantly to ruin her chances, and third, Janey's father Colonel Glenn will have none of it, so Janey has to sneak out after everyone thinks she has gone to bed. And Jeff has his own problem: it turns out that Natalie's dad owns the factory where Jeff's father works, and Mr. Sands puts pressure on Jeff to drop out, or else. But through all of this, Janey and Jeff begin to develop a relationship and eventually win the contest.

CAUTION: This film has a lot of coarse language and characters make quite a few sexual references.

GODZILLA VS MOTHRA

Paramount Home Video
1966
93 minutes
Directed by: Inoshiro Honda
Starring: Yu Fujiki, Yuriko Hoshi,
  Akira Takarada
MPAA rating: not rated

After a cataclysmic storm a huge egg washes up on Japanese shores. It is Mothra's egg and her emissaries, mysterious tiny twin girls, come to Japan to beg for its return. But they are too late; the egg has been purchased by unscrupulous entrepreneurs who plan to become wealthy by selling tickets to the hatching. Greater trouble strikes when Godzilla makes an appearance, destroying highways, dams and entire apartment blocks. The people of Tokyo need Mothra's help, but the Polynesian people who inhabit Mothra Island refuse to intervene (they've suffered much at the hands of the Japanese, the most recent imposition being a series of atomic tests conducted on their island that nearly destroyed all life there). Luckily, the tiny twin girls intervene, wake Mothra up (by singing!) and send her off to fight Godzilla. Mothra is old and tired, though, and she dies in battle. The safety of Japan now depends on the as yet unhatched Mothra. And at the thrilling climax, by an amazingly good stroke of luck, the egg hatches and a pair of larval Mothra twins emerge! They make quick work of Godzilla, restore peace to the Japanese countryside and swim home with the tiny twin girls in tow.

CAUTION: Godzilla loses. This can be a terrible shock to young fans who are accustomed to seeing Godzilla in the hero's role. The film is racist; the Polynesians seem to have the same kind of role as tribal Africans did in the old Johnny Weissmuller Tarzan flicks (except that when the Polynesians sing and dance there is a decidedly Broadway flavour to their choreography). There is some hand-to-hand combat with blood (not graphic).

GO: There are some great shots of Godzilla, who is unusually naturalistic.

GODZILLA VS THE SMOG MONSTER

Orion Home Video
1971
86 minutes
Original Japanese version directed
   by: Yoshimitu Banno; additional
   segments directed by: Lee Kresel
   for North American release
MPAA rating: G

Off the coast of Japan, an unknown monster is sinking ships. A fisherman takes what appears to be an unnaturally big tadpole to a local scientist who deduces that it was formed from a mineral (although later the monster is characterized as being born of sludge). He is able to generate more such tadpoles, and when he puts two together they join and grow larger, thus creating Hedora, a new and terrifying monster. Hedora develops the ability to fly and emits a sulphuric acid mist which makes him particularly dangerous. The death toll mounts, and the entire coastline is placed under a military alert. Meanwhile, the doctor, despite his deteriorating condition, has discovered that the monster can be destroyed by passing an electrical current through it. Godzilla has also come out of the ocean to battle this new opponent, and together with the help of the military, he defeats Hedora at the last possible moment as the powerlines are broken.

CAUTION: A young boy is shown playing with a very large knife, and people are dissolved instantly, leaving only their skeletons behind. This movie features the worst theme song of all time.

GODZILLA'S REVENGE

Studio
1969
70 minutes
Directed by: Inoshiro Honda
Starring: Machiko Naka,
   Kenji Sahara, Tomori Yazaki
MPAA rating: not rated

A lonely victim of neighbourhood bullies, Ichiro goes to Monster Island through the power of his imagination, where he meets Minia, the young son of Godzilla. Minia is a self-proclaimed coward who knows he must learn to fight his own battles, and at the insistence of Godzilla — whose anger Minia greatly fears — Minia gamely takes on a variety of monsters with varying degrees of success. (On Monster Island the chief entertainment seems to be fighting other monsters!) Encouraged by the lessons in self-defence, Ichiro returns home fully capable of dealing not only with the neighbourhood bullies, but with the evil thieves who kidnap him as well.

CAUTION: Much fuss is made about the fact that both of Ichiro's parents must go to work and Ichiro's social problems are all presented as stemming from this. Ichiro's mother even weeps from the guilt she experiences over neglecting her son. In one scene, possibly meant to depict the normal behaviour of a child, Ichiro talks with his mouth full of half-chewed food. A masterpiece of offensive dubbing, this film features both Ichiro and his young girl friend (possibly dubbed by the same person!) speak in irritating broken English. The voice characterization for Minia is especially frightful.

GO: *Godzilla's Revenge* is basically a showcase for scads of monsters, with some out-of-date social commentary that kids will love and parents will run screaming from.

✗ THE GOLDEN VOYAGE OF SINBAD

Columbia Home Video
1973
105 minutes
Directed by: Gordon Hessler
Starring: Tom Baker,
   John Phillip Law, Caroline Munro
MPAA rating: G

AGES 6 TO 10

When a strange bat-like gremlin flies over Sinbad's ship and one of his men fires an arrow at it, the creature drops a golden amulet on the deck. This, Sinbad recovers, and in so doing earns the everlasting enmity of Prince Koora, who is versed in every black art. Pursued by the evil prince, Sinbad comes under the protection of the masked vizier of a great city, a man who was terribly burned by the dark magic of that same evil prince. The vizier too, possesses an amulet and it turns out that if it and Sinbad's amulet are placed before a great spiritual power in the Temple of Many Faces, absolute power will be granted. And so, Sinbad begins his voyage to the islands of the Temple, accompanied by a drunk named Haroon and a beautiful slave-girl named Marianna, and followed by Prince Koora. After a host of adventures (including a battle with a six-armed Kali and a fight between a centaur and a huge griffin), Sinbad confronts Koora in the Temple. But Koora has arrived first and now possesses the power . . .

✗ **STOP:** At one point, a sinister witch invokes an incarnation of the devil with a frightening face and a malevolent voice.

CAUTION: The prince makes the figurehead of Sinbad's ship come alive and this may be too much for young viewers.

GO: Sinbad makes a distinctive statement about slavery and respect for others. He tells the slave girl that no human being has the right to own another.

GOONIES

Warner Home Video
1985
114 minutes
Directed by: Richard Donner
Starring: Sean Astin, Corey
   Feldman, Kerri Green, Anne
   Ramsey
OFRB rating: PG
MPAA rating: PG

A group of young outcasts called the Goonies is being forced to disband because their neighbourhood is being torn down by developers. (There has been a foreclosure on mortgages and none of their families has the money to buy their homes.) And on the last day they are together, the Goonies happened upon an authentic seventeenth-century treasure map in the attic of one of the boy's homes. Hoping to find the treasure and help their parents out (so the Goonies can stay together) they follow the map and encounter a counterfeiting gang, newly escaped from prison. They are chased through subterannean tunnels, lagoons and caverns, and they encounter a dead man in a freezer, lots of gruesome skeletons, booby-traps and a deformed man with piglet ears who turns out to be a good friend. They, of course, find the treasure, save their parents' homes from the developers and catch the counterfeiters. They even discover the value of paying attention during your piano lessons.

CAUTION: The film is very loud, with aggressive music, lots of screaming and noise from things blowing up and falling apart. In one scene, a boy is locked in a freezer with a dead man who is quite white and green, and in another, the counterfeiters threaten to put a boy's hand in a blender in an effort to make him "talk." There is some fighting and there are lots of skeletons with creatures crawling out of their mouths. Also of concern may be the actions of one teenage boy in the gang who's interested in one of the girls and even in dangerous situations manages to sneak long kisses.

GO: With extraordinary special effects, the film is generally good clean fun — an exciting adventure in true Spielberg style.

▲

GREASE

Paramount Home Video
1977
110 minutes
Directed by: Randall Keiser
Starring: John Travolta,
  Olivia Newton-John,
  Stockard Channing
MPAA rating: PG

High school students Danny and Sandy have a wonderfully innocent, romance-filled summer at the beach before Sandy has to go back to Australia. School starts again at Rydell High where Danny is the leader of a group of over-sexed, unruly and immature young men who call themselves the T-Birds. (Their girlfriends, the Pink Ladies, are their ideal counterparts.) Danny brags to his friends about his outrageous summer when he "scored" and is horrified to see goody two-shoes Sandy at school (her plans changed). Danny's jealous ex-girlfriend wastes no time in telling Sandy all about his reputation. Meanwhile Danny tries his best to reform in order to win Sandy's respect. But it doesn't quite work and it's up to Sandy to find a way to bring them together.

CAUTION: This film is replete with sexual vocabulary, most of which is in the lyrics to songs. Rizzo has sex with one of Danny's friends in a car; he has a condom, but it breaks and they go ahead anyway.

GO: In spite of its overt sexuality this film is a popular favourite with girls, mainly because the clothes, cars, hairdos and songs of the '50s are depicted in a fun way. There are fabulous song and dance numbers throughout the film and plenty of sight-gags.

GREASE II

Paramount Home Video
1982
114 minutes
Directed by: Patricia Birch
Starring: Maxwell Caulfield,
  Lorna Luft, Michelle Pfeiffer,
  Adrian Zmed
MPAA rating: PG

Stephanie Zinnoni, suffering from boredom, is fed up with being someone's "chick" and longs for something more exciting that the Pink Ladies. Excitement comes in the form of a mysterious and handsome motorcycle rider who appears out of nowhere whenever she is in need of help. She pines for this romantic vision, completely unaware that he is really the academic exchange student who is tutoring her.

CAUTION: The video includes the song "Reproduction" which is often edited out when the film is aired on television. There is some coarse language.

GO: With its silly sight gags and terrific song-and-dance routines, and with far less sexual innuendo than *Grease*, *Grease II* is a big favourite.

THE GREAT MUPPET CAPER

CBS Fox
1981
98 minutes
Directed by: Jim Henson
Starring: John Cleese,
    Charles Grodin, Diana Rigg,
    Jack Warden

When investigative reporters Kermit the Frog and Fozzie Bear completely miss the scoop on the robbery of fashion designer Lady Holiday's jewels, they are fired from the newspaper and vow to travel to England to interview Lady Holiday and catch the thieves themselves. Meanwhile, Miss Piggy arrives in London hoping to become a fashion model for Lady Holiday, but is hired as her secretary instead. And when Kermit arrives for his interview and mistakes Miss Piggy for Lady Holiday, Miss Piggy keeps up the charade until the real Lady Holiday is robbed again. Gonzo gets a shot of Lady Holiday's parasitic brother Nicky stealing her diamond

necklace, but the picture is destroyed. And when Miss Piggy goes on the runway as a last-minute replacement, Nicky plants the jewels on her and she is thrown in jail. In the end, Gonzo overhears Nicky and the models planning their next heist, and the Muppets (including Miss Piggy, who has broken out of jail) save the day.

CAUTION: The odd scene may be upsetting for small children. Miss Piggy is in jail with a group of snarly, scary-looking women and in the end she beats up Nicky and the thieves. In one scene, a man admits that he's out with another woman while his wife is at home.

GO: In the great Muppet tradition, the music is lively. This is a film that can be enjoyed by young and old alike.

GRYPHON

Public Media Video
1988
58 minutes
Directed by: Mark Cullingham
Starring: Amanda Plummer,
    Alexis Cruz, Nico Hughes
MPAA rating: not rated

Ricky Carreros is a tough kid who's continually getting into trouble both at school and at home because of his maliciously satirical drawings. But his life is transformed the day that the utterly bizarre Miss Ferenczi comes to his class as a substitute teacher, enthralling some students and repulsing others with her unorthodox lecture material. She teaches the class about magical things — mythical creatures, her family's royal ancestry, and angels that walk the earth in formal evening wear, listening to the sounds of humans singing — and Ricky is enthralled. He even researches these things when he's at home and, inspired by her description of a gryphon, makes a beautiful drawing of one and gives it to her. However, his new-found love of lore and learning causes a rift between himself and his former gang. Despite this falling out, Ricky finds that Miss Ferenczi's influence has somehow had a positive effect on his life. He develops a close friendship with another classmate, and also grows closer to his mother and his once-despised stepfather. In the end, a group art project initiated by Ricky brings him and his friend and gang leader Hector back together again. Based on a short story by Charles Baxter.

CAUTION: There is one non-graphic fist-fight between Ricky and Hector, but there are no bruises or broken bones.

GO: This is a wonderful story about the transformative power of trust, beauty and imagination.

■

THE HARDY BOYS: ACAPULCO SPIES (Vol. 8)

MCA
1977
47 minutes
Starring: Shaun Cassidy, Parker Stevenson
MPAA rating: not rated

Fenton Hardy, the boys' famous detective father, desperately summons his sons to Mexico to bring him an important file. Upon arriving, they are to register at their hotel under false names and await a

contact who will use a prearranged code. But when two American girls, Jackie and Sue, accidentally use the code phrase, Frank and Joe think they've met the contacts and there is some confusion. Then the boys receive a dinner invitation from a professed friend of their father's, Cartell, and they accept, only to become involved in a cat and mouse game with the evil enemy agent who holds their father prisoner. When that agent kidnaps Jackie, the boys go after him.

CAUTION: A thug kidnaps Fenton, and his jailers try to starve him. There is some mild innuendo when the boys think the girls are the contacts; the girls misunderstand what the boys are talking about (let's get down to business, etc.).

Other titles in the series are:
The Flickering Torch Mystery (Vol. 2)
The Mystery of King Tut's Tomb (Vol. 6)
The Mystery of the African Safari (Vol. 7)
The Mystery of the Flying Courier (Vol. 4)
The Mystery of Witches Hollow (Vol. 1)
The Secret of Jade Kwan Yin (Vol. 3)
Wipe-Out (Vol. 5)

GO: These made-for-TV adventures are harmless.

AGES 6 TO 10

HARRY AND THE HENDERSONS

MCA Home Video
1987
101 minutes
Directed by: William Dear
Starring: Don Ameche, Melinda Dillon, John Lithgow, Lainie Kazan
OFRB rating: Family—Swearing
MPAA rating: PG

An "average American family" meets a Sasquatch when they are on vacation. They accidentally hit "Harry" with the car, and figuring they've killed him, take him home on the roof-rack. But that night Harry regains consciousness. He creates havoc, and as he's trashing the Hendersons' house, hunting enthusiast George points his rifle at Harry. Their eyes meet, and George withdraws when he realizes that Harry is a sentient being. And even though they quickly grow to love him, it soon becomes obvious to the Hendersons that they must return Harry to his home — but not without difficulty, and not before he changes their and other people's attitudes toward creatures of the wild.

CAUTION: Startling scenes include those in which Harry pops his head into the car and surprises George while he is driving. Harry is shot at by an obsessed hunter, but he doesn't get hit. The Hendersons own a sports store that features guns. Minimal swearing.

GO: This is the film from which the television show originated. It is a comedy so none of the conflicts are particularly violent. Sympathy for creatures of the wild and the idea that ignorance can cause fear are explored. The family is a happy, solid one, and the ending is magical.

▲

HONEY, I BLEW UP THE KID

Walt Disney Home Video
1992
100 minutes
Directed by: Randal Kleiser
Starring: Lloyd Bridges,
    Rick Moranis, Daniel and
    Joshua Shalikar, John Shea,
    Marcia Strassman
OFRB rating: F
MPAA rating: PG

In the sequel to *Honey, I Shrunk the Kids*, Wayne Szalinski is up to his old inventing tricks, but this time, due to his previous successes, he has the backing of billionaire military-industrialist Clifford Sterling. However, things aren't going too well. A combination of the brightest minds in the country can't replicate Szalinski's original experiments, and when Szalinski puts in a little Saturday overtime (and sons come along) an experiment gone awry turns his two-year-old son, Adam, into a rapidly-growing mutant baby. Szalinski is then forced on a quest after his 100-foot son, to Las Vegas, of all places. But in the end, only Adam's mother can save him.

GO: The performances are universally excellent — especially that of the remarkable young twins who play Adam — and some of the effects are mind-boggling. This is a fun adventure film with tension but no violence.

HONEY, I SHRUNK THE KIDS

Walt Disney Home Video
1989
101 minutes
Directed by: Joe Johnston
Starring: Matt Frewer, Rick Moranis,
    Jarad Rushton,
    Marsha Strassman
OFRB rating: F
MPAA rating: PG

Wayne Szalinski is working on a device which will alter the size of objects, but despite his genius and dedication, the machine refuses to function. Then a neighbour's son, Ron, hits a ball through the Szalinski's upstairs window, striking the machine and accidentally making it fully functional. When Ron and his older brother, Russ, show up to get the ball and to apologize for the breakage, they and Wayne's children, Amy and Nick, go upstairs to the room and are instantly targeted by the machine and shrunk to the size of insects. Wayne returns to see the broken window and inadvertently sweeps up the children with the debris and puts them out with the garbage. The children emerge unscathed, but their only hope is to get back to the house, and to do this they must march through what has now become miles of backyard, a dangerous jungle full of unknown terrors. Meanwhile, Wayne finds the couch shrunk to miniature size, and when he sees that the kids are missing, realizes the terrible truth. While he and his wife conduct a frantic search in the backyard, the children, who couldn't get along at normal size, quickly unite and brave a succession of threats in their voyage to the house. After a full night in the yard, they grab onto the Szalinski's dog and ride him into the house, where Wayne sees Nick in his cereal just before he puts the spoon in his mouth. Wayne repairs the machine and restores the children to their normal size.

Tummy Trouble, the Maroon Cartoon that precedes this feature, is a madcap, slapstick send-up of the medical profession starring Roger Rabbit and Baby Herman.

CAUTION: On their trek the children narrowly survive often-terrifying encounters with giant bees, ants, scorpions, sprinklers, lawn mowers, dogs and cigarette butts. In one scene, Amy almost drowns (Russ saves her with CPR) and in another Ron's gigantic pet ant is killed defending the kids against a scorpion-like creature; the children's grief is evident.

GO: A good kids-working-together film, this movie features stunning special effects. All of the negative relationships become positive in response to the crisis.

▲

✗ HOOK

Columbia Tri-Star Home Video
1991
142 minutes
Directed by: Steven Spielberg
Starring: Dustin Hoffman,
  Bob Hoskins, Julia Roberts,
  Robin Williams
OFRB rating: F
MPAA rating: PG

Peter Banning, a successful acquisitions lawyer, takes his family to England where his philanthropist adoptive grandmother Wendy is dedicating a new wing for an orphans' hospital. While the Bannings are at the ceremony, their children are kidnapped, and a note from none other than Captain Hook is left, daring Peter to retrieve them. Granny Wendy faces the difficult task of convincing Peter that he is the real Peter Pan — the boy who would never grow up, but did — and that his children really have been taken by Captain Hook. Peter is highly sceptical, until he himself is forceably spirited to Never Land by his old friend Tinkerbell. Once there, he finds that his children are indeed in Hook's clutches, and a deal is struck: Peter has three days to get back into Pan-type shape and fight Hook for his children. And this means that Peter must rediscover the wonderful ageless qualities of the child he once was, and learn, once more, how to fly. Based on characters by J.M. Barrie.

✗ STOP: Many small children are terrified by the abduction scene, which in true Spielberg style is filled with amazing special effects; it has moments that are truly intense and sinister. Other potentially upsetting scenes include one in which a mutinous pirate is put into a box with a scorpion, and another in which the child-hero Rufio is killed by Hook.

GO: Staggering visuals and inventive plot twists all add to this family adventure film that was nominated for five Academy Awards.

HOUDINI

Paramount Home Video
1953
106 minutes
Directed by: George Marshall
Starring: Tony Curtis, Janet Leigh,
   Torin Thatcher
MPAA rating: not rated

This is a part-fact, part-fiction account of the life of the legendary escape-artist Harry Houdini. The film covers his life from the time he learns about the workings of locks in a manufacturing plant to the time of his death after debuting the famous Chinese Water Torture trick. We see some of Houdini's greatest illusions, increasing in complexity and risk as his career develops. A fair bit of time is devoted to the romantic relationship between Houdini and his wife, Bess.

CAUTION: This is not a truly authentic account of Harry Houdini's life and it may be too slow and mushy for magic fans. The re-creation of the incident in which Houdini was trapped under the ice and was presumed dead may upset some young viewers.

GO: A charming introduction to the life of the world's greatest magician, this film is for young people fascinated with legerdemain.

I CAN DANCE

Kultur Video
1989
30 minutes
Directed by: Ron Kanter
Starring: Diana Kettler

Professional dancer Deborah Maxwell designed this video specifically for boys and girls ages seven and up. It follows a child's first ballet lesson through a series of progressive levels of ballet. Pliés, centre work, the five basic positions and more are covered to familiarize children with the facts (and fun) of ballet.

I OWN THE RACECOURSE

Cineplex Odeon
1985
90 minutes
Directed by: Stephen Ramsey
Starring: Guly Coote, Tony Barry,
   Norman Kaye
MPAA rating: not rated

Andy Hoddel is considered a bit crazy; he has a chip on his shoulder, and he's always going on about owning things (bridges, the police station, and so on). He hangs out at the local racecourse where he picks up change off the stands after the races. One day, an old bum, who claims his father left the racecourse to him in his will, offers to sell it to Andy for twenty dollars. Andy assembles his spare change and purchases it. And when he brings the boys around to show "his" racecourse off, his friends are convinced he's lost it completely, and go looking for the bum who conned their friend. But Andy hangs around the racecourse so much that the employees start calling him "boss" and let him and his friends in free. Andy repays this trust when two crooks try to con him into putting an accelerant into one of the horses' feed, and he turns them in. But Bert, the kindly grounds-keeper, soon realizes that Andy is only risking his future by continuing to hang around, and he arranges to have the real owners "buy" the racecourse back from Andy. Based on the novel by Patricia Wrightson.

CAUTION: The pace of this film is too slow for most young children. It's filmed with grainy realism, almost in documentary style, making it less accessible to young viewers than it might have been.

GO: Developed with the assistance of the Australian Children's Television Foundation.

∎

IN SEARCH OF THE CASTAWAYS

Walt Disney Home Video
1962
98 minutes
Directed by: Robert Stevenson
Starring: Maurice Chevalier,
    Wilfrid Hyde-White, Hayley Mills
MPAA rating: G

In 1858, indomitable Mary Grant arrives with her brother Robert and their friend Professor Paganelle in Glasgow, Scotland. There they petition Lord Glenarbin and his dashing young son John (director of the ship line), to outfit an expedition to track down and rescue the children's father, Captain Grant, who has been shipwrecked and is presumed dead. At first His Lordship doesn't believe them, but soon Mary befriends John who wears his father down until at last he agrees to finance the search for Captain Grant. Thus begins an epic quest which takes them (among other places) to the southern latitudes of South America, up into the highlands of the Andes, through an earthquake, down a glacier, across the Indian Ocean and through a volcanic eruption.

GO: This is an improbable but exciting yarn for action fans of all ages. There is some platonic romance.

THE INCREDIBLE JOURNEY

Walt Disney Home Video
1963
80 minutes
Directed by: Fletcher Markle
Starring: Emile Genest,
    John Drainie, Tommy Tweed,
    Jan Rubes
MPAA rating: no rating given

Deep in the Canadian wilderness, John Longridge is caring for his godchildren's pets (Luath, a labrador retriever; Tao, a siamese cat; and Bodger, a bull terrier). One day when Longridge leaves on a duck hunting trip, the animals mistakenly think that he will not come back, and decide to make the long trek home alone — little knowing that home is 200 miles away. Luath leads the way, Bodger follows and Tao brings up the rear (when he feels like it). But Bodger finds the going rough and after the second day, the old dog is slowing down. Luath encourages him, and as the group struggles on they encounter a large black bear, dangerous rapids, a lynx, a porcupine and a hunter. And when Longridge returns, he realizes that the animals are on their way home, and begins to search for people who have sighted them. Sure that the animals have survived 100 miles at least, Longridge tells his godchildren what has happened, and they are devastated. But the family soon hears the barks of a dog and are delighted to see all of the animals come running home together, safe and sound after an incredible journey.

CAUTION: It is upsetting to some that the animals are hungry on their voyage and children may also be disturbed when the cat seems to be drowned in the river. This film may give some children the unrealistic hope that animals that run away will return home safely, even if they must travel great distances to do it.

GO: A wonderfully hopeful and fascinating story for animal lovers, *The Incredible Journey* shows the bond between animals and the bond between animals and their human caregivers. This film was remade in 1992 as *Homeward Bound: The Incredible Journey.*

■

THE INCREDIBLE MR. LIMPET

Warner Home Video
1963
99 minutes
Directed by: Arthur Lubin
Starring: Carole Cook,
    Andrew Duggan,
    Don Knotts,
    Jack Weston
OFRB rating: F

Bookkeeper Henry Limpet has one dream — to live as a fish. And after being rejected by the U.S. navy, a magical fall into the waters off Coney Island brings about some amazing circumstances. Henry is transformed into a fish and upon the discovery that he can detect Nazi U-boats with his underwater abilities, he becomes the navy's secret weapon. He finds fulfilment, success (in the form of a military decoration) and the love of a good fish in his new life under the sea.

CAUTION: A little dated, this film includes some female stereotyping and may be too slow for today's young audiences.

GO: The combination of live-action and animation makes this film accessible to young children.

IT'S A MAD, MAD, MAD, MAD WORLD

CBS/Fox
1963
155 minutes
Directed by: Stanley Kramer
Starring: Jim Backus, Milton Berle,
    Sid Caesar, Andy Devine,
    Jimmy Durante, Peter Falk,
    Buddy Hackett, Sterling Holloway,
    Buster Keaton, Don Knotts,
    Ethel Merman, Carl Reiner,
    Mickey Roony, Dick Shawn,
    Phil Silvers, Terry Thomas,
    The Three Stooges,
    Jonathan Winters, with cameos
    by many others
OFRB rating: PG
MPAA rating: G

When a spectacular car crash takes place in a mountainous desert region of California, the assembled passers-by struggle down the cliff to help the driver, who's been thrown clear. When they get to him, they find that he's fading fast. But the dying man has time to blurt urgently "there's this dough, see? There's all this dough, three hundred and fifty Gs! in the Rosita Beach State Park buried under this big W." And so the assembled onlookers climb back up to their cars and race off, each trying to find a way to get to the buried loot first. They tear up most of California in the process, picking up other treasure-seekers on the way. The action is fast and furious, with car chases, double-crosses, plane stunts, slapstick gags, some funky sixties dancing and hilarious performances by the all-star cast. (Literally every person who appears on screen is a star.) Finally, the madcap gang arrives at the park,

and eventually stumble upon the W (four palm trees at angles) and begin frantically digging and arguing. Meanwhile, Police Captain Culpepper stands calmly by and watches the manic proceedings. Then he tries to take off with the loot himself and the gang gives chase, leading to a wild and frantic finish in which it literally rains money.

GO: This is one of the all-time great comedies. For adults, it has scores of great comic stars of yesteryear and for children, it's what it has always been — a very funny movie. Note: A restored version of this film is available that includes 30 minutes of film which haven't been seen in 25 years.

✗ JASON AND THE ARGONAUTS

RCA/Columbia
1963
minutes
Directed by: Don Chaffey
Starring: Todd Armstrong,
    Nancy Kovack
MPAA rating: G

When the warlord Polias overthrows King Aristo, Polias is enraged to learn that he will, in turn, lose his throne to Aristo's son, Jason. (It is ordained by Zeus.) So when Jason appears, speaking of a golden fleece which hangs on a tree at the end of the world — a fleece that has the power to heal, bring peace and rid the world of plague and famine — Polias encourages Jason to go on a suicidal mission to retrieve it. And so, Jason holds games to determine the greatest champions in Greece (one of whom is Hercules), and he has the strongest ship built (the Argo). With the powerful ship and the mighty crew, he sets out into unknown waters. In the course of their adventures they encounter the living gargantuan statue of Talos; Phineas, a blind sage who is tormented by harpies; Medea, a high priestess of Caucus; the seven-headed Hydra and an army of skeleton warriors.

✗**STOP:** Polias stabs a woman (off-camera), and there is a blood-curdling scream and a realistic cleaving sound. This moment is totally out of character with the rest of the film.

CAUTION: The giant Talos, the hydra and the harpies may frighten young viewers.

GO: This is a more serious effort than the Sinbad movies, but with many of the same exciting characteristics and animation. Splendid sound effects add to the realism of the mythical characters.

▲

JAZZ TIME TALE

f.h.e.
1992
29 minutes
Directed by: Michael Sporn
Narrated by: Ruby Dee
MPAA rating: unrated

Rose (whose father is a talent scout) is always left at home when her father goes out. Feeling lonely one night, she hides in the back of his car when he goes to the Lincoln Theatre. She doesn't go in, but instead takes a walk down the street for some air. And as she walks she hears the "jumpiest" music she has ever heard coming from one of the houses. She goes to the house where she meets a girl named Lucinda and learns that the music is

that of a neighbour, Thomas Fats Waller. The girls become fast friends and when, at the Lincoln Theatre, the organist is unable to play, Fats takes over and Lucinda's family takes Rose along to hear him. Meanwhile, Rose's father has discovered that she is missing and after searching the streets finds her in the theatre. She introduces him to Lucinda's family who draws his attention to Fats on the organ. His jazz playing brings down the house, and the rest is history.

GO: Beautifully animated by Bridget Thorne, this film provides a terrific glimpse of New York City in 1919. There is even a cartoon movie within the cartoon!

THE JOURNEY OF NATTY GANN

Walt Disney Home Video
1985
101 minutes
Directed by: Jeremy Kagan
Starring: John Cusack, Lainie Kazan, Meredith Salinger, Ray Wise
MPAA rating: PG

During the Great Depression, Sol Gann is forced to travel west to the timberlands of Washington State to find work, leaving his young daughter, Natty, in the care of a sleazy hotel manager. But when life becomes unbearable, Natty strikes out west alone to find her father. Thus begins an incredible journey. On her way, Natty happens on a gruesome pit fight between a wolf and another dog. When the wolf wins, it escapes with a spectacular leap over the drunken spectators. Later that night, a chance encounter brings Natty face to face with the wolf; she shows it kindness, and it begins to follow her, even bringing her a rabbit when she is starving. Then Natty falls in with a group of thieving tramps, gets arrested and is sent to an orphanage (which is more like a prison camp). She makes her escape, finds her wolf and (after a considerable trek accompanied by a tough young drifter she meets on the way) is finally reunited with her father.

CAUTION: People are generally portrayed as being rude and hard (it is, after all, a hard time). Also of concern may be the pit fight and a scene in which Natty is molested by a truck driver when she accepts a ride.

GO: This is an exciting adventure film with a terrific musical score.

▲

JOURNEY TO SPIRIT ISLAND

C/FP
1991
93 minutes
Directed by: Laszlo Pal
Starring: Tony Acierto, Bettina,
    Gabriel Damon,
    Brandon Douglas,
    Tarek McCarthy, Nick Ramus,
    Marie Antoinette Rodgers
OFRB rating: PG

Controversy grips a northwestern reservation when the smooth-talking Bob Hawk brings in a group of white developers with plans to create a huge resort on Eagle Island (known to the elders as Spirit Island). The only thing standing in the developers' way is a mystic named Jimmy Jim. One day, Michael and Willie, the sons of a family friend, come up from Chicago to visit the reservation. The white boys are pleasant and amiable enough, but Maria (Jimmy Jim's granddaughter) is troubled by a visionary dream of peril. And when the four kids (Maria's brother Klim comes along) set out on a canoe trip through the island chain, disaster strikes. One of their boats is holed by a protruding log. The kids clamber into the remaining canoe, and the currents — or some unknown mystical power — carry them to Spirit Island. There they spend the night, and Maria tells the story of the great Tupshin, a shaman whose spirit roams the island in search of his lost son. The next morning, the canoe is gone, and the children are stuck on the island. They go exploring, find Tupshin's son's ancient bones, and give them the proper burial that will allow his spirit to leave. Then Hawk and a fellow thug show up on the island, and after a confrontation with him the children hide in a burial cairn which the thugs then seal with a big rock. But Maria follows her visions and finds another way out, and she and the others escape. The children then find their lost canoe, repair the kayak, rendezvous with Tom, and burst in on the tribal meeting in time to save Spirit Island.

CAUTION: At one point, Hawk captures Klim, and punches, slaps and threatens to kill him.

GO: This is a terrific adventure story. Both cultures are presented in a positive and non-patronizing light.

✘ KIDNAPPED

Walt Disney Home Video
1960
94 minutes
Directed by: Robert Stevenson
Starring: Peter Finch,
    James MacArthur, Peter O'Toole
MPAA rating: not rated

After his father's death, David
Balfour, an honest, high-spirited
young man, sets out across the
highlands of Scotland. On the
strength of a letter delivered to him
after his father's death, David goes
to his mysterious uncle Ebenezer's
half-finished castle, the House of
Shaws (cursed twelve hundred and
nineteen times by a witch), and
stays with the suspicious skinflint.
But when Ebenezer arranges an
"accident" for David, David begins to
suspect the worst. Sure enough,
Ebenezer conspires with the sinister
Captain Hosesan to trick David
aboard Hosesan's ship, intending to
send him to the Carolinas and sell
him off as an indentured servant.
Enroute, an accident brings rebel
fighter Alan Breck Stewart aboard,
and when Hosesan and his evil first
mate Mister Shawn plot to kill him,
David stands with Stewart against
the entire crew. They triumph, but
Stewart himself is a vainglorious,
quarrelsome handful, and David is
subsequently drawn into a
harrowing series of events which
lead him into the maelstrom of
Scottish clan feuding and,
eventually, back to the House of
Shaws and a confrontation with his
miserly uncle.

✘ **STOP:** During the voyage, the kind cabin
boy is abused and killed by Mister Shawn.
There is a bloodcurdling scream, and then
the boy's body is carried out of the deck-
house.

CAUTION: There is heroic violence. Alan
and David hold off an entire crew of sailors
at half-sword and the fighting is intense. In
one scene, David dangles from the highest
parapet of the castle.

GO: This is a stirring, action-packed adventure replete with colourful characters
(including a debut cameo by Peter
O'Toole).
■

THE KNIGHTS OF THE ROUND TABLE

MGM/UA
1953
116 minutes
Directed by: Richard Thorpe
Starring: Felix Aylmer,
    Stanley Baker, Anne Crawford,
    Mel Ferrer, Ava Gardner,
    Rod Taylor
MPAA rating: not rated

In feudal England, Morgan le Fey
and her champion Mordred meet
Arthur and Merlin to contest the right
of kingship of Britain. (Arthur is the
illegitimate son of the last king,
while Morgan is the king's legitimate
daughter.) They put their claims to
the test against Excalibur, a sword
embedded in a stone, and Arthur
prevails by pulling the sword clear.
Knights from all over flock to
Arthur's standard, including
Lancelot and his companions. Soon
thereafter, Arthur and Lancelot
journey to Stonehenge for a
conference of rival barons, which
breaks down and turns into a
skirmish. War rages between the

rival factions, but Arthur wins the climactic battle and pardons his foes, including Mordred. Arthur then creates the famous round table and, as time passes, he and his knights survive campaigns and adventures. All the while, though, Lancelot wrestles with his love for Arthur's bride, Guinevere. When Morgan and Mordred become suspicious of his desires, they spring on the lovers, leaving them no option but to flee. Lancelot returns and tries to explain to Arthur, but the king sends Guinevere to a convent and has Lancelot banished. Then Mordred and Arthur war on each other, and Lancelot returns again, too late; Arthur lies dying. It is up to Lancelot to seek out Mordred and settle the issue in a combat to the death.

CAUTION: There is minimal heroic violence.

GO: This not very accurate rendition of Malory's *Morte d'Arthur* should at least get children interested in the legend. And certainly, it's got enough good clean knights-in-armour action for young fans of chivalry. ■

✗ LABYRINTH

Nelson
1986
102 minutes
Directed by: Jim Henson
Starring: David Bowie,
   Jennifer Connelly
OFRB rating: F
MPAA rating: PG

Teenager Sarah lives in a fantasy world. She is constantly acting out the part of heroic princesses from books. And when she must baby-sit her baby half-brother, Toby, and he

wails and cries interminably, Sarah's fury knows no bounds. She grabs her little brother and screams a poetic entreaty to the Goblin King to come and take the baby away. Nothing happens, of course, but as Sarah pauses in the doorway of her brother's room, she turns back and quietly adds that she really *does* wish that the goblins would come. And sure enough, seconds later, Toby's crying abruptly stops. Sarah rushes back into the room and Toby is gone; there are goblins all over the house. Then the sinister Goblin King appears and informs her that her wish has been granted. Sarah tries to explain that she didn't really mean it, at which point the Goblin King lays down the law. In the land of the goblins, she will have thirteen hours to solve the Labyrinth, reach the Goblin King's castle and rescue her brother. If she is unable to complete the test in the time allotted, Toby will become one of the goblins. Sarah has no choice; she sets out through the enormous maze, encountering a host of bizarre characters (some of which she befriends) and resisting the Goblin King's crafty intrigues along the way. In the end, Sarah makes it through the Labyrinth in time, besieges the goblin castle with her brave friends and confronts the Goblin King in his eerie sanctuary. There, she pronounces the words which will send the King to oblivion, and return her and her brother to safety.

✗STOP: The scene in which the goblins come into Sarah's house is definitely too scary for little ones.

CAUTION: Certain images in this film may disturb or frighten the young crowd. In one scene, Sarah, in a daze, encounters Muppet witches who resemble bag ladies and who burden her down with toys and stuffed animals in a replica of her room. In another,

Sarah takes a bite of a poisoned apple and, in the grip of a trance, dances with the Goblin King at a strange party.

GO: This is a terrific film about shedding selfishness and growing up, without losing the essential joy of youth. A plethora of Henson creatures and visual ideas make this a top favourite film with kids six to ten.
▲

THE LAST UNICORN

J2
1982
84 minutes
Directed by: Jules Bass,
    Arthur Rankin
Starring the voices of: Alan Arkin,
    Jeff Bridges, Mia Farrow,
    Angela Lansbury, Christopher
    Lee, Keenan Wynn
MPAA rating: G

The Last Unicorn, having become lonely in her solitude, bids farewell to her beautiful forest and sets out on an epic journey to look for other unicorns. Her journey spans many seasons, and on the way she encounters Mommy Fortune's Midnight Carnival and is imprisoned. There she learns of the Red Bull, a huge magic-spawned monster who (at the bidding of King Haggard) has been hunting down all of the unicorns and pushing them to the ends of the earth. And so, after escaping the carnival with the help of a not-very-good magician named Shmendrick, the Last Unicorn, Shmendrick and a hardened outlaw named Molly Grue venture into the desolate domain of King Haggard. That very night the monster is released, and as it is closing on the Unicorn, Shmendrick in desperation yells out the spell: Magic! Do as you will! And the Unicorn is mysteriously transformed into a young woman, whom they name the Lady Amalthea. The trio go to the fortress, where they meet King Haggard and his son, Prince Leer, and where they learn more about the destruction of the unicorns. It turns out that a prophecy has foretold that a unicorn will bring about Haggard's doom, so he has been getting rid of the unicorns by throwing them into the sea where they become the surging white crests of the waves. When King Haggard realizes who Amalthea really is, he unleashes the Red Bull again. But Prince Leer (who has fallen in love with Amalthea) comes to her aid, and when he is struck down, the Unicorn finally fights back, driving the Red Bull into the sea, freeing all of the unicorns and sending King Haggard plunging amidst his crumbling castle to his doom.

CAUTION: This animated film has scared a lot of kids, and the Red Bull is really terrifying. A huge harpy kills Mommy Fortune, and we see from the back the vulture-like form hunched over her body, obviously feeding. A tree turns into a lascivious creature and hugs the young wizard suggestively. Some children are upset at the loneliness of the unicorn.

GO: The children who like this film really like it — possibly because of its overwhelming romanticism.

LET'S DRAW!

```
Random House Home Video
1992
35 minutes
Directed by: Malcolm Hossick
Narrated by: Brett Ambler
```

Based on the books by Colin Caket and Leon Baxter, this guide shows even the youngest artists how to find a way to draw by using basic principles and familiar shapes and figures.

■

LET'S GET A MOVE ON! A KID'S VIDEO GUIDE TO A FAMILY MOVE

```
Kidvidz
1990
30 minutes
Directed by: Jane Murphy,
   Karen Tucker
```

This is a well-paced live-action video about moving house. Using songs, animation and recreated situations the video deals with the concerns children will have about such things as prospective buyers who visit the home, watching a room being taken apart and saying good-bye. Children are reminded that home is where the family is. Recommended for children aged four to ten, this tape includes an activity guide.

THE LION, THE WITCH AND THE WARDROBE

```
Public Media Video
1988
165 minutes
Directed by: Marilyn Fox
Starring: Sophie Cook, Richard
   Dempsey, Barbara Kellerman,
   Jonathan R. Scott, Sophie Wilcox
OFRB rating: no rating available
```

During World War II, four children, Peter, Susan, Lucy and Edmund, are evacuated to a sprawling manor house in the English countryside. While exploring the house, Lucy happens upon a wardrobe and finds an entrance to Narnia, a strange and magical world. In Narnia it is "always winter and never Christmas" because it is under the control of the evil White Witch. After a series of events, the children finally come into Narnia together, where Edmund falls under the spell of the Witch and betrays his siblings. Peter, Susan and Lucy escape and, guided by a pair of friendly beavers, begin a gruelling march through the countryside in search of the great lion Aslan, the champion of truth and goodness. As the children travel, the Witch's magic begins to weaken, and the snow melts with the coming of spring. This predicates Aslan's great sacrifice to save Edmund, and Aslan's resurrection by a Deeper Magic. The great lion then leads the forces of goodness to victory, and the children are made kings and queens of Narnia. (In the end, they return to England safe and sound.)

Other films in the Narnia series are:

Prince Caspian and the Voyage of the Dawntreader
The Silver Chair

CAUTION: Some viewers may find the intensely evil White Witch frightening, and Edmund's treachery, creepy. The complex story, with its archetypal religious theme and ponderous length, may leave some very young children behind.

GO: This BBC production, made in association with Wonderworks, is a credible attempt to bring the first book of the Narnia series to life.

■

✗ LITTLE HEROES

Select Home Video
1991
78 minutes
Directed by: Craig Clyde
Starring: Raeanin Simpson,
   Katherine Willis
OFRB rating: F
MPAA rating: G

Ten-year-old Charley Wilson's family is poor, and she worries because, although her parents love each other, they fight about the situation. At school Charley is taunted by the other more affluent girls and her only real friends are her dog, Fuzz, and Alonzo, the elderly farmer who lives next door. One day, Charley is invited to Carol Evans's birthday party, and Charley's mother uses her mad money to buy fabric and make Charley a dress. But Carol's mother uninvites her, and Charley, humiliated and unable tell her mother what has happened, dresses up anyway and pretends to go to the party. A few days later, Charley finds Alonzo in the field; he has just cut his thumb off in a farm machine. Charley runs to get help and is later surprised to see Mrs. Evans at the hospital. It turns out that Alonzo is Mrs. Evans's father. She explains to Charley that she was mean to her because Charley's poverty reminded her of her own tough childhood. And in the end, when Fuzz is found dead (poisoned by a piece of meat Alonzo left out to catch a fox), Alonzo and Mrs. Evans find a way to thank Charley for her kindness by buying her a new puppy. This film is based on a true story.

✗STOP: The dog dies! There is a sentimental montage with music reminiscing about the good times Charley and Fuzz had together. The box cover gives the impression through photos and words that this is more of an action film; it is, however, a relationship film about tolerance and prejudice.

GO: The film shows a gentle slice of life and the moral is a good one.

LITTLE WOMEN

MGM/UA
1933
116 minutes
Directed by: George Cukor
Starring: Joan Bennett,
   Spring Byington, Frances Dee,
   Katherine Hepburn,
   Peter Lawford, Edna May Oliver,
   Jean Parker
MPAA rating: no rating given

During the American Civil War, wildly independent Jo March lives with her mother and her sisters

Meg, Amy and Beth in Massachusetts. It's Christmas, their father is at the front, and the girls are living day to day. Then Laurie, a dashing young man who ran away from school to join the army and was wounded, moves in across the way. He and Jo strike up a friendship, but despite her deep affection for Laurie, Jo refuses his offer of marriage, preferring instead to pursue her writing career in New York City. But when Jo learns that Beth is dying, she returns, and through her contact with her courageous sister, matures enough to recognize that to be loved is a precious gift. Then Jo writes a serious work, based on the truth and beauty she knows in her heart: *My Beth*. This film is black and white.

CAUTION: Beth dies on camera, and the family's grief is depicted.

GO: This may be the stronger of the two versions; the beginning is certainly more atmospheric, giving a stronger impression of poverty and the hardships of war.

■

LITTLE WOMEN

MGM/UA
1949
122 minutes
Directed by: Mervyn LeRoy
Starring: June Allyson, Mary Astor,
  Rossano Brazzi, Peter Lawford,
  Janet Leigh, Margaret O'Brien,
  Elizabeth Taylor, Lucile Watson
MPAA rating: no rating given

The plot of the 1949 version of *Little Women* follows almost exactly the plot of the 1933 version described in the previous review.

CAUTION: Beth dies. The death is not overtly depicted, but anyone over five is going to get the idea.

GO: *Little Women* is an American paean to innocence, independence, and the true heart.

■

LOOK WHAT I FOUND: MAKING CODES AND SOLVING PROBLEMS

Pacific Arts Video/MCA Home Video
1992
45 minutes
Starring: Amy Purcell

Host Amy Purcell shows kids how to become junior detectives with fingerprint games, secret codes, tin can telephones, code wheels and treasure hunts. Recommended for children aged five to twelve.

LOOK WHAT I GREW: WINDOWSILL GARDENS

Pacific Arts Video/MCA Home Video
1992
45 minutes
Starring: Amy Purcell

Amy Purcell's easy-to-do gardening experiments include seed viewers, sprouting vegetable tops, apple finger puppets, terrariums and garden journals. Suitable for children aged five to twelve, this film is recommended by the National Gardening Association.

LOOK WHAT I MADE: PAPER PLAYTHINGS AND GIFTS

Pacific Arts Video/MCA Home Video
1990
45 minutes
Starring: Amy Purcell

Amy Purcell teaches children to make piñatas, origami, paper hats, flower bouquets, newspaper hammocks and more. Winner of the Parent's Choice Award and the 1990 Action for Children's Television award, this video is recommended for children aged five to twelve.

LOOKING FOR MIRACLES

Walt Disney Home Video
1989
104 minutes
Directed by: Kevin Sullivan
Starring: Zachary Bennett,
    Joe Flaherty, Greg Spottiswood
OFRB rating: F

Sixteen-year-old Ryan Delaney is determined to go to university — even though it's the middle of the Great Depression and he doesn't have any money. Ryan earns a scholarship, but his widowed mother cannot give him money for expenses. In fact, she doesn't even have enough money to keep Ryan's younger brother, Sullivan, at home.

And when her relatives are unable to continue caring for Sullivan they send him back and Ryan is forced to get a steady job to help support the family. Ryan hears about a job opening for a counsellor at a summer camp, and he manages to convince the camp director that he is an eighteen-year-old expert on Indian lore. He is given the position of head counsellor (for which he is ill-equipped) and, with Sullivan in tow, moves to the camp, where he soon sees that the hardest part of his job will be to look as if he knows what he is doing. One ornery camper nicknamed Ratface, realizing at once that Ryan can't swim or paddle a canoe, promptly begins to make the counsellor's life miserable. And things aren't going well for Sullivan either as his older brother continues to ignore his every effort to please. Sullivan's only friend is Grace Gibson, the owner of the camp, who teaches him to swim. And when Ryan is fired for spending an evening at a neighbouring girls' camp, Sullivan goes to Miss Gibson and explains everything about Ryan's scam and his desperate desire to go to university. And in the end, Ryan realizes how much his little brother means to him. Filmed in Toronto and throughout Southern Ontario, this movie is based on the book by A.E. Hochner.

CAUTION: The boys' father is dead.

GO: This film truly is a coming-of-age film, with the delightful flavour of another time.

■

THE LORD OF THE RINGS

```
HBO
1978
133 minutes
Directed by: Ralph Bakshi
MPAA rating: PG
```

In an indeterminate, ancient age, man shares the world, Middle Earth, with a variety of other intelligent bipeds — elves, dwarves, orcs (goblins) and hobbits (little furry-footed folk). In the story, a hobbit named Frodo Baggins unwittingly comes into the possession of the Ruling Ring (a plain gold ring which is a token of enormous power). The Ring is being sought by its owner, the dreadful Sauron, who has already sent his ghastly servants, the Ringwraiths, out into Middle Earth to look for it. With this horrible crew closing in on him, Frodo takes to the road, and thus begins an epic journey through peril and war, as the film chronicles the adventures of Frodo and the companions he gathers with him on his quest to destroy the Ring.

CAUTION: This animated film based on the popular book is a remarkable effort, but it's incomplete, telling the story approximately until the halfway point, to the first stage of Frodo and Sam's journey into the dreadful realm of Mordor, and the seige of Helm's Deep. There are elements in this story which are likely to frighten small children; the ringwraiths, for example, are blood-curdling, red-eyed incarnations of evil.

GO: The look of the animation in this film is both unique and striking. (Frodo's ride to the river near Rivendell, with the dreadful Ringwraiths in swift pursuit is especially breathtaking.) Of course, when an animator takes on a masterpiece, read by millions, that animator risks coming under some criticism. But certainly this is a worthy effort, and perhaps a way to introduce young people to the epic.

■

THE LOVE BUG

```
Walt Disney Home Video
1969
108 minutes
Directed by: Robert Stevenson
Starring: Buddy Hackett,
    Dean Jones, Michele Lee,
    David Tomlinson
MPAA rating: G
```

Down-on-his-luck racecar driver Jim Douglas has cracked up so many cars that his sponsor is dumping him. And his best friend and room-mate Tennessee Steinmetz (a modern sculptor who uses the pieces of Jim's wrecks to create art), is trying to convince him to quit before he destroys himself on the track. But Jim is immovable and as he is drooling over a Jaguar at a local import dealership a little Volkswagen nuzzles up to him; in fact, the car won't leave him alone. It follows him home, and as a result he is arrested for grand theft the next morning, and forced to purchase the car. It soon becomes obvious that the "Love Bug" has a life of its own. And when they race, Herbie leaves the opposition in his dust. But Jim begins to attribute his new-found success solely to his own abilities, and it's up to his friends, and Herbie, to set him straight.

Other Herbie movies to try are:
Herbie Goes Bananas
Herbie Goes to Monte Carlo
Herbie Rides Again

CAUTION: One of the characters, Mr. Wu, is not portrayed in a particularly favourable light (he will not speak English until the subject of money is broached); in fact, there are a number of rather unfortunate depictions of Chinese-Americans in the film.

GO: This is a wonderful comic effort in the Disney tradition, with a terrific performance by Tomlinson as the villainous Thorndike.
●

MAC AND ME

Orion
1988
99 minutes
Directed by: Stewart Raffill
Starring: Christine Ebersole,
    Jonathan Ward, Katrina Caspary,
    Lauren Stanley
OFRB rating: F
MPAA rating: PG

The film opens in a distant solar system, where a family of aliens is scratching out a meagre existence on an arid world. There a United States spacecraft lands, evidently taking samples, and inadvertently sucks up the curious family. And when the craft is recovered, the terrified aliens burst out of the compartment and escape from the scientific facility. One of the younger aliens hides in a van belonging to Janet and her sons Michael and Eric. The family is moving from Illinois to Sacramento, and they inadvertently take the alien with them. When they arrive at their new home, the alien moves in with them, causing quite a bit of havoc (for which Eric, who uses a wheelchair, is usually blamed). But Eric is suspicious and he and his new friend Debbie finally see the strange little alien, whom they call MAC (Mysterious Alien Creature). MAC's hijinks soon begin to attract attention, however, and a government capture group shows up when the teens go to a local burger joint. Eric is forced to flee with MAC on his lap and his older brother, Michael, shows up just in the nick of time with the van. They follow MAC's directions to the desert, where they find MAC's family hiding in an abandoned mine. The kids bring the alien family back,

but when frightened police officers open fire on them in a parking lot and several cars are blown up, the massive explosion apparently kills them, and Eric as well. But, the aliens miraculously walk out of the fireball, revive Eric and stay to become American citizens.

CAUTION: The scene in which MAC is stuck to the windshield of a car may upset young viewers and the fire at the end of the film is also scary. *MAC and Me* is a blatant commercial for a certain fast-food chain.

GO: Not much reference is made to Eric's disadvantage; he is simply treated like any hero. Nor does the film fall into the soppy trap of having the aliens cure Eric of his disability.

▲

THE MAGICAL BIRTHDAY PARTY

Abilities Research Inc.
1992
20 minutes
Starring: Brian Glow

Have world-class Canadian magician Brian Glow bring his show to your home. On this tape, aimed at children aged four to eleven, Brian demonstrates some of his best illusions and teaches children how to perform some tricks themselves (although he does trick the children in the process). In order to do the tricks child will need some equipment, all of which can be obtained at any magic store or through catalogues.

GO: Many children are fascinated by doing magic and there are very few videos which have a tempo and clarity that the child can follow.

THE MAGNIFICENT SIX-AND-A-HALF

MVA
1987
91 minutes
Starring: Michael Audreson,
  Ian Ellis, Brinsley Forde,
  Lionel Hawkes, Len Jones,
  Kim Tallmadge, Suzanne Togni
MPAA rating: no rating given

When Toby, Steve, Liz, Dumbo and Stodger are walking beside the river one afternoon, they spot two other children, Whizz and Pee Wee, on the bank. A dog is in trouble in the water, and Dumbo clumsily falls in to save it. It turns out that the dog belongs to a junk-yard owner, so the children return it to its master and ask permission to use an old van in the junk-yard as their gang's hideout. And when Whizz and Pee Wee want to join the gang, Pee Wee is turned away (she's too young) and Whizz is told that he must spend the night in a local haunted house to prove his worth. The rest of the gang, of course, decides to give him a good scare, but it backfires when they discover that there is a someone — or something — in the house. That someone turns out to be Pee Wee who snuck in by herself. This is just one of the many adventures included in this film.

CAUTION: There is a lot of slapstick humour in this film.

GO: *The Magnificent Six-and-a-Half* is curiously reminiscent of the famous Our Gang series of early film history.

THE MAN FROM SNOWY RIVER

CBS/Fox
1982
115 minutes
Directed by: George Miller
Starring: Tom Berlinson,
   Kirk Douglas, Sigrid Thornton
MPAA rating: PG

When a great wild stallion causes a stampede, killing Jim Craig's father, Jim leaves their small mountain ranch to learn about ranching in the lowlands. There, he seeks employment with a rich rancher named Harrison who has just purchased a colt worth a thousand pounds. And when the dangerously unruly colt nearly tramples Harrison's headstrong daughter, Jessica, Jim comes to her aid and Harrison hires him. Eventually, Jim tames the colt, and he and Jessica become close. Then one day, Harrison slaps Jessica during a heated discussion, and she rides off into the high country and falls from a cliff. Jim saves her, and on their way back to the ranch introduces her to Spur, a friend of Jim's who also happens to be her uncle and Harrison's twin brother. At home, Jessica's aunt tells her the long-guarded family secret. Twenty years ago, Jessica's father and her uncle quarreled over a spirited young woman named Matilda. Harrison won her hand, but she still cared enough for Spur that Harrison wasn't sure that Jessica was his daughter and, in a jealous rage, he shot off his brother's leg. For bringing the long-buried story to

life, Jim is told to leave the ranch. And after Jim beats up two other hands who picked a fight with him, the hands set the colt loose and Jim is blamed. Jim retrieves the colt, captures the great wild stallion and, vowing to return for Jessica, rides off to reclaim his ranch.

CAUTION: There is some coarse language and during a fight in the bunkhouse Jim thumps a couple of bullies (no blood). Harrison slaps his daughter's face.

GO: This is an exciting adventure with a minimum of violence, incredible riding and spectacular scenery.

THE MIGHTY DUCKS

Touchstone
1992
104 minutes
Directed by: Emilio Estevez
Starring: Joss Ackland,
   Emilio Estevez, Joshua Jackson,
   Heidi Kling, Lane Smith,
   Josef Sommer
OFRB rating: F
MPAA rating: PG

Gordon Bombay is a ruthless young Minnesota trial lawyer who lives his life on the edge. And when he is arrested for drunk driving and reckless endangerment, his powerful boss Gerald Duckworth gets him off relatively lightly . . . with community service. This service turns out to be time spent coaching the local hockey team, District Five. The team is pathetic and, once a pee-wee superstar himself, the competitive Bombay believes he's been consigned to his own personal hell; worse, Gordon's old team, the Hawks, is still coached by Coach

Reilly, a success-oriented ogre who ruined Gordon's own youthful hockey experience. At first, Gordon is determined to beat him with his own win-by-any-means attitude. But when young Charlie Conroy refuses to cheat and quits the team, Gordon has second thoughts. He apologizes to his young charges, then proceeds to drill them in the fundamentals of good hockey. He gets them properly outfitted with the Duckworth firm's financial backing and District Five becomes the Ducks. The Ducks soon become the terror of the league, and despite pressure from his boss and friends Gordon sticks with his new-found principles. He and his team sneak into the playoffs, resulting in a final confrontation with Reilly and the Hawks.

CAUTION: There is minimal sport violence (body-checks, pucks in the head) and at the film's climax, two of the Hawks are ordered to knock the Ducks' star player out of the game. (He is viciously cross-checked into the goal post and taken out on a stretcher.) In one scene the boys ogle some discarded *Sports Illustrated* swimsuit issues and make generally rude comments.

GO: In an interview, Estevez indicated that he wanted to make a film that his own children could see, and he has succeeded. This is a rousing Cinderella sports epic, in which the sad-sack team effects a miraculous turn-around and rises to become champions. There are few suprises, but this a welcome entry for the six and up crowd.

MOM AND DAD SAVE THE WORLD

Warner Bros
1992
88 minutes
Directed by: Greg Beeman
Starring: Teri Garr, Eric Idle,
    Kathy Ireland, Jeffrey Jones,
    Jon Lovitz, Wallace Shawn
OFRB rating: PG
MPAA rating: PG

Tod, Emperor of Spengo, planet of idiots, has plans to destroy the planet Earth. But even as their visual detectors zero in on Woodland Hills, California (Earth's most vulnerable spot), Tod sees what he believes to be the most beautiful woman he has ever seen, frumpy Marge Nelson exercising beside the pool in her sweats. The nefarious Tod decides to delay the destruction of Earth for a single day, while he kidnaps the object of his affections. Meanwhile, Marge and her chronic complainer of a husband, Dick, are preparing for a fun anniversary weekend, but before they get very far, Tod has beamed the Nelsons across the galaxy. Marge is taken to a gilded tower and pampered in preparation for her upcoming wedding, while Dick is tossed in the dungeon. Thanks to Marge, Dick eventually escapes in a weird little aircraft. When he is shot down in the desert, he meets some not-very-intelligent tribesmen with whom he organizes a resistance. Using subterfuge only a moron would fall for, Dick and his followers enter Tod's fortress, rescue Marge and save the world; or rather, they would have saved the world, if it had ever really been in danger in the first place. And they have some great photos of their trip.

CAUTION: In one scene, Dick, bound and gagged, is jolted with electric current, and in another, guards surround him and punch him.

GO: Despite the few above-mentioned concerns, this is a perfect film for seven-year-olds, especially boys.

THE MOON STALLION

BBC
1985
95 minutes
Directed by: Dorothea Brooking
Starring: James Green, David Haig, Sarah Sutton
MPAA rating: no rating given

While accompanying her father on an archaeological dig in northern England, young blind Diana Purwell encounters the Moon Stallion, a magnificent wild white horse with whom she shares a strange, almost psychic relationship. The horse, it turns out, is the servant of the lunar goddess Diana, and it's being hunted down by Professor Purwell's patron, Sir George Mortenhurze, who wishes to exploit its tremendous power. The Moon Stallion engages Diana in a dangerous and mysterious adventure with mythological repercussions.

CAUTION: Sir George Murtenhurze dies, leaving behind his teenage daughter (Diana's friend) who is very upset. At the film's climax, an evil antagonist is stomped to death by the Stallion.

■

THE MOUSE AND THE MOTORCYCLE

Strand VCI
1986
42 minutes
Directed by: Ron Underwood
Starring: Mimi Kennedy, Thom Sharp, Phillip Walker, Ray Walston
MPAA rating: no rating given

When the Gridleys arrive at the Mountainview Inn, eight-year-old Keith discovers that he has no one to play with. He does, however, have a couple of great toys, the best of which is a snazzy model motorcycle. The moment Keith leaves the room Ralph, a mouse who lives at the inn, tries it on for size and almost immediately becomes trapped in a garbage can. Sure he'll be thrown out with the trash, Ralph is relieved to be discovered by Keith, and the two become friends. With Keith's blessing, Ralph races around the inn and, despite his friend's warnings, loses the bike. Keith is upset; however, even though he is ill, he forgives Ralph for his carelessness. Then Keith becomes progressively sicker, and the required medicine is not available. But Ralph remembers having seen some in a cubbyhole in the inn, and after an epic search, finds the medicine and borrows Keith's toy ambulance to pick it up. And in a last happy scene, the motorcycle is discovered in a bin full of dirty laundry, and Keith generously gives it to Ralph for keeps. See our review for the sequel, *Runaway Ralph*. Based on a novel by Beverly Cleary.

AGES 6 TO 10

GO: This film features a lively, humorous story and absolutely superb pixilation.

■

THE MYSTERIOUS ISLAND

1961
101 minutes
Directed by: Cy Endfield
Starring: Michael Callan,
   Michael Craig, Joan Greenwood,
   Herbert Lom
MPAA rating: unrated

In 1865 five men escape from a Confederate prison in a hot air balloon and are wrecked over a supposedly deserted volcanic island. They are soon joined by two woman who survive a shipwreck and together they must battle some bizarre creatures, including a giant crab, a giant bee and a chick large enough to ride on. They find that these animal anomalies are the product of the infamous Captain Nemo's experimentation. And they must make an agreement with Nemo in order to escape the island before the volcano erupts. Special effects by Ray Harryhausen.

CAUTION: Pirates are shot and some people are lost at sea. There are skeletons. Nemo is crushed by a falling beam and dies with his eyes open. And for the most part the women in this film wear scanty clothes and run around being help-less.

GO: It's a great adventure film that holds up well for young viewers who are interested in an exciting movie that isn't too scary.

THE MYSTERY OF THE MILLION DOLLAR HOCKEY PUCK

Dal Productions
1975
89 minutes
Directed by: Jean Lafleur,
   Peter Svatek
Starring: Angele Knight,
   Michael Macdonald,
   Jean-Louis Millette
OFRB rating: PG

Pierre, a promising young hockey player who adores the Montreal Canadiens, lives with his sister, Catou, at the Chicoutimi Orphanage. One day, he is sent to the florist's to pick up some daffodils, but he forgets his wallet in the shop and returns to overhear the details of a sinister plot. Gangsters, operating out of the back of the shop, plan to smuggle a fortune in stolen diamonds into the United States inside one of the Canadiens' team hockey pucks. Startled, Pierre knocks over a flowerpot, and in his haste to get away, leaves his wallet behind again. Unable to convince the nuns of the trouble afoot and with the gangsters hot on his trail, Pierre collects his sister and gets ready to run. The gangsters arrive at the same moment, and the resourceful children wait until the gangsters have gone inside then climb into the back of their truck. And so, as stowaways, they begin their trek to Quebec City where they beat the gangsters to the jewels. Finally, during the confusion of a narrow escape at a Canadiens-Detroit Red

Wings hockey game, the million dollar puck ends up on the ice in the middle of the action.

GO: This is a sweet film, exciting without violence, and great for young mystery fans. Pierre, initially worried about bringing his sister along, learns to appreciate her foresight and courage.

NANCY DREW: THE MYSTERY OF THE DIAMOND TRIANGLE (Vol. 2)

MCA
1977
47 minutes
Directed by: Noel Black
Starring: Pamela Sue Martin,
    George O'Hanlon, Jean Rasey
MPAA rating: no rating given

AGES 6 TO 10

When trying for the coveted Diamond Triangle Award for airplane pilot excellence, Nancy Drew and her friend George see an automobile run off the road. But in their resulting investigation they find no trace of the car, and they learn that the road has been closed for a long time. Determined to unravel the mystery, Nancy finds the owner of the car — a car that he thought was locked up in his garage, but which now appears to have been stolen. Unfortunately, Morgan's car was a restored antique and the book value of the insurance is nowhere near the value of the car. And while Nancy's father, a lawyer, works out the insurance claim, the sheriff suspects Morgan of trying to swindle the insurance company (particularly when parts that were supposedly used to improve the

vehicle are found still in the garage). In the end, when Nancy sets out to prove that Morgan has been framed, she discovers that a ring of car thieves have been operating in cahoots with an upstanding member of the community.

CAUTION: The music is a bit intense, and there is pushing and shoving.

GO: Nancy is shown as an intelligent, capable young woman.

Titles in the series are:
The Mystery of Pirate's Cove (Vol. 1)
A-Haunting We Will Go (Vol. 3)
Secret of the Whispering Walls (Vol. 4)
The Mystery of the Fallen Angels (Vol. 5)
The Mystery of the Ghostwriters' Cruise (Vol. 6)
The Mystery of the Solid Gold Kicker (Vol. 7)
Nancy Drew's Love Match (Vol. 8)

GO: The Nancy Drew series is, from a violence standpoint, quite mild. Some episodes contain moderately intense scenes of Nancy being held captive, and the viewer can generally count on a chase scene or two per episode.

THE NEVERENDING STORY

Warner Bros.
1984
94 minutes
Directed by: Wolfgang Petersen
Starring: Noah Hathaway,
    Patricia Hayes, Barrett Oliver,
    Tami Stronach
OFRB rating: F—Frightening
    scenes
MPAA rating: PG

When a bookseller in a queer little bookshop warns Bastian not to read *The Neverending Story* (for those who read it become strangely intertwined with the destiny of the characters in the story), Bastian is intrigued and steals the book away to read in the school attic. Sure enough, as he reads, Bastian is drawn into the world of Fantasia, a land that is slowly being destroyed by an evil force called The Nothing. Fantasia's only hope is the Empress, who is dying with her world and who chooses a boy named Atreyu to be the last great warrior. As Bastian reads, he and Atreyu become one, and together they discover that the reason Fantasia is dying is that people no longer use their imaginations. And they also discover that the only way to save Fantasia is for Bastian (a human boy) to give the Empress a new name; which, at the last possible moment, Bastian does, and Fantasia rises again. Based on the book by Michael Ende.

CAUTION: There is an intense scene when a storm rages against the attic. Atreyu's horse drowns in a bog of quicksand and Atreyu cannot save him. (Although the horse does reappear at the end of the film when Fantasia is recreated.) Atreyu stabs a creature and when he withdraws his hand there is blood. Creatures of Fantasia at first appear grotesque although they become more endearing as the film progresses. In one scene, rays from the Southern Oracle's eyes pierce a knight and his visor flips up revealing a charred and bloody face. Bastian's mother is dead and he reads in order to escape the reality of his relationship with his father. Fans of the book be warned: the film is based only on one third of the original text.

GO: One of the best films available in the fantasy film genre, this is the story of courage and the power of imagination.

■▲

THE NEVERENDING STORY II: THE NEXT CHAPTER

Warner Bros.
1989
90 minutes
Directed by: George Miller
Starring: Clarissa Burt,
   Jonathan Brandis,
   John Wesley Shipp
MPAA rating: PG

At the advent of his second adventure into Fantasia, Bastian is suffering from a crisis of courage. He's desperate to make the school swim team, but the very first test is a dive from the tower, and when he gets up to the top, he finds he's looking out over a huge waterfall, thundering into an abyss. So, the next day he goes into K. Koreander's shop, looking for a book on how to jump from very great heights. But when he sees *The Neverending Story* he changes his mind and decides to take that instead. Bastian finds a safe place and begins to read. And he enters Fantasia again, this time on a mission to save the childlike Empress. He finds that he has the power to wish for anything he chooses. But is unaware that every time he makes a wish, Xayide, the sorceress of emptiness, will steal one of his memories until he has forgotten his world, and his mission. In the end, through the love he bears for his friend Atreyu, Bastian breaks Xayide's spell and triumphs. But a final test of courage remains: the giant waterfall of his vision. (This video also contains the G-rated

Bugs Bunny cartoon *Box-office Bunny*.)

CAUTION: Xayide's minions are hostile beetle-like giants and they may be too intense for small children. Also, the sophisticated nature of the plot may leave young viewers baffled. This sequel to *The Neverending Story* is loosely based on more of the book by Michael Ende, but it still doesn't tell the complete story.

GO: All in all, this is an engaging fantasy film with strong themes of courage, resistance to temptation and reconciliation.

■ ▲

THE NEW ADVENTURES OF BLACK BEAUTY

Morningstar Entertainment Inc.
1960
70 minutes
Directed by: John Crone
 Starring: Stacy Dorning,
  William Lucas, Amber McWilliams
MPAA rating: No rating given

When Victoria Denning's widowed father returns from Australia with his new wife, Jenny, and her beloved black horse, Beauty, Victoria finds a friend. The two women are very much alike — energetic, independant and head-strong, with a great love and knowledge of horses (Jenny is a vet). Then tragedy strikes. Victoria's father (on his return to Australia to prepare them a home) is reported lost at sea, and the women, refusing to believe that this could be true, journey to the homestead to begin the search for him. They find their property in disrepair and only a young man named Manfred to help them. Then one night a mysterious

black horse arrives. Vicky presumes its appearance is an answer to her wish for a horse of her own just like Black Beauty, but it turns out that he belongs to an unfriendly neighbour. This story is continued in a newly released video called *The Further Adventures of Black Beauty*. Based loosely on characters from the book by Anna Sewell.

CAUTION: The horse which is supposedly the original Black Beauty, now over twenty years old, dies. This is an episode from the made-for-television series and is not a complete story in itself. Viewers never find out if Vicky finds her father or if she keeps the new Black Beauty from falling back into the hands of his cruel owner and the loose ends are bound to frustrate some young viewers. Commercial blacks disrupt the story even more.

GO: Updated music and beautiful scenery of England in the 1900s make this British production appealing. There are two good female role models in this film — Jenny is a veterinarian and the blacksmith is also a woman. Vicky and her stepmother Jenny have an excellent relationship. Parts of the film were shot on location in New Zealand.

NEWSIES

Walt Disney Home Video
1992
121 minutes
Directed by: Kenny Ortega
Staring: Christian Bale,
 Max Cansella, Robert Duvall,
 David Moscow, Bill Pullman
MPAA rating: PG

Newsies is a full-scale big-budget musical, set in New York City in the early part of this century. During a newspaper war between Joseph Pulitzer and William Randolph

Hearst, Pulitzer decides to beef up his profits by increasing the wholesale cost of the paper to the newsies (the disadvantaged youngsters who peddle his papers on the street). This triggers a full-scale revolt among the boys, who, led by ringleaders Jack Kelly and Dave Jacobs, and aided by reporter Bryan Denton, stand up to the newspaper baron and his henchmen, no matter how tough the going gets.

CAUTION: There is one close-up of a face being punched, and there are fist-fights between goons and newsies, in which noses and lips bleed.

GO: This is a terrific film about kids making a difference and can also serve as an introduction to the historical reality of child labour. The song-and-dance sequences are spectacularly staged.

THE NIGHT TRAIN TO KATHMANDU

Paramount Home Video
1988
102 minutes
Directed by: Robert Wiemer
Starring: Eddie Castrodad,
   Milla Jovovich, Pernell Roberts
MPAA rating: No rating given

Fourteen-year-old Lily McLeod's parents are Princeton archaeology professors, and when they agree to spend a year in Kathmandu in Nepal, Lily and her nine-year-old brother Andrew must go with them. Lily is unhappy to be leaving her school and her friends, but on the last leg of their journey (on the night train to Kathmandu) she meets a handsome, mysterious young man named Johar, who is aboard without a ticket. Lily saves him from being thrown off the train by telling the guard that he is her servant — much to Johar's indignation. Lily and Andrew then persuade their parents to allow Johar to accompany them to Nepal, where he agrees to work for them. But Johar is more than he seems; in fact, he is a prince of the mythical Invisible City (a city in the remote Himalayas which appears periodically for a single moon, allowing one of royal birth to leave and experience our world). In Kathmandu, the City is regarded as legend, but two academics, Hadley-Smithe and Dewan, both suspect that the city is very real. With the arrival of Johar they quickly deduce his true identity. At the film's climax, Johar must find his way back to the Invisible City before the new moon appears. In the end, it's up to Lily alone to help her friend return before he perishes.

CAUTION: Lily's parents won't listen to her when she goes to them for help.

GO: The film is a little slow moving in the middle, but it's an excellent attempt to make an interesting family film in an exotic location. There is no violence or swearing.

✗ OLD YELLER

Walt Disney Home Video
1957
84 minutes
Directed by: Robert Stevenson
Starring: Chuck Connors, Tommy
   Kirk, Dorothy McGuire,
   Fess Parker
MPAA rating: G

In the 1860s, a Texas pioneer leaves his wife and sons, Travis and Arliss, for four months while he goes to bring in a herd of cattle. While he is away, a stranger comes to the homestead searching for his "big yeller dog." He finds the dog, but recognizing Arliss's affection for Yeller, allows the family to keep it. The dog proves to be a protector and a playmate to both boys. However, after saving Travis from an attack by a rabid wolf, the dog develops "hydrophobia" and must be shot. The dog is replaced by one of its pups, but the boys know it will never grow to be like Old Yeller.

✗STOP: In spite of the G rating, this is a tough film for animal lovers. Old Yeller has vicious fights with wild pigs and a wolf; he gets covered with blood and in one scene has to be sewn up. Travis shoots a buck for dinner (the deer is shown falling) and he carries the dead animal home. And Travis also has to shoot Old Yeller because he contracts rabies, which makes for a very sad but realistic ending.

GO: Featuring a stable household and loving and sensitive relationships, this film shows just how hard the pioneers worked. The children are encouraged to "look for something good to replace the bad" when Old Yeller dies.

■▲

PADDLE-TO-THE-SEA

NFB
1966
28 minutes
Directed by: Bill Mason
MPAA rating: no rating given

An Indian boy, who lives in a small village north of Lake Superior, has a vision during the long winter nights,

and painstakingly begins to carve and paint the small wooden figure of a man in a canoe. On the bottom of the hull, he inscribes the request: I am Paddle-to-the-Sea, please put me back in the water. Then the boy leaves Paddle-to-the-Sea on the ice of a frozen river. With the spring, the ice melts, and the little wooden figure's epic journey through the great lakes begins. Paddle-to-the-Sea has many adventures, and though it occasionally seems that his journey will not be completed, he reaches the sea at last. There he is found by a lighthouse-keeper, who respectfully touches up the wooden man's faded paint, and sends him out into the Atlantic on a new journey to unknown shores.

GO: Holling C. Holling's children's story is beautifully interpreted in this Oscar-nominated short, a travelogue which has charmed and educated generations of young children.

■

THE PARENT TRAP

Walt Disney Home Video
1961
127 minutes
Directed by: David Swift
Starring: Brian Keith, Hayley Mills, Maureen O'Hara
MPAA rating: not rated

Susan, a rough-and-tumble girl, lives with her father on a ranch in California, while Sharon, who is more of an artist, lives with her upper-class mother in Boston. When the two meet at an exclusive summer camp for girls, they instantly loathe each other, which is ironic . . . because they look exactly alike. But this doesn't stop them from playing tricks on each other, and one prank leads to another, escalating in severity until a war is raging. Finally, the exasperated camp directors sentence the pair to the ultimate punishment: bunking together until they sort out their differences. Before very long, the two discover that they actually quite like one another, and as their friendship deepens and they learn more about each other's pasts, they come to a startling revelation: they are twins, the children of estranged parents who separated while the girls were infants, each parent raising one child. The girls vow to reconcile their parents, and to this end, switch identities and set in motion their grand conspiracy to ruin their father's upcoming marriage to a super-sophisticated social climber, and get their parents together again.

CAUTION: This film can be a problem for children of separated parents who are clinging to the fantasy that their parents will reconcile.

GO: *The Parent Trap* is one of the all-time great Disney classics, a consumate blend of slapstick humour, childhood antics and rekindled romance suitable for everyone from the age of five and up.

✗ PEE-WEE'S BIG ADVENTURE

Warner Brothers
1985
92 minutes
Starring: Elizabeth Daly,
   Mark Holton, Paul Reubens
Directed by: Tim Burton
MPAA rating: PG

Pee-Wee Herman lives a kid's fantasy. He has his own house, jam-packed with amazing toys. And his prize possession is his bicycle. Francis Buxton, a rich spoiled brat, wants it for his own, but Pee-Wee won't sell at any price. Then, horror of horrors, Pee-Wee's bike disappears! Of course, Francis is the prime suspect, but breaking into the Buxton mansion and threatening Francis doesn't get Pee-Wee anywhere. And after a huge unsuccessful search, Pee-Wee trudges through the rain to a bogus fortune teller, who tells him that his bike is in the basement of the Alamo. So Pee-Wee hitchhikes to Texas, accepting rides from a convict and a ghostly truck driver. After befriending a waitress at a truck stop and repeatedly dodging her jealous boy friend, he finally finds his bike on a set at Warner Brothers Studios. Pee-Wee steals the bike and leads his pursuers on a wild chase, stopping only to rescue pets from a burning pet store. Impressed by his heroism, the studio executives reward Pee-Wee by giving him back his bike and making a movie out of his story. And all of the friends he made along the way come to the drive-in to see it.

✗**STOP:** Large Marge, the ghostly truck driver, suddenly transforms into a horrible bug-eyed apparition right at the climax of her story. This is done in claymation.

CAUTION: There are a couple of incidents of innuendo, subtle enough that most little children will not pick up on them, and in one scene, Pee-Wee has a nightmare in which dark, evil clowns tear apart his bike — one even pulls down his mask to reveal a leering face.

GO: This is an irresistably charming and infectiously humorous film, as popular with cult fans as it is with children. The more you watch it, the funnier it gets.

▲

THE PHANTOM TOLLBOOTH

MGM
1969
90 minutes
Directed by: Chuck Jones,
    Abe Levitow (animation),
    David Monahan (live action)
Starring: Butch Patrick
Starring the voices of: Mel Blanc,
    Hans Conreid, June Foray
MPAA rating: G

Nine-year-old Milo is always bored. When he's in school, all he wants is to get out, and when he's not in school, he just wants to be somewhere else. Then one afternoon he hears the sound of something heavy drop, and turns to see that a large striped package has appeared in his bedroom. There is a label on the package which says: If bored, pull tab marked tab and step back! Milo does, and in so doing becomes the proud owner of one Turnpike Tollbooth, which comes equipped with a galvanized automobile, a map and a gramophone horn which instructs him to select a destination. Sceptical, Milo picks "The Castle in the Air," and upon entering the gate turns immediately into a cartoon. He proceeds forward and finds himself in an animated world on the road to Dictionopolis. There he has a number of exciting adventures, encountering a host of eccentric characters along the way (including a watchdog with a real watch in his stomach, named Tock). He discovers that in this world, you have to *think* your way out of difficulties, and he discovers that, in

spite of the fact that he hasn't had much practice thinking, he actually has a flair for it. Based on a book by Norton Juster.

GO: This is an excellent production of a clever story that emphasizes the necessity (and fun) of education.

■

POLLYANNA

Walt Disney Home Video
1960
134 minutes
Directed by: David Swift
Starring: Richard Egan,
    Hayley Mills, Agnes Moorehead,
    Jane Wyman
MPAA rating: G

Pollyanna Whittier is the irrepressibly cheerful orphan of a church missionary, who is sent to live with her stern aunt, Polly Harrington. The matriarch and virtual dictator of the small mid-western town of Harrington, Aunt Polly's control is so complete that she even shapes the content of the Reverend Ford's sermons. But before very long, Pollyanna's sheer joy of living begins to rub off on everybody, breaking the spell of habitual misery which has fallen over the town. Coinciding with Pollyanna's arrival is the reappearance of her aunt's old suitor, Dr. Chilton. (Their long-lost love, as it turns out, is the source of Aunt Polly's bitterness.) And when the doctor learns that the town badly needs a new orphanage, and that Aunt Polly refuses to allow one to be built, the issue becomes a symbol of her control over the community, and he urges the people of Harrington to stand up to her. The townsfolk plan a fund-raising affair, which Aunt Polly fights tooth and nail. But it's Pollyanna's inadvertent influence on the Reverend Ford that turns the tide, and with him on their side, the townsfolk go ahead with their celebration. Aunt Polly angrily forbids Pollyanna to attend the party, but the child climbs out the window and down a tree. On her return, Pollyanna falls and is seriously hurt, and it's only then that Aunt Polly realizes how much she has come to love the child. After the accident, Pollyanna is paralysed; worse, she has lost the will to live. But the entire town comes to wish her well, and return the love she has instilled in them; thus encouraged, Pollyanna's recovery is assured. Based on the novel by Eleanor H. Porter.

CAUTION: Pollyanna's fall from the third floor eaves is agonizingly realistic, and her subsequent black depression may be very upsetting for some children.

GO: A wonderful film for any age. Mills won an Honorary Academy Award for the Most Outstanding Juvenile Performance of the Year.

■

PRANCER

Orion
1990
103 minutes
Directed by: John Hancock
Starring: Sam Elliott, Rebecca Harrell, Cloris Leachman
OFRB rating: F
MPAA rating: G

Nine-year-old Jessica, daughter of an embittered, down-on-his-luck farmer, takes a short-cut through the woods where she sees a great reindeer that allows her to go up and pet it. But no one believes her story until the next night, when she and her father are driving through the snowy forest and their truck hits the reindeer. Realizing that the animal is wounded, Jessica's father takes out his rifle to mercifully kill the deer. But Jessica begins to scream, momentarily distracting him, and when he looks around again, the creature is gone. At home, Jessica dreams of the reindeer falling from the sky, and when she looks out her window, she sees that the barn door is open, and soon discovers that Prancer (who is indeed one of Santa's reindeer) has taken refuge inside. She keeps him hidden, bringing him feed, and even gets a vet to come over and look at him. And all the while, Jessica plans to take the lost reindeer up to the ridge on Christmas Eve, where Santa can come and get him. But word gets out, and one day Jessica returns home to find an army of people gawking at Prancer. Her father sells the deer, and Prancer is taken away and caged as a Christmas exhibit. Jessica and her brother try to set Prancer free, but during the attempt Jessica falls and is badly hurt. Instead of escaping, Prancer stays by her side, and saves her life. In an emotional final scene, Jessica's father expresses his love for her, and when he buys Prancer back, they go together to the ridge and release him.

CAUTION: The scene in the woods is lonely and scary, and many young viewers will be upset when the truck strikes the reindeer.

GO: *Prancer* features a stirring theme of hope despite poverty and adversity.

THE PRINCE AND THE PAUPER

Walt Disney Home Video
1962
120 minutes
Directed by: Don Chaffey
Starring: Donald Houston,
    Laurence Naismith, Sean Scully,
    Guy Williams
MPAA rating: G

Based on Mark Twain's classic novel of social injustice, *The Prince and the Pauper* is the story of two boys who look exactly alike. One, Edward Tudor, is born into kingly wealth and privilege, while the other, Tom Canty, is born into the most abject poverty sixteenth century London could offer. One day, when Tom goes to the palace to try to catch a glimpse of the prince, and the guards rough him up, the outraged prince orders that Tom be brought in to his apartments for a sumptuous meal. While he is there, the boys realize how much alike they look, and devise a clever plan: they will switch clothes and get a taste of each other's life. But Tom, subjected to an endless succession of state duties, hasn't been in the prince's shoes for an hour before he's ready to trade back. And worse, no one will believe him when he tells them he isn't the prince; they simply think he's mad. Meanwhile, Edward has disappeared into the streets of London, only to end up in Tom's evil home, where he soon knows that he too has had enough of the charade. But it isn't until a gallant knight, Sir Miles, becomes convinced that

Edward really is the king that each boy is returned to his rightful place.

Versions of this story are also available from:
Media Home Entertainment
Storytime Video
Walt Disney Home Video (starring
    Mickey Mouse)
Warner Home Video

CAUTION: Tom's father bludgeons a priest and the abuse in his slovenly home is frightful. There are a number of swordfights.

GO: Probably the most accessible of all the versions of this tale, this film presents a fascinating look at the times, with a lot of action thrown in.

■

PRINCE CASPIAN AND THE VOYAGE OF THE DAWNTREADER

Public Media Video
1988
165 minutes
Directed by: Alex Kirby
Starring: Warwick Davi,
    John Hallam, Jonathan R. Scott,
    David Thwaite, Sophie Wilcox
MPAA rating: no rating given

Prince Caspian begins in the Land of Narnia, where Caspian, nephew of King Miraz, is the heir to the throne; however, when the Queen gives birth to a baby, Caspian is informed by a loyal friend that his life is in danger. He flees the castle, and in the forest encounters a multitude of talking animals (both familiar and mythological), all bent on recovering their kingdom from the nasty King Miraz (who, as it turns out, also murdered Caspian's father). The forest creatures rally around Prince Caspian, but a surprise attack by Miraz's army puts their entire cause in jeopardy. They are forced to hide in a cavern, and there Caspian blows the horn which will summon help. Sure enough, Lucy, Susan, Peter and Edmund are whisked from an English train station into the land of Narnia. There the children encounter Aslan, and join up with Caspian in time to triumph in battle over the evil Miraz. And after establishing the Prince as King Caspian X of Narnia, Aslan returns Lucy, Susan, Peter and Edmund to the train station.

The Voyage of the Dawntreader begins with the arrival of Lucy and Edmund at the country house of their unpleasant cousin Eustace. Soon all three are transported through the beautiful picture of a ship and plunked into an ocean in Narnia. They are taken aboard the ship and are greeted by Caspian himself, now a number of years older. The young king is on a mission to find the seven lost lords of Narnia, who were banished by evil king Miraz, and to do it he plans to sail to the Lone Islands, and after that into uncharted waters. After a series of fantastic adventures, they find five of the seven lords. The last two, however, can only be awakened if one brave traveller will journey beyond the end of the earth to Aslan's country. And after much debate, it is agreed that the brave mouse Reepicheep will make the fateful trip. He sets out in a small boat, and Lucy, Edmund and Eustace are returned home.

CAUTION: Like the first film in the series, *The Lion, the Witch and the Wardrobe, Prince Caspian and the Dawntreader* is leisurely paced, and may leave the little ones far behind. It doggedly follows the narrative, lending credence to the notion that the best film adaptations of books are not those which stick religiously to the text.

Also, the fighting scenes in the Narnia series are suprisingly violent (particularly considering the understated nature of the rest of the production).

GO: These videos succeed in capturing the spirit of the C.S. Lewis books and are richly produced. This is a BBC Television production in association with Wonderworks.

■

THE PRINCESS BRIDE

Nelson Home Entertainment
1987
98 minutes
Directed by: Rob Reiner
Starring: André the Giant,
    Cary Elwes, Christopher Guest,
    Mandy Patinkin, Chris Sarandon,
    Wallace Shawn, Robin Wright
MPAA rating: PG

When a young boy is sick in bed, his grandfather reads him a story called *The Princess Bride*. And as he reads, the action unfolds as if through the child's mind's eye. The story begins on a farm in a far away place where Buttercup and her desperately poor attendant Westley grow to love each other. But before they marry, Westley decides to go to sea to seek his fortune. And when his ship is captured by the Dread Pirate Roberts (who takes no prisoners), the word is that Westley is dead and the grief-stricken Buttercup is subsequently betrothed to not-so-nice Prince Humperdinck. While she is out on a ride one day, Buttercup encounters three strange characters, the diminutive Vizzini, the giant Fezzik, and the master swordsman Inigo Montoya. It turns out that the three are agents, intent on starting a war with Gilder, the country across the sea, and they kidnap Buttercup, sailing away in a small ship. But they are pursued across eel-infested waters and even up the Cliffs of Insanity by a mysterious masked man in black, who defeats Inigo in a sword fight, Fezzik in a duel of strength, and finally Vizzini in a battle of wits. The masked man is revealed as none other than Westley, back from the dead and with an amazing (and hilarious) tale to tell. But the adventure is not over yet as the evil Prince pursues them. Westley and Buttercup must brave the Fire-forest and the Rodents of Unusual Size. And finally, Westley must come back from the dead, join new allies and take Prince Humperdink's castle. Based on the book by William Goldman.

CAUTION: Some images may frighten small children. Hideous Screaming Eels rush at Buttercup to devour her and Westley is tortured with a strange machine and writhes in pain as the life is sucked out of him. In an intense battle Wesley stabs a huge rat repeated with a sword. And the final confrontation between Inigo and his arch-foe Count Rugen is violent and bloody (swords pierce arms and legs, and slash faces with blood).

"BUT MOM ALWAYS LETS US WATCH THIS!"

GO: Despite the cautions, this is surely one of the great films of the eighties, full of wry humour and wit and splendid performances including a vignette with Billy Crystal and Carol Kane. An enchanting tale which can be enjoyed by viewers of a wide range of ages over and over again.
■ ▲

THE QUEST

MCA
1986
93 minutes
Directed by: Brian Trenchard-Smith
Starring: Henry Thomas,
Tamsin West
OFRB rating: F
MPAA rating: PG

In a bog in Australia, fourteen-year-old Cody and his friend Wendy witness some mysterious occurrences which, according to an old Aboriginal folk legend, are caused by the spirit of "Donkegin." Cody is compelled to uncover the mystery and his inquisitiveness gets him into dangerous trouble when he's trapped underwater in the bog. Then it's up to Wendy to unravel the mystery and save him.

CAUTION: The children come upon a gruesome skeleton of Cody's old friend, and when Cody disappears underwater, he is gone so long that everyone presumes that he has drowned (this is not a movie for children who are afraid of water). There is one instance of coarse language.

GO: The children in this film are intelligent, inventive, resourceful and courageous.

RAGS TO RICHES

Studio
1986
96 minutes
Directed by: Bruce Seth Green
Starring: Joseph Bologna, Tisha
  Campbell, Blanca DeGarr, Kimiko
  Gelman, Bridget Michele,
  Douglas Seale, Heidi Zeigler
MPAA rating: no rating given

Nick Foley is a self-made
millionaire. He has a mansion, a
beautiful fiancée and a devoted
butler. Now he's ready for that last
move which will take him to the top
of the heap — the Big Merger. But
his prospective partner, billionaire
Baldwin, has problems with Nick's
image. Meanwhile, across town at
the orphanage, the six girls in Room
204 have gained a reputation for
trouble, and since the orphanage is
about to go down the tubes, things
don't look good for the girls. But
they vow to stick together, and
when their leader, Rose, calls the
papers to advertise their plight,
Nick's right-hand man, Freddy, sees
an opportunity to turn Nick into a
family man by acquiring an instant
family. And so he does. But the girls
— feisty Rose, appearance-oriented
Diane, Nina (with a biker boyfriend),
Patty (with reading problems),
financial wizard Marva and tiny
Nicky — prove more than a handful.
The girls don't exactly fit in, and
Nick cynically plans to send them off
to a boarding school as soon as
they've served their purpose. But
despite himself, Nick grows to care
deeply for them. He starts to look
forward to Saturday outings with the
girls. And when Nina takes off with
her biker boyfriend, Nick goes
halfway across the country to get
her back. But when Nick's
scheming, jealous fiancée decides
to implement Nick's original plan to
send the girls away, the girls revolt
and destroy Nick's deal-signing
party, even ripping off Baldwin's
toupée. The girls are promptly
shipped back to the orphanage; that
is, until Nick suddenly realizes
where his priorities, and his heart,
lie.

CAUTION: There is one fight scene, in
which Nick takes on the bikers, but it's brief
and not too violent.

GO: This made-for-TV movie is a popular
little film, featuring the music of the girls
and their band.

THE RAILWAY CHILDREN

Thorn EMI
1970
104 minutes
Directed by: Lionel Jeffries
Starring: Jenny Agutter, Bernard
  Cribbins, Iain Cuthberston,
  Dinah Sheridan, Sally Thomsett,
  Gary Warren
MPAA rating: not rated

The Waterbury children, Roberta,
Phyllis and Peter, live in rural
Edgecombe Villa at the turn of the
century with their wonderful mother
and their father, who is simply
perfect. But when Christmas comes
and mysterious circumstances lead
to Mr. Waterbury's arrest by
Scotland Yard, things go from
perfect to horrid. The family moves
to a country house in Yorkshire, and
the house proves to be a drafty

affair, especially in the cold season. And despite Peter's best efforts (he steals coal from the local railway yard), their mother falls ill with influenza. The children must provide for themselves, and somehow get money for their mother's medication. Then salvation arrives, when the ingenious children befriend an elderly gentleman they have seen regularly, on a passing train. (He sends them a basket of food.) And when the children help avert a catastrophe by reporting a landslide on the tracks, they receive commendations for their efforts. Later, by accident, Bobbi discovers the truth about their father: he has been falsely arrested for selling state secrets and sentenced to five years in prison. In the end, the elderly gentleman works tirelessly to clear Mr. Waterbury's name, and the children's father is returned to them. Based on the story by E. Nesbit.

GO: This is an utterly delightful, charming and gentle film.
■ ●

THE RED BALLOON

Embassy Home Entertainment
    (Children's Treasures)
1956
34 minutes
Directed by: Albert Lamorisse
Starring: Pascal Lamorisse

This is the story of Pascal, a young French boy who, on his way to school, saves a red balloon from certain death by untangling its string from a lamppost. It soon becomes obvious that this is no ordinary balloon; it comes when he calls and Pascal doesn't even have to hold its string — it just follows him! But no one else seems to appreciate the balloon (he's not permitted to take it on the bus, to school or even into his house). And when, after a chase through the narrow streets of Paris, a gang of bullies uses slingshots to take turns shooting at the balloon, Pascal urges the balloon to go, but it will not leave him at the mercy of the bullies. After a well-aimed shot the balloon is done for. The air slowly leaves the beautiful red balloon and a bully delivers the final blow by stepping on it. Then something strange and magical happens: suddenly, all of the balloons in Paris fly from their owners' hands, passing over the rooftops in multicoloured splendour to converge around a delighted Pascal. He holds as many strings as he can in his little hands, and the balloons lift him up into the air for the ride of his life.

CAUTION: Because it had such a personality, and because the outcome is so unfair, the balloon's death will disturb some viewers.

GO: The film has no dialogue and can be followed purely as the story unfolds. The film also provides a delightful glimpse of Paris in the '50s.
●

✗ RETURN OF THE JEDI

CBS/Fox
1983
132 minutes
Directed by: Richard Marquand
Starring: Harrison Ford,
    Mark Hamill, Carrie Fisher,
    Billy Dee Williams
MPAA rating: PG

After liberating his friend Han Solo from his frozen state in the fortress of Jabba the Hutt, Luke Skywalker returns alone to the Dagobah system to resume his studies with Yoda. But Yoda informs Luke that his training is now complete and tells him that it's time for him to return to face Darth Vader. Meanwhile, the Imperial Forces under Vader's command race to complete the new Death Star near the forest moon of Endor. Luke joins his friends with the rebel fleet to prepare for a surprise attack. Their first priority is to travel to the surface of Endor and knock out the force field generator which guards the half-completed Death Star. But when they arrive on the forest moon, Luke and company lose the element of suprise when they encounter an Imperial patrol on rocket-sleds. Realizing that his presence (which Vader can sense) is jeopardizing the mission, Luke gives himself up in hopes of turning Vader from the Dark Side. And while the fighting reaches a frenzied climax, Luke is brought into the presence of the awful Emperor, where he must duel with Vader and avoid being brought over to the Dark Side himself.

✗STOP: Jabba the Hutt and his cronies delight as a girl is thrown into a pit to be eaten by a hideous, drooling monster — in fact, a number of bad guys fall to their deaths in similar fashion. Luke removes Vader's helmet to reveal his face (scarier in its anticipation than in its reality). And at the climax of the film, Vader's hand is cut off, and the evil Emperor repeatedly zaps Luke as he lies writhing on the ground in agony.

GO: A great finish to a now-classic trilogy, this is the one that features the teddy bear-like creatures, the Ewoks, and the chase scene through the forest, which is, without question, a special-effects landmark.

▲

THE RETURN OF THE KING

Solar Home Video
1991
96 minutes
Directed by: Jules Bass
Starring the voices of: Orson Bean,
   William Conrad, Hans Conreid,
   John Huston, Roddy McDowell
OFRB rating: not rated
MPAA rating: not rated

This effort, named after the third part of J.R.R. Tolkien's famous epic, begins with the Companions, Gandalf and the hobbits, Merry, Pippin, Samwise and Frodo, returning to Rivendell, home of the northern elves. There they meet Bilbo Baggins, who asks about the Companions' adventures and what has befallen his magic ring. Gandalf and the minstrel of Gondor then tell the tale, giving the viewer a brief synopsis of the first half of the original tale, and beginning it in earnest during the scene in the tower of Cirith Ungol. The orcs have captured Frodo, but Sam holds the Ring of Power, and he proceeds gamely into the grim fortress to rescue his friend. But first, he puts on the Ring, and wanders through a psychological morass of bombastic, megalomaniacal ravings and stinky songs. Meanwhile, Gandalf directs the defense of the city of Minas Tirith, which is besieged by hordes of orcs and eastern warriors under the terrifying King of the Ringwraiths. While the Riders of Rohan and Aragorn's forces relieve the siege of the city, Sam rescues Frodo and the pair proceed into the dreary land of Mordor. From there, the plot is straightforward. Frodo and Sam strike for smouldering Mount Doom, where the Ring is to be destroyed, while Gandalf, Aragorn and the Companions lead a host into certain death to distract the Dark Lord's omnipresent attention.

CAUTION: This is, as Tolkien himself described, a history of the War of the Ring, and it is filled with violent combat and images which may be frightening to young children. Also, it is probably necessary to have either read *The Lord of the Rings*, or have watched Ralph Bakshi's film of the same name, to make any real sense of this effort, synopsis notwithstanding. The songs, and there are lots of them, are the worst.

∎

✗ RETURN TO OZ

Walt Disney Home Video
1985
109 minutes
Directed by: Walter Murch
Starring: Fairuza Balk, Mott Clark,
   Jean Marsh, Nicol Williamson
MPAA rating: PG

Six months after her legendary visit to Oz, Dorothy Gayle is still going on about ruby slippers and scarecrows, and still no one believes her; moreover, she's having difficulty sleeping and her worried aunt finally takes her to the sanitorium of Dr. J.B. Worley, who is convinced that shock therapy is the answer. But Dorothy is terrified in the creepy mental institution, and escapes to the nearby river, where she (along with her pet chicken, Billina) is swept away in the torrent, and carried to Oz. There, Dorothy returns to the Emerald City, but finds it in ruins and soon realizes

that everyone there has been turned to stone. She learns that the Gnome King has conquered the Emerald City, and that only the sinister Princess Mombi knows where the Scarecrow is. When Dorothy approaches the Princess she is thrown into the tower prison. (Mombi, who changes her heads as it pleases her, intends to lock Dorothy in a tower for a few years until the girl's head is ready to be taken.) There, Dorothy meets a living Jack O'Lantern named Jack. Together they escape and make their way to the Gnome King's castle. But the evil king (who's terrified of eggs) has foreseen their coming, and draws them into the bowels of the mountain. Dorothy saves the Scarecrow and in the nick of time, Billina literally lays an egg, and Oz is saved. Based on characters and situations from *The Marvelous Land of Oz* and *Ozma of Oz* by L. Frank Baum.

✗STOP: The sanitorium is terrifing; thunder rattles in the distance as the lunatics shriek and wail. Mombi's head-changing scene is bizarre and even when she isn't wearing them they all have the ability to move and speak. And when the Wheelers, army of the Gnome King, reach the deadly desert, they turn to stone and crumble into sand. The final confrontation with the Gnome King is intensely frightening; gnomes grow out of every nook and cranny and threaten the fleeing companions.

CAUTION: Not to be compared with the musical feature *The Wizard of Oz*, The Disney Corporation printed a warning on the box: Portions of this material may not be suitable for small children. Parental discretion advised.

GO: This film is sombre, but the special effects are dazzling, with claymation by Will Vinton.

∎

✗ RING OF BRIGHT WATER

CBS/Fox
1969
109 minutes
Directed by: Jack Couffer
Starring: Virginia McKenna,
   Bill Travers
OFRB rating: F
MPAA rating: G

When London resident Graham Merrill notices an otter in a pet shop window, it seems to him that the otter has singled him out. So he buys the creature and names it Mij. Graham and the otter get along well, but Mij proves to be more than a handful. He tears around Graham's place, getting into and upsetting everything, and soon Graham is forced to customize his entire home to accommodate the animal. But this very reorganization brings Graham to the realization that both he and Mij are prisoners in London, and he decides to move to the west coast of Scotland to complete his life's dream of writing a book. The hijinks begin before he even gets there, as Mij gets away during the train ride and causes mass panic. And so otter and owner are put off the train, and forced to travel the rest of the way by bus. When they finally do arrive, Graham sees a young woman freeing a trapped swan, and later discovers that she is Mary, the town doctor. She and Graham soon become fast friends, and their lives become more and more intertwined, while Mij seizes the opportunity to find a mate of his own. Then, Mij is killed by a roadside worker and Graham is devastated by the news. Still, he begins to write, and one magical day, sees Mij's mate and three baby otters that he knows belong to Mij. And while watching the otters at play in Mij's pool, Graham receives the inspiration for a book.

✗STOP: Mij is killed.

GO: This is a gentle, leisurely paced film with quiet, thoughtful characters and a poignant envrionmental message.
■

ROAD TO AVONLEA

Astral Video
1989
45-57 minutes (each multi-episode
  volume)
Starring: Jackie Burroughs,
   Sarah Polley, Gema Zampogna

This television series is based on the Lucy Maud Montgomery stories of *The Story Girl*. In nineteenth century Prince Edward Island, little Sarah Stanley must go to live with her deceased mother's family while waiting for the outcome of her father's embezzlement scandal. Things do not start off well, but slowly Sarah makes friends and finds a new life in the lovely rural town of Avonlea. Volumes 1 and 2 are available in French.

Titles in the series are:
Aunt Abigail's Beau; Malcolm and the
  Baby (Vol. 4)
The Blue Chest of Arabella King; The
  Witch of Avonlea (Vol. 6)
Conversions; Felicity's Challenge (Vol. 5)
The Journey Begins: The Story Girl
  Earns Her Name (Vol. 1)
Nothing Endures But Change (Vol. 7)

Old Lady Lloyd; Proof of the Pudding
(Vol. 3)
Quarentine at Alexander Abrahams; The
Materialization of Duncan McTavish
(Vol. 2)
■ ▲

isn't until Ralph is back at home that
he is truly happy.

CAUTION: Ralph is caught by the cat.

RUNAWAY RALPH

Strand VCI
1986
42 minutes
Directed by: Ron Underwood
Starring: Conchata Ferrell, Sara
Gilbert, Kellie Martin, Summer
Phoenix, Fred Savage, Ray
Walston
MPAA rating: no rating given

In this combined live-action and
pixilated sequel to *The Mouse and
the Motorcycle*, a boy named
Garfield and his parents arrive to
spend the night at the Mountainview
Inn. (Garfield will be heading to
Happy Acres summer camp the
next day and he isn't exactly
thrilled.) Meanwhile, Ralph, a
motorcycle-riding mouse who lives
with his family at the inn, is
grounded for refusing to give rides
to the smaller mouse kids and
decides to run away. Eventually
Ralph ends up at Happy Acres
camp himself. And after a
frightening run-in with a ferocious
cat, Ralph is rescued by Garfield
and put in a cage. Ralph loathes the
green pellets Garfield brings him,
and realizes at once that he was
much better off at the inn. He
introduces himself to the surprised
Garfield, and though the two
become friends (Ralph outwits a cat
to clear Garfield's name when a
watch goes missing at the camp), it

✗ RUSSKIES

Lorimar
1987
100 minutes
Directed by: Rick Rosenthal
Starring: Peter Billingsley,
Whip Hubley, Leaf Phoenix
MPAA rating: PG

Three young Florida boys, Danny,
Adam and Jason, are fans of
Sergeant Slammer, a jingoistic
commie-bashing comic-book hero.
They have a secret clubhouse in an
abandoned bunker on the coast,
where they read Sergeant Slammer
with great relish, and fantasize
about a Communist invasion. Then
one day, after a storm, the boys
discover a ruined Russian raft and a
Russian code book. They also
discover an injured Soviet sailor
named Misha, hiding in their bunker.
When the boys try to warn their
parents about what they believe is a
Russian invasion, no one believes
them. So they return to the
clubhouse and try to decide what to
do with their real live Russian.
Danny and Jason leave Adam with
their prisoner, and while they go off
to assemble their "gear," Adam
befriends the sailor. And by the time
the others get back, Adam and
Misha are playing cards. Jason, too,
quickly become friends with Misha,
but Danny, whose grandfather was
killed by Russians in the Hungarian
revolution of 1956, is immovable.
Meanwhile, two Russian agents,

who also survived the wreck, turn up in town and rendezvous with a traitor, who is supposed to deliver them a device. And at the same time, the boys' parents finally begin to believe the boys' story. Soon the entire U.S. military is after Misha, and the boys must find a way to get Misha back to the rendezvous point before he is captured for real.

✗STOP: Some copies of *Russkies* include a trailer for *Return of the Living Dead II* at the beginning (go figure).

CAUTION: Many of the characters are rough marine types who use some coarse language and there is one punch-up, in which Misha and the boys take on an obnoxious off-duty soldier and his buddies. Shots are fired near the end of the film.

GO: This is an excellent film which explains that, although people may be perceived as evil enemies, they are simply human beings.

THE SEA GYPSIES

Warner Bros
1978
102 minutes
Directed by: Stewart Raffill
Starring: Mikki Jamison-Olsen,
    Robert Logan, Heather Rattray
MPAA rating: G

In order to bring himself and his daughters closer together, Travis McClean takes them on a voyage around the world in a large schooner (accompanied by an attractive female reporter named Kelly). They are well underway when the youngest daughter, Samantha, discovers a stowaway, Jesse, and agrees to keep mum

about it. But when Jesse falls overboard, Sam is forced to reveal the truth to get her family to go back for him. And then a tremendous gale blows up and dashes them onto the coast of a remote part of Alaska. Shipwrecked, they have lost almost everything in the storm and the going is tough at first. But gradually they begin to eke out an existence, and as the weeks pass, the group survives attacks by grizzlies and a killer whale. And finally, with the Arctic winter coming on, and knowing that they could never survive it, they work feverishly to build a boat that will take them to civilization. In the end, the lucky group is picked up by the Coast Guard.

CAUTION: Some of the animal attacks may be a little much for young viewers.

GO: This is an excellent adventure story without combat.

THE SECRET GARDEN

MGM/UA
1949
92 minutes
Directed by: Fred M. Wilcox
Starring: Margaret O'Brien,
    Dean Stockwell
MPAA rating: PG

When Mary Lennox's parents die of cholera, she must leave her home in colonial India to live with her uncle, Archibald Craven, in his sprawling mansion on the moors of England. Accompanied only by sullen servants, Mary is very unhappy at first, and she's frightened by the muffled screams which echo from somewhere in the huge, dark house. And when she finally sees her reclusive uncle before he leaves on a trip, and asks him why the house is so empty, he explains that his wife died ten years before (killed by a falling branch in the garden), and that ever since his only wish is to live alone. Unsure about what to do, Mary then explores the grounds, where she finds a secret garden, locked up and enclosed by high, vine-covered walls. Her investigations also lead her to the source of the mysterious screams — a room beyond a forbidden door, where her crippled cousin, Colin, lies in bed. But because Mary won't put up with Colin's nonsense, he finds new reason to live and begins to make efforts to get up and about. When Mary and Dickon (a local boy with a bright personality) find the key to the garden, they restore it to its original splendour, and take Colin out to see it. It is soon revealed that Colin isn't really crippled; rather, his father's desire to die had been transferred to him. And when Archibald returns home, intending to sell the house and leave with his son, he sees Colin walking, and his wish to escape from the house vanishes. This film is shot mostly in black and white, but goes to colour when Mary enters the garden.

Other versions of this story are available from:

Playhouse Video
Republic Pictures Home Video

CAUTION: When Mary is told of her parents' death, her grief is intensely expressed. Colin's screams are ghastly and frightening.

GO: O'Brien and Stockwell are brilliant, handling the sophisticated dialogue with impressive ease. The theme — the renewal of life and hope — is positive.

∎

✗ THE SECRET OF N.I.M.H

MGM/UA
1982
84 minutes
Directed by: Don Bluth
Starring the voices of:
    John Carradine, Dom DeLuise,
    Elizabeth Hartman, Derek Jacobi,
    Arthur Malet, Paul Shenar,
    Peter Strauss
MPAA rating: G

The rats of N.I.M.H. (The National Institute of Mental Health) were once ordinary animals, but a laboratory experiment has given them intellects comparable to humans. The story begins four years after their escape from the lab, as Nicodemus, an elder rat, recounts that a mouse named Jonathan Frisby has been killed while helping with the Plan. (The Plan revolves around the rats' preparations to become a self-sufficient farming community in the isolation of a nearby valley.) Meanwhile, Moving Day is also at hand for the widow, Mrs. Frisby, who is left alone with her children. (Every spring when the farmer begins to till the field the creatures who live there are forced to move.) But this year, grief for her lost husband is compounded by the fact that one of her sons is too sick to be moved. So, Mrs. Frisby braves a visit to the great owl for advice. The great owl tells her that in order to keep her son safe, her entire house must be moved, and that only the rats of N.I.M.H can do it. And when the rats learn that Mrs. Frisby is Jonathan Frisby's wife, they devise an ingenious plan to help. Meanwhile, the scientists have located the rats, and are planning to exterminate them. In the end, only Mrs. Frisby's courage of the heart, and the legacy of her departed husband, can save them. Based on Robert C. O'Brien's book *Mrs. Frisby and the Rats of N.I.M.H.*

✗STOP: In the climactic swordfight between one of the friendly rats and a dissident rat the struggle is extremely intense, and the blades leave visible cuts in the bodies of the victims. In the scene in the laboratory, the animals are in obvious distress, and the rats are given injections in their abdomens; it is scary.

CAUTION: The farmer's cat is very frightening and when the tractor starts up, the creatures of the field are in obvious panic. At one point, the Frisby house begins to sink into the mud, and the terrified children are suffocating.

GO: This film features brilliant animation, great voice-overs, and an important theme.

■

THE SEVENTH VOYAGE OF SINBAD

RCA/Columbia
1958
94 minutes
Directed by: Nathan Juran
Starring: Kathryn Grant,
  Kerwin Matthews
MPPA rating: G

On the island of Colossa, Sinbad encounters the evil black-robed magician, Sikura, who is pursued by a huge cyclops. And while Sinbad and friends hold off the cyclops, the magician produces a lamp and rubs it. Out comes a genie in the form of a small boy who protects the group.

But in the chaos that follows, the magician drops the lamp and it is recovered by the cyclops. Sikura wants to go back to retrieve it, but Sinbad adamantly refuses. (He is on a critical mission to deliver the princess Parisa to the Caliph of Bagdad, in order that the two should marry, thereby ensuring peace between their two kingdoms.) Once in Bagdad, the evil Sikura shrinks Parisa, then bargains with Sinbad. A secret potion will restore the princess to her normal size, but the critical ingredient (made from the shell of a Roc's egg) can only be found on the island of Colossa. With little choice, Sinbad sets sail for Colossa again, where he and a few of his men are promptly caught and locked up by the hungry cyclops. But the tiny princess picks the lock on their cage, and Sinbad escapes to find the desired ingredient. At this point Sikura betrays Sinbad, forcing a final confrontation in which, among other things, Sikura unleashes a huge dragon upon Sinbad and his men.

See reviews for these Sinbad movies:
The Golden Voyage of Sinbad
Sinbad and the Eye of the Tiger

THE SHAGGY D.A

Walt Disney Home Video
1976
90 minutes
Directed by: Robert Stevenson
Starring: Tim Conway, Dean
  Jones, Suzanne Pleshette,
  Keenan Wynn
MPAA rating: G

When Wilby Daniels discovers that crooks disguised as movers have stolen everything from his home, he decides to run for the office of District Attorney on an anti-corruption platform. The incumbent, Honest John Slade, is in cahoots with a gangster and together they are robbing the town blind; Wilby, meanwhile, has another encounter with the ring of Lucretia Borgia, which causes him to change into a dog right before his first campaign speech. To make matters worse, his enemies get control of the ring and gain the ability to turn him into a dog any time. They even get him sent to the pound, where he is sentenced to "the chamber." But Wilby arranges a jailbreak with his new dog buddies, and after the usual zany sequences all is set right. Sequel to *The Shaggy Dog*.

CAUTION: When Betty acts as Wilby's campaign manager, she is presented as clearly out of her depth, and comments are made intimating that her incompetence stems from the fact that she is a woman. In the dog pound, it is evident that the animals are all awaiting execution.

basement. During a clandestine visit to the town museum, Wilby meets the bizarre Professor Plumcut, who tells him all about shape-shifting. As he is leaving, Wilby knocks over a display of ancient artifacts, and returns home to discover that he has a strange ring in the cuff of his pants. He reads the inscription on the ring: *In Canis Corpore Transmuto* . . . and promptly turns into a dog. Now he's in a fix, and when the Professor explains that Wilby will drift in and out of the spell indefinitely, the shenanigans begin (particularly as he tries to conceal the truth from his dog-hating father). And when, in his altered form, Wilby learns that their neighbour is a spy, Wilby must take matters into his own hands . . . er, paws. This film is black and white.

CAUTION: Married life and women are not particularly well-represented — when Wilson Daniels eats breakfast he orders his wife around like he's some potentate. Wilby's friend Buzz is absolutely revolting in his treatment of young women and he lies to everyone.

GO: A fun film, this was the forerunner of a number of transformation films that followed (*Teen Wolf*, etc.). It seems Disney did it all before everyone else.

THE SHAGGY DOG

```
Walt Disney Home Video
1959
101 minutes
Directed by: Charles Barton
Starring: Annette Funicello,
   Jean Hagen, Tommy Kirk,
   Fred MacMurray
MPAA rating: no rating given
```

Wilby Daniels is a brilliant boy-inventor who, among other things, builds missile interceptors in his

SHIPWRECKED

```
Walt Disney Home Video
1991
93 minutes
Directed by: Nils Gaup
Starring: Gabriel Byrne, Stian
   Smestad
OFRB rating: PG—Frightening
   Scenes
MPAA rating: PG
```

In 1859 in Norway, young Haakon Haakonsen goes to sea to pay his family's debts and save their homestead. As Haakon's ship goes through pirate territory, a villain named John Merrick gains entry onto the ship by impersonating an officer. Merrick poisons the Captain and takes over the ship, crewing it with his own men. Before long, though, a great storm wrecks the ship on an island where Haakon finds a treasure and evidence of Merrick's treachery. Haakon is soon reunited with his friends (Jens, a shipmate, and Mary, a stowaway who taught him how to read), and together they scuttle the bad guys, escape with the treasure and return to Norway to pay the family debts and reclaim the homestead. Based on the Book *Haakon Haakonsen* by O.V. Falck-Ytter.

CAUTION: Gabriel Byrne's character may be too frightening (or too threatening) for young children.

GO: Featuring excellent cinematography, this is a pirate movie with plenty of adventure but no gratuitous violence. Potentially threatening situations are treated with humour, and there is an excellent role model in the character of Mary.

■

THE SILVER CHAIR

Public Media Video
1988
165 minutes
Directed by: Alex Kirby
Starring: Tom Baker,
    Richard Henders, Camilla Power,
    David Thwaites
MPAA rating: no rating given

Eustace and his friend Jill return to a rather nasty boarding school, where they are pursued by a gang of bullies. The pair escapes through a previously locked garden door, on the far side of which, they find themselves in the magical land of Narnia. But they soon become separated and Jill meets the great lion, Aslan, alone. Aslan explains that they have been called to perform a difficult task — to find a long-lost prince, or die trying. Aslan then gives Jill four signs to guide her in her quest; the first of which is that Eustace must greet an old and dear friend as soon as he sets foot in Narnia, in order to get the help they will need. But it's too late. Without the benefit of Aslan's instructions Eustace has already failed to recognize his friend (the now-aged King Caspian) and the old man has boarded a ship and set sail. The pair, having missed the first sign, are forced to spend the night at King Caspian's city of Cair Paravel. Their luck does improve, however, and they set out to find Caspian's long-lost son, Prince Rilian. As each of the signs is revealed, the children survive encounters with cannibal giants, and a treacherous witch, who rules a grim underground domain. The children free Rilian from the witch's spell and return home.

CAUTION: The film is slow and long and will probably leave little ones far behind. Eustace and Jill provide a less than positive example as they are rude to each other during most of their stay in Narnia.

GO: The locations and the sets, while obviously created on a limited budget, are magnificent, and the special effects are decent enough. It has been remarked that the cast of the Narnia series isn't particularly charismatic, but they are generally true to C.S. Lewis's protagonists. This is a BBC Television Production in association with Wonderworks.

SINBAD AND THE EYE OF THE TIGER

Columbia
1977
113 minutes
Directed by: Sam Wanamaker
Starring: Kurt Christian,
  Taryn Power, Jane Seymour,
  Damien Thomas,
  Patrick Troughton, Patrick
  Wayne, Margaret Whiting
MPAA rating: G

Sinbad and his men arrive in port only to discover (to their disgust) that the city is closed. And after fighting off an assortment of evil creatures, Sinbad saves the Princess Farah and together they tearfully explains that her brother, Crown Prince Kassim, has been turned into a baboon by the evil witch, Xenobia. And so, Sinbad sails to find the great sage Melanthias, a man of mythical wisdom, who will help Sinbad restore Kassim to his human shape. It's an exciting adventure from that point on, as Sinbad encounters giant wasps, bronze minotaurs and friendly troglodytes (all made wonderfully real by Ray Harryhausen's amazing effects). And when Sinbad and his friends find the sage and get the advice they need, they sail to the ice-locked land of Hyperborea, where Kassim is restored and the showdown with Xenobia, who turns into a giant sabre-toothed tiger, takes place.

For other Sinbad reviews see:
The Golden Voyage of Sinbad
The Seventh Voyage of Sinbad

CAUTION: Young children may find some situations too intense, and the fight at the end of the film between the giant tiger (which is killed) and a troglodyte is particularly realistic.

GO: Once again, Sinbad is an excellent adventure from the Ray Harryhausen school of special effects.

THE SNOW QUEEN

BFS Video
1992
56 minutes
Directed by: Andrew Gosling
Starring: Linda Slater,
  Joshua Le Touzel
MPAA rating: unrated

When demons decide to take the devil's mirror (which makes beautiful things ugly, and hearts turn to ice) up to reflect the face of God, they laugh so hard that they drop it on the way and it shatters into thousands of pieces and falls to Earth. There, a small piece becomes lodged in the heart of Kay, a young boy who is out walking with his good friend Gerda. One night as Gerda's grandmother tells the children about the Snow Queen on Christmas Eve, Kay becomes unusually belligerent and runs off into the snowy night. There the Snow Queen finds him and whisks him away to her ice palace, where she tells him that if he solves a puzzle he will gain a new pair of skates. Meanwhile, Gerda searches high and low for her friend and eventually becomes hostage to some gypsies. The gypsies finally give Gerda a reindeer that she can ride to the Snow Queen's palace.

When she arrives she melts the ice fragment in Kay's heart and the spell is broken. On Christmas morning Kay receives his new skates. Based on a story by Hans Christian Andersen.

CAUTION: This film is probably too scary for young children — the faceless witch, in particular. In one scene a robber is shown with a blood-covered knife, and in another a coachman is shown dead with a knife sticking out of his stomach. The sound track is ominous.

GO: An effective combination of animation and live-action, in this production the people are superimposed against painted backgrounds.

■

THE SOUND OF MUSIC

CBS/Fox
1965
174 minutes
Directed by: Robert Wise
Starring: Julie Andrews,
    Christopher Plummer
MPAA rating: G

When a young nun named Maria has trouble fitting in at the convent, she tries her luck at being a governess, taking an assignment with the von Trapp family. Baron von Trapp is an Austrian aristocrat and a captain in the Austrian navy, and his children are notorious for making short work of governesses. But the children soon learn that Maria is as tough as they are, and as she is by far the most entertaining nanny they have ever had, they befriend her. And when the Baron sternly expresses his reservations about Maria's casual style, she even stands up to him,

and he is both dumbfounded and much-impressed by her strength of character. But as soon as Maria realizes that she is falling in love with the Baron (who is engaged to someone else), she returns to the convent, and the whole von Trapp family is crestfallen. But Maria can't stay away long and returns to confess her feelings for the baron (feelings which are mutual) just as the baron is being forced to command a ship in the German navy. The baron makes plans for the family's escape to Switzerland. And after nearly being captured by Nazi soldiers (alerted by the boyfriend of the eldest von Trapp girl), they receive help from Maria's friends at the convent, and escape Austria over the alps. This film is based on a true story.

CAUTION: You may have to do a little explaining about Nazis. The film is very long, so you may want to spread it over two nights.

GO: One of the great musicals of this era, its list of hit songs includes: "The Sound of Music," "My Favourite Things," "Sixteen Going on Seventeen."

STAR WARS

CBS/Fox
1977
121 minutes
Directed by: George Lucas
Starring: Carrie Fisher,
    Harrison Ford, Alec Guiness,
    Mark Hamill
MPAA rating: PG

In another galaxy, in the distant past, the democratic Republic has been undermined from within, by evil men using the enormous power of the dark side of the Force. To cement control of their Empire, the evil rulers design and build the Death Star, an enormous battlestation capable of destroying an entire world. Then, by chance, two droids, R2-D2 and C-3P0, carrying stolen schematics of the Death Star, come into the hands of a farm boy named Luke Skywalker; this attracts the attention of the evil Lord Vader whose minions will the stop at nothing to track the droids down and retrieve the plans. And when R2-D2 goes to the desert home of Obi Wan Kenobi (one of the few remaining members of the nearly extinct mystical order of Jedi Knights), Luke follows and learns that his own father was once a Jedi, but was betrayed and killed by the evil Vader. He also learns that the droid contains critical schematics of the Death Star (sent by princess Leia, who's being held at the battlestation). Luke returns home, where he finds that the agents of the Empire have destroyed the farm and murdered his aunt and uncle. Luke vows to become a Jedi like his father. He and Obi Wan enlist the services of swashbuckling smuggler, Han Solo, to help them cross the galaxy, rescue Princess Leia and get the plans to the rebels.

See reviews for other titles in the Star Wars trilogy:
The Empire Strikes Back
Return of the Jedi

CAUTION: This is a film about the struggle between good and evil and consequently features a lot of combat. Darth Vader is certain to be a figure of terror for very young viewers and Obi Wan, a beloved central character, is killed in a duel with Darth Vader.

GO: This ground-breaking space opus is already considered to be a classic and a visionary effort. Its incredible effects (made on a modest budget, compared to today's standards) are still as vital and fantastic as they were in 1977.

▲

THE SWISS FAMILY ROBINSON

Walt Disney Home Video
1960
128 minutes
Directed by: Ken Annakin
Starring: James MacArthur, Dorothy McGuire, John Mills, Tommy Kirk
MPAA rating: G

In the nineteenth century, a family headed for a colony in New Guinea is shipwrecked on a tropical island. Salvaging items from the ship, the father, mother and two teenage boys build a tree-house complete with running water. The addition of a young woman from another ship (saved by the boys during a reconnaissance trip) causes some conflict between them, but this pales in comparison to the battle the family faces when an invading ship of sabre-wielding oriental pirates arrives on the island. Based on the book by Johann Wyss.

CAUTION: Some young animal lovers may be upset by scenes in which animals from the ship are attacked by sharks; large dogs attack a tiger, and a zebra in quicksand is surrounded by hyenas. Also, pirates with sabre-like swords converge on one of their own with hacking motions, and the family is obliged to defend itself by shooting pirates (no blood).

GO: Baby monkeys, tigers, a baby elephant, dogs, sea turtles, ostriches, parrots and lizards are all featured in this exciting family adventure. Kids are sure to like the family's clever inventions, too.

■

TALES FOR ALL SERIES

Cinéma Plus/HBO Cannon Video/
  Astral Home Video
1984-1993
90-100 minutes (each volume)

Produced by Québécois filmmaker Rock Demers and Les productions la fête, the *Tales for All* series of fourteen films (with more to come) has garnered more than 135 international awards. The films feature many different writers and directors; many have magical or mystical elements, and all are generally geared for family viewing. In the majority of the films, there is no coarse language and almost no violence. (See our section for children aged ten to thirteen for more reviews in this series.)

The Case of the Witch That Wasn't (Tale #10)

Penpals Melanie and Florence spend the summer together, befriend an eccentric old woman and solve a mystery in what turns out to be a season of great change for everyone. Winner of the Most Popular Film Prize at the Beauvais Festival in France. (Astral Home Video, 1990)

✗ The Dog Who Stopped the War (Tale #1)

In a small Quebec town, school has just let out for the Christmas holidays. Mark and Luke and the rest of the kids arrange war games and divide into two armies, the main rule being that hostilities end at sundown. Luke is overbearing, bossy and generally a tyrant, while Mark is quieter and devoted to his beautiful St. Bernard, Cleo. Mark has the smaller force, but his intellectual friend Warren designs a massive snow-fort, and newcomer Sophie lends courage and tenacity. And so the great war begins, set to last for the entire Christmas holidays. After Mark's force builds the biggest snowfort of all time, Luke's swelling army besieges it. Meanwhile, Luke and Sophie begin to grow fonder of each other, to the point of after-dark meetings, when hostilities are suspended. But the war goes on, and assault after assault is repelled by the great fort, until the climactic attack. Also available in French under the title *La Guerre des Toques*. (HBO Cannon Video, 1984)

✗**STOP**: Mark's dog dies, smothered by the fort as it collapses on her, and Mark is absolutely crushed by grief — as will many young viewers be who are caught unprepared for this shocker.

GO: Winner of Golden Reel Award in 1984 and the 1986 Grand Prize at France's Festival of Films.

▲

The Great Land of Small (Tale #5)

A little man named Fritz, from the Great Land of Small, comes to the woods of northern Quebec, with mystic gold which can bring great good to the world. He gives the gold to a rough pub owner, Flannigan, warning him: Use it wisely for the good of all, or it will cause your own downfall. But Flannigan is greedy, and when his daughter Sarah also receives a gold nugget he steals it from her. Convinced that Sarah and her friends, Jenny and David, are connected in some way to the little man, Flannigan chases them. Jenny and David escape in a canoe with Fritz, and are caught in the rapids and presumed drowned. In truth, the kids have travelled, for a time, to the Great Land of Small. Their return provokes a final confrontation with Flannigan, who, in the end, comes to realize that he cares more for his daughter than anything else. Also available in French under the title *C'est pas parce qu'on est Petit qu'on peut pas être Grand*. (Cinéma Plus, 1987)

✘**STOP:** Flannigan enters his daughter's room, paws through her things, and takes her gold nugget.

CAUTION: Some of the characters in the Great Land of Small are pretty strange, and Fritz, who is rather gross, has a propensity to burp. At the end of the film, Fritz, now out of magic, is stranded on Earth, where he must wait under every rainbow for his brother the king to save him.

▲

Reach for the Sky
(Tale #12)

Corina is a ten-year-old who dreams of winning an Olympic gold in gymnastics, so she begs her coach to allow her to apply to the prestigious school in Deva, Romania. It takes her two years to gain acceptance into the school and even then the tough Romanian coach disapproves of her. Soon the pressures of maintaining her marks and improving her skills as a gymnast become almost impossible

to bear. But when the time for the world championship competition arrives, Corina finally realizes her dream. Also available in French under the title *La Champion*. (Astral Home Video, 1992)

CAUTION: In one emotional scene, a budding gymnast breaks her wrist and her career is over. This film was made with actors from the country of its origin and was dubbed into English. (Children find this technique less irksome than adults.)

GO: This is a true-to-life account of the hard-working and unglamorous world of gymnastics, which is not at all romanticized. Excellent for the budding athlete.

Tadpole and the Whale
(Tale #6)

Daphne, known as Tadpole, is a twelve-year-old girl with extraordinary powers. She is completely comfortable underwater; moreover, she can hear and understand the songs of whales. Her best friends are Grandpa Thomas, a salty old seadog, and a dolphin, Elvar, with whom she can communicate. She keeps busy recording the enchanting songs of humpback whales from Grandpa Hector's home, Old Manor. But when Grandpa Hector decides to sell the manor to a consortium which is planning to put in a resort, Daphne is inconsolable. Then the trouble is compounded when a young couple are stranded at sea. Daphne rushes to their aid only to hit her head and sink into the water. Then it's up to Elvar to save Daphne. Also available in French under the title *La Grenouille et La Baleine*. (Cinéma Plus, 1987)

GO: Beautiful underwater photography highlights this exciting and informative adventure, which appeals to a very broad age range. (For young viewers this is a non-violent film, featuring lots of dolphins and whales at play, and for older children, it's an entertaining way to learn about marine mammals, their origins, senses and behavioural patterns.)

▲

Tommy Tricker and the Stamp Traveller (Tale # 7)

Tommy Tricker is a young scamp who helps support his huge fatherless family with stamp-related scams. When he tricks fellow stamp enthusiast Ralph James into giving up Ralph's father's prize Bluenose stamp, "The Man in the Mast," a strange chain of events is set into motion. Ralph and his sister discover a cryptic letter hidden in the cover of an old stamp album, they learn of the existence of another stamp album which is hidden in Australia and which contains a fabulous fortune in rare stamps. The children also find an incantation which, when spoken, will cause the speaker to shrink onto a stamp. The "stamp traveller" can then be mailed anywhere in the world, and upon reaching his or her destination, will be restored to normal size. But there is a danger: If the stamp traveller does *not* reach the address on the letter, he or she must remain on the stamp forever. Tommy Tricker also learns the incantation, and he and Ralph engage in a race for the Sidney Stamp and Coin Shop, where the fortune is allegedly hidden. And after an exciting (and thoroughly informative) trip, the boys retrieve the valuable album and return home on a letter bound for Canada. Also available in French under the title *Les Aventuriers du Timbre Perdu.* (Cinéma Plus, 1988)

GO: Besides being a unique adventure

which appeals to children of all ages, *Tommy Tricker and the Stamp Traveller* has inspired many a youngster to take up stamp collecting. Winner of the 1989 Parents' Choice Award for Best Children's Film of the Year, this film features original music by Kate, Anna and Jane McGarrigle.

▲

The Young Magician (Tale # 4)

Pierrot, a devotee of the art of magic, discovers, to his infinite surprise, that he possesses real telekinetic powers. At first, this proves a major problem for him, as he is completely alienated from his peers and from society in general. But when a military weapon of enormous destructive power is accidentally dropped from an aircraft and ends up lodged in a factory roof, Pierrot is called upon to save the day. Also available in French under the title *Le Jeune Magicien.* (Cinéma Plus, 1986)

■ ▲

✗ TEENAGE MUTANT NINJA TURTLES: THE MOVIE

Releasing Home Video/Alliance
1990
95 minutes
Directed by: Steve Barron
Starring: David Forman,
    Judith Hoag, Elias Koteas,
    Josh Pais, James Saito,
    Michelan Sisti, Leif Tilden
Starring the voices of: Kevin Clash,
    Corey Feldman, David McCharen,
    Robbie Rist, Brian Tochi
OFRB rating: PG—Martial Arts:
    Violence
MPAA rating: PG

When a highly organized gang of masked martial artists is recruiting young men and terrorizing New York City, only TV reporter April O'Neill has the courage to publicly identify the scourge. And in so doing she earns the attention of the evil head of the gang, Shredder. But Shredder's plans are thwarted when, as his gang ambushes April in a subway station, Raphael, a Teenage Mutant Ninja Turtle, intervenes and rescues her. She is taken to the Turtles' secret hideout where she meets the rest of the company (Leonardo, Donatello and Michelangelo, and their mentor, a mutant rat named Splinter), and learns about their radioactive origins. Then things get tense when Splinter is kidnapped and April's troubled teenage son Danny runs away to join the gang. But with the help of April and a fellow martial-artist, Casey Jones, the Turtles still manage to save the day.

✗**STOP**: There is fighting throughout, and it's often accompanied by realistic sound effects. April is slapped and punched senseless by a group of masked thugs: twice. Casey refers to April as Broadzilla.

CAUTION: One complaint we have is that the Turtles, despite the efforts of their mystic teacher, are relentlessly low-brow. Also, the bad guys are hardly original: they've

been stolen from every martial arts movie of the past twenty years, and the endlessly derivative evil folks do tend to get a bit tiring.

GO: It's action packed, good and evil are clearly defined, and April's son Danny learns a valuable lesson about family values and hanging around with the right sort of people.

▲

THAT DARN CAT

Walt Disney Home Video
1965
115 minutes
Directed by: Robert Stevenson
Starring: Dean Jones,
    Roddy McDowall, Hayley Mills,
    Dorothy Provine
MPAA rating: G

Two daring bank-robbers kidnap a teller during a heist, and hide out a mere block and a half from where they pulled the job. When one of them stops off at the local fishmonger's, ultra-intelligent and ever-mooching feline D.C. (Darn Cat) tags along in hopes of a freebie. He gets into the robbers' hide-out where the resourceful teller scratches a message on her watch and slips it around D.C.'s neck. And that night, when D.C.'s owner sees the message "Hel . . ." she realizes what has happened, and goes to the FBI. Then a high-powered team of agents are instructed to tail D.C. And inevitably, shenanigans and hijinks galore follow, as D.C. leads the FBI to the bad guys. Based on the book *Undercover Cat* by the Gordons.

CAUTION: The bank robbers are a little scary, and at one point one of them raises

his fist to strike the helpless teller. There is a fairly rough fist-fight at the climax.

GO: This is an entertaining comedy-mystery in the classic Disney tradition. ■

GO: *The Three Caballeros* was one of the first full-scale films to combine animation and live-action, and is a great way (if a tad dated) to introduce young viewers to the Latin cultures. The music is fantastic, too. ▲

THE THREE CABALLEROS

Walt Disney Home Video
1964
71 minutes
Directed by: Norman Ferguson
Starring: Donald Duck, Joe Carioca, Panchito
MPAA rating: G

It's Friday the thirteenth, Donald's birthday, and his Latin American friends send him a huge present which includes, among other things, a projector and a reel of film containing an assortment of stories. The first is the story of Pablo, a little penguin whose burning desire is to move to tropical shores, but who freezes whenever he moves away from his stove. The second is a film in which viewers learn all about a variety of South American birds. And the third tells the tale of an old gaucho from Uruguay who, as a little gauchito, found the most amazing bird in history, a small burro with a functional pair of wings. Donald is then joined by his friend Joe Carioca, a parrot who teaches him about Brazil, and by the Mexican bird, Panchito, who sings the legendary hit "We're Three Caballeros" and who takes Donald and friends on a tour of Mexican tradition and culture.

CAUTION: Some of the animation is downright psychedelic, representing a real exploratory phase in the company's history.

✗ THE THREE LIVES OF THOMASINA

Walt Disney Home Video
1964
97 minutes
Directed by: Don Chaffey
Starring: Susan Hampshire, Patrick McGoohan
MPAA rating: not rated

A new vet has moved into the small town of Inveragh, Scotland, in 1912. He is Dr. Andrew MacDhui, a most difficult man, full of newfangled medical ideas. He is also a widower and the father of young Mary MacDhui. Mary's pride and joy is a self-satisfied orange tabby named Thomasina, the narrator of the tale. And when a chance encounter with an otherwise gentle guide-dog named Bruce leaves Thomasina at death's door, MacDhui decides to put her to sleep. Thomasina travels into another world — to the dark, cat-filled domain of the goddess Bast. But Bast sends Thomasina back, and the cat finds herself in the care of Laurie MacGregor, a beautiful, mysterious young woman who lives in the glen and has a way with animals. Laurie nurses Thomasina back to health, but the cat has lost all knowledge of her former life. Mary, meanwhile, is crushed by grief, and won't even speak to her father. Desperate to reach his daughter, MacDhui breaks out of his cold shell, and, as Mary is failing, turns to Laurie for help. But in the end, it's all up to Thomasina.

✗STOP: Thomasina dies and Mary reacts violently to the cat's death.

CAUTION: Thomasina's mystical voyage to the domain of Bast is a little eerie, and may provoke some questions about the hereafter. In one scene a badger is shown with his bloody paw caught in a leg-hold trap and in another MacDhui fights with thugs at the circus. Also, some people are irritated by the way Mary treats her father.

GO: This is a magical tale in the Disney tradition.

THE TIME MACHINE

MGM/UA
1960
103 minutes
Directed by: George Pal
Starring: Rod Taylor,
    Yvette Mimieux
MPAA rating: G

The Time Machine opens in London at the turn of the century, where a brilliant young inventor named George builds a fabulous time machine which takes him into the distant future. He passes through World Wars I and II, and finally World War III, in which he witnesses the apocalypse. He barely makes it back to his machine, and as he starts forward, again into the future, he is buried in rubble. Centuries go by, and finally the rubble falls away, revealing a green and pleasant land. And George, finally able to stop the device, finds himself in the year 802,701 A.D., outside a bizarre temple-like structure. He then begins to explore the beautiful but

terrible world. Humanity has apparently subdivided into two species; the first of which is a dull-eyed, stupid race called the Eloi, who are bred like cattle to feed the second species, a dreadful race of misshapen mole-like creatures called Morlocks who live underground. (The Eloi are so utterly passive, in fact, that when a young Eloi woman named Weena is drowning in the river, no one but George will save her.) And when the Morlocks drag George's time-machine into their temple, luring him into an obvious trap, George enters the temple, fights off the Morlocks and returns to his own time. In the end, though, he returns to Weena. Based on the novel by H.G. Wells

CAUTION: There are images and concepts in this film which may frighten little ones. The Morlocks' subterranean cannibal domain is laughably antiseptic compared to how it could have been presented, but the idea may still be fairly intense for young children. In one scene, a face melts and turns into a skeleton.

GO: This is an exciting sci-fi adventure (admittedly with something of a slow beginning) that still holds up after all these the years.

■

THE TREASURE

Malofilm
1990
95 minutes
Directed by: Robert Cording
Starring: John Weisbarth,
    Freddy Rible, Frank Jimison
MPAA rating: no rating given

Emerald Cove's lighthouse keeper vanishes on a windy July night in 1959, and his disappearance is a mystery. It is rumoured that a secret passageway connects the lighthouse to some old pirate caves, but no one is sure. The lighthouse, in the meantime, is declared a historical landmark. Thirty years later, the hero and narrator of the tale is David Shipper, a tall, fair-haired son of the town. He's looking forward to a great summer, until he learns that his overweight, bespectacled city-boy cousin Jonathan is coming to visit for the whole two months. David figures the summer is a total loss and so plans a camping trip on the beach to separate the men from the boys. But enroute to their camping spot, they stop to inspect the boat graveyard. While aboard one wreck, they are joined by David's best friend, Freddy, and promptly discover a mysterious treasure map. Then, pursued by comical villains, and startled by the brief appearance of a ghostly apparition of a young woman, they boys solve the mystery of the treasure, the missing lighthouse keeper and the mysterious apparition.

CAUTION: The villains are pretty mean when they talk to each other (no swearing, just a lot of insults). There is some fighting.

GO: For fans of films like *The Hardy Boys* and *Encyclopedia Brown*, this is a fun little mystery.

TREASURE ISLAND

Walt Disney Home Video
1950
96 minutes
Directed by: Byron Haskin
Starring: Bobby Driscoll,
    Robert Newton, Basil Sydney
MPAA rating: G

When a former shipmate of the blood-thirsty pirate captain John Flint shows up at the Admiral Benbow Inn and promptly dies, Jim Hawkins, the son of a tavern

mistress, comes into possession of a map which reveals the location of Flint's immense treasure. Local gentlemen outfit a ship to sail to Treasure Island but, exhibiting a stunning lack of good judgment, manage to hire a crew composed almost entirely of the late Flint's former shipmates. These knaves are led by the one-legged Long John Silver, and wherever Silver is, murder, treachery and savage combat are never far behind. Yet despite Silver's horrific past and intemperate nature, he has a soft spot in his heart for the brave and honest Jim.

CAUTION: The most intense moment is the famous scene in which Jim is pursued up into the rigging of the ship by the knife-wielding, homicidal Israel Hands, and in which Jim is forced to shoot the other, taking a dagger in the shoulder in the process.

GO: In this version of the classic tale, Robert Newton so popularized the character of Long John Silver that a television series was created featuring him and his scurvy mates. The violence is tame by today's standards, but represents a perfect example of exciting action contained within the boundaries of good taste.

■

THE TROUBLE WITH ANGELS

RCA/Columbia Home Video
1966
110 minutes
Directed by: Ida Lupino
Starring: June Harding, Hayley Mills,
    Rosalind Russel, Camilla Sparv
MPAA rating: no rating given

Two teenage girls from wealthy families are sent to St. Francis convent school. Rachel Devery comes from a loving family, but Mary Clancy is an orphan, cast away by her playboy uncle. The two become fast friends, and the film follows their three-year career at St. Francis, where their various spectacular pranks serve to infuriate the convent's Mother Superior, earning them constant kitchen duty and penance in the chapel. Finally, when the pair smoke a couple of left-over cigars in the basement and cause a full-scale fire alert, the Mother Superior is ready to expel the girls. But when she meets Mary's uncle, she decides to grit her teeth and hang on. The course of Mary's life begins to change when, deserted at Christmas, she stays over at the convent for the holidays and experiences the simple beauty of the nuns' celebration; then, she discovers that her ideal, the radiantly-beautiful Sister Constance, is leaving to teach in a leper colony. Mary is profoundly touched by Sister Constance's selfless courage. Finally, after much agonized soul-searching, Mary makes the difficult decision to stay on and become a novice after graduation. At first, Rachel is devastated. She feels so betrayed that she won't even talk to Mary. But finally, the two are reconciled, and Rachel departs for the world with Mary harbouring the hope that one day Rachel will return for good. If that should happen, the Mother Superior warns her: I quit!

CAUTION: One of the Sisters dies, and there is a scene of mourning.

GO: This is a gentle, humorous and touching tale for anyone over six. Mary's transformation from a hellion to a sensitive young woman is straightforward enough to be understood even by younger children.

THE UNDERCOVER GANG

MCA Home Video
1986
73 minutes
Directed by: Peter Sharp
Starring: Darryl Beattie,
   Alix Chapman, Peter Hayden,
   Miles Murphy, Jon Trimmer,
   Emma Vere-Jones
MPAA rating: no rating given

During World War I, in the small town of Jessop, New Zealand, a mysterious figure is sabotaging buildings. And while inspiring teacher Clippy Hedges is trying to give the children of Jessop a decent education, and Miss Bolton is busy directing a patriotic play, children Noel and Kitty Wix, Phil Miller and Irene, are doing their best to track down the perpetrator. While on a school swimming outing, Noel and Miller discover an incriminating oil-can at the bottom of the river. Meanwhile Edgar Marwick, the suspected firebug, is preparing another arson, and when the boys follow him, they prevent a destructive fire; however, nothing can be proven to the satisfaction of the law, and the sergeant even begins to suspect the boys. So Miller and Noel team up with Irene and Kitty to scout out the Marwick place. But things get hot quickly, and Kitty is captured. The gang does get the police out quickly enough to save her, but not quickly enough to incriminate the evil Marwick. Then the Undercover Gang really goes to work, keeping Marwick under surveillance until they can catch him red-handed. But catching a madman red-handed is not without perils of its own.

CAUTION: The Marwicks consistently accuse the children of lying and Hedges and Marwick duke it out, with bloody noses as the result.

GO: This is an intriguing period mystery for young fans of the genre, and a good example of kids making a difference.

✗ THE WATCHER IN THE WOODS

Walt Disney Home Video
1981
84 minutes
Directed by: John Hough
Starring: Carroll Baker, Bette Davis,
   Lynn-Holly Johnson,
   David McCallum
MPAA rating: PG

From the novel *A Watcher in the Woods* by Florence Engel Randall. When the Curtis family rents a beautiful, secluded manor house in the country, everything seems a bit strange. Mr. Curtis, a pianist, and Mrs. Curtis, a writer of children's books, like it very much, but their older daughter, Jan, is uneasy. Immediately she feels that someone is watching her. Mrs. Aylwood, the eccentric lady of the manor, lives in a secluded cottage on the property and communicates with unseen entities. Jan sees a terrifying apparition in a mirror (a blindfolded girl reaching out to her); her younger sister Ellie hears voices and writes the name Karen backwards in the dust on a window. Jan learns that Karen was Mrs. Aylwood's daughter, who disappeared in a terrible fire in an old chapel. After a series of terrifying supernatural

events, Jan begins an investigation
to find out exactly what happened to
Karen. She begins to put pressure
on the three people who last saw
the young woman, and learns that
Karen was going through an
initiation rite at the chapel, and
vanished. The paranormal
phenomena become more and
more intense until, during a total
eclipse of the sun, the dreadful
mystery is revealed. Karen and a
mysterious being from another
dimension exchanged places during
the strange rite, and now the three
original participants must be
assembled, and the rite re-enacted,
in order to bring Karen back.

✗**STOP:** Don't be deceived by the Disney
label. This is a horror movie. Frightening
events are introduced with sudden shock
value and accompanied by loud bursts of
spooky music. An apparition beckons and
gestures from the wrong side of mirrors on
several occasions, a blindfolded maiden
lies in an ancient coffin, windows suddenly
break. And there are lots of cheap false
alarm moments. Ellie is possessed by a
spirit and the final transformation is fraught
with terror and peril. There is also a near-
drowning sequence which is grotesque
and extremely frightening for young
children.

CAUTION: Even for grown-ups, this is a
pretty intense effort.
■

WE ALL HAVE TALES

Rabbit Ears Productions Inc./Sony
1988-1992
30 minutes (each volume)
Directed by: C.W. Rogers
Starring: (see individual credits
below)

These videos are productions of
fairy tales and legends and are not
fully-animated. Motion is simulated
by the camera moving over the
quality illustrations. Top film stars
provide the narration while the
music is played by noted musicians.

Titles in the collection are:
Anansi (told by Denzel Washington,
music by UB40)
The Boy Who Drew Cats (told by William
Hurt, music by Mark Isham)
Brer Rabbit and the Wonderful Tar Baby
(told by Danny Glover, music by Taj
Mahal)
East of the Sun, West of the Moon (told
by Max Von Sydow, music by Lyle Mays)
The Emperor and the Nightingale (told
by Glenn Close, music by Mark Isham)
The Emperor's New Clothes (told by Sir
John Gielgud, music by Mark Isham)
Finn McCoul (told by Catherine O'Hara,
music by Boys of the Lough)
The Fisherman and His Wife (told by
Jodie Foster, music by Van Dyke Parks)
The Fool and the Flying Ship (told by
Robin Williams, music by The Klezmer
Conservatory Band)
The Gingham Dog and the Calico Cat
(told by Amy Grant, music by Chet
Atkins)
How the Leopard Got His Spots (told by
Danny Glover, music by Ladysmith Black
Mombazo)
How the Rhinoceros Got His Skin (told
by Jack Nicholson, music by Bobby
McFerrin)
Jack and the Beanstalk (told by Michael
Palin, music by David A. Stewart)
King Midas and the Golden Touch (told
by Michael Caine, music by Ellis
Marsalis & Yo-Yo Ma)
Koi and the Kola Nuts (told by Whoopi
Goldberg, music by Herbie Hancock)
The Legend of Sleepy Hollow (told By
Glenn Close, music by Tim Story)
The Monkey People (told by Raul Julia,
music by Lee Ritenour)
The Night Before Christmas; Best-Loved
Yuletide Carols (told by Meryl Streep,
music by The Edwin Hawkins Singers
and others)
Paul Bunyan (told by Jonathon Winters,
music by Leo Kotke with Duck Baker)

AGES 6 TO 10

244

Peachboy (told by Sigourney Weaver, music by Ryuichi Sakamoto)

Pecos Bill (told by Robin Williams, music by Ry Cooder)

Puss in Boots (told by Tracey Ullman, music by Jean-Luc Ponty)

Rumplestiltskin (told by Kathleen Turner, music by Tangerine Dream)

The Three Billygoats Gruff; The Three Little Pigs (told by Holly Hunter, music by Art Lande)

Thumbelina (told by Kelly McGillis, music by Mark Isham)

The Tiger and the Brahmin (told by Ben Kingsleym, music by Ravi Shankar)

CAUTION: These are beautifully produced videos. However, they are not fully-animated and may be too slow for some children.

GO: Between them these videos have won sixteen Parents' Choice Awards, two Grammy Awards and seven Action for Children's Television Awards.

WILLIE THE OPERATIC WHALE
(with Ferdinand the Bull and Lambert, the Sheepish Lion)

Walt Disney Home Video
1951, 1956
30 minutes
Directed by: Hamilton Luske and
   Clyde Geronimi
MPAA rating: G

Willie the Operatic Whale When news of a singing whale reaches the scientific community, they react by proposing the theory that the whale has somehow swallowed an opera singer, and send out an expedition, led by the impressario Tetti-Tatti, to kill him. Willie, under the mistaken impression that he has finally been discovered, races to his audition

and is harpooned, but continues his career in heaven.

Ferdinand the Bull While all the other bulls run and jump and bang heads, Ferdinand sits quietly in the shade, smelling the flowers. But when the men in the funny hats come to pick the bulls for the bullfight in Madrid, Ferdinand accidentally sits on a bumblebee. The men erroneously think that Ferdinand is the monster they've been looking for and put him into a bullfight. The result is a pacifistic fiasco, and Ferdinand is summarily retired to his flower garden.

Lambert, the Sheepish Lion It's the old stork mix-up routine in the pasture, as Lambert the Lion accidentally gets delivered to a flock of sheep, and has to adapt to a life as a herbivore. Lambert can't do anything right, and he is the butt of many pasture pranks. But as time goes by, and everyone grows up, and a wolf threatens the flock, Lambert recalls his heredity and saves the day.

CAUTION: *Willie the Operatic Whale* is billed as a Wagnerian-style tragedy and the ending is desperately sad.

THE WIZARD

MCA
1990
100 minutes
Directed by: Todd Holland
Starring: Beau Bridges,
   Luke Edwards, Sam McMurray,
   Fred Savage, Will Seltzer,
   Christian Slater
MPAA rating: PG

Jimmy Woods is a traumatized little boy who is more than a handful for his mother, and she and her new husband intend to put him in a home. While his father Sam and his older brother Nick are screaming at each other, Jimmy's brother Corey slips out to collect Jimmy and together, armed only with Corey's skateboard, they stow away aboard an ice-cream truck heading for California. Jimmy's mother and step-father then hire Putnam, a cold-hearted hunter who specializes in tracking down runaways, and Sam and Nick set off after the boys as well. At a stopover in a little midwestern town, Corey gives Jimmy a quarter for a video game to keep him amused. Jimmy racks up a huge score. It turns out that Jimmy is a video game wizard. And when he beats their new friend Haley, she and Corey realize that Jimmy has one hope: to get to Video Armageddon, the video championships in L.A., and win the big prize. So off they go, chased across the country by Putnam, and financing their trip by setting up video suckers on their way. In the course of their adventures, the reason for Jimmy's condition is revealed. Finally, the kids reach the championship, chased by everyone, and Jimmy takes on the best players in the country with his future at stake. In the end he prevails, the family is reconciled, and the central mystery of Jimmy's life, his constant urge to return to California, is solved.

CAUTION: The reason Jimmy has withdrawn from life is that he witnessed his twin sister drowning; certain unflattering references are made to Jimmy's state. At one point, to delay Putnam, Haley points at him and yells: He touched my breast! — a little unsettling as it gives kids the idea that they can use a false accusation of sexual abuse as a form of power.

GO: Haley is a good role model for girls. She is tough and resourceful and smart. And Corey must be the best brother in the history of the world.

WIZARDS OF THE LOST KINGDOM

Astral
1986
78 minutes
Directed by: Hector Olivera
Starring: Bo Svenson
MPAA rating: PG

It was an age of magic, an age of sorcery, an age of chaos, an age of cheesy special effects; it was an age of poorly choreographed swordfights and pompous musical accompaniment, when wizard fought wizard, warrior fought warrior, for yet another great sword of power, and yet one more ring of . . . yes, power. They lost the sword, but they kept tabs on the ring, and for a time, King Tyler ruled in peace. Simon is the son of a court magician. When the castle comes under attack from evil wizard-type Shirka, both the king and Simon's dad are killed, and Simon's girlfriend Laura is imprisoned. Simon escapes with the ring and his servant Gofax, and promptly falls into one of Shirka's traps. But he is rescued by the warrior Kor the Conqueror (Bo Svenson visibly reads cue cards in this appearance). And together he and Simon wander around for awhile, kick a few butts, and reclaim the castle and the girl. Hooray!

CAUTION: Humans over the age of twelve should not watch this film. Shirka turns people into mice, and his midget pet monster pounces on them.

GO: One eight-year old boy we know solemnly informed us that this is the greatest film ever made.

THE WONDERFUL WORLD OF DISNEY: AN ADVENTURE IN COLOR (Vol. 1)

Walt Disney Home Video
1959-1981
100 minutes
Directed by: Hamilton S. Luske,
   William Reid

An Adventure in Color (1959)
This is a Disney special that originally came out when everyone was starting to get colour television. Walt talks about how cartoons started, and how after *Steamboat* *Willie* and *Silly Symphonies*, the next big revolution was colour. Then he hands the proceedings over to the inimitable Professor Ludwig von Drake, who talks about how colour affects us, how colour and light are related and what happens to colours when they are mixed. He even sings the "Green with Envy, Red with Anger, Purple Passionate Blues," and includes a version for people with black and white televisions. He sort of explains how televisions receive colour, and his explanation is followed by a rich montage of colour-filled, live-action nature scenes. Then Disney introduces another fascinating subject, and Donald Duck guides us into Mathemagic Land.

Mathemagic Land Donald is introduced to the origins of some rather sophisticated mathematical

ideas, like the Pythagorean theorem and the Golden Section. Although this film can be enjoyed purely for the cartoons, much of the content makes it more appropriate for viewers over twelve.

The Illusion of Life (1981) This section is hosted by Hayley Mills, who is in the studio to do voice-overs for *The Black Cauldron*. Pearl Bailey's owl character in *The Fox and the Hound* is also featured. Disney's animators talk about characters they have done, and about how they acheived their life-like effects through a process of transforming rough drawings into moving, talking, life-like animations.

Other titles in *The Wonderful World of Disney* series are:

The Bluegrass Special; Runaway on the Rogue River (Vol. 6)

Call It Courage; The Legend of the Boy and the Eagle (Vol. 9)

Dad, Can I Borrow the Car?; The Hunter and the Rock Star (Vol. 7)

Ducking Disaster with Donald and His Friends; Goofing Around with Donald Duck (Vol. 3)

Fire on Kelly Mountain; Adventure in Satan's Canyon (Vol. 8)

The Plausible Impossible; The Ranger's Guide to Nature (Vol. 4)

The Ranger Brownstone; It's Tough to Be a Bird (Vol. 2)

Three on the Run; Race for Three on the Run; Race for Survival (Vol. 10)

The Yellowstone Cubs; Flash, the Teenage Otter (Vol. 5)

CAUTION: *The Illusion of Life* is fascinating for older kids and adults, but it may go over the heads of young viewers.

GO: All three sections are highly informative, fast-moving and educational.

●

ZORRO: THE LEGEND CONTINUES

Malofilm
1989
92 minutes
Directed by: Ray Austin
Starring: Patrice Camhi,
    Duncan Regehr,
    Efrem Zimbalist Jr.
MPAA rating: no rating given

In this remake of the traditional story, Zorro is thrown from his horse during a clash with the colonial soldiers, and lands in a rocky pit, hitting his head. When Felipe, his young deaf-mute servant, clambers down to rescue him, Zorro recalls his origins. Once known as Don Diego, the son of wealthy landowner Don Alejandro, Zorro was sent to Spain for four years to study with the greatest swordsman in Europe, in order to prepare him to lead the resistance against the oppressors of California. We then follow Don Diego's return to California, where he immediately earns the enmity of the evil governor, the Acalde, and, as the man in black, takes on the government troops single-handedly.

CAUTION: Certain scenes may be a little intense for young children.

GO: This film is a bit bland, but will entertain young swashbucklers.

Chapter 8

VIDEOS FOR AGES TEN TO THIRTEEN

If your child is between the ages of ten and thirteen, you are probably now in the area of quasi-adult films. So, for the purposes of this chapter, we are primarily concerned with films which fall under the PG heading, although we will include a handful of AA-rated films.

As we've already mentioned, the PG category is extremely broad and you can expect to find vastly different content from one film to the next. So you can't simply judge a film's suitability by its rating. (See chapter 3 for more information on ratings.)

WHAT WE'RE UP AGAINST

Peer pressure

Your child is now in social situations every bit as stressful as your own. He or she doesn't want to be perceived to be a loser. And having to hide the fact that mom and dad have disallowed *Terminator 2*, when it seems that everyone else has seen it, makes things tough. Visits to the video store often turn into battles. You want your child to watch *Treasure Island* because it's a great movie and you loved it when you were ten. But now he or she is ten, and in the nineties, Arnold Schwarzenegger is cool.

AGES 10 TO 13

Star attraction

Pre-teens sometimes become attracted to an actor or actress and wish to watch everything that star appears in. However, often the films in which these teen stars play aren't even *remotely* suitable for your ten-year-old. So be careful. Check the ratings. Child star does not necessarily equal child viewing (a good example of this is *My Own Private Idaho*, an R-rated film featuring Keanu Reeves and River Phoenix).

The shrinking screen and other misconceptions

When the movies we've seen in the theatre are transferred to video and shown on our television screens, we often succumb to the mistaken impression that the movies have been somehow magically transformed, losing their impact. And suddenly it seems all right to allow children to see a film that we wouldn't have considered taking them to in the theatre.

But think again. Whether it's shown on the big screen or on your TV, it is *exactly* the same movie; the content is still the same. In fact, certain scenes of graphic or suggestive footage that were removed to lower the film's rating in the theatre may, at the director's request, have been put back in in the video version, in effect making it even *more* unsuitable for child viewers!

THE CARE-GIVER'S LAMENT

Someone's not playing by the rules

If a family member or a baby-sitter is renting unsuitable films for your child, then while you are working hard at guiding your child's viewing, it is being undermined. (Sometimes even to score points with the child.)

Lay down the law and stick to it. (We have included a blank page at the back of this book for you to list forbidden films, so that your baby-sitter can refer to it.)

Heading off the "can we get a horror movie?" request

Often when pre-teens get together they want to watch films that have the allure of the forbidden. Here are a few ways you can handle the situation:

You might prefer to settle for a comedy with a slightly racy theme, one which is obvious enough to make the older kids feel grown-up, but subtle enough that the younger ones simply won't get it. After all, children really like comedies and while they tend to associate horror films with being more mature, there are many light-hearted films that will serve the same purpose.

Empower your child to battle peer pressure by finding some more obscure films in different genres that your child can then introduce to his or her friends. It gives a child prestige to be able to say, "You mean you've never heard of this movie? It's great! Where have *you* been?"

Most stores have a VCR and a television out front. And generally, even a stubborn ten-year-old will agree to take a film after seeing a few minutes of it. (Especially if you don't recommend it too strongly!)

I give up

A lot of parents just give up and let their children see anything they want, wearily resigned to the fact that "if they don't see it at home, they'll see it somewhere else." But there are two very good reasons for maintaining your own standards in your own home. The first is that, if your children are warching grossly unsuitable material in your home as well as elsewhere, they are certainly going to be seeing a lot more of it. Research has given every indication that there is a direct correlation betweeen the amount of inappropriate viewing and the damage it can do. The second reason is that, without wishing to seem overly moralistic, it's one thing to acknowledge the inevitability of your child being exposed to unsuitable material, and it's quite another to be a contributor, especially in your child's eyes. And finally, while you're wrestling with this dilemma, keep in mind that you're not alone, and that consciousness of this problem is growing rapidly, spearheaded by the efforts of such celebrities as Arnold Schwarzenegger, Chuck Norris, and Emilio Estevez. Even now, plans are in effect to provide violence warnings on U.S. television programming.

When the genie is out of the bottle

There is a big jump in intensity from PG to AA and then again from AA to R. And once you've seen the next grade up, the previous rating does seem tame. So what do you do when your twelve-year-old has seen an R-rated action film and now everything in the PG category bores him? Following are a few suggestions:

- ▶ Choose PG films with an R feeling; that is, action-packed, fast moving and exciting films.
- ▶ Choose AA films or PG—Warning films, and agree to compromise in one area. (It may be language.)
- ▶ Steer your child toward comedies, even cartoons. Kids love comedies and are usually satisfied with a good laugh.
- ▶ Ask your retailer to suggest a title (within your specifications, of course).

One inventive fifteen-year-old we know puts the onus on herself. When she doesn't want her nine-year-old brother to see a film that's too advanced for him, she says it frightens her. He then feels very grown-up and, wanting to protect her, agrees to rent something else.

THE ADDAMS FAMILY

Paramount Home Video
1991
102 minutes
Directed by: Barry Sonnenfeld
Starring: Angelica Huston,
    Raul Julia, Christopher Lloyd
OFRB rating: AA
MPAA rating: PG-13

The Addams family is a macabre inversion of the normal North American family; immensely rich, they dwell in a sprawling run-down mansion straight out of a horror movie. The movie begins when Gomez Addams and his wife, Morticia, receive a visit from their crooked lawyer, Tully. Tully has been trying for years to swindle the wealthy eccentrics (without success), and when he is confronted by the evil Abigail Craven and her hulking son Gordon — who just happens to bear an uncanny resemblance to Gomez's long-lost brother Fester — a sinister plot is hatched: Gordon will impersonate Fester in order to gain access to the family's vault and its immense wealth. The delighted Addams family (although slightly suspicious) accepts the bogus Fester instantly, and the hijinks begin as Gordon must endure life with the Addamses. Oddly, he comes to cherish his new family, and a final showdown puts his loyalties to the test.

CAUTION: Overt sadism coupled with off-beat humour make this film unsuitable for some children. And the constant abuse in the Addams family's home — however satirical — leads one to speculate just how funny a child from a truly abusive household would find this film.

GO: This film is a big-budget extravaganza with superb casting. Connoisseurs will be struck by the uncanny resemblances of Julia, Huston and Lloyd to Charles Addams's original comic-strip characters.

ADVENTURES IN BABYSITTING

Touchstone Home Video
1987
102 minutes
Directed by: Chris Columbus
Starring: Maia Brewton, Keith
    Coogan, Anthony Rapp,
    Elizabeth Shue
MPAA rating: PG-13

Chris Parker's easy baby-sitting job becomes complicated when a flaky friend calls and pursuades Chris to pick her up at the bus depot, taking the kids with her. On the way, the family station wagon blows a tire, and when the spooky one-armed truck driver who gives them a lift makes a detour to take pot-shots at his wife's lover, Chris and the kids become mixed up in all kinds of trouble. In short order, they make a daring escape from stolen-car dealers, sing the blues, battle street gangs, negotiate an inner city hospital, attend a wild university party, meet the living embodiment of Thor, confront the bad guys and get home before their parents do. It's all in a night's work for the greatest baby-sitter in history.

CAUTION: The children are frequently in peril. There is some racial stereotyping.

GO: This is a charming adventure that's

AGES 10 TO 13

low on swearing and violence (by today's standards), and high on excitement and fun. In one scene there is a significant message about the dangers of street life.

▲

✗ THE ADVENTURES OF BARON MUNCHAUSEN

RCA/Col
1988
126 minutes
Directed by: Terry Gilliam
Starring: Winston Dennis, Eric Idle,
  Charles McKeown, John Neville,
  Sarah Polley, Jonathan Pryce,
  Jack Purvis, Oliver Reed,
  Uma Thurman, Robin Williams
OFRB rating: PG
MPAA rating: PG

In the late eighteenth century, as the Sultan's army beseiges a European city, the play "The Adventures of Baron Munchausen" is being performed by a travelling theatre group. Suddenly, the play is interrupted by the real Baron Munchausen, who (accompanied by a young stowaway named Sally) sets out in a hot air balloon in hopes of finding his lost companions with whom he will raise the siege. Those companions are: Berthold, who can run faster than a bullet; Albrecht, the strongest man on earth; Adolphus, who can see and shoot farther than a telescope; and Gustavus, who can hear over impossible distances and exhale harder than a hurricane. In the course of their search, the Baron and Sally visit the moon, where a jealous King holds him captive; they fall into a volcano and find themselves in the domain of Vulcan and his slinky wife Aphrodite; and they are swallowed

by a sea-monster and expelled back to the city just in time to defeat the Sultan's forces and save the day.

✗STOP: In one scene, the Sultan plays an organ which produces screams instead of music as the victims trapped inside are tortured. Death is a frightening, skull-faced black angel and the eyes of the Sultan's executioner have been sewn shut.

CAUTION: The scene in Vulcan's domain has some very racy moments and the king of the Moon (when body and head are attached) is very carnal. There are noisy combat scenes throughout.

GO: A dazzling effort, *Baron Munchausen* has some incredible visual effects.

■

✗ ANGEL SQUARE

C/FP
1990
104 minutes
Directed by: Anne Wheeler
Starring: Ned Beatty, Marie Gaudry,
  Jeremy Radick,
  Guillaume Thivierge
OFRB rating: G

Christmas, 1945. Sammy Rosenberg's father, the railway watchman, is knocked unconscious and taken to the hospital in a coma. When the police investigation goes nowhere, he and his friend Tommy conduct their own investigation. They discover that two boys who were on the railroad grounds the night of the assault saw a comic book fall to the ground. Tommy locates the comic, but when he fingers the wrong man even his policeman friend Ozzy tells him to drop it. Then on Christmas Eve,

Tommy solves the case. Based on the book by Brian Doyle.

✗STOP: In one scene, Tommy's boy-crazy friend Florette gives him an elementary lesson in the biological differences between males and females with some drawings in the snow and in another, he asks a girl if she has ever French-kissed.

CAUTION: The film talks about anti-semitism and opens with a realistic war dream, involving boy soldiers who suffer realistic bullet wounds. The boys' evil teacher's head swivels right around and Tommy comments on the difficulties of having a sister with Down Syndrome. (He says, "...it's like having a younger sister for life.")

GO: This is an entertaining Canadian film.
■

✗ BABY: SECRET OF THE LOST LEGEND

Touchstone Home Video
1985
92 minutes
Directed by: B. W. L. Norton
Starring: William Katt, Patrick
    McGoohan, Sean Young
OFRB rating: PG
MPAA rating: PG

When Dr. Eric Kiviat learns that giant apatosaurs still inhabit the African rainforest, he will stop at nothing (murder included) to get credit for the greatest scientific discovery of all time. So when his assistant, Susan, discovers an apatosaurus skull, he convinces her that she's actually found the skull of a giraffe. But Susan suspects that Kiviat is concealing something, and that night she charters a helicopter into the interior. Her husband George follows, and finds Susan helping neolithic villagers who are dying after having eaten the flesh of what is apparently a dead apatosaurus. Meanwhile, Kiviat hires a boat of trigger-happy government soldiers, and the next day, when George and Susan come into close proximity with a family of apatosaurs, Kiviat and his party arrive, tranquilizing one of the adults and killing the other. George and Susan decide to take the baby apatosaurus back to the civilized world, but it gets away from them and after numerous adventures George and Susan trail Kiviat and his soldiers to their military base for a final violent confrontation.

✗STOP: Automatic weapons fire, grenades explode and an arrow pierces a soldier's neck. Kiviat brutally murders the soldiers' commander with a tranquilizer gun and a apatosaurus kills Kiviat, who dies screaming horribly — considerable violence for a film associated with the Disney studios.

CAUTION: There is one love-making scene (partial nudity) and some coarse language.

GO: This film is amazingly popular with young children who seem to be able to overlook the carnage and concentrate on the antics of the cute baby dinosaur.
▲

BACK TO THE FUTURE

MCA
1986
116 minutes
Directed by: Robert Zemeckis
Starring: Michael J. Fox,
    Crispin Glover, Christopher Lloyd,
    Lea Thompson, Thomas F.
    Wilson
OFRB rating: PG—Swearing
MPAA rating: PG

When lunatic inventor "Doc" Emmett Brown creates a plutonium-powered time machine in the body of a DeLorean, he invites his friend, high school student Marty McFly, to help him test it. The testing is going well until terrorists, looking for the plutonium, interrupt at the critical point; Doc is gunned down and Marty flees in the DeLorean with the terrorists in hot pursuit. When Marty hits eighty-eight miles an hour, the machine is activated and he's zapped into the year 1955. There he meets his parents as teenagers and, through a series of fluke accidents, alters the future when his own mother falls in love with him. Dumbfounded, Marty does the only thing he can think of. He tracks down Doc, thirty years younger, and after finally convincing the scientist that he really is from the future, explains that the DeLorean is out of fuel. Doc devises a plan to power the DeLorean back to 1985 with a bolt of lightning. But first, Marty must attend the high school dance to make sure his mother and father get together or his very existence will be in jeopardy.

CAUTION: Doc is shot. There is the odd fight and some coarse language.

GO: Impressive art direction and a complex story-line make this film watchable many times over.

BACK TO THE FUTURE II

MCA
1989
108 minutes
Directed by: Robert Zemeckis
Starring: Michael J. Fox, Christopher Lloyd, Lea Thompson, Thomas F. Wilson
OFRB rating: PG
MPAA rating: PG

Marty has only just returned to his own time when Doc reappears in the DeLorean. He's come from the year 2015 to take Marty and his girlfriend Jennifer back to the future where there are serious problems with their children. When they arrive, Doc puts Jennifer to sleep to prevent her from seeing more than she should. Then, Marty impersonates his own son to foil the criminal designs of Griff, his present-day nemesis Biff's psychotic grandson. His mission complete, Marty buys a sports almanac, intending to make a fortune on betting when he gets back to his own time. Meanwhile, the police discover Jennifer's unconscious body, identify her and take her to her 2015 home. While Marty and Doc frantically try to rescue her, Biff discovers the time machine and uses it to take Marty's almanac back to his own younger self in 1955. Marty and Doc retrieve Jennifer and return to 1985 to find that the world has been horribly altered and that the man in charge is millionaire Biff, the Luckiest Man Alive. They return to 1955 to steal the almanac back from young Biff and at the climax of the film, the

DeLorean is struck by lightning and Doc is blasted into 1885, leaving Marty stranded in 1955.

CAUTION: You may have to wrestle with a plot explanation for young viewers. There is some fighting and some coarse language.

▲

BACK TO THE FUTURE III

MCA
1990
118 minutes
Directed by: Robert Zemeckis
Starring: Michael J. Fox,
   Christopher Lloyd, Mary
   Steenburgen, Lea Thompson,
   Thomas F. Wilson
OFRB rating: PG
MPAA rating: PG

Marty and the young Doc of 1955 receive a letter from the Doc of 1855 describing the location of the DeLorean. They find and repair the car, then Marty races to the Old West. But when he arrives, he ruptures a fuel line and he and the Doc of 1855 realize that the only way to get the DeLorean up to the critical eighty-eight miles an hour is to hijack a locomotive and push the car. Barroom brawls and gunfights at sunrise aren't enough to keep them from their work. But when Doc falls in love with a young teacher named Clara Clayton, things get horribly off-schedule. And when Clara shows up unexpectedly, Doc must stay behind to save her, and Marty returns to 1985 alone where even more surprises are in store.

CAUTION: There is some coarse language.

GO: The special effects are incredible, and the dazzling, madcap story features terrific performances by Fox, Lloyd, Steenburgen and Wilson. There is something for everyone.

✗ BATMAN

Warner Home Video
1989
126 minutes
Directed by: Tim Burton
Starring: Kim Basinger,
   Michael Keaton, Jack Nicholson,
   Jack Palance
OFRB rating: PG
MPAA rating: PG-13

The futuristic metropolis of Gotham City is ravaged by crime and virtually run by criminal gangs, most notably that led by the evil Grissom and his chief henchman Jack Napier. But help comes in the form of the mysterious caped crusader Batman, alias Bruce Wayne, a troubled multi-millionaire whose parents were killed by a thug when he was just a child, and who is now exacting his revenge on the criminal community of Gotham. Wayne is indeed a tortured soul, but a little sunshine enters his life when he begins a relationship with the lovely photographer Vicki Vale. The plot thickens as Grissom discovers that Napier is having an affair with his own mistress, Alicia, and arranges to set Napier up to be busted. Napier escapes the trap but falls into a vat of toxic waste and is transformed into the Joker, a hideously deformed psychotic hellbent on avenging himself on just about everybody. The Joker knocks off Grissom, consolidates the forces of evil and prepares to take over Gotham City. Only Batman stands in his way.

✘STOP: People are killed in violent fashion. The Joker is grotesque and homicidal. In one scene, the Joker repeatedly pumps bullets into Grissom. In another, Alicia has obviously been tortured and disfigured. There are extended scenes of peril. At the climax, Batman and Vicki are suspended from the lofty heights of a cathedral steeple as the Joker tries to kill them. The Joker falls to his own death.

CAUTION: The mood of this film is relentlessly haunted, dark and brooding, like much of the work of Tim Burton who seems obsessed with deformity and alienation. And while this is a genuine tribute to the original Dark Knight, it will very likely be far too intense for the younger viewers. As an alternative, try *Batman: The Movie*.

GO: An exciting, action-packed adult fantasy.

▲

✘ BATMAN RETURNS

Warner Home Video
1992
126 minutes
Directed by: Tim Burton
Starring: Danny DeVito,
    Michael Keaton, Michelle Pfeiffer,
    Christopher Walken
OFRB rating: AA—Violence/
    Frightening Scenes
MPAA rating: PG-13

Batman Returns opens three decades before the present, where the Christmas season heralds the birth of a hideously deformed infant. After the infant eats the family's pet cat, his desperate parents dump him into the sewer, where he sails into a subterranean cavern beneath the Gotham City Zoo and is met by a flock of penguins. The film then returns to Christmas present, and the office tower of city big-shot Max Shreck. Shreck, who routinely abuses his mousy secretary Selina Kyle, is just about to give his annual holiday address when an army of heavily armed clowns machine-guns the city centre, driving Shreck into the catacombs below. There he meets the Penguin (the once-abandoned infant who has grown to become the loathsome ruler of the sewers), and the pair forms an unholy alliance to rule Gotham. As their plot unfolds, Shreck pushes Selina Kyle out a window of his skyscraper. On the ground, she is resurrected by a swarm of alley cats to become the Catwoman; she then proceeds to terrorize the streets of Gotham and exact her revenge on Shreck. She also cuts a deal with The Penguin to destroy Batman. The Penguin then double-crosses Catwoman, is subsequently double-crossed by Shreck and undertakes to wreak vengeance on all of Gotham. Amidst this maelstrom of shifting alliances, Batman does violent battle with just about everyone, while his alter-ego Bruce Wayne has a neurotic romance with Selina Kyle.

✘STOP: This is not a film for children. De Vito's superb Penguin is a grotesque, tortured sociopath who eats raw fish, drools black blood and bites off the noses of people who annoy him. The violence level is extreme and the special effect of falling from great heights appears absolutely real.

CAUTION: The sets are magnificent, the effects are spectacular and the performances are mostly wonderful; unfortunately, all of this only contributes to the menacing impact of the film. Previewing by a parent is strongly advised. You might want to consider renting *Batman: The Movie* instead if you have young children who are Batman-crazy. (See the 6-10 section.)

✗ THE BEAR

Columbia/Tri-Star
1989
92 minutes
Directed by: Jean-Jacques Annaud
Starring: Tcheky Karyo,
Jack Wallace
OFRB rating: PG
MPAA rating: PG

After his mother is killed in a rock slide, a little bear cub befriends an adult male grizzly and together they try to outrun hunters.

✗**STOP:** This is a social comment film and *not* a cute animal movie for young children. Concern has been raised about the manipulation of animals to tell this story of man against beast.

CAUTION: The male grizzly mates while the baby watches, and the baby bear has hallucinations after eating poisonous mushrooms.

GO: The film has a worthwhile message.

AGES 10 TO 13

BEBE'S KIDS

Paramount
1992
74 minutes
Directed by: Bruce Smith
Starring the voices of: Nell Carter,
Rich Little, Tone Loc
OFRB rating: PG
MPAA rating: PG-13

Based on characters created by the late comedian Robin Harris, this is a full-length animation about a man who meets an attractive woman named Jamika at a friend's funeral. He pursues her until she agrees to go out with him, but she insists that it be someplace appropriate for her and her young son. Her son is nice enough, but when Robin goes to pick Jamika up she has custody of three more children, her friend Bébé's kids. Robin and Jamika end up taking the whole gang to Funland, where Bébé's uncontrollable children set the amusement park on its ear. When Robin finally gets Bébé's children home, he finds that they live in a crack-infested dump and that their mother doesn't care about them.

CAUTION: The opening scene takes place in a bar with hookers where the main character is trying to drink away his troubles. This is a social comment film; the humour is gross and there is some coarse language.

GO: This video also contains the seven minute featurette cartoon, *Itsy Bitsy Spider*, which is a funny, well-animated look at the battle between an exterminator and a very resourceful spider.

✘ BEETLEJUICE

Warner Home Video
1988
92 minutes
Directed by: Tim Burton
Starring: Alec Baldwin, Geena
    Davis, Jeffrey Jones, Catherine
    O'Hara, Winona Ryder
OFRB rating: PG—Frightening
    Scenes
MPAA rating: PG

Adam and Barbara Maitland are spending their vacation fixing up their home in Winsome River, Connecticut. When on a quick errand to the general store, they accidentally run their car into the river, and it isn't until they return home, soaking wet, that they discover they are dead. But the hereafter is totally unexpected. The Maitlands can't leave the house and the house's new owners are intent on customizing it to their own excessive tastes. Desperate, the Maitland's consult a copy of *The Handbook for the Recently Deceased* which tells them how to find their case-worker, Juno. But when they meet with Juno and she refuses to help, they turn to Beetlejuice, a free-lance bio-exorcist, and an expert at driving unwanted living people out of houses. Beetlejuice, however, has his own sinister agenda.

✘**STOP:** This film is full of potentially disturbing images. In the waiting room of the afterlife, people appear as they did when they died (for example, an explorer has a shrunken head), and while this is quite amusing for adults, it may terrify some young children. Beetlejuice also takes on some fairly frightening manifestations in the film.

CAUTION: In our experience, any film which is based in its entirety on a depiction of the afterlife — satirical or not — is bound to raise many questions for young people. Even teenagers have come to us with questions prompted by this film.

GO: This quality production features a stellar cast and plenty of Tim Burton's characteristic incredible special effects. Best suited to kids in their mid-teens and up; we recommend young children stick with the animated version.

BETTER OFF DEAD

Key Video
1985
97 minutes
Directed by: Steve Holland
Starring: John Cusack, Kim Darby,
    Diane Franklin, Anne Ramsey
OFRB rating: PG
MPAA rating: PG

Things aren't going well for sixteen-year-old Lane. His family (and everyone else in his hometown) is decidedly strange, and he's just lost the girl of his dreams because his popularity is sliding. After a series of wacky misadventures during which he contemplates suicide, he manages to get his life together with the help of a female foreign exchange student. And he soon comes to realize that the girl who cares about him enough to help him impress another girl is the *real* girl of his dreams.

CAUTION: The main characters are high school students, so expect gross behaviour and some sexual innuendo.

GO: Despite its title, this is a comedy. The female foreign exchange student is intelligent, capable and sensitive and she demonstrates positive values.

BEYOND THE STARS

IVE
1989
94 minutes
Directed by: David Saperstein
Starring: F. Murray Abraham,
  Olivia D'Abo, Martin Sheen,
  Christian Slater
OFRB rating: PG
MPAA rating: PG

Suspended from high school for smashing a window with a model rocket, astronaut hopeful Erik Nichols goes to visit his father in Cedar Bay. There, he meets Mara who introduces him to her friend (and Erik's hero) Col. Paul Andrews, a retired astronaut who's been on the moon. Andrews is a bitter alchoholic, unable to reconcile something in his past. At first rude to Erik, Andrews is eventually won over by Erik's ideology and youthful enthusiasm. Erik's father, however, dislikes Andrews and what he represents (he harbours much bitterness about his own experiences with NASA) and refuses to allow Erik to continue visiting. Soon the men see how their animosity is hurting Erik and, after a violent verbal exchange, apologize to each other and to Erik. It turns out that Andrews is suffering from leukemia (contacted from exposure to radiation during the moon mission), but before he dies he reveals to Erik the secret of what he found on the moon and asks Erik to

return the object when he becomes an astronaut himself.

CAUTION: In spite of the title this is not a film about space exploration, but rather about a rocky father-and-son relationship. There is some coarse language.

GO: The relationship between Erik's divorced parents is civilized. Messages about earth conservation are included in the film.

BIG GIRLS DON'T CRY . . . THEY GET EVEN

New Line
1992
93 minutes
Directed by: Joan Micklin Silver
Starring: Griffin Dunne,
  Adrienne Shelley, Hillary Wolf
OFRB rating: PG—Mature Theme

Laura Chartoff has big family problems. Her parents are divorced and her mother has just married a high-powered executive with three children: Josh, the eldest, has never reconciled himself to his mother's death and has run away from home; Kurt is a thirteen-year-old military fanatic; and Corinne is just like Laura's own mother, shallow and obsessed with the trappings of wealth. Desperate for advice, Laura calls her father, who has also remarried, but he's no help. Neither is his *other* ex-wife, Barbara. The only family friend Laura really has is her new step-brother Josh. So, when Laura is unjustly blamed for breaking some expensive china, she stows away on Josh's truck. By the time he discovers her it's too late, and she ends up travelling with

AGES 10 TO 13

him to his mountain cabin. Her parents track her down, but she escapes into the woods. Then it's up to the whole bickering clan to find her. But first they must begin the painful process of learning to understand one another.

CAUTION: Laura is extremely critical of her father's many marriages. Family members are rude to each other and Laura's mother blatantly favours Corinne. There is some coarse language.

GO: For older kids, this is an excellent film about overcoming animosity.

BIG MAN ON CAMPUS

Vestron Home Video
1989
102 minutes
Directed by: Jeremy Paul Kagan
Starring: Melora Hardin, Allan Katz,
  Corey Parker, Tom Skerritt,
  Cindy Williams
OFRB rating: PG
MPAA rating: PG-13

When an uncivilized hunchback swings down from the clock tower to save a beautiful university student named Cathy Adams, he is captured and taken into custody. At his hearing, psychologist Dr. Fisk claims that the creature is unable to fit into society, but the university's Dr. Webster disagrees, insisting that it's necessary to study him further before making such a conclusion. The university wins custody on the condition that if the creature exhibits any signs of hostility he's to be institutionalized. At the university, Cathy's boyfriend, Alex, is enlisted to baby-sit and civilize the creature and Dr. Diane Girard is brought in to teach him speech. Together they agree to call him Bob and lessons progress so well that when Dr. Webster is invited to bring him onto a talk show meant to discredit him, she accepts the offer as an opportunity to show the world how Bob has evolved. The show will, of course, make Dr. Fisk look like a total fool, so in order to save her reputation she calls Bob and tells him that Cathy is in trouble. He rushes to the dormitory to save her, causing a commotion and resisting arrest on the way. And it seems to many that Dr. Fisk was correct after all. But Bob manages to make it to the studio in time and during the outrageous live show discredits Dr. Fisk and finds true love.

CAUTION: The creature chants Cathy's name repeatedly and the doctor explains that this is "another form of masturbation." Also of concern may be a scene in which Bob gets an explanation of French-kissing from Dr. Girard.

GO: Alex has continual one-liners and there are a lot of sight gags. In spite of the sexual references this is a very funny film, suitable for viewers of a great range of ages.

BINGO

RCA/Columbia Home Video
1991
90 minutes
Directed by: Matthew Robbins
Starring: David Rasche, Robert J.
  Steinmiller Jr., Cindy Williams
OFRB rating: F
MPAA rating: PG

When Bingo, the world's smartest dog, runs away from the circus, he saves the life of a young boy named Chuckie and the two promptly become best friends. But Chuckie's mom won't have a dog in the house, so Chuckie is forced to conceal the dog's presence. And as if this weren't bad enough, Chuckie's dad, a place-kicker for the Denver Broncos, gets himself traded to Green Bay. Still, the intrepid boy and his dog have the move all worked out and even design a secret compartment in which Bingo will travel. But Bingo thwarts the plan when, after spending the night wining and dining the friendly lady dog next door, he sleeps in and misses the departure. Then follows one hilarious adventure after another as Bingo pursues his beloved master thousands of miles across America. He meets evil kidnappers, escapes a food stand featuring hot dogs made from real dogs and even ends up in jail.

CAUTION: This is a spoof on all of the dog movies in which dogs are shown to be smarter than humans, and its satirical humour may be lost on young children. There are some frightening scenes and there is some coarse language.

GO: A silly but fun movie, this is a nice attempt by a director to try something new.

BODO THE WHIZ KID

MCA Home Video
1989
90 minutes
Directed by: Gloria Behrens
Starring: Gary Forbes,
    Martin Forbes, Andreas Vitasek,
    Jake Woods
OFRB rating: PG

Bodo Blinker, a fourteen-year-old inventor-genius, is faced with some typical problems: his marks are low, the girl he likes (Nova) doesn't even know he exists and there are obnoxious bullies at school. To complicate matters, his father, in the middle of a work-sponsored samurai program, and his mother, an exercise junkie, have Bodo attending sessions with an aggression therapist who's intent on turning Bodo into a lean, mean corporate raider. When Bodo is tormented by a bully named Alex, he retaliates by turning Alex's motorbike into a rocket and, knowing that a counterstrike is inevitable, he uses science to defend himself. He taps into a major computer centre and creates Bodo 2, an ultra-confident, macho-man version of himself with a mean streak a mile wide and a real eye for the ladies. Soon, however, the clone becomes a bigger problem than all of his other problems put together, causing chaos and confusion everywhere he goes. In the end, Bodo 1 and Bodo 2 each learn a valuable lesson from the other: Bodo 1 gains courage and Bodo 2, sensitivity and understanding.

CAUTION: When Bodo 2 proves to be a tough fighter, Nova falls for him (not such a great message for either sex). Also, Bodo's Mom is a bit lascivious, and Bodo's clone makes a weird pass at her. There is some coarse language.

parents in a plane crash and his resulting confinement in the mental institution is upsetting to watch. There is some swearing.

GO: Millie and her brother have a good relationship and their family is strong in spite of its difficulties. This is a movie about "magic" possibilities.

THE BOY WHO COULD FLY

Karl-Lorimar
1986
108 minutes
Directed by: Nick Castle
Starring: Bonnie Bedelia,
    Lucy Deakins, Colleen Dewhurst,
    Fred Savage, Jay Underwood
OFRB rating: PG
MPAA rating: PG

After her father's suicide, fourteen-year-old Millie moves with her mother and brother into a new neighbourhood. There she meets Eric, who is strangely mute and rumoured to be able to fly. Millie shows him some kindly interest and each day discovers something new about Eric. Then she has an accident that puts her in hospital, and is convinced that Eric's "magical qualities" saved her life. She begins to escape from the pain and grief of her father's death only to learn when she returns that Eric has been taken to the State Institution. Eric escapes and Millie runs away with him, and when they are cornered by state troopers it's discovered that Eric really can fly as he rises above the startled spectators with Millie in tow. In the end, Eric realizes that he cannot stay now that his secret has been revealed, so he flies off into the sunset, never to be seen again.

STOP: This is not a film for young children. It's emotionally disturbing and includes a confusing blend of fantasy and reality. Millie's father committed suicide (because he had cancer), and the family has trouble coming to grips with the situation. Eric's problems are a reaction to losing his

✗ BUFFY THE VAMPIRE SLAYER

20th Century Fox
1992
86 minutes
Directed by: Fran Rubel Kuzui
Starring: Rutger Hauer, Luke Perry,
    Paul Reubens, Donald
    Sutherland, Kristy Swanson
OFRB rating: PG—Violence
MPAA rating: PG-13

According to ancient tradition, only the Slayer, a young woman trained by the Watcher, can stem a plague of vampires. And sure enough, when Los Angeles is rocked by a series of bizarre murders (not only are the bodies drained of blood, but they're also vanishing from the morgue), Buffy, a California airhead, is approached by a man who tells her that she is the chosen one. Buffy thinks he's crazy. But he is, in fact, the next Watcher, and he knows that she is to be the Slayer. Reluctantly, she agrees to hear him out and accompanies him to the graveyard; after killing a couple of vampires, she is eventually convinced of her birthright and begins rigorous training. Then, night after night she's on the streets, secretly knocking off the undead, all the while undergoing a complete personality change. And in the final confrontation, at the big high school dance, Buffy battles a horde of vampires, led by their evil leader, Lothos.

✗**STOP:** The rating is appropriate. This is not a film for young children; it's full of frightening images and violent murders and combat. Spikes are plunged into vampire chests with realistic crunching noises, and growling vampires claw from fresh graves.

CAUTION: There are spooky white vampire faces with fangs and bloodshot eyes, and a lot of bloody neck-biting. There is some coarse language.

GO: For teens and adults this is a camp-a-thon, Paul Reubens' death scene in particular.

Klopek's scary mansion and discover . . . nothing. But things aren't over yet, as this zany farce lurches to its madcap conclusion.

✗**STOP:** This is a black comedy, and the morbid elements are probably too frightening for anyone under the age of nine. In the end, it's revealed that Ray's suspicions were right all along as Professor Klopek tries to kill him with an injection in a frantic fight in an ambulance. Other scenes that may upset viewers are one in which Professor Klopek comes up from the basement covered in blood and another in which Ray has a nightmare about a satanic ritual.

GO: For kids thirteen and up, this film is definitely among the ranks of the great dark comedies.

✗ THE BURBS

MCA
1989
101 minutes
Directed by: Joe Dante
Starring: Bruce Dern,
    Rick Ducommun, Carrie Fisher,
    Henry Gibson, Tom Hanks
OFRB rating: AA
MPAA rating: PG

Ray Peterson's quiet vacation at home is disrupted when the Klopeks, creepy, mad-scientist types, move into the dilapidated house next door. Bolstered by his suburbanite buddies, a neighbourhood busybody and a crazed Vietnam vet, Ray does some major league snooping and becomes more and more convinced that the Klopeks are committing unspeakable atrocities in their basement. Ray's wife thinks he's gone crazy, but Ray persists, and he and his friends sneak into the

✗ CAN'T BUY ME LOVE

Touchstone Home Video
1987
94 minutes
Directed by: Steve Rash
Starring: Patrick Dempsey,
    Dennis Dugan, Amanda Peterson
OFRB rating: PG-Coarse Language
MPAA rating PG-13

When Cindy Mancini, the most popular girl in school, accidently ruins her mother's best dress and needs $1000 to replace it, "nowhere-man" Ronny Miller comes to her rescue on one condition: that she pretend to be his girlfriend, thereby helping him achieve popular status. Reluctantly she agrees, and in the time they spend together Ronny opens her eyes to things that are much more important than money and clothes. Conversely, Cindy introduces him to all of her friends and soon Ronny becomes so popular himself that he no longer needs her. But that's not the end of it. Rejected by her own friends and now by Ronny, Cindy makes it known that Ronny bought his way into popularity by buying her, and every single person Ronny knows instantly loses respect for him. It's in this way that Ronny makes everyone else understand that money can't really buy popularity — it's being yourself that makes you loved.

✗STOP: Keep in mind that this film is about senior high school students so there's a fair amount of sexual activity, although it's within the PG limits. Also expect coarse language and some offensive behaviour.

GO: The entire film is a message about the teenage struggle for popularity. There is a poignant portrayal of the stupidity of peer pressure.

▲

✗ CHRISTOPHER COLUMBUS: THE DISCOVERY

Warner Home Video
1992
121 minutes
Directed by: John Glen
Starring: Marlon Brando,
   George Corraface, Tom Selleck,
   Rachel Ward
OFRB rating: AA
MPAA rating: PG-13

Genovese mapmaker Christopher Columbus is a proud, half-crazy visionary. Inspired by the tale of Marco Polo and tempted by maps of India, he is convinced there must be a way to reach Asia by sailing west. He finally secures financing from Queen Isabella herself, but Columbus's biggest challenge is convincing anyone to man his three ships (no one believes they will ever make it back) and he's eventually forced to hire criminals. His preparations made, Columbus sets off due west with favourable winds and a grumbling crew. But thirty-two days and twenty-four hundred miles later, the crew is ready to mutiny. And even as his men prepare to do him in, a heavenly wind arises, and land is sighted. The explorers go ashore and are soon greeted by the natives. Columbus then establishes Natividad, and the oppression of the new world begins.

✗STOP: In the citadel of the Inquisition, it's clear that someone is being tortured as screams sound in the background. On the voyage, a traitor is hung out in the sun to make him talk, and is found one morning with a knife in his side. And at the end of the film, the murderous Spaniards are killed by the natives. (Spaniards are shown hanging and butchered.)

CAUTION: One of the ship's officers makes advances to a cabin boy. The natives are scantily clad (women are bare-breasted).

GO: A good way to introduce older children to the history of this cataclysmic episode in human history. The Spaniards are certainly not glorified in this film.

✗ CLASH OF THE TITANS

MGM/UA
1981
118 minutes
Directed by: Desmond Davis
Starring: Harry Hamlin,
   Laurence Olivier, Maggie Smith
MPAA rating: PG

King Acletius of Argos, jealous of his daughter Danae's beauty, keeps her locked away from the sight of men; however, this is no protection from the amorous attentions of the mighty god Zeus. And when Danae bears Zeus a son (Perseus), the furious king casts her and the boy adrift on the ocean. Zeus exacts terrible revenge on Acletius, killing him and unleashing the monstrous Titan Kraken upon his kingdom. Thus begins this epic, which chronicles the adventures of Perseus whose quest for the hand of his beloved Andromeda pits him against the sea-goddess Thetis, her deformed son Caballos, Medusa the Gorgon and the huge Titan Kraken.

✗**STOP:** This film is likely to terrify little ones right from the first scene, when Danae and her child are locked in a chest and cast onto the waters. Many of the mythological creatures featured are grotesque and one battle is extremely graphic.

CAUTION: The story is so long and complex that anyone under the age of eight will probably fade out.

GO: Some of Ray Harryhausen's finest special-effects are featured in this film. (The scene in which Perseus battles the Medusa is a masterpiece of stop-animation.) *Clash of the Titans* will appeal to young people with a taste for fantasy and will serve to provide a loose introduction to Greek mythology.

✗ CLOAK AND DAGGER

MCA
1984
101 minutes
Directed by: Richard Franklin
Starring: Dabney Coleman,
    Michael Murphy, Henry Thomas
OFRB rating: PG
MPAA Rating: PG

Davey copes with his mother's death by immersing himself in fantasy role-playing. He substitutes an imaginary hero named Jack Flack for his practical air force

colonel father (played by Dabney Coleman in a dual role). But the fantasy suddenly becomes real when Davey witnesses a murder and is forced to handle the situation alone as the hit men close in. The climax of the film brings with it the realization that life is no game, that Jack Flack is by no means the hero Davey had imagined and that the true hero is Davey's down-to-earth real father.

✗**STOP:** Davey is thrown into the trunk of the car along with a dead friend (killed off-camera) and is later forced to shoot a villain in self-defense. Some children are disturbed by a scene in which the villain tells Davey in lurid, terrifying detail how he is going to kill him.

GO: The film is a great good guy vs bad guy yarn, extremely suspenseful — every boy will love it.

✗ CROCODILE DUNDEE

Paramount Home Video
1986
98 minutes
Directed by: Peter Faiman
Starring: Mark Blum, Paul Hogan,
    Linda Kozlowski
OFRB rating: PG—Swearing
MPAA rating: PG-13

Sue Charlton, a glamorous and adventurous reporter, travels to the wilds of northern Australia to get the big scoop on famed croc-hunter Mick Dundee. In the process she learns how to survive in the hinterland, and she discovers the truth behind the legend of "Crocodile Dundee." Sue then brings Mick back to New York City, where he in turn discovers a different kind of wilderness, one for which he too must learn new rules of survival.

✗**STOP:** Although this is a comedy there are fist-fights and much sexual innuendo. The New York scenes show drug use, transvestites, prostitutes and muggers.

CAUTION: Sue attends a party in a revealing dress (her bottom is exposed), and many of the kids we know hooted and howled when they saw it. Blacks are given limited on-camera time in the city scenes, and are represented primarily as pimps and muggers.

GO: The film shows our own urban culture in a fresh light.

✗ CROCODILE DUNDEE II

Paramount Home Video
1988
110 minutes
Directed By: John Cornell
Starring: Paul Hogan,
    Linda Kozlowski
OFRB rating: PG—Mature Theme
MPAA rating: PG

In this film, the sequel to *Crocodile Dundee*, Mick saves his abducted girlfriend, Sue, from big-time Columbian drug lords. Beginning in New York and ending in Australia, *Crocodile Dundee II* doesn't have the light comic touch that the first film did.

✗**STOP:** In one of the many violent scenes, an informer is shot in the head, execution style.

CAUTION: Although the MPAA rating of this film is lower than that of the first Crocodile Dundee film, the violence is far more serious.

CURLY SUE

Warner Home Video
1991
102 minutes
Directed by: John Hughes
Starring: Jim Belushi, John Getz,
    Kelly Lynch, Alison Porter
MPAA rating: PG

Shiftless Bill Dancer and his young friend Curly Sue are a down and out con-artist team, who figure they have it made when they spot a rich lawyer named Grey Ellison and set her up for the old car-hits-pedestrian scam. They manage to score a meal and that's all, but the next evening Grey hits Bill again, and this time it's for real. So Bill and Curly Sue become fixtures in Grey's life; they stay at her apartment and take advantage of the benefits of her largesse. But charity has its limits and when Grey's jealous boyfriend calls the Children's Aid Society, Bill is thrown in jail and Curly Sue is taken to a children's hostel. By this time, Grey realizes that she loves the child and takes the necessary steps to become her legal guardian. Thus relieved of his responsibility, everyone expects Bill to leave, but he doesn't, and in the end Bill, Grey and Sue live happily ever after.

CAUTION: The film may raise some questions for children about derelicts and street people. There is some coarse language.

CURSE OF THE VIKING GRAVE

CFP Video
1991
120 minutes
Directed by: Michael Scott
Starring: Evan Adams, Jay Brazeau,
    Nicholas Shields, Cedric Smith,
    Michelle St. John
OFRB rating: PG

When Martin Connolly, a treasure hunter with a dubious reputation, learns of Jamie McNair's discovery of a Viking grave, he's convinced it belonged to famous Viking raider Kunar, son of Ragnor. (Kunar was supposedly buried with the White Christ, a priceless artifact.) So Connolly approaches Jamie, asking to see the site and offering to pay for the guides. Jamie accepts, but he regrets his decision as Connolly's agenda becomes clear: he intends to rob the grave. Jamie's friends, Awasis and Angeline, expecting the worst, set out after Jamie, but they too fall into Connolly's hands. And while Jamie and Awasis are sealed in the viking grave, Connolly and his accomplice take Angeline hostage. Jamie uses his knowledge of Norse rune symbols to find a way out and, aided by the Curse of the Viking Grave, returns the White Christ to its resting place.

CAUTION: Connolly kills his accomplice (off-camera) and ghostly apparitions haunt Connolly and drive him mad.

GO: Based on the book by Farley Mowat, sequel to *Lost in the Barrens.*

■

up in bed with a young woman and can't remember her name. There is some coarse language and some sexual innuendo.

GO: Moira Kelly proves herself to be a fine comedian in places, and the overall story is a positive one for teens and preteens.

THE CUTTING EDGE

MGM/UA
1992
102 minutes
Directed by: Paul Michael Glaser
Starring: Moira Kelly, D.B. Sweeney
OFRB rating: PG—Language May
   Offend Some
MPAA rating: PG

At the 1988 Olympics, amateur hockey superstar Doug Dorsey is crushed on the boards and his injuries knock him out of hockey forever. At the same time, star pairs figure-skater Kate Mosley is dropped by her partner forty-five seconds from the end of a gold-medal performance. Doug returns to his brother's bar in Minnesota and plays hockey in a bar league; Kate, meanwhile, goes through eight partners in two years, and the only qualified skater left vows never to skate with her again. In desperation, Kate's Russian coach invites Doug to try figure-skating. Reluctantly, Doug agrees and he and Kate fight from the first moment they meet. But neither has a choice: Doug's hockey career is over and no one else will skate with Kate. They must work together. And as their relationship evolves, Doug proves his intense dedication to his new endeavour and Kate manages to overcome the bitterness which has dogged her since her childhood. The climax of the film comes when Kate and Doug go to the 1992 Olympics in Albertville, France.

CAUTION: In the first scene Doug wakes

D.A.R.Y.L.

Paramount Home Video
1985
100 minutes
Directed by: Simon Wincer
Starring: Mary Beth Hurt, Michael
   McKean, Barrett Oliver
OFRB rating: PG—Swearing
MPAA rating: PG

D.A.R.Y.L. is a "Data Analysing Robot Youth Lifeform" that looks like a human being. After a memory loss, he becomes disoriented and is taken in by Andy and Joan, a kind couple who desperately want a child of their own. Soon, though, D.A.R.Y.L.'s "real" parents (the scientists who created him) find him and take him to a military base where they discover that he is now more human than they realized. Disturbed when the military orders them to destroy the "experiment," they contact Andy and Joan and ask them if they still want to raise D.A.R.Y.L. Then they fake the robot's death, and using his remarkable brain D.A.R.Y.L. escapes to live with the foster parents who have learned to love him for his human qualities.

CAUTION: D.A.R.Y.L. looks human but isn't, so it's a little disconcerting when the military performs tests on him. D.A.R.Y.L.'s "father" (the scientist who created D.A.R.Y.L.) is killed by police while trying to help his "son" escape. He dies with his eyes open; there is blood.

GO: The film shows that some scientists (a much-maligned profession in films) are concerned with "things of the heart."

CAUTION: Jet is involved in two accidents which may be hard on horse lovers. There is some fighting.

GO: Actress Ari Meyers gives the best fifteen-year-old-with-an-attitude looks. This film about overcoming difficulties has a happy ending.

DARK HORSE

Live Home Video
1992
98 minutes
Directed by: David Hemmings
Starring: Ed Begley Jr.,
    Samantha Eggar, Tab Hunter,
    Ari Meyers, Mimi Rogers
ORRB rating: PG
MPAA rating: PG

Following the death of her mother, Allie moves with her father and brother to a small town, where in an attempt to fit in with her peer group she gets into trouble and is arrested. The sentence is ten weekends of community work at local veterinarian Susan Hadley's ranch. There, Allie feels a kinship with a dark horse named Jet and asks Susan to teach her to ride. As the weeks go by, Allie not only learns to ride but is happier about herself. Inevitably, though, the horse must go back to its owner and on the way Susan and Allie are involved in a serious accident. Allie and Jet fall down a steep cliff and Allie is left with severe damage to her spinal cord. The horse, too, is seriously injured, but Susan refuses to destroy it, preferring instead to rehabilitate it for Allie's sake. And with Jet to motivate her, Allie finds the strength to stand again. Based on a story by Tab Hunter.

DATE WITH AN ANGEL

HBO
1987
114 minutes
Directed by: Tom McLoughlin
Starring: Emmanuelle Beart,
    Phoebe Cates, Michael E. Knight
MPAA rating: PG

Jim Saunders and Patty Winston are about to get married, but at their engagement party Jim is having trouble mixing with her socialite friends. Then *his* friends arrive (disguised as terrorists) and take him away for a night of wild fun. The next morning, a blinding flash of light and an explosion of water wake Jim up, and he's surprised to find a beautiful mute woman floating in the pool. Even more surprising is the fact that she has wings (one of which was broken in her fall, rendering her incapable of leaving). His friends immediately begin planning ways of capitalizing on the angel's misfortune. Patty's psychotic father, meanwhile, is after Jim and the whole time Patty is drinking herself into a stupor. Chase scene follows chase scene, then at the film's climax Jim realizes that the angel is an angel of death and that she has come for him. He has one hope, though: through the course of their misadventures, the angel has fallen in love with him.

CAUTION: The morning after his stag, Jim is shown asleep holding a Love Doll. The film also includes an extremely negative representation of a Roman Catholic priest. Jim's friends are revolting and there is coarse language.

GO: Not bad, but it's rude.

DEFENSE PLAY

Trans World Entertainment
1988
95 minutes
Directed by: Monte Markham
Starring: Monte Markham, David
    Oliver, Susan Ursitti
OFRB rating: PG
MPAA rating: PG

When Scott Denton is joy-riding near the U.S. military base, he watches as a miniature helicopter (a Dart) explodes in midair. Scott then learns more about the Dart when he meets Karen, daughter of Professor Vandemeer who's heading the helicopter development project. That night, while the professor is analysing data from the explosion, somebody activates one of the Dart prototypes and Professor Vandemeer is killed. Scott, who was on the phone with the professor at the time of his murder, is stunned to hear that the death is recorded as an accident. So, he and Karen break into the physics lab, uncover the mystery, and race to identify a Russian spy and destroy the rocket before it's launched.

CAUTION: Professor Vandemeer is cornered and killed by one of the Darts.

The film is somewhat jingoistic in tone and there is some coarse language.

GO: Especially for young video-game fans, this is an exciting spy mystery with a minimum of violence.

DON'T TELL MOM THE BABYSITTER'S DEAD

Warner/HBO
1991
142 minutes
Directed by: Stephen Herek
Starring: Christina Applegate,
    Joanna Cassidy, Keith Coogan
    OFRB rating: PG—Mature Theme
    MPAA rating: PG

When their mother decides to take a much-needed vacation, Sue Ellen and the rest of the kids are left in the care of what appears to be a very nice old lady. But the baby-sitter turns out to be a tyrant who makes the kids wear weird clothes and muster for roll call. And when she sees Sue Ellen's brother's rock-and-roll posters, she promptly dies from shock. Afraid of spoiling their mother's vacation and seeing the possibilities of the situation, the kids put the baby-sitter in a box and leave her outside a funeral home. All well and good, except for one thing: the baby-sitter just happened to have the money for the entire summer in her pocket. With no other alternatives, Sue Ellen and her brother toss to see who will get a summer job. Sue Ellen loses, and hits the work force armed with her mother's slightly altered resumé. By a series of comic misunder-standings she lands a job as an executive assistant in a svelte fashion house, and her dream career skyrockets. But success brings with it a heaping helping of adult stress, and while Sue Ellen copes with burn-out her brother is undergoing a conversion of his own (from rock-and-roll animal to dedicated homemaker). The charade can't go on forever, though; Sue Ellen's company launches its new line of teen clothes at a party in her house, and the whole thing comes to an abrupt end when mom returns home.

CAUTION: There is some coarse language, and at the beginning of the film Sue Ellen's brother smokes a joint with his friends.

GO: This is a terrific little movie featuring teenage characters who display surprisingly good values. They learn to take responsibilty for themselves and for their younger siblings and there is a nice reversal of roles when Sue Ellen becomes the breadwinner and her brother stays home to run the household. We can't understand why this film would receive a "mature theme" warning when other, more extreme films don't.

✗ EDWARD SCISSORHANDS

AGES 10 TO 13

CBS/Fox
1990
100 minutes
Directed by: Tim Burton
Starring: Alan Arkin, Johnny Depp,
    Anthony Michael Hall,
    Vincent Price, Winona Ryder,
    Dianne Wiest
OFRB rating: PG—Frightening
    Scenes
MPAA rating: PG-13

Kim, now an old woman, tells her grandchildren the story of a kind old inventor who lived in the mansion at the top of the hill. In her story the inventor makes many wonderful things, including a man (Edward). But the inventor dies before Edward is complete, and the poor creature is left alone with scissors instead of hands. Then one day, an Avon lady named Peg goes to the mansion on a whim. There she finds Edward and, sorry for his situation, takes him home with her. Peg, her husband Bill and their daughter Kim soon grow to appreciate their house guest. And Edward, meanwhile, proves himself to be the master hedgeclipper of all time, crafting stunning likenesses of dinosaurs and people out of the local trees and bushes. When one of the ladies asks him to trim her hair, Edward's place in the community as a master hairdresser seems assured. But then things begin to go wrong. When Kim's evil boyfriend, Jim, tricks Edward into using his marvelous hands to help him rob his father, Edward is arrested. And as the town turns against him, he's forced back to his mansion and into a final confrontation with Jim which ends in Jim's death.

✗ STOP: In one sense this is a Frankenstein movie about deformity and alienation. There is a close-up of Jim's horrified face as he is impaled by one of Edward's blades and falls from a window.

CAUTION: Edward is highly unusual and may cause some unease for young viewers. (His scissor hands are very sharp and he is always cutting himself.) The inventor's death scene is intense and in the end, Edward is forced back into seclusion.

GO: This film is uniquely different.

GO: Though probably the weakest of the Ernest films, *Scared Stupid* still features Jim Varney's great shtick, and its ending (in which the kids save the day) is a positive one for children.

◄ ERNEST SCARED STUPID

Touchstone Home Video
1991
92 minutes
Directed by: John Cherry
Starring: Jim Varney
OFRB rating: PG—Frightening
  Scenes
MPAA rating: PG

Long ago in Briarville, Missouri, a demonic, child-stealing monster is captured by a group of outraged pioneers (led by Phineas Worrell), who bury the creature alive under a young oak tree. But just before they begin to shovel the creature in, it utters this chilling prophecy: When the face of death covers the moon, one with your blood will release me. Sure enough, years later, that descendant arrives in the form of Ernest P. Worrell, Briarville's outrageous garbageman. Ernest is sent to clean up the Hackmore place, a spooky, run-down mansion inhabited by a pyromaniac witch. There, Ernest stops his work to help two young friends build a tree house and in so doing, unleashes the monster. Then only Ernest (and the witch) can stop it.

✗STOP: Many of the images at the beginning of the film will frighten young viewers. A terrified child is pursued through the woods by a nameless horror, and there's a really scary look-around-and-see-a-monster-in-your-bed scene.

CAUTION: The hideously misshapen, child-stealing monster turns its victims into dolls and new trolls are shown growing up out of the ground and dragging adults away.

THE ESCAPE ARTIST

Vestron Home Video
1982
96 minutes
Directed by: Caleb Deschanel
Starring: Desi Arnaz, Teri Garr,
  Raul Julia, Griffin O'Neal
MPAA rating: PG

Son of the late Harry Masters, famous magician and escape artist, Danny Masters is a magician himself. On a visit to the local magic shop, Danny runs into Stu, the mayor's bully of a son, and during the ugly confrontation, steals Stu's wallet. The wallet, it turns out, belongs to the mayor, and it's full of stolen money. So when the mayor demands Stu return the wallet and Stu replies, "If I had it, I'd give it to the FBI," the mayor has his own son thrown in jail. As part of a plan to expose the mayor, Danny hides both the wallet and his lock-picking utensils in the elevator at the jail house. Then he proceeds to the local newspaper, where he issues a challenge: he will escape from the "escape-proof" jail just one hour after being locked up. But the sheriff is as corrupt as everyone else, and after the reporters have gone he warns Danny not to try to escape or he'll end up like his father. (Danny's father is alleged to have become a crook and died trying to escape from the town jail.) Despite the threat, Danny effects a dramatic escape, during which he comes to terms with his father's death (symbolically represented in a surreal scene), and he uses the confidence he has gained from the experience to successfully crack the mayor's safe and place the incriminating money inside.

CAUTION: Danny is often treated badly and he struggles to come to terms with his father's death. The mayor has his thugs beat his own son, and in a poignant scene Danny "witnesses" his father's death.

GO: Danny is spirited, independent and intelligent. This film was produced by Francis Ford Coppola of *Black Stallion* films.
▲

FAR AND AWAY

MCA
1992
140 minutes
Directed by: Ron Howard
Starring: Tom Cruise, Nicole
    Kidman, Colm Meany
OFRB rating: PG—Not Recom-
    mended for Children
MPAA rating: PG-13

In Ireland at the turn of the century, Joseph Donnelly's father dies, and during the funeral, agents of the family's landlord, Mr. Christie, burn the family farm for want of unpaid rent. Joseph decides to exact his revenge by killing Christie himself. But his plan goes awry when his gun misfires, and Joseph ends up a prisoner recuperating in the Christie household. There he meets Christie's willful daugher Shannon, who hopes to make her way to Oklahoma, where one hundred and sixty acres of free land is being offered to each and every

able-bodied man and woman who wants it. The two decide to go together and, after a narrow escape from Shannon's family, make their way to Boston. There they work in a chicken-plucking factory until Joseph's skill as a fighter earns him the favour of local kingpin Mike Kelly. Joseph's renown grows as he wins fight after fight, but his concern for Shannon proves his undoing and he loses the greatest fight of all. The two are then ostracized, forced to wander the streets of the city in the frigid winter. And when Shannon is shot and wounded by an angry homeowner, Joseph returns her to her family (now in Boston) and goes to work on the railroad. Unable to forget the land, Joseph eventually makes his way to Oklahoma where he's reunited with Shannon and the two stake a claim together.

CAUTION: Shannon stabs Joseph in the thigh with a pitchfork and Joseph is involved in numerous bloody fights with the realistic impact of fists on faces, stomachs and backs. Shannon is felled by a rifle-shot in the back and at the film's climax, a horse rolls over Joseph. There are some sexual

situations as Shannon and Joseph, posing as brother and sister, share a room in a brothel.

GO: Based on an actual event in American history, this is a visually stunning epic, full of romance and adventure and featuring strong performances. One thirteen-year-old viewer we know remarked, "We studied the Oklahoma Land Rush in school but it wasn't anywhere near as exciting as this!"

FATHER OF THE BRIDE

Touchstone Home Video
1992
105 minutes
Directed by: Charles Shyer
Starring: Diane Keaton,
    Steve Martin, Martin Short,
    Kimberly Williams, B.D. Wong
OFRB rating: F
MPAA rating: PG

When George's daughter, Annie, returns home after a summer in Rome and announces that she's engaged, George doesn't handle the news very gracefully — even when "Mr. Right" also appears to be "Mr. Perfect." (Annie's fiancé is a wealthy, handsome computer whiz who's so successful that no single firm can afford to keep him on staff.) And while George's wife and daughter plan an extravagant wedding with the help of two ultra-campy wedding co-ordinators, George marches steadily to the brink of madness. The climax comes when George is arrested in a grocery store because of a dispute over hotdog buns. Then it's up to his good-humoured, sensible wife to set him straight. On the surface, the film appears to be an almost scene-for-scene remake of the 1950 effort starring Spencer Tracy and Elizabeth Taylor. The plot unfolds in nearly identical fashion, and many scenes are presented as virtual replicas. However, the grating sexism of the original has been eradicated and Martin's George Banks (unlike that of his 1950 counterpart) is something of a neurotic flake.

CAUTION: Some people who have been through the same grotesque wedding expenditure fail to find the film amusing. As a parent of a young child, you may end up having to explain what a condom is.

GO: *Father of the Bride* is a family film; that is, adults will want to see it and many children will end up watching it simply because it's not grossly unsuitable.

FERRIS BUELLER'S DAY OFF

Paramount Home Video
1986
103 minutes
Directed by: John Hughes
Starring: Matthew Broderick,
    Alan Ruck, Mia Sara
OFRB rating: PG—Swearing
MPAA rating: PG-13

Easy-going high school senior Ferris Bueller devises an elaborate plan to play hooky, and he takes his girlfriend Sloane and his best friend Cameron along. Ferris bullies Cameron into borrowing his father's prized Ferrari and the three make their way to downtown Chicago where they attend a ballgame, have lunch in an expensive restaurant, visit a museum and even take part in a parade. And after a day of adventure and self-discovery, they return the Ferrari only to discover, to

AGES 10 TO 13

their horror, that they cannot reset the odometer to its original reading. Instead, in a fit of rage against a father who pays more attention to a car than to him, Cameron pushes the Ferrari through the window and into the ravine. His courage mustered after a day of risk-taking, Cameron is now prepared to face his father and discuss their problems.

CAUTION: Ferris takes advantage of his parents' kindness and gullibility without a second thought. There is a *lot* of coarse language in this film.

GO: In spite of the language, *Ferris Bueller's Day Off* is a funny, light-hearted movie. Don't forget to watch the film to the very end of the credits!

FORBIDDEN PLANET

MGM/UA
1956
99 minutes
Directed by: Fred McLeod Wilcox
Starring: Anne Francis,
    Leslie Nielsen, Walter Pidgeon,
    Warren Stevens
OFRB rating: PG
MPAA rating: G

Commanded by J.J. Adams, United Planets Cruiser C57D is headed for the planet Altair IV, where a group of scientists landed twenty years before. It is the ship's mission to search for survivors, and when they arrive they're relieved to make contact with Edward Morbius, the only surviving scientist. But Morbius is suprisingly irritated by the rescue team's appearance, and only reluctantly agrees to meet with the ship's officers (Adams and Ostrow)

before sending them back. As Adams' unease with the situation grows, he decides to contact Earth Base; this, however, will require dismantling part of their own ship to create a transmitter, and before that can be done, the ship is sabotaged by a mysterious entity. When Adams and Ostrow press Morbius for an explanation, they learn about the Krell, ancient inhabitants of the planet who designed a machine that uses sheer intellectual power to transport matter. In the end, Ostrow sacrifices his life to learn the terrible truth: when they built their machine, the Krell failed to consider the power of the Id, and now Morbius's subconcious has become a monster.

CAUTION: The attack scenes are frightening and one of our nine-year-old friends had many serious questions about the nature of the invisible entity, and why it attacked and killed people.

GO: The film is moody and atmospheric, with a great score. An all-round great effort, one can only wonder what would have been created with a modern budget.

✗ FRANKENWEENIE

Walt Disney Home Video
1984
27 minutes
Directed by: Tim Burton
Starring: Shelley Duvall,
    Barret Oliver, Daniel Stern
MPAA rating: PG

When Victor Frankenstein's beloved dog, Sparky, is hit by a car, the boy cannot contain his grief and his parents don't know what to do. Then, in science class, Victor sees a demonstration of electricity moving a dead frog's legs, and decides to try the same thing on Sparky. He goes to the graveyard and digs the dog up, and after fitting him with some electrodes, jolts him back to life. Victor tries to keep Sparky a secret, but soon the rambunctious dog gets outside, and he isn't exactly a hit with the neighbours. (He's covered with large stitches from the accident.) In an effort to restore the peace, Victor's parents invite everyone over to introduce them all to the newly-resurrected dog. But the whole thing goes terribly wrong when Sparky panics and runs off. The villagers pursue him to an abandoned mini-golf course where Victor is trapped inside a windmill. When the windmill catches fire, and Sparky rescues his friend at the cost of his own life, the townspeople help to reanimate the dog again. This film is black and white.

✘STOP: Sparky is killed twice in this film.

CAUTION: Adults will find this is a brilliantly witty spoof on all of the great horror films, but young children may be upset by the scary music, gloomy images and frightening scenes.

GHOST DAD

MCA
1990
104 minutes
Directed by: Sidney Poitier
Starring: Ian Bannen, Bill Cosby,
   Brooke Fontaine, Salim Grant,
   Denise Nicholas, Kimberly
   Russell, Raynor Scheine
OFRB rating: PG
MPAA rating: PG

Widower Elliot Hopper must balance a high-pressure career with the job of raising his children, Diane, Danny and Amanda. With a critical deal coming up, Elliot stands to take a giant step up the corporate ladder. But his plans are short-circuited when he gets into a cab piloted by a madman cab driver who crashes on a bridge, causing them to plunge into the watery depths. Elliot climbs back up to the road and makes his way home where he discovers that his kids can only see him in the dark and that they can't hear him or touch him. He communicates his situation to them (first through charades, and then through the sheer will to talk to them), but in the middle of the conversation is sucked away by the actions of a British medium. The medium tells Elliot that he won't last long in his current state and that it will be a miracle if he makes it to the big meeting on Thursday. Determined to get his promotion, Elliot bluffs his way through meetings and appointments and even discovers a few advantages of his ghostly state. (He can frighten away his daughter Diane's obnoxious would-be boyfriend.) Then when Diane falls and suffers a life-threatening concussion, Elliot encounters her spirit in the hospital and after a reconciliation they both return to their respective bodies.

✘STOP: The film presents negative depictions of the afterlife and Elliott's use of his ghostly form to frighten people may frighten little ones.

CAUTION: There is coarse language.

AGES 10 TO 13

✘ GHOSTBUSTERS

RCA/Columbia
1985
105 minutes
Directed by: Ivan Reitman
Starring: Dan Aykroyd,
   Rick Moranis, Bill Murray,
   Harold Ramis, Sigourney Weaver
OFRB rating: PG—Coarse
   Language/Frightening Scenes
MPAA rating: PG

When paranormal experts Doctors Peter Venkman, Egon Spengler and Ray Stantz lose their research grant at a large New York university, they open Ghostbusters, an agency for the removal of unwanted phenomena. Unfortunately, no one seems to need their services, and Ghostbusters lurches towards bankruptcy. But just when all seems lost, Dana Barrett, a violinist with a strangely behaving fridge, seeks their help, and the Ghostbusters are flooded with calls as paranormal activity in New York takes a sudden upsurge. They locate the source of the paranormal emanations (Dana Barrett's apartment building) and with time running out, and both Dana and her ultra-nerd neighbour possessed, the Ghostbusters go head to head with an ancient entity in the form of a hundred-foot marshmallow man, and save the world.

✘STOP: In the opening scene, the ghost of a librarian becomes a hideous, demonic apparition. There is coarse language and sexual innuendo as in one scene Dana, possessed by a demon, tells Peter, "I want you inside me."

CAUTION: A number of the ghost scenes, funny for adults and older children, may be too intense for young viewers.

GO: *Ghostbusters* is a wild and wacky, fast-paced comic-fantasy.

✘ GHOSTBUSTERS II

RCA/Columbia
1989
102 minutes
Directed by: Ivan Reitman
Starring: Dan Aykroyd,
   Peter McNichol, Rick Moranis,
   Bill Murray, Harold Ramis,
   Sigourney Weaver
OFRB rating: PG
MPAA rating: PG

Five years after their first success, the down-and-out Ghostbusters reunite when they discover a river of psychically active slime running through an abandoned subway tunnel. Meanwhile, a gigantic eerie portrait of Vigo the Carpathian (also known as Vigo the Impaler) has been moved into the Metropolitan Museum. It turns out that the sorcerer Vigo is preparing to come back and rule the twentieth century. He sends his toady to kidnap Dana's baby as the chosen vessel for his return, and encases the entire Museum, with the baby inside, in an impenetrable slime mold. To break through, the Ghostbusters need a living symbol of goodness and purity. So they animate the Statue of Liberty, and crash through the roof to save the day.

✘STOP: When the boys are advancing on Vigo's stronghold, they find themselves surrounded by severed heads on stakes.

AGES 10 TO 13

CAUTION: Some of the ghosts are pretty scary and there is some coarse language.

THE GIRL WHO SPELLED FREEDOM

Walt Disney Home Video
1985
90 minutes
Directed by: Simon Wincer
Starring: Jade Chinn,
    Mary Kay Place, Wayne Rogers
MPAA rating: not rated

In September of 1979, Cambodian refugees Fann Yann and her six children are taken in by an American family. Then comes the long process of forgetting the atrocities of war and adapting to a new culture. This film is a dramatization based on events in the life of Cambodian refugee Linn Yann; facts were obtained from newspaper articles and personal interviews.

CAUTION: This is an intense film. Scenes of Fann Yann's family struggling in Cambodia are juxtaposed with scenes of their American host family's idyllic life. No one is shot or killed (on screen).

GO: The film serves to enlighten North American audiences to the plight of southeast Asian refugees and offers positive solutions.

THE GODS MUST BE CRAZY

20th Century Fox
1980
109 minutes
Directed by: James Uys
Starring: NIXau, Sandra Prinsloo,
    Louw Verwey, Marius Weyers
OFRB rating: PG
MPAA rating: PG

In the deep Kalahari, Xi and his tribal family of Bushmen have never seen, or even heard of civilization. Then one day, a pilot throws a Coke bottle out of the window of his plane, and Xi sees it land and takes it back to his people. The bottle is

the most beautiful thing they've ever seen — and the most useful. (It can be used to grind food *and* carry water.) And it soon becomes apparent to everyone in the tribe that the gods have made a mistake in sending only one of the object. They become angry and jealous (once foreign emotions) and Xi decides that the only way to restore peace is to take the thing to the end of the world and throw it off. And after countless encounters (some comical, some nail-biting) with all kinds of people from "civilization," Xi reaches the end of the world (Angel Falls) and throws the bottle away.

CAUTION: A rather bloody assasination attempt is portrayed in slow motion, and is shockingly out-of-character with the rest of the film.

GO: This film is a splendid, light-hearted compassionate look at nomadic (and civilized) life.

THE GODS MUST BE CRAZY 2

RCA/Columbia
1990
98 minutes
Directed by: James Uys
Starring: Lena Faruga, NlXau, Hans Strom
OFRB rating: F
MPAA rating: PG

When Xixo's young children happen on a poacher's vehicle and clamber aboard (they assume it's some strange kind of animal), it unexpectedly starts up and carries them away. Xixo realizes the children have been stolen by a mysterious thing and gives chase. Meanwhile, Dr. Anne Taylor arrives

in Africa to give a seminar on corporate law and accepts an offer to go on an aerial sight-seeing jaunt with a zoologist named Stephen. But a freak storm forces them out of the sky, and not only is Anne unable to give her seminar, but she's forced to rough it in the deep Kalahari with the rugged Stephen. Improbable adventures occur, and after a brief encounter with Xixo and his children, (who by this point have finally managed to get away from the poacher's truck) everyone goes home.

GO: A splendid film, *The Gods Must Be Crazy II* is far less violent than its predecessor, with lots of great jokes for old and young.

A GIRL OF THE LIMBERLOST

Wonderworks
1990
105 minutes
Directed by: Burt Brinckerhoff
Starring: Joanna Cassidy, Heather Fairfield, Annette O'Toole
MPAA rating: no rating given

Embittered widow Kate Comstock struggles to run a farm with only her teenage daughter Elnora to help. Despite her mother's misgivings that she won't fit in with those frilly town girls, Elnora is resolved to attend high school. And with her mother's grudging permission, Elnora goes. She's a good student with the heart of a poet, but Elnora can't even afford books, and the rigorous demands of the farm are a massive obstacle. Then Elnora meets Mrs. Gene Stratton Porter, a naturalist photographer who requires butterflies and moths for her studies, and hires Elnora to catch some. Elnora is delighted to have found a way to earn some money. But suddenly, the taxes on the farm skyrocket. Then a miracle saves the day: Elnora finds the rarest of butterflies and sells it to make the taxes.

CAUTION: Grief, pain and anger are central elements in this story, and they are intensely portrayed. Elnora's stormy relationship with her mother is reconciled only after Elnora learns that her father died in an accident the night she was born.

GO: A moving story about self-discovery, reconciliation and emotional healing, this film has an environmentalist undercurrent.
■

GREMLINS

Warner Bros
1984
106 minutes
Directed by: Joe Dante
Starring: Hoyt Axton, Phoebe Cates,
    Corey Feldman, Zach Galligan,
    Judge Reinhold
MPAA rating: PG

When Billy's dad gives him a tiny creature called a mowgway, Billy is delighted. His dad explains that this is an unusual kind of pet and warns him to remember three important things: Billy must keep the mowgway away from bright lights and from water, and most important of all, he must never feed his mowgway after midnight. Of course, it isn't long before Billy's younger friend Pete spills water on the creature, and out pop five new mowgway. But these aren't like the original; they're mischievious. And

when Billy's clock stops and he inadvertently feeds them after midnight, they go through a strange and terrible metamorphosis, turning into a nasty crew of mean-spirited little gremlins. Led by a particularly horrible gremlin named Stripes, an army of the creatures terrorizes the town — even the local law enforcement officers are helpless — and in the end it's up to Billy and his girlriend Kate to stop the dreadful little monsters.

✗**STOP:** This is a horror movie, albeit a darkly funny one, and not a film for children. The gremlins kill a lot of people and many of the gremlins themselves meet a horrible end. (One is ground to bits in a blender while another blows up in the microwave.) *Gremlins II* is more of the same and was rated PG-Frightening Scenes.

✗ HOME ALONE

Fox
1990
103 miuntes
Directed by: Chris Columbus
Starring: Macaulay Culkin,
    John Heard, Catherine O'Hara,
    Joe Pesci, Daniel Stern
OFRB rating: PG
MPAA rating: PG

A few days before Christmas, as his family prepares for a clan visit to relatives in Paris, eight-year-old Kevin is feeling ignored. That night before bed he wishes out loud that he didn't have a family, and the next morning when he's all alone in the house he believes that his wish has come true. (In truth, a severed power line prevented the alarms from going off, and in the chaos that ensues, Kevin is missed in the head count as his family leaves for the airport. It isn't until they're over the Atlantic that Kevin's mother realizes he's not with them.) For a while at least, Kevin is in kid heaven, playing with his older brother's stuff, tobogganing inside the house and so on. He even learns to do the laundry and goes shopping. Then burglars target the house and it's up to Kevin to outsmart them.

✘STOP: Some of Kevin's booby-traps — although hilarious in the film — could be extremely dangerous and children have been known to imitate them. (He sets off firecrackers in a kitchen pot, shoots one of the burglars with an air gun, heats a door-knob with a barbeque starter, etc.)

CAUTION: Kevin's siblings treat him miserably, and when he acts in self-defense he is punished. (His uncle angrily calls him a jerk.) Some children are upset because they get the impression Kevin is being locked in the attic for being bad; however, he is, in fact, sleeping there because all of the bedrooms are full of house guests. There is some coarse language.

GO: Kevin has a charming, realistic and insightful conversation with his next door neighbour. This is a comedy with some attention given to the value of family.

✘ HOME ALONE II: LOST IN NEW YORK

20th Century Fox
1992
90 minutes
Directed by: Chris Columbus
Starring: Macaulay Culkin,
    Tim Curry, Brenda Fricker,
    John Heard, Catherine O'Hara,
    Joe Pesci, Daniel Stern
OFRB rating: PG
MPAA rating: PG

One year after his traumatic Christmas home alone, Kevin McCallister and his family wake up late on the morning of their vacation — again. And this time, the resulting chaos leaves Kevin alone on a plane to New York City (his family goes to Florida). However, he is armed with his father's flight bag, money and credit cards and Kevin soon cons his way into the swanky Plaza Hotel, where he proceeds to run up huge bills. Finally, the grown-ups catch on and Kevin is forced to flee into the unfriendly streets of the Big Apple. Meanwhile, the Wet Bandits (his adversaries from the first film) have escaped from jail and are planning to rob a toy store on Christmas Eve. They encounter Kevin, who lures them to his uncle's empty house which is loaded with booby traps.

✘STOP: Kevin's booby traps, while hilariously cartoonish, have been known to occasionally generate copy-cat pranks by children too young to know better.

CAUTION: Kevin makes no effort to contact his family once he's lost; rather, he cheerfully goes into New York City alone. The burglars are partially electrocuted, smashed with a steel bar, shot in the face with a staple gun, etc.

GO: This is a straight-ahead box-office comedy smash that's too similar to its predecessor to have any surprises.

HOT SHOTS!

20th Century Fox
1991
83 minutes
Directed by: Jim Abrahams
Starring: Lloyd Bridges, Jon Cryer,
 Kevin Dunn, Cary Elwes,
 Valeria Golino,
 Charlie Sheen
ORFB rating: PG
MPAA rating: PG-13

When former navy pilot Topper Harley is asked to return to the service for a secret mission (Operation Sleepy Weasel), Harley agrees, and finds himself with the weirdest flight group ever assembled. It becomes immediately obvious that the group's lead pilot, Kent Gregory, despises Harley. (Harley's father allegedly caused Gregory's father's death.) And Harley becomes so crippled by his family's shameful history that the mere mention of his father's name is enough to induce a psychotic episode. Navy psychiatrist Ramada Thompson plans to have Topper grounded, but his commander keeps him in the air. (He hopes the unpredictable pilot will contribute to the failure of Operation Sleepy Weasel, so the navy will buy more sophisticated fighters.) In the end, Harley learns the truth about his father and after some more than incredible flying, saves the day. But don't let this seemingly normal plot description fool you; this movie is a joke-every-five-seconds send-up.

CAUTION: The movie includes a spoof of a scene from the film *Nine-and-a-Half Weeks*, in which Harley puts food on Ramada's naked stomach. (She is in her underwear.) There is some coarse language.

GO: Suitable for the older crowd, this film includes hilarious send-ups of such films as *Top Gun, Dances With Wolves, Superman, Marathon Man* and *The Fabulous Baker Boys*. The jokes are literally non-stop.

✗ INDIANA JONES AND THE LAST CRUSADE

Paramount
1989
126 minutes
Directed by: Steven Spielberg
Starring: Sean Connery,
 Denholm Elliott, Harrison Ford,
 John Rhys-Davies
OFRB rating: PG
MPAA rating: PG-13

Philanthropist Walter Donovan has uncovered a twelfth-century tablet which indicates a possible location of the Holy Grail in the catacombs of Venice. But when Donovan's project leader, Dr. Jones Sr., is abducted, he hires Dr. Jones Jr. (Indiana Jones) to take up the search. In Venice, Indiana meets his father's associate, Dr. Elsa Schneider, who takes him to the place where his father vanished. There, Jones and Elsa are attacked by a group of fanatics who have defended the secret location of the Grail for a thousand years. They manage to assure the group that they are interested only in finding Dr. Jones Sr., and learn that he's being held by the Nazis in an Austrian castle. Indiana rescues his father, and after several narrow escapes and wild chases involving motorcycles, dirigibles and a Nazi tank, the Joneses ends up in a secret temple where they face the three deadly traps protecting the Grail's sanctuary. And with his father's life now on the line, Indiana must avoid the traps and face the terrible secret of the Grail. This is the last film in the Indiana Jones trilogy.

✗STOP: When Donovan chooses the wrong chalice (in one of the tests of the Grail), he ages in seconds and decomposes while still alive.

CAUTION: This film has the violence you would expect from an Indiana Jones movie (punching, shooting, killing, people being run over with tanks). There are many, many rats.

GO: Once again, Indiana Jones is a big-budget action adventure.

✗ INDIANA JONES AND THE TEMPLE OF DOOM

Paramount Home Video
1984
118 minutes
Directed by: Steven Sielberg
Starring: Harrison Ford,
    Kate Capshaw, Ke Huy Quan
OFRB rating: PG-Warning
MPAA rating: PG

In this "pre-quel" to *Raiders of the Lost Ark*, daredevil archeologist Indiana Jones embarks on a journey to India. There he hopes to find the Ankara Stone and bring it back to a museum. But a mysterious cult has enslaved all of the children of the village and, after numerous harrowing experiences, "Indy" saves

the children and returns them and the stone to the village where they belong.

✗STOP: This film is not for young children. The violence is frequent and often gratuitous. One of the more disturbing scenes features a horrible cult ceremony, during which a beating heart is ripped out of a live victim. Also watch for gruesome skeletons, dead bodies and a banquet at which eyeball soup and fried beetles are served.

CAUTION: Indiana's female companion is a poor role model and she tends to be more of a problem than a help.

GO: The violence is so extreme and situations are so impossible that the fact that Indiana always come out unscathed gives the film a comic book-like atmosphere.

✗ JURASSIC PARK

Universal
1993
125 minutes
Directed by: Stephen Spielberg
Starring: Richard Attenborough,
    Laura Dern, Jeff Goldblum,
    Sam Neill
OFRB rating: PG—Frightening
    Scenes
MPAA rating: PG-13

Note: At the time this book was printed, this video had not yet been released. Jurassic Park has seriously frightened many children, but yours will clamour to see it.
Previewing is recommended.

Jurassic Park is a prehistoric wildlife sanctuary-cum-theme park featuring an array of genetically engineered dinosaurs. The park is financed by philanthropist John Hammond. After an accident resulting in a worker's death, Hammond must convince his nervous investors of the park's safety, and to this end he invites a trio of scientists to take a tour. Paleontologist Dr. Alan Grant, paleobotanist Dr. Ellen Sattler and "chaotician" Ian Malcolm are joined by Hammond's grandchildren, Tim and Alexis, and his anxious lawyer. Things soon go awry. The group becomes separated, and glitches in the electrical systems are compounded by a raging tropical storm; then the park's computer programmer, Dennis Nedry, turns off the defense systems in order to smuggle some dinosaur embryos off the island. A tyrannosaur quickly breaks out of its enclosure and attacks the tour, wounding Malcolm, devouring the lawyer and tossing the car around with the children trapped inside. Grant saves the children in the nick of time, and as they struggle back through the park toward the central control centre, Sattler and the park's chief ranger Muldoon take a jeep and go out in search of the tour, finding only Malcolm and bringing him back with them to the centre. Meanwhile, Nedry has been killed, leaving all the computers locked; Hammond orders them shut down, but when Sattler and Muldoon venture out to restore power and restart the systems, they discover that the vicious predatorial velociraptors have escaped. In the climax, the survivors find themselves hunted by the intelligent raptors.

✗STOP: This film is not for children under ten! The dinosaurs appear real and they may terrify even older kids. One character is eaten by a dilophosaur which spits a deadly venom all over his face, while a second is horribly killed by raptors. The lawyer is swallowed by a tyrannosaurus, and in a startling scene, Dr. Sattler grabs onto a severed human arm. In its intensity, this film rivals any other Spielberg production (eg. *Poltergeist*).

CAUTION: The scene in which Tim and Alexis are trapped in their car by the tyrannosaurus is particulaly unnerving, as is the scene in which Tim is nearly electrocuted on a high-voltage electric fence.

GO: The effects are remarkable, employing full-scale, full-motion dinosaur replicas and highly realistic computer-generated imagery. The film draws on much of the latest scientific information about dinosaurs. There's even a quick remedial science lesson to remind viewers what DNA is. The film contains strong female role models; Doctors Sattler and Grant are clearly on equal footing and Alexis is the computer hacker who eventually brings the defense systems back online.

◼

✗ K-9

MCA
1990
111 minutes
Directed by: Rod Daniel
Starring: James Belushi, James Handy, Mel Harris, Ed O'Neill, Kevin Tighe
OFRB rating: AA
MPAA rating: PG-13

When narcotics cop Mike Dooley needs a dog to help him bust powerful drug lord Kent Lyman, he acquires Jerry Lee, a fierce and incredibly intelligent German Shepherd. Not only does Jerry Lee sniff out the drugs, he takes on a pool hall full of thugs, runs down the bad guys and saves Dooley's life more than once. But Lyman proves to be harder to nail than Dooley had expected. When Dooley's girlfriend Tracy is kidnapped, Dooley and his dog must intercept a drug shipment to rescue her. In the final confrontation, Jerry Lee is shot while trying to save Dooley.

✗STOP: This film is not for young children. In one disturbing scene, a villain describes a Columbian neck-tie (which involves cutting a victim's throat and pulling his tongue out through the wound), and in another, Lyman cruelly teases an intended victim, then coldly executes him.

CAUTION: The dog gets shot, and while he pulls through in the end, for a time viewers are made to think he has died. In an opening shot of a parking lot, sexual activity is implied through rain-drenched car windows.

GO: *K-9* is exciting, but definitely not for kids under twelve.

THE KARATE KID

RCA/Col
1984
126 minutes
Directed by: John G. Alvidsen
Starring: Martin Kove,
    Ralph Macchio, Pat Morita,
    Elisabeth Shue, William Zarka
MPAA rating: PG

Teenager Daniel LaRusso moves to Los Angeles with his mother, who is looking for a new start in life. But things aren't so good for Daniel. Soon after his arrival, he meets a charming girl at a beach party and is promptly beaten up by her jealous ex-boyfriend, Johnny. And this is only the beginning of a campaign of terror against him, as Johnny and his friends pound Daniel mercilessly at every opportunity. When Daniel goes to the local karate school to seek some training to defend

himself, he discovers that his tormentors are already students there, under the tutelage of a merciless sensei, John Kreese. The bullies finally catch him, and are in the process of beating him within an inch of his life when Daniel is rescued by the building's mysterious caretaker, Mr. Miyagi, who also turns out to be a master of karate. After convincing Kreese and his students to leave Daniel alone until the All-Valley karate tournament, Miyagi himself trains Daniel in the fundamentals of karate. Against nearly impossible odds, Daniel enters the tournament and defeats opponent after opponent until in the final match he must face Johnny himself. Available in French as *Moment de verité*.

CAUTION: Many of the fight scenes are brutal. There is some coarse language.

GO: This is an inspiring tale of an underdog, graced by a spiritually sensitive teacher, who earns self-respect and wins the day.

▲

THE KARATE KID PART II

RCA Columbia
1986
113 minutes
Directed by: John G. Avildsen
Starring: Daniel Kamekona,
    Ralph Macchio, Nobu McCarthy,
    Pat Morita
OFRB rating: PG—Martial
    Arts Violence
MPAA rating: PG

When Miyagi's father is dying, he returns home with considerable trepidation. When last he was there, he broke with tradition and announced to the whole village his intention to marry Yuki, who was already promised to his best friend Sato. This brought shame and dishonour to Sato who had no option but to challenge Miyagi to a fight. But because he did not believe in fighting, Miyagi left the island (and his great love) behind and moved to the United States. Now Miyagi must return to face a dying father, Sato (who has not forgotten) and Yuki (who has never married). Daniel accompanies his mentor on his trip and he, too, runs into problems. Sato's cruel nephew takes an instant dislike to him and begins a feud with him. And in a brutal climactic fight Daniel realizes that this time the fight is not a competition for points, but for his life. This is the sequel to *The Karate Kid.*

CAUTION: There is a lot of fighting in this film. Daniel's delicate girlfriend is savagely punched in the face by Sato's cruel nephew and the climax is brutal and bloody.

GO: Alongside all of the violence are the poignant and tasteful love stories of Miyagi and Yuki and Daniel and Komiko. The importance of "true honour" is demonstrated and hate and revenge are shown to be wrong.
▲

THE KARATE KID PART III

RCA/Col
1989
Directed by: John G. Alvidsen
Starring: Thomas Ian Griffith,
    Daniel Kamekona, Sean Kanan,
    Ralph Macchio, Pat Morita
OFRB rating: PG—Martial Arts
    Violence
MPAA rating: PG

After losing to Miyagi and Daniel at the All-Valley karate tournament, John Kreese has lost all of his students and his school. So when his old army buddy and fellow karateka, Terry Silver, bails Kreese out, together they plot his revenge against Miyagi and Daniel: Daniel will be invited to defend his All-Valley title against killer karateka Mike Barnes. But when Miyagi refuses to allow Daniel to enter the tournament, Mike and Silver's thugs literally force Daniel to sign the entrance form. Still, Miyagi refuses to participate, prompting Silver to pose as a well-meaning sensei who agrees to take over Daniel's training. In reality, this is just a ruse designed to ruin all of Miyagi's hard work with Daniel. But Daniel's inner strength allows him to resist Silver, and he eventually breaks off the relationship. Only then does Miyagi agree to conduct the training. And again, we return to the karate championships, where Daniel faces the fierce Mike in a final showdown.

CAUTION: There is violent fighting

throughout. At one point, Mike coldly kicks a female friend of Daniel's in the stomach.

▲

✗ LADY JANE

Paramount
1985
140 minutes
Directed by: Trevor Nunn
Starring: Helena Bonham Carter,
    Carey Elwes, Warren Saire,
    Patrick Stewart, John Wood
MPAA rating: PG-13

During the reign of the frail teenage king Edward the Sixth, powerful barons, looking beyond the young king's imminent death, maneuver for power. They plot to install Lady Jane Grey as the next ruler, hoping to marry her off to Gilford Dudley, thereby uniting their two houses. But Gilford is wild and Jane is quiet and studious, and at first the two can barely get along. Then they discover that they do have much in common, in particular a thirst to see a just and equitable government over England. But when the idealistic Jane finally becomes Queen of England, the coalition which keeps her on the throne crumbles, and her reign is over in nine days. She and Gilford are arrested, and like so many others before them, eventually go to the headsman.

✗**STOP:** In one disturbing scene, Jane's mother forces her to lift her skirts and bend over a chair, where her mother gives her a savage and prolonged beating.

CAUTION: When they are married, Jane and Gilford are shown sitting up in bed, naked and facing each other. (They can be seen from the hips up.) The Machiavellian plottings of the barons may be too confusing for young viewers and the film's ending, too traumatic.

GO: A skilfully crafted love story about two people who put their lives on the line when they get a chance to really make a difference, this is a splendid depiction of a rich period in English history.

✗ LADYHAWKE

Warner Home Video
1985
121 minutes
Directed by: Richard Donner
Starring: Matthew Broderick,
    Rutger Hauer, Leo McKern,
    Michelle Pfeiffer, John Wood
OFRB rating: PG—Violence
MPAA rating: PG-13

When a beatiful woman named Isabeau rejects the advances of the corrupt Bishop of Aquila, she and her true-love Navarre are placed under a terrible curse: she is transformed into a hawk by day and he, into a wolf by night. And so they are always together, but eternally apart. Navarre and the hawk have been travelling for two years when they encounter Phillipe "The Mouse" Gaston (a petty thief, whom Navarre believes is his guiding angel). Now sure that the curse cannot be broken, Navarre plans to kill the Bishop, and convinces Phillipe to join him in seeking his revenge. But their plans are delayed when the hawk is wounded, and Phillipe is forced to take her to the old priest, who had originally betrayed their trust and who is the only one who knows how to heal her. In a moment of remorse, the priest tells Phillipe that the lovers' curse can be broken when "day is in night and night is in day," and the Bishop casts his eyes on both Isabeau and Navarre in human form. This seems impossible, but Phillipe goes along with Navarre to the castle hoping to dissuade him from his plan to kill the Bishop, just in case. There, to his amazement the moon covers the sun in a solar eclipse and Isabeau changes into human form to stand beside Navarre in full view of the Bishop. The lovers are reunited.

✗STOP: There are some rough battle scenes in this film. Navarre impales the Bishop and the Captain of the Guard. (There is blood, and it is violent.) A wolf trapper is killed when his head is caught in one of his own traps.

GO: Full of adventure and romance, the story is based on a thirteenth century legend and features a modern but impressive musical score. There is no coarse language.

math teacher at a posh high school in a privileged neighbourhood, and at night he teaches at Galaxy High, where classes are held in the sleazy night-club after hours. Suddenly seeing him as sexy, Sandy incurs the ire of her jealous boyfriend by making advances toward Kevin. And in the end, in an effort to prove that he really is teaching math at the dance club, Kevin pits his Galaxy High students in a math contest against his students from Stonewood High.

CAUTION: There is a fist-fight between the kids from the rival schools in which both boys and girls throw punches, and there is some coarse language.

GO: Don't be fooled by the sexy cover and the title; this film is not a dance movie. It's about a sympathetic teacher who puts his career on the line for his students, and it's about appreciating an education. Watch right through the credits!

LAMBADA

✗ LANTERN HILL

Warner Home Video
1990
104 minutes
Directed by: Joel Silberg
Starring: Shabba Doo,
   Melora Hardin, J. Eddie Peck
OFRB rating: PG
MPAA rating: PG

Astral Video
1989
111 minutes
Directed by: Kevin Sullivan
Starring: Mairon Bennett,
   Zoe Caldwell, Colleen Dewhurst,
   Sarah Polley, Sam Waterston
OFRB rating: F

When high school student Sandy Thomas goes to a new dance club in East L.A., she makes two shocking discoveries: the first is a new dance craze called the Lambada, and the second is that the strait-laced teacher she knows as Kevin Laird is leading a double life. By day, he's her conventional

During the Great Depression, while her mother is recovering from polio, twelve-year-old Victoria Jane Stuart lives with her domineering grandmother. She hears nothing but negative stories about her absent father (he was involved with a woman named Evelyn, who mysteriously disappeared). Then one day her father sends a letter, asking Jane to come and visit him on Prince Edward Island. There, Jane learns the truth about her parents, and when she finds a letter from Evelyn explaining what really happened, she goes about reconciling her parents. Based on the book *Jane of Lantern Hill* by Lucy Maud Montgomery.

✗**STOP:** Jane's friend, a grandmother figure, dies in a heart-wrenching scene.

CAUTION: This ghost story/romance is too sophisticated for little ones. Jane's situation is not a happy one and there are some spooky elements.

GO: This is a sensitive film about family relationships.
■▲

✗ THE LAST STARFIGHTER

MCA
1984
100 minutes
Directed by: Nick Castle
Starring: Lance Guest,
    Dan O'Herlihy, Robert Preston,
    Catherine Mary Stewart
OFRB rating: PG
MPAA rating: PG

Alex Rogan is an expert at the videogame "Starfighter." Unbeknownst to him, the game has been installed by aliens who are seeking recruits for their interstellar forces, and when Alex breaks the game record, one of the aliens arrives and takes him to the planet Rylos. There, because of his talent, Alex is recruited to be a Starfighter, where he will take part in an action against the black terror of the Kodan, which is threatening the rapidly collapsing frontier. But Alex has no desire to become a Starfighter for real, and when he pleads to be returned home he is given two choices: return to Earth and live like everyone else until the Kodan's evil forces arrive and destroy the planet, or stay and become the last Starfighter, the only man who can save the galaxy.

✗**STOP**: The action is intense and often gruesome. In one scene, a clone of Alex develops a deformed head and bulging eyes and in another, the Star League's greatest spy, his neck bound to the wall, has his face disintegrated. There is some sexual suggestion and a little swearing.

GO: Ron Cobb (*Alien, Star Wars, Conan the Barbarian*) did an amazing job with the production design, and the computer-generated special effects are superb. The story will be especially appealing to science fiction and video-game buffs.

✗ LEAN ON ME

Warner Home Video
1989
109 minutes
Directed by: John G. Avildson
Starring: Morgan Freeman,
    Robert Guillaume, Beverly Todd
OFRB rating: PG—Mature Theme
MPAA rating: PG-13

Once considered one of the finest schools in America, Eastside High has fallen into ruin. Teachers are brutally beaten, guns are carried and drugs are dealt openly. Faced with the prospect of losing the school to the state, the Superintendant of Schools hires a gifted, arrogant teacher named Joe Clark to clean it up and raise the students' basic skills level; he gives Clark 110 school days in which to do it. Clark begins by expelling all of the trouble-makers and chaining the school doors shut to keep the remaining students safe. Convinced that the students will live up to what is expected of them, Clark bullies the staff into raising their expectations and reminds them that if they don't like his methods they can quit. After much work, the school is cleaned up, the students gain some self-respect and the Basic Skills test is written. But before the marks even come in, the parents of the expelled students have Clark arrested for disobeying the fire chief's order to unchain the doors. The entire student body demonstrates outside the jail where the glowing Basic Skills test scores finally arrive. This film is based on a true story.

✗**STOP:** During the opening credits a teacher is repeatedly kicked and his head is slammed into the floor; it is bloody. There is some coarse language.

GO: Most of the violence in the film is shown during the opening credits. (There is only one other fight.) This is an inspiring feel-good movie.

✗ LEGEND

MCA
1986
89 minutes
Directed by: Ridley Scott
Starring: Tom Cruise, Tim Curry,
    Mia Sara
MPAA rating: PG

In a magical place, in another time, the Dark Lord plots his return to dominion over the world of light. However, standing in his way are a pair of unicorns, in whose souls the light is harboured, and who are beyond his evil grasp because they can only be found by pure-hearted mortals. One of the pure-hearted is Jack, who lives with his lady-love Lily in a marvellous forest. When Jack shows Lily the unicorns, the young woman is so enchanted that she touches one, setting off a cosmic catastrophe. Everything freezes and the stallion unicorn becomes trapped in ice, enabling the goblins to catch it and cut off its horn. The world of light is immediately locked in a terrible winter; the goblins capture Lily and the mare unicorn, and Jack and his fairy friends are forced to follow the goblins into the dreadful realm of the Dark Lord. There, they pass through all the perils of hell, rescue Lily from the clutches of the demon ruler and use the power of the remaining unicorn and the sun itself to restore order to the universe.

✗STOP: *Legend* is not for most children. The film opens in hell, where writhing figures strapped to tables are beaten with whips. Later, a huge ogre carries away a shrieking dwarf and a swamp troll is beheaded.

CAUTION: The Dark Lord and his goblin servants are hideous. The plot is relentlessly grim, and the landscape, desolate.

GO: The performances are excellent; the costumes and sets are stunning, and the atmosphere, soundly established.

LEGEND OF THE WHITE HORSE

CBS Fox
1985
91 minutes
Directed by: Jerzy Domaradzki, Janusz Morgenstern
Starring: Allison Balson, Christopher Lloyd, Dee Wallace Stone
MPAA rating: no rating given

When environmental impact consultant Jim Martin is hired by a developer to survey a property in remote Karistan, he and his son move there and stay with the local witch and her blind adopted daughter, Jewel. Jim soon hears of the existence of a mysterious cave on the property, and learns that Jewel is the only person who can enter it safely past the watchful eye of the white horse/dragon that

guards it. (The horse/dragon turns all others who try to enter into stone.) It turns out that the witch and her evil partner need Jewel to get into the cave where precious jewels and the secrets of youth and immortality await. In the end, the witch and her partner meet a grisly death when they turn on Jewel inside the cave. Then it's discovered that the mysterious horse/dragon is none other than Jewel's biological mother transformed. Jim exposes the developer's unscrupulous plans to the government in order to preserve the mystery of the white horse and the integrity of the land. Based on the book *Dark Horse, Dark Dragon* by Robert C. Fleet

CAUTION: The actors' accents are inconsistant and the music is invasive and inappropriate. In order to gain immortality, Jewel must die, so the witch kills Jewel with a knife. (Jewel comes back to life.) People are machine-gunned and die with their eyes open and blood coming from their mouths, and bad guys are vaporized by the dragon. Also of concern may be the fact that Steve's mother dies before the film begins.

■

LICENSE TO DRIVE

Studio
1988
90 minutes
Directed by: Greg Beeman
Starring: Corey Feldman, Heather Graham, Corey Haim, Carol Kane, Richard Masur
OFRB rating: PG—Coarse Language
MPAA rating: PG-13

When sixteen-year-old Les Anderson meets Mercedes, he knows he's found the perfect girl. Now all he needs is the perfect car — and his driver's license — to make his dream complete. But the second half of his dream is slow in coming when, after sleeping through every one of his driver's education classes, Les fails the written portion of his test. Upset by his failure, and doubly mortified by his twin sister's success at *her* test, Les is further disgraced when his pregnant mother discovers his results and grounds him. Determined to see his dream girl, Les takes his grandfather's prize Cadillac and sneaks out. Almost immediately things begin to go wrong. Mercedes gets drunk and dances on the hood of the car, causing significant damage, before passing out. Friends help Les repair the damage then convince him to take *them* for a ride. They put Mercedes in the trunk and from there on in it's just one disaster after another until they finally manage to get what's left of the Cadillac home. Soon after, Les's mother goes into labour and Les has one final chance to prove his driving ability by getting his excited family to the hospital.

CAUTION: The boys try to decide in what kind of car a girl would be willing to lose her virginity; one of the boys lifts Mercedes's dress while she is passed out and takes photos; and a drunk vomits in the car. The teens in this film are out all night and there is coarse language.

GO: Despite the language and some sexual innuendo, this film is basically inoffensive, and there's something in it for everyone.

✗ LIONHEART

Warner Home Video
1986
104 minutes
Directed by: Franklin J. Schaffner
Starring: Gabriel Byrne, Nicola
  Cowper, Dexter Fletcher,
  Eric Stolz
OFRB rating: PG
MPAA rating: PG

In late twelfth century France, during a pitched battle with a rival fiefdom, a young knight named Robert Nera loses his nerve and flees. Haunted by his shame, he sets off to join the crusade of Richard I and encounters two young circus runaways on the way. The trio set out for Paris together, stopping at an abbey for shelter during a storm. There Robert first sees the Black Prince, a shadowy black-garbed warrior who prowls the roads looking for wayward children. Robert gathers many of these children under his protection as he travels. Once they reach Paris, he discovers a society of orphans hiding in a catacomb under the protection of a good but sickly knight. The knight convinces Robert to take the children south to the warmth of the sun and the sanctuary of Richard's armies. And so, tracked by the Black Prince and accompanied by his friends, Robert shepherds his charges through plague and peril, until a final confrontation with his enemy tests his skills and courage to the limit.

✗**STOP:** Robert wrenches open a confessional door, and the body of a priest tumbles out, his throat slit.

CAUTION: This film has some intense battle scenes. The Black Prince is a fearsome man who kills his own unarmed brother and commits sacrilege by throwing a knife into the statue of Christ.

GO: This film features two very positive role models for young women — one has a strange gift with animals and the other is a fierce, independent knight.

✗ LITTLE MAN TATE

Orion
1991
99 minutes
Directed by: Jodie Foster
Starring: Jodie Foster,
   Adam Hann-Byrd, Dianne Wiest
OFRB rating: PG
MPAA rating: PG

Fred Tate is a seven-year-old supergenius who paints like Raphael, plays advanced piano, writes opera and instantly visualizes the solutions to higher-order math problems. Alienated from his peers — and even from his own loving but uneducated mother, Deedee — all Fred really wants is someone to eat lunch with. Then he is interviewed by Dr. Jane Grierson of the Grierson Institute, a school specialized in meeting the educational needs of extremely gifted children, and things begin to change. The doctor instantly recognizes Fred's enormous potential, and invites him to attend a summer seminar course where he finally meets kids who are just like him. Upon his return, Fred's relationship with his mother is strained, and when she lands a job in Florida it's agreed that he will stay behind to attend university and live with Dr. Grierson. But Fred finds the university to be an achingly lonely place and Dr. Grierson isn't good with children. The crisis builds to a climax in which everyone comes to realize that no matter how immensely powerful his intellect, Fred is still a little boy who needs his mother.

✗STOP: While there are no particular scenes of concern, this film is unlikely to interest anyone under the age of nine.

CAUTION: In one scene, Fred walks in on a college friend in bed with a young woman. And throughout the film, Fred is afflicted with nightmares, one of which is depicted.

GO: The film is light, realistic and unsentimental. The performances are excellent, and there's a refreshing absence of villains. Altogether, an amazing effort from first-time director Jodie Foster.

✗ LITTLE MONSTERS

MGM/UA
1989
103 minutes
Directed by: Richard Allen
   Greenberg
Starring: Howie Mandel, Ben
   Savage, Fred Savage,
   Daniel Stern, Frank Whaley,
   Margaret Whitton
OFRB rating: PG—Frightening
   Scenes
MPAA rating: PG

Brian Stevenson has a major problem: his parents are separating. So when his little brother Eric complains about monsters under his bed, Brian assumes it's a reaction to the family turmoil and gallantly offers to trade rooms with him. However, he soon discovers that there really are monsters under his brother's bed and sets a trap to catch one. Brian and his prisoner monster, Maurice, quickly become friends and embark on a nightly spree of mischievous capers until Brian notices that he's turning into a monster himself. Then, to make matters worse, Eric is kidnapped and Brian must go into the heart of the monsters' lair to rescue his brother and turn himself back into a boy.

✗**STOP:** This movie is not for young children or for children who suffer from night terrors. In the final confrontation, the monster leader's face falls off, revealing a ghastly visage beneath.

CAUTION: Brian's parents are having marital problems throughout. This movie may give younger children some not-so-nice prank ideas, so be sure to debrief them afterwards.

GO: This film has helped some children deal with the "monster under the bed" problem.

LOST IN THE BARRENS

C/FP
1991
94 minutes
Directed by: Michael Scott
Starring: Evan Adams, Lee J.
  Campbell, Graham Greene,
  Nicholas Shields
OFRB rating: PG

When Jamie McNair's trust fund runs out, he's forced to move from the boarding school at St. George's College to live with his uncle, a gruff woodsman named Angus Stewart who makes his living crafting canoes in Stewart's Landing, Manitoba. Jamie soon finds that he isn't suited to rustic living and is frustrated by the fact that his three-year stay will probably ruin his plans for a higher education. Angered by his predicament, he carelessly throws down a rifle and accidentally shoots Angus in the leg. With no choice but to do Angus's work for him, Jamie goes on a hunting expedition with Angus's native friend Menwanis, Menwanis's son, Awasis, and other members of their tribe. Their travels take them north into the Barrens where Jamie and Awasis separate from the group to go exploring. They happen on an ancient grave-site and, true to Awasis's fears of invoking a curse, emerge to find that their canoes have drifted away. Their only hope of rejoining the rest of the group is to cross the Barrens, a desolate wasteland reputedly populated with cannibals and made trecherous by the approaching winter. Still, they are plucky and resourceful, and in the end, they receive aid from their perceived enemy, the Inuit.

CAUTION: Angus is shot and, on the expedition, Awasis kills a caribou with a knife.

GO: *Lost in the Barrens* is a great adventure story about two young men who overcome vast cultural differences to help each other.

■

LUCAS

CBS FOX
1986
100 minutes
Directed by: David Seltzer
Starring: Kerri Green, Corey Haim,
   Winona Ryder, Charlie Sheen
OFRB rating: PG—Coarse Language
MPAA rating: PG-13

When Maggie, a sixteen-year-old cheerleader, falls for the captain of the football team instead of for him, Lucas, a small fourteen-year-old with a keen interest in science, decides to prove his worth by trying out for the football team himself. He makes the team and steps in during a big game, hoping to be a hero. Instead, Lucas ends up under a pile of football players twice his size, embarrassed and seriously injured. In the end, Maggie, the captain of the football team and the rest of the school admire Lucas for his courage, and Lucas realizes the importance of just being himself.

CAUTION: In the locker room, when the boys are taking showers there is full nudity from the back. There is coarse language during one key scene.

GO: The film talks about peer pressure and the value of friendship and has a stand-up-and-cheer ending.

▲

MAID-TO-ORDER

I.V.E.
1987
92 minutes
Directed by: Amy Jones
Starring: Beverley D'Angelo,
   Michael Ontkean, Valerie Perrine,
   Dick Shawn, Ally Sheedy,
   Tom Skerritt
OFRB rating: PG
MPAA rating: PG

Jessie is a rich, spoiled brat who's used to getting whatever she wants, whenever she wants it. Her philanthropist father is fed up with her expensive, irresponsible habits and absently remarks that sometimes he wishes he never had a daughter. A star flashes outside the window and his wish comes true; all record of Jessie's existence is erased. Stella, a cigarette-smoking jogger claiming to be Jessie's fairy godmother, explains to Jessie what's happened and cynically remarks that some princesses deserve to be maids. Jessie thinks the woman is crazy until, when she tries to go home, she's chased away by the outraged staff — even her father doesn't recognize her. Starving and filthy, she wanders into an employment agency and lands a job as a maid in the mansion of a bizarre Hollywood agent. Jessie is, of course, the worst maid in the world and she drives her co-workers crazy. But as time passes their kindness and generosity rub off on her and she becomes compassionate and respectful of both them and herself. She even develops a romance with the chauffeur — who's also an aspiring composer. And when her father organizes a charity benefit and the lead singer is knocked out by a coconut, Jessie inserts her friends into the musical program and they're a smash hit. In the end, Jessie's new-found selflessness wins her back her life.

CAUTION: There is some (non-sexual) nudity when Jessie goes skinny-dipping. Jessie is arrested with a vial of cocaine. Minimal coarse language.

GO: Jessie learns to appreciate what she has, and to love and respect others.

THE MAN WHO WOULD BE KING

CBS/Fox
1975
128 minutes
Directed by: John Huston
Starring: Michael Caine,
   Sean Connery,
Christopher Plummer
MPAA rating: PG

In Colonial India, yet another caper by adventurers Peachy Carnehan and Daniel Dravot goes awry. Only the influence of their friend and fellow Freemason (an ancient order dedicated to the brotherhood of man) Rudyard Kipling can save them both. The three — now fast friends — return to Kipling's where Peachy and Danny reveal the details of their next scheme. They will enter Kafiristan, go into the service of one of the leaders of its warring tribes, use their military knowledge to make that tribe ascendent and take over the whole country. To do this they'll have to go over the Khyber Pass and cross the Hindu Kush — a trek no white man has managed since Alexander the Great. They endure the hardships of the inhospitable mountains, waging nonstop tribal warfare until the natives believe that Danny is a god. Thanks to his Freemason's amulet (the symbol of Alexander the Great), Danny comes to be worshipped as Alexander's son, and the vast treasures of Alexander are handed over to him. Peachy and Danny plan to sit out the winter and make off with the treasure in the spring, but Danny comes to prefer governing to wealth and marries one of the natives. This proves to be Danny's undoing, and he and Peachy must fight their way out of the city and journey home through a bitter, hostile land.

CAUTION: Danny is killed by being thrown from a cliff. In one scene, Peachy reveals Danny's severed, rotting head and in another, the troops play polo with the head of a defeated enemy in a canvas bag. There is some combat violence.

GO: This is a splendid, sprawling epic which may encourage young people to learn more about colonial history and the Indian subcontinent.

MANNEQUIN

Warner Home Video
1987
90 minutes
Directed by: Michael Gottlieb
Starring: G.W. Bailey, Kim Cattrall,
   Carole Davis, Estelle Getty,
   Andrew McCarthy, James Spader,
   Meshach Taylor
OFRB rating: PG
MPAA rating: PG

Mannequin opens in ancient Egypt, where a young Egyptian woman, refusing to marry a camel-dung dealer, prays for help from the gods. Her prayers are answered and she's transported into a twentieth century department store in the United States, where she inhabits the form of a newly made mannequin. In that very same department store, Jonathan Switcher, assistant to the outrageous window dresser Hollywood Montrose, makes a startling discovery: the mannequin, who comes alive and introduces herself as Emmie. Emmie, it turns out, has a real flair for window design, and she and Jonathan spend their nights creating dazzling displays. The only problem seems to be that whenever anyone other than Jonathan looks at Emmie she turns back into a mannequin. And, as the department store windows attract more and more customers, vice-president Richards and his manic security guards do their best to find out what Jonathan is up to. They finally decide that the mannequin must be connected to Jonathan's success, and kidnap her. This precipitates a wild chase, in which Emmie regains her human form when Jonathan risks his life to rescue her.

CAUTION: In one scene, Emmie opens her coat to reveal that she's wearing only lingerie underneath, and in another, Jonathan's former girlfriend is shown doing up her blouse after what was obviously a sexual encounter with a business associate. Hollywood Montrose is a stereotype of the gay window-dresser.

GO: Values of love, loyalty and persistence are highlighted. There is a sequel, *Mannequin II.*

MORGAN STEWART'S COMING HOME

HBO
1987
92 minutes
Directed by: Alan Smithee
Starring: John Cryer, Viveka Davis, Paul Gleason, Nicholas Pryor, Lynn Redgrave
MPAA rating: PG-13

Morgan Stewart, a self-declared "orphan with parents," has been shunted from boarding school to boarding school since he was ten. Now, at seventeen, he learns that his parents, a prominent Republican Senator and a cold, ambitious socialite, suddenly want him to come back and live with them in their sprawling Washington mansion. But Morgan soon learns that the decision was purely political and was prompted by Jay, a new assistant who's orchestrating the Senator's family-oriented campaign. Things seem to improve when Morgan meets Emily, a fellow horror fan, at an autograph appearance, and he steals his parents' car to take her out. But when Morgan's parents find out, he's grounded, and worse, his mother has closed-circuit cameras installed in his bedroom. The last straw comes when Morgan and Emily defy the grounding and Jay plans to have Morgan sent to military school. Morgan runs away, but returns when, after going to the bank to clear out his account, he discovers that Jay has been embezzling campaign funds.

CAUTION: Most of the adults in this film are portrayed as stupid, insensitive people. There is some mild language.

GO: Morgan remains loyal to his parents despite the neglect he has suffered and his relationship with Emily is based on mutual interest and respect. Emily is also a good role model.

MY BODYGUARD

20th C Fox
1980
97 minutes
Directed by: Tony Bill
Starring: Matt Dillon, Ruth Gordon, John Houseman, Chris Makepeace, Martin Mull
MPAA rating: PG

On the first day at his new school, Cliff Peache is approached by bully Big M Moody. (He's collecting money in return for protection.) Cliff is not easily conned or intimidated, but when his father calls the school and Big M is given a week of detentions, things get much worse. The intimidation continues until Cliff convinces the hulking Ricky Linderman (who is rumoured to have committed murder) to be *his* bodyguard. Intrigued by his new protector, Cliff follows him to an auto shop where Linderman shows him the motorcycle he's lovingly been rebuilding and the two become friends. Meanwhile, Big M has hired a bodyguard of his own, a thug named Mike who roughs up Linderman and his motorcycle. Cliff, unable to understand why Linderman wouldn't fight back, confronts him and learns the real story of his new friend's past. The next day at a chance meeting in the park, Mike and Linderman fight it out. And when Cliff and Big M get mixed up in the brawl, Cliff fights his own battle.

CAUTION: Linderman's emotional problems are caused by an accident in which his brother is shot while they are playing with their father's gun. Linderman describes "the blood pouring out of the side of his head." The fist-fight at the end is realistic and there is blood when Cliff breaks Big M's nose. Mild language.

GO: This is a warm film with heart-quality about a problem some kids face at school, and is a cautionary tale about the perils of keeping a firearm in the house. Look for a young Jennifer Beales and Joan Cusack.

✗ MY GIRL

Col/Tri-Star
1992
102 minutes
Directed by: Howard Zieff
Starring: Dan Aykroyd, Anna Chlumsky, Macaulay Culkin, Jamie Lee Curtis
OFRB rating: PG—Mature Theme
MPAA rating: PG

Vada, eleven-year-old daughter of the town funeral director, Harry Sultenfuss, is a hypochondriac obsessed with death (a condition stemming directly from the premature death of her mother). She imagines she's developing the symptoms of the dead people who are brought to the funeral parlour where she and her father live. Her best friend, Thomas Jay, is allergic to practically everything and, despite the mild abuse she directs his way, is devoted to Vada. When make-up artist Shelley Devoto answers Harry's want ad for a cosmetician, the Sultenfusses go through a period of upheaval. Harry and Shelley start a relationship, and Vada must resolve her feelings of jealously and guilt. Then tragedy strikes: Thomas Jay dies after being repeatedly stung by a horde of wasps, and during his funeral Vada completely breaks down. It's only through Shelley's healing influence and Harry's new-found courage that Vada is able to reconcile her grief and overcome her preoccupation with death.

✗**STOP:** For any child who has recently had to deal with the death of a loved one, this film is a definite NO. Thomas Jay is stung to death by a horde of wasps, and in a wrenching scene, Vada is informed of the tragedy and is subsequently crushed by grief.

CAUTION: This film is about coming to grips with the passing of a loved one, and about the changes that time and life inevitably bring — pretty weighty stuff for young children. In one scene Shelley talks to Vada about menstruation and there are scenes in the mortuary, where Harry and his assistant are working on bodies. Thomas Jay is shown in his coffin.

GO: This film contains one of the great last lines of all time. (Too bad the kids won't get it!)

✗ MY SCIENCE PROJECT

Touchstone
1985
94 minutes
Directed by: Jonathan Betuel
Starring: Dennis Hopper,
    Fisher Stevens, John Stockwell,
    Danielle Von Zerneck
OFRB rating: PG—Too Intense for
    Young Children
MPAA rating: PG

The film begins in the 1950s when the military discovers a crashed flying saucer, the burned-out hulk of which they cut into pieces and store away. The scene then shifts to the present, where Mike Harlan, a high school senior, interested only in cars and Bruce Springsteen, has learned that he will not graduate if he doesn't have a science project ready before the end of term. He visits a graveyard for outdated military equipment, hoping to chance upon something he can use for the much-despised project, and finds a bizarre machine in a container marked "top secret." After a number of strange incidents occur, he takes the machine to his science teacher, who identifies it as a time warp generator, and is promptly sucked into another dimension. General chaos ensues as Mike and his friends race against time, the authorities and a collection of teen-age villains, to stop the gizmo from destroying the universe. The film comes to a climax when a time warp envelopes the entire school, bringing together past, present and future in a violent final confrontation.

✗ STOP: This film is definitely not for young children. The climax of the film is nothing more than one graphic killing after another, which comes as something of a shock because up to this point the film isn't violent at all. Viewers will see a gladiator die a gory death, Viet Cong machine-gunned, futuristic mutants annihilated by blasters and a dinosaur's stomach blown open.

CAUTION: Mike's father's girlfriend is portrayed as a sleazy, gold-digging floozie, the police are represented as idiotic Nazis, and all of the women (except the heroine) are interested only in chewing-gum and sex. There is extreme coarse language and some of Vinnie's chauvinistic "girl advice" could be construed as offensive.

GO: The main characters display sensitivity, tolerance and understanding and there are reconciliations between enemies in the finale. The plot is well-paced, the special effects are dazzling and the story line is interesting.

NATIONAL GEOGRAPHIC VIDEO SERIES

Vestron Video
1980-1990
60 minutes (each volume)

National Geographic videos are a treasure-trove of information, and are a terrific way to educate kids and inspire a continued interest in various topics. Several of these videos are available in French.

Titles in the series are:
Africa's Stolen River
African Wildlife
Amazon: Land of the Flooded Forest
Among the Wild Chimpanzees
Antarctic Wildlife Adventure
Atocha: Quest for Treasure
Australia's Aborigines
Australia's Improbable Animals
Baka: People of the Forest

Ballad of the Irish Horse
Born of Fire
Cameramen Who Dared
Creatures of the Mangrove
Creatures of the Namib Desert
Crocodiles: Here Be Dragons
Egypt: Quest for Eternity
Elephant
Explorers: Century of Discovery
For All Mankind
Gorilla
The Great Whales
The Grizzlies
Hawaii: Strangers in Paradise
Himalayan River Run
Hong Kong: A Family Portrait
Iceland River Challenge
In the Shadow of Vesuvius
The Incredible Human Machine
The Invisible World
Jerusalem: Within These Walls
Land of the Tiger
Lions of the African Night
Living Treasures of Japan
Love Those Trains
Man-eaters of India
Miniature Miracle: The Computer Chip
Mysteries of Mankind
Polar Bear Alert
Rain Forest
Realm of the Alligator
Reptiles and Amphibians
Return to Everest
The Rhino War
Rocky Mountain Beaver Pond
Save the Panda
The Search for the Battleship Bismarck
Search for the Great Apes
The Secret Leopard
Secrets of the Titanic
Serengeti Diary
The Sharks
The Soviet Circus
Strange Creatures of the Night
Superliners: Twilight of an Era
Those Wonderful Dogs
The Tropical Kingdom of Belize
Volcano!
White Wolf
The Wilds of Madagascar
Yukon Passage
Zebra: Patterns in the Grass

✗ STOP: As many of the videos in this series contain graphic live footage, pre-screening is highly recommended.

NECESSARY ROUGHNESS

Paramount
1991
108 minutes
Directed by: Stan Dragoti
Starring: Scott Bakula,
    Hector Elizondo,
    Harley Jane Kozak, Robert
    Loggia, Larry Miller, Sinbad
OFRB rating: PG
MPAA rating: PG-13

A massive corruption scandal has virtually destroyed the Texas State Fighting Armadillos; the coaches have been fired and the players, suspended. Ed "Straight Arrow" Ginero has been hired to take over as head coach and brings his friend Wally Riggendorf onto the team. And what a team it isn't. They have so few decent prospects they have to play Iron Man football (players play both offense and defence). And they recruit thirty-four-year-old former high school quarterback star Paul Blake, who for personal reasons never enrolled in college. Blake meets journalism teacher Dr. Suzanne Carter and gets off on the wrong foot right away. Things go even worse on the field as the Armadillos lose every game. But Blake and Suzanne eventually develop a relationship, and the Armadillos get better until finally, in the last game of the season, they have a chance to win.

CAUTION: There's some fairly graphic fighting, and Suzanne and Blake are shown naked in bed (under the covers). In one scene, a player's face mask is knocked off and blood pours from his mouth. There is coarse language.

GO: The central theme, that fair play is more important than winning, is strongly stressed. Unfortunately titled, this is not a negative movie.

NEVER CRY WOLF

Walt Disney Home Video
1983
105 minutes
Directed by: Carroll Ballard
Starring: Brian Dennehy,
    Charles Martin Smith
OFRB rating: F
MPAA rating: PG

Tyler, a biologist, goes to the Arctic alone where he hopes to disprove the theory that wolves are a threat to people. He studies them for months before discovering that the wolves are catching and eating mice to survive. He even cooks and eats some mice himself (as an experiment, at first) and soon develops a taste for them. After many months of study, Tyler concludes that the wolves are more charitable and interesting than most humans. Based on the book *Never Cry Wolf* by Farley Mowat.

CAUTION: Wolves attack, kill and eat a caribou, and Tyler has nightmares about being attacked himself. In one scene, Tyler goes skinny dipping, and in another he falls through the ice and is trapped underneath. There isn't a great deal of action in this film — it's more a story about a man's growing understanding of and appreciation for nature — so young children may not be engaged.

GO: This gentle story gives a new view of the much-maligned wolf.

■ ▲

✘ ONE MAGIC CHRISTMAS

Walt Disney Home Video
1985
88 minutes
Directed by: Phillip Borsos
Starring: Harry Dean Stanton, Mary
   Steenburgen, Jan Rubes
OFRB rating: PG
MPAA rating: G

Every year, a Christmas angel named Gideon is assigned the task of helping someone get into the Christmas spirit; this year that person is Ginnie Granger. Work is hard at the supermarket where she is employed; her husband's been laid off and they're being forced out of their home. Gideon reveals his assignment to Ginnie's daughter, Abbie, and tells her not to be afraid, no matter what happens. The next day, Ginnie's husband, Jack, is shot trying to foil a robbery and the thief makes a getaway in Jack's car, taking Abbie and her brother Cal with him. Desperate, Ginnie follows in the robber's car just in time to see the car with the children inside plunge into the river. Returning to an empty house, Ginnie realizes the most important thing in her life was her family. When her children are returned to her unharmed, she is grateful but must tell them that their dad is dead. Abbie goes to Gideon for help, but Gideon send her to Santa Claus who tells her that only her mom can "make [Jack] not dead." Santa gives her something to take to her mother that causes a transformation in Ginnie and restores the family.

✘STOP: In spite of its innocent title, this is not a film for children. The film is emotionally trying. Jack is shot violently and the children's plunge into an icy river is shocking.

GO: A wonderful, magical film for everyone who feels overworked and has lost the sense of childhood wonder.

OPPORTUNITY KNOCKS

MVA 1990
103 minutes
Directed by: Donald Petrie
Starring: Julia Campbell,
   Dana Carvey, Todd Graf,
   Robert Loggia, Milo O'Shea,
   James Tolkan
OFRB rating: PG
MPAA rating: PG-13

On the run from the mob, small-time con man Eddie Farrell hides in a deserted suburan house until the owners, Milt and Mona Malkin, come home and mistake him for a friend of their son, David. They lend him five hundred dollars, give him a fancy car and clothes, and even introduce him to their gorgeous doctor daughter, Annie. Before Eddie knows it, he's been offered a vide-presidency in Milt's company, and Annie is beginning to fall in love with him. He has the perfect opportunity to work the ultimate con, settle things with the mob and set himself up for life. But as he begins to care more and more for the Malkins, he's compelled to change his ways and save Milt and his company instead. In the end, when his true identity is revealed, the Malkins come to love Eddie for the person he is.

CAUTION: There is minimal violence and some coarse language, but the PG-13 rating was most likely earned by the mature theme. Carvey's South Asian and Chinese impersonations may be considered offensive.

GO: The film has a decent redemption theme.

✗ PROJECT X

CBS Fox
1987
101 minutes
Directed by: Jonathan Kaplan
Starring: Matthew Broderick,
   Helen Hunt
OFRB rating: PG
MPAA rating: PG

Jimmy Garret is an ambitious pilot who, after a disciplinary action, is relegated to assisting in a top-secret military project involving chimpanzees. At first he's reluctant to participate in the project, considering it to be a waste of time, but changes his mind when he realizes that it has extremely serious implications. He discovers that one of the chimps, Virgil, can communicate in sign language (a skill acquired from a young psychologist named Terry MacDonald in a previous training project) and is horrified to learn that the chimp is doomed to annihilation. Jimmy calls Terry to help him free Virgil and the other chimps in the lab (who have already devised an escape plan of their own). Jimmy and Terry are caught, but the chimps make use of their simulated flight training and escape for good to the Everglades.

✗STOP: The whole issue of experimenting on animals is very complex and may upset some children. In one scene a chimp is exposed to an enormous dose of radiation, wears an agonized expression and eventually dies. The U.S. air force use the word "Russian" as synonymous with "enemy."

CAUTION: The film is based on U.S. military tests of human endurance in the event of nuclear war. A chimp is shot and there is some swearing.

GO: This film caused some controversy about experimenting on animals when it was released. The musical score is excellent.

✗ RAIDERS OF THE LOST ARK

Paramount
1981
115 minutes
Directed by: Stephen Spielberg
Starring: Karen Allen, Harrison Ford,
   John Rhys-Davies
OFRB rating: PG—Some Scenes
   May Frighten
MPAA rating: PG

Indiana Jones, Ivy League professor, archaeologist and adventurer, is contacted by the U.S. government about a mission of extraordinary importance. A possible site of the Ark of the Covenant has been located in the lost city of Tanis, and the government is racing to find it before the Nazis do. However, the Ark is hidden in the Well of Souls and can only be located with the help of another artifact, an amulet called the Staff of Ra. Jones finds the amulet with archeologist's daughter Marion Ravenwood, and together they race to Egypt where the Nazis already have a huge excavation underway (supervised by Jones' nemeis, Belloq). Jones and Marion infiltrate the digsite, sneak into the map room and find their way to the Well of Souls where Belloq and the Nazis discover them, take the Ark and imprison them in the Well. Jones and Marion escape, and after a number of spine-tingling fights, chases and more escapes, find themselves prisoners again on a remote Mediterranean island. There they are present when the Nazis test the Ark and meet a grisly end.

✗ STOP: A man is shown impaled on spikes. When the Ark is opened, the faces of the evil melt like wax, and apparitions with angelic faces turn hideous and impale the Nazi soldiers. In one fight a mechanic is chopped up by a whirling propeller (blood splatters), and throughout people die with their eyes open, blood dribbling from their mouths.

GO: Blood and gore aside, this is surely one of the greatest action films of all time.

the project, has given the team four months in which to complete their work and as the deadline approaches he becomes increasingly more nervous. He forces the team to spend every spare moment in the lab, but despite their efforts, the laser will not work. Then Chris, supergenius and party animal of the the group, has a moment of brilliant inspiration and finds a way to make the necessary adjustments. They test the laser — it punches a hole through half the town — and the question comes up: Why does Hathaway need so much power? The team realizes it's been duped into building a weapon and, with Hathaway's unwitting help, sabotages the military test turning the weapon's demonstration into the biggest practical joke of all time.

CAUTION: There is coarse language, and sexual remarks are made.

GO: Ingenuity reigns supreme in this genuinely funny film. There is no violence and there are no disturbing scenes.

REAL GENIUS

RCA Columbia
1985
106 minutes
Directed by: Martha Coolidge
Starring: William Atherton,
 Gabe Jarret, Val Kilmer,
 Michelle Meyrink
OFRB rating: PG
MPAA rating: PG

Mitch, a brilliant fifteen-year-old scientist, is accepted into the prestigious National Science Institute where he joins a team of the best minds on campus to work on a top-secret laser project. Professor Hathaway, who's heading

✗ RETURN TO SNOWY RIVER

Walt Disney Home Video
1988
99 minutes
Directed by: Geoff Burrows
Starring: Tom Burlinson,
 Brian Dennehy, Sigrid Thornton
OFRB rating: PG
MPAA rating: PG

Jim Craig returns to Snowy River with a stake of beautiful horses, where he intends to find his true love Jessica Harrison, marry her and set up a ranch. (He lets the great stallion run free, in hopes that it will cover his new mares.) To that end, Jim attends a horse race on the Harrison property, where he not only sees Jessica, but upperclassman Alistair Pattan and Jessica's father as well, who promptly informs him that he is not welcome on his ranch. Jim and Jessica continue their relationship nonetheless, while Alistair's banker father pressures Harrison to help him drive the local land-owners out of the prime Snowy River grazing area. Alistair hires a gang of thugs to rob Jim. And when Jim goes after Alistair and his goons, Alistair shoots Jim's horse out from under him, knocking Jim out. When Jim comes to, the great stallion appears; Jim mounts him and renews the chase, encountering Harrison, Jessica, the mountain folk and the lowlanders on the way — all of them willing to help him recover his stock. Jim then catches up with Alistair, and with the help of the great stallion, beats him in a fight. In the end, Jim lets the great stallion go free once more. This film is the sequel to *The Man from Snowy River*.

✘**STOP**: Jim's horse is shot and dies.

CAUTION: During a fight at the end of the movie, Jim is cut with a sabre and hit in the

face with a branch. There are realistic punches and bloody faces.

GO: The riding and scenery are spectacular in this great sequel.

✘ THE ROCKETEER

Walt Disney Home Video
1991
109 minutes
Directed by: Joe Johnston
Starring: Alan Arkin, Bill Campbell, Jennifer Connelly, Timothy Dalton
OFRB rating: PG—Violence
MPAA rating: PG

In Los Angeles, in 1938, Clifford Secord, a daring young stunt pilot, is racing his Piper over California farmland when he accidentally becomes a target in a shoot-out between federal agents and the crooks who've just stolen Howard Hughes' latest aviation miracle, a rocket pack. When a fleeing crook dumps the pack on Cliff's airfield, Cliff and his partner Peevy test the pack by strapping it to a statue — it flies! Peevy then designs a helmet for Cliff, and when an aviation stunt goes wrong and Cliff dons the rocket-pack to save the day, the Rocketeer is born. Neville Sinclair, a Nazi agent masquerading as a big-time Hollywood celebrity, learns about Cliff's discovery and is intent on securing the rocket pack for himself. (He and his henchmen plan to rule the world with an army of Nazi rocketeers.) They kidnap Cliff's girlfriend in a huge dirigible and, after an intense nail-biting confrontation, are defeated by the

Rocketeer. Based on the novel by Dave Stevens.

✗STOP: A huge Nazi assassin with a grotesque, disfigured face murders a wounded gangster in his hospital room.

CAUTION: Shoot-outs, death threats and punch-ups abound. One nine-year-old boy we know remarked, "Too much kissing, not enough flying."

GO: The special effects are great and the flying sequences are spectacular.
■ ▲

SISTER ACT

Touchstone
1992
100 minutes
Directed by: Emile Ardolino
Starring: Whoopi Goldberg,
    Harvey Keitel, Maggie Smith
OFRB rating: PG
MPAA rating: PG

When two-bit night-club singer Deloris Van Cartier goes to break off her affair with her gangster boss Vince, she inadvertently bursts into his office while he is having his driver "eliminated." Unconvinced that she will not spill the beans, Vince sends his thugs to kill her, but Deloris escapes to the police and tells all. Placed in protective custody until the hearing, Deloris is disguised as Sister Mary Clarence and sent to the San Francisco convent of St. Catherines. The Mother Superior will have none of it at first, but her small convent is in danger of closing, and the police promise a generous donation. So Deloris is admitted and she and convent life meet in a head-on clash, during the course of which Deloris is forced to come to grips with her own shortcomings. But those shortcomings are nothing compared to those of the deplorable convent choir which Deloris rebuilds and turns into a spiffy, jazzy musical ensemble that drags the local populace into the church. Deloris incurs the ire of the Mother Superior, but also attracts huge crowds to the convent — even the Pope decides to stop by during his North American tour. The climax comes when the gangsters find and kidnap Deloris, taking her back to Reno to finish her off. The nuns then spiritually blackmail a helicopter pilot into flying them to Reno, and as Deloris escapes her captors, everyone converges in the casino.

CAUTION: Staunch Roman Catholics may be a bit put off by some of the film's antics. One gangster is shot.

GO: This is a wildly-popular and generally inoffensive film.

✗ SOMETHING WICKED THIS WAY COMES

Walt Disney Home Video
1983
94 minutes
Directed by: Jack Clayton
Starring: Diane Ladd,
    Jonathan Price, Jason Robards
OFRB rating: PG
MPAA rating: PG

Fall comes to a small town in the mid-west, and with it comes Mr. Dark's Pandemonium Carnival. Mr. Dark isn't just an impressario; he can also see and grant the heart's desire. However, each wish is fulfilled with a terrible price and one by one the townspeople fall victim to his temptations. A plain spinster who wishes to be beautiful is granted beauty, but made blind. A war amputee and former football star who wants to be whole again is granted his wish, but turned into an evil child. And so on. The town librarian's son and his best friend spy on the carnival and discover the dreadful truth — that Mr. Dark and his infernal accomplices intend to destroy the whole town. The agents of hell try to kill the boys with a plague of spiders and when that doesn't work, Mr. Dark himself comes for the boys. They hide in the library, and during a confrontation with Mr. Dark, the courageous librarian resists the ultimate Faustian temptation, setting up a violent climax which releases a long-awaited rainstorm, destroying the satanic carnival. Based on the book by Ray Bradbury.

✗STOP: Frankly, this is not a children's film. One of Mr. Dark's henchmen is turned into an evil child and Mr. Dark crushes the librarian's hand to a pulp while demanding to know the location of the boys. During the assault on the house, the boys are trapped by hundreds of huge spiders.

CAUTION: This tale of a modern Mephistopheles, who grants wishes for souls is replete with haunting images. There is a

strained relationship between father and son, a key element in the film.

■

SPACE CAMP

Vestron
1986
116 minutes
Directed by: Harry Winer
Starring: Kate Capshaw,
    Tate Donovan, Leaf Phoenix,
    Kelly Preston, Lawry B. Scott,
    Lea Thompson
OFRB rating: PG—Swearing
MPAA rating: PG

Andy is an astronaut assigned to teach kids at a space camp, simulating NASA flights and training them to be astronauts. She has four special students: Katherine, who dreams of becoming the first female shuttle commander; Tish, who has an incredible memory and who wants to contact alien life-forms in the universe; Rudy, who's fiercely determined even though he's of average intelligence; and Kevin, whose father has forced him to go to the camp and who doesn't take anything seriously. It's up to Andy to teach her students to work together as a team on a spacecraft. At first, the team works badly together and it's only when Andy and her group are accidentally sent up into space, and the kids are forced to handle re-entry by themselves, that they finally learn to work together as a team.

CAUTION: Andy's injuries in the accidental launch are traumatic. There is some mild language.

GO: Based on a real NASA summer camp, this is a terrific film for young fans of ad-

venture and science fiction. Positive female role models highlight this film.

SPACEBALLS

MGM/UA
1988
97 minutes
Directed by: Mel Brooks
Starring: Mel Brooks, John Candy,
    Rick Moranis, Bill Pullman,
    Joan Rivers, Daphne Zuniga
MPAA rating: PG

This spoof on the *Star Wars* trilogy manages to poke fun at a few other epics as well, including a hilarious final vignette based on *The Planet of the Apes.* Under the command of the fiendish Darth Vader clone Dark Helmet, the evil Spaceballs of the Planet Spaceball have a clever plan: They will kidnap the Druish Princess Vespa and force her father, King Rolland, to give them the combination to the air-shield of Planet Druidia (which protects the precious atmosphere the Spaceballs desire). But their plans are thwarted by the renegade Lone Star and his sidekick Barf, who rescue Vespa and her robot Dot Matrix. With the stumblebum Spaceballs in hot pursuit, the four flee across the galaxy in search of the mystic Yogurt, master of the Schwartz. After numerous chases, duels and corny jokes (when they comb the desert for the fugitives, the Spaceballs use a real comb), everyone lives happily ever after — except the Spaceballs, of course.

CAUTION: Sexual innuendo, double entendres, crude jokes and coarse language permeate this film. President Scroob is obnoxious and leering, and his female chief in command is a real dominatrix.

GO: Young kids don't seem to get many of the mature jokes. This is one of those films that's perfect at sleep-overs for kids eight and up; it gives them that racy, forbidden feeling without going to extremes.

SPACED INVADERS

Touchstone Home Video
1990
100 minutes
Directed by: Patrick Read Johnson
Starring: Douglas Barr, Royal Dano,
    Ariana Richards, Gregg Berger
OFRB rating: PG
MPAA rating: PG

In Big Bean, Illinois, new sherrif Sam Hocksley takes his daughter Kathy to a Halloween party to help her adjust to her new home town. Meanwhile, The Martian Imperial Atomic Space Navy has programmed new Enforcer Drones to oversee all of its starships, and launches an ill-fated attack on the Arcturus system. The Space Navy is completely destroyed, and its last forlorn distress signal is picked up by a lone Martian patrol ship. The crew scans for the source of the distress signal and picks up a Halloween broadcast of Orson Welles' "War of the Worlds" instead. They come to the mistaken conclusion that the attack on Arcturus was just a feint, and that the real assault is on the insignificant planet Earth. So the Martians land in Big Bean, Illinois on Halloween night, where they intend to join up with their armada, which they assume is taking over Earth.

There, some of the Martians join Kathy's group of trick-or-treaters and it doesn't take long for Kathy to determine the truth (these kids aren't from around here). She follows the Martians as they head off to destroy what they believe is one of Earth's missile defense systems (a granary). And from that point on, the film careens from one wild episode to another as the mixed-up Martians are chased by practically everyone, including their own Enforcer Drone. Eventually, the town manages to defeat the Enforcer Drone, saving both the Martians and Earth, and they send the little green guys home.

CAUTION: The Martians are kind of rude, and their Enforcer Drone might be a little spooky for some kids. The Martian captain is hit by a truck (he survives).

GO: All in all, a fun flick for kids over six.

Placement Calculus Exam they will all be assured of college entrance. He threatens, wheedles, begs and cajoles; he encourages them to believe they can accomplish anything. When the exam day arrives they write the test and they all pass. But the results are so revolutionary that the Board of Education suspects Jaime and his students have cheated. An inquiry is made and Jaime convinces the class that the only way to prove their innocence is to write the exam again. Apprehensive, they undergo the ordeal a second time and achieve even better results. This film is based on a true story.

CAUTION: The film contains a little coarse language and Jaime has a heart attack (he survives).

GO: This is a truly inspiring film for teachers, students and anyone with a math phobia.

▲

STAND AND DELIVER

Warner Home Video
1988
103 minutes
Directed by: Ramon Menendez
Starring: Andy Garcia,
    Edward James Olmos,
    Lou Diamond Phillips
OFRB rating: PG
MPAA rating: PG

Jaime Escalante quits his upscale job to teach calculus at a high school in East Los Angeles only to find that the senior students can't even do basic arithmetic. Determined to teach his students what they need to know, Jaime tells them that if they pass the Advanced

✗ STAR TREK II: THE WRATH OF KHAN

Paramount
1982
113 minutes
Directed by: Nicholas Meyer
Starring: Kirstie Alley,
    Ricardo Montalban, Leonard
    Nimoy, William Shatner
MPAA rating: PG

A Federation starship is conducting a survey to find a suitable test-world for the top-secret Genesis Project, when its landing party inadvertently stumbles upon a group of sinister genetic mutants (marooned by Kirk fifteen years before). The mutants, led by the vengeful Khan, take over the Federation Starship and the Genesis Orbital Station. From there they send out a distress call, which is picked up by Admiral Kirk and the Enterprise. Khan then ambushes the Enterprise and a harrowing game of cat and mouse ensues. In the final confrontation, Khan sets the Genesis device to explode, planning to destroy both his own vessel and the Enterprise. The crew's fate appears sealed until Spock enters a lethally irradiated chamber and repairs the starship's drive. The crew escapes, but Spock dies in the process. However, the movie does end with a message of hope.

✗ **STOP:** There are a great many scenes in which people are tortured, burned, crushed and disintegrated. Kirk is reunited with his son — a son from a relationship with a woman to whom he was obviously never married. And Spock, a universally popular character, dies as he is slowly disfigured by radiation poisoning.

GO: The film is replete with positive messages and features a number of women in positions of authority. The special effects are spectacular.

✗ STAR TREK III: THE SEARCH FOR SPOCK

Paramount
1984
105 minutes
Directed by: Leonard Nimoy
Starring: DeForest Kelly,
  Christopher Lloyd, Leonard
  Nimoy, William Shatner, George
  Takei
OFRB rating: PG
MPAA rating: PG

Kirk and his companions have paid a heavy price for the defeat of Khan and the creation of the Genesis planet; Spock is dead and McCoy is inexplicably being driven insane. Then an unexpected visit from Spock's father, Ambassador Sarek, provides a startling revelation: McCoy is harbouring Spock's living essence, placed in his mind by Spock himself just before his death. And in order to release that essence they must retrieve Spock's body. Kirk and his crew have no choice but to steal the Enterprise, defy Starfleet's quarantine and go to the Genesis planet. There they unexpectedly encounter a resourceful group of Klingons who are determined to seize the secret of the Genesis torpedo to use it as a weapon. A desperate struggle follows in which the Enterprise is destroyed and the rapidly regenerating body of Spock, now a small boy, is discovered. Subsequently, Kirk's son is killed and the battle culminates in a brutal hand-to-hand fight between Kirk and the Klingon commander. Kirk triumphs and he and his companions take Spock's new body and his essence to the planet Vulcan, where the two are reunited.

✗ **STOP:** In one tense scene, the Klingons prepare to kill a hostage — and do.

CAUTION: The battle scenes and hand-to-hand combat are brutal (often the innocent are victimized) and there is some coarse language.

GO: Friendship and loyalty are positively portrayed.

✗ STAR TREK VI: THE UNDISCOVERED COUNTRY

Paramount
1991
110 minutes
Directed by: Nicholas Meyer
Starring: Kim Cattrall, Iman,
Leonard Nimoy,
Christopher Plummer,
William Shatner, David Warner
OFRB rating: PG
MPAA rating: PG

When an explosion on a Klingon moon, caused by overmining and insufficient safety precautions, critically pollutes the atmosphere of the Klingon homeworld, the desperate Klingons have no option but to sue for peace. Klingon Chancellor Gorkon is summoned to discuss the terms, and the Enterprise is chosen to escort his battlecruiser into Federation space. Soon after the rendezvous, the Enterprise inexplicably fires photon torpedoes at the Klingon ship. The craft is badly damaged, though no order was given and the Enterprise still retains its full complement of torpedoes. Then two masked commandos board the Klingon vessel and kill the ambassador. In order to prevent an incident, Kirk and McCoy surrender themselves and are taken to the Klingon world where they are tried and sentenced to a frozen prison planetoid. But Kirk and McCoy soon make some unusual allies and plan an escape with Martia, a bizarre shape-changing being. The arrangements turn out to be a set-up, but Kirk and McCoy are rescued by the Enterprise. Now

aware of the conspiracy afoot, they race to the site of a major peace conference where they defeat General Chang, a Romulan conspirator who is lurking in a cloaked warship near the planet.

✗STOP: This film features relatively graphic violence. The commandos shoot Klingons with beam weapons which sever arms and punch holes in bodies, leaving globules of blood floating in a weightless environment.

CAUTION: A hapless wretch is tossed out into the snow on the prison planetoid and left to die. Spock interrogates a fellow-Vulcan with a brutal telepathic method that causes her obvious trauma. During the assassination attempt, an assassin lies dead in a pool of blood.

STAY TUNED

Warner Bros.
1992
89 minutes
Directed by: Peter Hyams
Starring: Pam Dawber,
Jeffrey Jones, Eugene Levy,
John Ritter
OFRB rating: PG
MPAA rating: PG

Roy Knable isn't exactly a success story — he sells plumbing supplies door-to-door. Threatened by his wife Helen's success (she's a big-time advertising executive), Roy lives in front of the television in order to escape. Helen has had enough, and the night comes when she decides to leave him. But that same night, a shadowy figure named Spike shows up and gives Roy a huge home entertainment centre, complete with a satellite dish guaranteed to bring in six hundred and sixty-six channels. But the television only seems to pick up grotesque shows with names like *Three Men and Rosemary's Baby*. And when Roy goes out to adjust the dish to fine-tune the reception, he and Helen are sucked into a satanic television nightmare called Hell Vision (run by Spike) in which the acquisition of lost souls is turned into high entertainment for The Boss Down Below. Roy and Helen must survive twenty-four hours in Hell Vision, living through a succession of macabre send-ups, gruesome game-shows and even a Bugs Bunny/Tom and Jerry style cartoon. Meanwhile, their children Darryl and Diane discover the enormous new set, and gradually begin to catch on: Their parents are trapped in the television. As Roy and Helen travel through the infernal world, Roy gains strength and confidence in his resourcefulness and, with the help of the children, they draw ever closer to the twenty-four hour deadline. But when a technicality sends Roy home without Helen, he has to prove himself by returning voluntarily to rescue his wife, setting up the final confrontation with Spike.

CAUTION: While the tone is mild, the satirical humour in this film may be lost on young children. There are numerous grotesque images, and the lead characters are in peril throughout. The film is bound to raise questions about the hereafter in the minds of some young viewers and there is some coarse language.

GO: For teens and adults this is a light-hearted romp through send-ups of many familiar shows and movies. The theme is hopeful and the special effects are great.

STRANGE BREW

MGM/UA
1983
91 minutes
Directed by: Rick Moranis,
    Dave Thomas
Starring: Rick Moranis,
    Dave Thomas, Max Von Sydow,
    Paul Dooley, Angus MacInnes
MPAA rating: PG
OFRB rating: PG

When their irritated father orders them to get more Elsinore beer, Doug and Bob Mackenzie plan to trick the store into giving them some free; they will use the old "mouse in the bottle" ruse. They take their complaint right to the brewery, a huge castle located next to the Royal Canadian Institute for the Criminally Insane. There, by a stroke of luck, they save the life of Pamela, daughter of the company's late president, and promptly land jobs at the brewery. It turns out that only one day after the president's recent passing, his brother Claude married his wife and took over the whole brewery. (Holy Hamlet!) Meanwhile, Brewmeister Smith, an evil genius, is conducting experiments on the patients in the asylum next door and has laced Elsinore Beer with a powerful drug, which will enable him to rule the world. When the boys unwittingly expose his plans, Smith sets the boys up as Pamela's kidnappers, hoping to get rid of all three of them. He arranges for the boys' van, with Pamela inside, to crash into the river. Pamela is left totally traumatized, the boys are blamed and all three end up in the Institute for the Insane. Bob and Doug manage to escape, save Pamela and defeat the evil doctor before his beer drug completely ruins Oktoberfest.

CAUTION: Beer-drinking, burping and generally gross behaviour are all part of this film.

GO: It's a silly film, but it's funny.

SUPERMAN

Warner Home Video
1978
127 minutes
Directed by: Richard Donner
Starring: Marlon Brando,
  Gene Hackman, Margot Kidder,
  Christopher Reeve
OFRB rating: PG
MPAA rating: PG

On the advanced planet Krypton, Jor-El has discovered that his home world will be destroyed within 30 days. When the ruling council of the planet refuses to believe him and commands him to keep silent, he arranges to send his son to the primitive planet Earth, where the child will have extraordinary powers and an excellent chance of survival. The tiny spaceship carrying the toddler escapes just before the planet is destroyed. It lands in the mid-western United States and is discovered by Martha and Jonathan Kent, who name the baby Clark. When the baby saves Jonathan by holding up a toppling pickup truck, Jonathan realizes that Clark is here for a reason. Later, Clark suffers over having to hide his special gifts

when he is a teenager. After Jonathan dies, Clark is woken in the middle of the night by some strange static. An artifact from his spaceship, long hidden, has come to life. Clark travels up into the arctic, flings the crystal into the white wastes and watches it explode, creating the Fortress of Solitude. Clark remains there and discovers the nature of his origin. Then he moves to the city of Metropolis, getting a job as a reporter at the *Daily Planet*, masquerading as an ineffectual wimp, and hanging around star reporter Lois Lane. As Superman rescues Lois from certain death and performs other heroic acts (rescuing cats, saving airplanes) he attracts the attention of the evil super-villain Lex Luthor. Luthor deduces that meteorite fragments of the exploded planet Krypton will be lethal to Superman, and takes steps to obtain some. Then he arranges to divert the flight path of two nuclear missiles during a test, his master plan being to nuke the San Andreas fault, drop California into the sea, and become the owner of thousands of miles of newly waterfront property. When Superman arrives to stop him, Luthor tricks him into exposure to Kryptonite; but Luthor has made a fatal error in judgment and Superman has an unexpected ally, allowing him to race to the aid of the country. But in the end he is forced to violate one of his father's decrees in order to save Lois.

CAUTION: Lex Luthor has an FBI agent pushed in front of a subway train. Lois is smothered to death in a car which is trapped in a cave-in. During the earthquake resulting from the missiles, many people are shown in peril.

▲

✗ SUPERMAN II

Warner Home Video
1980
127 minutes
Directed by: Richard Lester
Starring: Gene Hackman, Margot
   Kidder, Christopher Reeve,
   Terence Stamp
OFRB rating: PG
MPAA rating: PG

When an explosion in space shatters The Phantom Zone (a floating exile chamber created by the leaders of Krypton to imprison their worst criminals), General Zod, Ursa and Non are released and make their way to Earth. And when Superman's old foe, Lex Luthor, encounters them, he enlists their help to battle Superman. (He tells them that Superman is their jailor's son, and together they vow to destroy him.) Unaware of the trouble afoot, Lois finally comes to the realization that Clark Kent and Superman are one and the same, and she and Superman fall in love. He takes her to the Fortress of solitude where a holographic image of his deceased mother tells him that in order to be with the woman he loves, he must become an ordinary mortal. He undergoes the change and, now unable to fly, drives Lois back to the city. On the way, after stopping at a diner, he sees the President on TV submitting to Zod and pleading for Superman's help. Recognizing his responsibility to mankind, Superman returns to the Fortress of Solitude and regains his powers. Then the four super-beings battle it out above the streets of New York. Eventually, Superman renders the villains powerless and, when order is restored, gives Lois a kiss of forgetfulness so that his true identity will remain a secret. This is a sequel to the very successful *Superman* film.

✗**STOP:** Because this is a movie about battling super-beings, the violence is on a grandiose scale. The speical effects are so believable that they will frighten some children. People are crushed, shot and hurled through windows.

CAUTION: Clark and Lois are shown sleeping naked together, covered by sheets. It may be disturbing to some that earthlings are totally helpless against the super-beings.

GO: The film has great special effects and the plot is exciting and clever. There are the usual in-the-nick-of-time rescues and some fun stuff as Lois gradually figures out Clark's true identity.

▲

SUPERMAN IV: THE QUEST FOR PEACE

Warner Home Video
1987
90 minutes
Directed by: Sidney J. Furie
Starring: Jon Cryer, Gene Hackman,
    Mariel Hemingway, Margot
    Kidder, Christopher Reeve
OFRB rating: PG
MPAA rating: PG

When the *Daily Planet* is purchased by a press tycoon with a reputation for turning his papers into money-making tabloids, the staff anticipates trouble. Sure enough, trouble comes in spades, especially for Clark Kent. The tycoon's daughter develops an inexplicable crush on the bumbling Kent, and to make matters worse, she and Lois arrange for a double date with him and Superman. This, needless to say, necessitates some very quick changes for the Man of Steel. Meanwhile, there's trouble of a much more serious nature brewing as Lex Luthor, Superman's arch enemy, sets in motion an ingenious plan to prevent Superman from ridding the world of nuclear weapons. He and his nephew clone Superman's genetic material and fire it along with a nuclear missile into the sun; the evil Nuclear Man is born. Nuclear Man is as powerful as Superman and serves Lex Luthor as a devoted servant. His only weakness is darkness. In their first fight, Nuclear Man scratches Superman on the back of the neck, and Superman is forced into hiding, where he grows progressively weaker from radiation sickness. But

Superman receives aid from a surprising source, and returns to defeat Nuclear Man by creating an eclipse, then dropping the hapless villain down the exhaust vent of a reactor.

CAUTION: There is violence throughout the film, including punching and smashing and so on. When Superman is ill, the scenes of his sickness may cause concern among very young children.

GO: The story ends on a hopeful note.
▲

TALES FOR ALL SERIES

Cinema Plus
1985-1992
90-100 minutes (each volume)

Produced by Québécois filmmaker Rock Demers, the *Tales for All* series has garnered more than 135 international awards. The films feature many different writers and directors; many have magical or mystical elements, and all are generally geared for family viewing. There is no coarse language and almost no violence. (See our section for children aged six to ten for more reviews in this series.)

Bach and Broccoli
(Tale #3)

A young orphan named Fanny is sent to live with her eccentric Uncle Jonathan. (Jonathan was in love with Fanny's mother, who married his brother instead.) An organist practicing almost single-mindedly for a music festival, Jonathan finds

Fanny's resemblance to his lost love almost too much to bear, but agrees to take her in until a proper foster family can be found. Despite his unwillingness to change his ways, Jonathan comes to appreciate Fanny more and more. Then comes the day when a foster family is found, and Jonathan realizes he must chose between the solitude he once prized so highly, and the little girl he has come to love. (Available in French under the title *Bach et bottine*).

CAUTION: This might not be a good choice for a child who has recently lost a loved one.

GO: This is a good story about appreciating the important things in life.

▲

Bye Bye Red Riding Hood (Tale #9)

Fanny lives in the forest with her meteorologist mother where she meets an apparently kind wolf, a city boy named Nicholas and an ornithologist who bears a striking resemblance to the father who abandoned her long ago . This is a modern retelling of the Red Riding Hood story. (Astral Home Video, 1989). Available in French under the title *Bye, Bye, Chaperon Rouge*.

CAUTION: There are some frightening and disturbing scenes. The wolf is shot and the great-grandmother dies

▲

✗ The Peanut Butter Solution (Tale #2)

One morning, eleven-year-old soccer star Michael Baskin wakes to learn that there has been a fire in the neighbourhood's spooky old house, and that two street people were killed inside. He dares to enter the burned-out house and sees something so terrible that his hair falls out. Hoods, hats, wigs and all the efforts of medical science do not help. Then one night, the ghosts of the street people come to see Michael. Sorry for his condition they give him the Peanut Butter Solution (a disgusting recipe that includes dead flies, rotten eggs and peanut butter) to make his hair grow back. He's warned not to use more than a spoonful of peanut butter, but when the mixture won't stick Michael ignores the warning and adds more. The tonic works too well; in fact, his hair won't stop growing. Strangley, his creepy art teacher, decides that Michael's hair will make perfect paint brushes and kidnaps him, taking him to a sweatshop where other students are also being held. It's up to Michael's sister, Suzy, and his friend, Connie, to find him and rescue him. Also available in French under the title *Operation Buerre de Pinottes.*

✗STOP: Young viewers may be disturbed by the creepy art teacher who kidnaps his own students and by some of the ghost scenes.

GO: This is a rather strange film, but it *is* a ghost story without the elements of horror.

▲

The Summer of the Colt (Tale #8)

When Laura, Daniel and Phillipe visit their grandfather Don Federico's horse ranch in South America, Laura notices at once that her grandfather is avoiding her. (It turns out that Laura, having grown, now bears an uncanny resemblance to her grandmother, Don Federicos's long-lost love, and Don Federico can hardly stand to look at the girl.) There is more promise of a happy summer for Daniel, however, when Martin, the ranch foreman's son, shows him a new stallion named Fiero. Stunned by its beauty, Daniel asks his grandfather if he can have the horse. And his grandfather agrees on the condition that Daniel break the horse himself. But Martin has already broken the stallion in secret, and when Daniel tries to ride it, he's thrown off and hits his head on a fence. He tells his grandfather he doesn't want to ride the horse anymore, but thinking that his grandson is a coward, Don Federico demands that Daniel continue to ride. Angrily, Laura intervenes, and when her infuriated grandfather banishes her to her room, Laura takes a horse, and rides off into the wild. Then it's up to Daniel and Martin and Don Federico to find her.

CAUTION: There is a great deal of angst in the relationship between Don Federico and his grandchildren. Laura tells her aunt that she has had her period.

GO: This is a moving tale of people learning to understand one another, with plenty of stuff to interest horse lovers.

Vincent and Me
(Tale #11)

Thirteen-year-old Jo's work bears such a striking resemblence to that of Van Gogh that unscrupulous people plan to use her talents to help them pull off the art con of the century. But Jo goes back in time to the nineteenth century, and Van Gogh himself helps her thwart the criminals. The paintings of the master are prominently featured in the film. (Astral Video, 1991)

GO: Winner of the 1991 Parents' Choice Award for Best Children's Film of the Year and of the 1992 Emmy Award for Best Children's Special.

TEEN WOLF

Paramount
1985
92 minutes
Directed by: Rod Daniel
Starring: Michael J. Fox, James Hampton, Scott Paulin, Susan Ursitti
OFRB rating: PG
MPAA rating: PG

Scott, a player on his high school's losing basketball team, is alarmed by the way his body is changing. Wolf-like hair has begun to sprout on his chest; he develops a growl that sends chills through the toughest bully; he can even hear a dog whistle. Desperate, he turns to his father for help, only to learn that his condition runs in the family — his father is a werewolf, too. Scott finds little comfort in his father's words until he discovers that his new-found werewolf strength makes him a great basketball player. His teammates, however, soon come to resent his abilities (they hardly ever get to play) and it isn't until Scott begins to work with the rest of the team that they are victorious.

CAUTION: A game of dares is played in which losers must perform tasteless acts, and partying teens are shown smoking and drinking. Scott's transformation may upset young children. The film includes mild innuendo, some fighting and coarse language.

GO: Scott rejects superficial rewards and develops confidence and self-respect.

TEEN WOLF TOO

Paramount
1987
95 minutes
Directed by: Christopher Leitch
Starring: John Astin,
  Jason Bateman
  Kim DarbyOFRB rating: F
MPAA rating: PG

In the *Teen Wolf* sequel, Scott's cousin, Todd Howard, is forced to accept a boxing scholarship to get into university. There, shocked by his own transformation into a werewolf (a condition that runs in the family), he finds the extraordinary strength that makes him the regional boxing champion. Success, however, makes Todd unpopular with his friends, as he becomes obnoxious, coasting on the strength of his athletic abilities. Todd's Uncle Harold talks to him about responsibility. And when his boxing team makes it to the championships, Todd apologizes to his friends and, using only his strength as a human, is victorious.

CAUTION: There are boxing matches throughout the film, with plenty of punching. Todd fondles a girl's behind.

GO: This film emphasizes the importance of being yourself. There is no swearing.

THE THREE AMIGOS

Orion
1986
105 minutes
Directed by: John Landis
Starring: Alfonso Arau,
  Chevy Chase, Steve Martin,
  Patrice Martinez, Martin Short
MPAA rating: PG

In 1916, a little Mexican village is easy prey for the villainous El Guapo and his murderous banditos. In a direct send-up of *The Magnificent Seven* the desperate villagers gather what money they can, and send the beautiful Carmen to seek out and hire The Three Amigos — Lucky, Dusty and Ned — gunfighters famous for helping the downtrodden. The villagers don't know that The Three Amigos are just actors who, among other things, have just been dropped by their studio. The Amigos, happy for the work and thinking that they've been hired to act in a movie, head south, hilariously unaware that the offer was real; that is, until one of El Guapos's henchman grazes Lucky with a real bullet. Then the truth dawns on the terrified thespians and they beg for mercy. El Guapo scornfully lets them live and rides off with the beautiful Carmen as his captive. Much shamed, the heroes recover their nerve and vow to become The Three Amigos for real. They follow a bizarre set of instructions and sneak into the fortress of El Guapo during his birthday party. There they save Carmen, make a narrow escape and use some good old-fashioned trickery to finally defeat the bandit leader and his men.

CAUTION: There is the odd off-colour joke and people do get shot, although nothing is graphic.

GO: This movie contains some first-rate comedy, and is sophisticated enough for adults while retaining enough physical humour for the eight to twelve set.

THREE MEN AND A LITTLE LADY

Touchstone Home Video
1990
103 minutes
Directed by: Emile Ardolino
Starring: Christopher Cazenove,
    Ted Danson, Steve Guttenberg,
    Tom Selleck, Nancy Travis,
    Robin Weisman
OFRB rating: PG
MPAA rating: PG

In this film (sequel to *Three Men and a Baby*), Peter, Michael and Jack are still living with Sylvia Bennington and her daughter Mary. They're the three best fathers any little girl ever had and everybody's happy; that is, until Sylvia, who has fallen in love with Peter, begins to demand a more passionate, conventional family life. Worried that Mary is confused by her extended family, and confused herself by the situation, Sylvia accepts her director friend Edward's proposal of marriage and moves to England. Soon after the big move, Michael talks to Mary on the phone and, realizing that she's desperately unhappy, the men decide to go to England. When they get there, Peter is horrified by Edward's

attitude towards Mary, especially when he begins to suspect that Edward plans to shunt her off to a boarding school. But more importantly, he discovers that he's always loved Sylvia and goes to extraordinary lengths to get her (and Mary) back.

CAUTION: Mary mentions the word penis, and an embarrassed Peter mumbles an inadequate biological explanation. There is some sexual innuendo.

GO: This is a light, comical film about how an unconventional family can be just as happy as a more conventional one, and about how the weight of responsibility can sometimes cloud the expression of love.

▲

✗ THREE NINJAS

Touchstone Home Video
1992
85 minutes
Directed by: John Turteltaub
Starring: Rand Kingsley,
    Alan McRae, Chad Power,
    Max Elliott Slade,
    Michael Treanor, Victor Wong
MPAA rating: PG

The Douglas brothers spend their summers with their Japanese grandfather, Mori Tanaka, who trains them in the positive aspects of the ancient ninja arts. The boys' father, Sam Douglas, is an FBI agent who hates martial arts. (He's trying to track down arms dealer and expert ninja Hugo Snyder.) After a close call with the Feds, Snyder threatens Tanaka in an attempt to force Sam off the case. When that fails, Snyder hires three thugs to kidnap the boys. The Douglas boys easily defeat the comic villains in a style reminiscent of *Home Alone*, but more formidable goons soon arrive and take the kids to Snyder's ship in the harbour. Tanaka follows and sneaks onboard, and in the mayhem that ensues, Tanaka and Snyder face each other in a final showdown.

STOP: At one point, Snyder turns to an associate and says: "I'm going to crush your head until a slimey ooze comes out of your eyeballs."

CAUTION: There is violence throughout, though most of it slapstick. Punches and kicks don't draw blood, and are accompanied by absurd sound effects. (When a villain is knocked out, we hear tweety-bird noises.)

GO: This is a fun, action-packed film which stresses the positive aspects of martial arts.

TREASURE ISLAND

Malofilm/Turner Home
   Entertainment
1990
132 minutes
Directed by: Fraser C. Heston
Starring: Christian Bale,
   Julian Glover, Charlton Heston,
   Richard Johnson, Christopher
   Lee, Oliver Reed, Clive Wood
OFRB rating: PG

A grog-swilling seaman armed with a treasure map arrives at the Admiral Bensbow Inn and after he meets a grisly end the map comes into the possession of Jim, the innkeeper's son. Jim shows the map (which reveals the location and geography of Treasure Island) to Squire Trelawney, who resolves to

outfit a ship and set sail for the Spanish Main. But the squire cannot hold his tongue, and news of the treasure attracts a scurvy crew of pirates led by Long John Silver. Despite the crew, the voyage proceeds uneventfully until Jim overhears Silver plotting to take over the ship and the treasure. He informs the officers of the planned mutiny and when they reach the island, they are prepared for the pirates' assault. Jim then sneaks back aboard the lightly guarded ship, and, to prevent the pirates from escaping, runs her aground on another part of the island. In the end, the pirates follow the map only to find that the treasure has been moved to safety, and after a final battle, Jim lets Silver escape.

✗STOP: A blind pirate's blindfold is ripped off, and his terrible, disfigured features are revealed; he is later run over in the road as he pathetically calls for his mates to help him. There is a graphic close-up of a pirate lying dead with his throat brutally cut.

CAUTION: The action is more extreme than in previous versions; musket balls thud into chests and produce exit wounds and swords and knives cut into flesh.

GO: Jim is honourable to a fault. All in all, an exciting adventure.

■

✗ TRON

Walt Disney Home Video
1982
95 minutes
Directed by: Steven Lisberger
Starring: Bruce Boxleitner,
   Jeff Bridges, Cindy Morgan,
   David Warner
MPAA rating: no rating given

In the world of virtual reality, sinister Master Control has established a totalitarian state. There, all programs must have permission just to travel around their own microcircuits, and belief in the Users (the humans in the physical world) is considered to be a false belief subscribed to only by religious lunatics. As Master Control dominates more and more programs, he sends those who defy him to The Game Grid, where they're forced to play an evil program called Sark and are destroyed. But one human is trying to break in from the outside. Determined to retrieve the innovative game programs he designed, video game wizard Flynn is intent on getting into his former employer Encom's system. Flynn's old rival at Encom, Allan Bradley, has also noticed something strange going on in the system. He creates a security program called Tron which will operate independently of Master Control. And when Encom shuts Allan down too, Flynn and Allan go to the company at night to confirm their suspicions. Master Control manipulates a laser matter transmission device, and Flynn is sucked into the computer world of virtual reality, taken prisoner and sent to the Games Grid to be destroyed. There he meets Tron and, during a team game, the two escape. After a chase of epic proportions, Flynn and Tron finally reach the sanctuary of the master program where, with the fate of the world at stake, Tron goes up against Sark and Flynn pits his will against Master Control.

✗STOP: Master Control tortures one of Flynn's programs to try to make him reveal his User; the program's death is protracted and obviously painful.

 CAUTION: Violent combat is a central ele-

ment of this film. There are intense battle scenes.

GO: This is a staggering achievement with an interesting story and concept. The animation is superb and the theme of courageous resistance to tyranny is inspiring.

TROOP BEVERLY HILLS

RCA/Col
1989
105 minutes
Directed by: Jeff Kanew
Starring: Mary Gross, Shelley Long,
  Craig T. Nelson, Betty Thomas
OFRB rating: PG
MPAA rating: PG

On the verge of a divorce, wealthy Beverly Hills socialite Phyllis Nefler is chosen to lead her daughter's Wilderness Girl troop. There are two obstacles standing in her way, however: One, the wealthy and pampered girls aren't typical Wilderness Girl recruits, and two, local Red Feather leader and reverse-snob Velda Plender intends to have the Beverly Hills troop disbanded. To this end, Vera sends her assistant to spy on the troop's unorthodox activities (which include a stay in a luxury hotel after a camping trip is rained out, and badges for gem identification and shopping instead of knot-tying). But when it comes to seeing which troop can sell the most Wilderness Girl cookies, Phyllis refuses to bend the rules and allow the girls' parents to buy the whole lot, and the girls are forced to come up with some original ideas to sell more than their share of cookies. The real test comes during the wilderness trek when the girls in Troop Beverly Hills must prove they have all the qualities necessary to be real Wilderness Girls.

CAUTION: Some references are made to the size of one woman's bust. Phyllis and her husband are divorcing, and he is going out with a younger woman. There is some mild swearing.

GO: The family reconciles. This is a great sleep-over movie for girls.

own life to save Scott's. Scott is devastated to lose his new friend. But there are puppies on the way.

✘**STOP:** Hooch dies at the end.

CAUTION: A hood's leg and throat are cut. (The camera pans away, but we hear him gag horribly.) Amos is stabbed in the back.

GO: An excellent film, with a lot of warm-hearted humour. Some events may be too intense for young children.

TURNER AND HOOCH

Touchstone
1989
99 minutes
Directed by: Roger Spottiswoode
Starring: Tom Hanks,
    Mare Winningham
OFRB rating: PG
MPAA rating: PG

Scott Turner is a healthy living neatness freak and a cop in a small town. When his elderly friend, Amos, complains about strange noises at the seafood plant next to his house, Scott doesn't take him seriously. Then hoods operating out of the plant murder Amos. Scott is left with an unsolved case, few leads and Hooch, Amos's gigantic mastiff-type dog, who proceeds to destroy Scott's home. Hooch's one saving grace is that he brings home an attractive collie belonging to Emily Carson, a vet with whom Scott becomes involved. In time, destruction aside, Turner comes to love Hooch and Hooch, as it happens, is the only one who can I.D. the bad guys. He turns out to be a pretty good cop too, giving his

TWINS

MCA
1989
107 minutes
Directed by: Ivan Reitman
Starring: Danny DeVito,
    Kelly Preston,
    Arnold Schwarzenegger
ORFB rating: PG
MPAA rating: PG

When a group of scientists conducts a test-tube research experiment to produce the perfect human, things don't go quite as expected. Instead of one perfect baby, twins are born: Julius is perfect and Vincent is anything but. It's decided that the twins must be separated. Julius is taken to a remote, tropical island where he learns to speak twelve languages, develops physically and spiritually and helps his foster-father with his scientific experiments. Vincent is abandoned as an orphan. But when the cloistered Julius is thirty-five, his foster father reveals to him the secret of his birth and tells him that he has a twin brother. Julius instinctively senses that his brother is in trouble and sets out to find him in jail for unpaid parking tickets and on the lam for a debt of $20,000. Julius bails him out and after failing to convince Vincent of his true identity, naively becomes involved in Vincent's illicit business ventures. Pursued by angry loan sharks and a vengeful assassin and accompanied by their girlfriends, Julius and Vincent visit the scientist who headed the test-tube experiment. He verifies Julius's story and Vincent is finally convinced of the truth. In the end, Julius puts his life on the line for his brother, and Vincent sacrifices a fortune for Julius. They find their mother and, now heirs to immense wealth, marry their respective girlfriends and have twins of their own.

CAUTION: There are fist fights and shootings and a brief sexual situation between Julius and his girlfriend.

✗ UHF

AGES 10 TO 13

Orion
1989
97 minutes
Directed By: Jay Levey
Starring: Victoria Jackson,
    Kevin McCarthy,
    Weird Al Yankovic
OFRB rating: AA
MPAA rating: PG-13

When George Newman's uncle wins a television station in a poker game, George is hired as the manager. Channel 69 is teetering on the verge of bankruptcy and all of George's efforts to turn the station around (which include a host of bizarre programs like a do-it-yourself show on which the guest star accidentally cuts off his own thumb) only result in lower ratings. And after inadvertently angering a psychotic competitor and losing his long-suffering girlfriend, George gives up and turns his children's program, *The Uncle Nutsy Show*, over to the station janitor. Incredibly, the bizarre Spadowski turns out to be a kids' show genius, and *Stanley Spadowski's Playhouse* rockets to number one, taking channel 69 with it. George's network enemies then plot his demise, and hilarious chaos follows.

✗ STOP: Elements of the dark humour in this film are certain to be too extreme for young children; for instance, on a show called *Raoul's Wild Kingdom* poodles are "taught" to fly.

CAUTION: A depiction of an Oriental karate school teacher might be considered stereotyping. Weird Al's off-the-wall satire is definitely not for little ones.

GO: This is a great comedy for pre-teens and young teens.

UNCLE BUCK

MCA
1989
100 minutes
Directed by: John Hughes
Starring: John Candy,
    Macaulay Culkin, Amy Madigan,
    Jay Underwood
OFRB rating: PG
MPAA rating: PG

When Cindy Russell's father has a heart attack and she and her husband Bob are forced to go to her parents, the only person available to baby-sit their three children is Bob's brother Buck. Buck is a notorious ne'er-do-well who's been making his living on fixed races at the track. He's also a classic stumblebum, and when he shows up at the Russell house with his smoke-belching old car, the children are stunned. Maisy and Miles quickly come to like him, but a real battle of wills develops between Buck and fifteen-year-old Tia. Tia rejects Buck's assessment of her odious boyfriend Bug until, in a final act of defiance, she sneaks out with him to a party where she discovers that Buck was right all along, and leaves in disgust. Buck, meanwhile, gives up his old ways to search for her and they meet on the street and reconcile.

CAUTION: There is some coarse language and Bug has a hard time taking no for an answer.

GO: Buck is persistent and patient with Tia, and the fact that he cares about her transforms her. The film features a very positive message about accepting responsibility.

VICE VERSA

RCA/Columbia
1988
97 minutes
Directed by: Brian Gilbert
Starring: Swoosie Kurtz,
    Judge Reinhold, Fred Savage
OFRB rating: PG—Coarse
    Language
MPAA rating: PG

Somewhere in Thailand, a thief steals a skull from a mountain temple. The priceless artifact is eventually brought into the United States by unwitting businessman Marshall Seymour, who, after discovering it in his luggage, decides to keep it in his apartment until the rightful owner comes to claim it. Meanwhile, Marshall's ex-wife goes on vacation and leaves his eleven-year-old son Charlie with Marshall. But Marshall is so busy that he doesn't have time for Charlie and the two just can't seem to get along. During one argument, while holding the skull, Charlie wishes he could change places with his father. And when Marshall replies that he wishes he could change places too, a magical transformation takes place: Charlie changes into Marshall, and Marshall changes into Charlie. Unable to change each other back, Charlie must impersonate his father in his high-pressure job and Marshall is forced to return to the terrors of sixth grade. All the while, the smugglers are after the skull. In time, Marshall sets new school test records, while Charlie revolutionizes his father's department store. The climax comes when the villains kidnap Marshall and Charlie must find a way to save his father.

CAUTION: There is some coarse language.

GO: This is a terrific film about the value of human relationships and about remaining young at heart.

✗ WATERSHIP DOWN

Warner Home Video
1978
90 minutes
Directed by: Martin Rosen
Starring the voices of:
    Richard Briers, Denholm Elliot,
    John Hurt, Zero Mostel,
    Ralph Richardson
MPAA rating: PG

Fiver, a rabbit visionary, senses terrible destruction (a land development) is coming to the warren, so he and his brother Hazel and a friend called Bigwig go to the chief rabbit to try to galvanize the warren into leaving. They manage to persuade only a few to accompany them, and leave to start a new warren. They are later joined by a survivor from the old warren who describes the terrible destruction. Painfully aware that their warren will not survive without female rabbits, they infiltrate a nearby warren where many of the females with no chance of finding mates wish to leave, but are forbidden to do so. Hazel and some others help them escape, fight a ferocious battle and triumph with intelligence and ingenuity. In the end, the new warren flourishes and the Black Rabbit of Death comes for Hazel. Based on the novel by Richard Adams.

✗STOP: The story is a social commentary and not suitable for children. Death is everywhere and no effort is made to reduce the tension for young viewers.

CAUTION: The film is violent. Hawks swoop out of the sky, talons extended, striking with blood-curdling shrieks; rabbits are buried alive and crushed to death by construction; combat between rabbits is bloody and graphic; and in the end, the lead character dies.

GO: A fantastic score, great voice-overs and superior animation are the hallmarks of this production.
■

✗ WAYNE'S WORLD

Paramount
1992
93 minutes
Directed by: Penelope Spheeris
Starring: Dana Carvey, Rob Lowe,
    Mike Myers
OFRB rating: PG—Coarse
    Language
MPAA rating: PG-13

Wayne Campbell still lives with his parents in Aurora, Illinois and has never had a career — although he's quick to point out his considerable collection of hair nets and name tags. The one thing in life that is going well for him is the public access television show he has on Cable 10: *Wayne's World*, a hilarious basement talk show which he hosts with his best friend Garth Algar. But when Benjamin, an ambitious, unscrupulous TV executive, sets out to acquire the rights to *Wayne's World*, Wayne and Garth are tricked into signing the show away for five thousand dollars each and things begin to go terribly wrong. Wayne is fired from the show for insulting the sponsor on the air and Benjamin has plans to steal Wayne's girlfriend away. The only thing that can save Wayne's career and his relationship is a special edition of *Wayne's World*.

×STOP: Viewers who are not yet able to read will miss the rudest elements of this film.

CAUTION: Coarse language, stereotypes and crude behaviour abound, but, thanks to all of the hype, it's a major attraction for young children.

GO: Lowe is perfect as the amoral executive, and there are wonderful cameos from Ed O'Neill (*Married With Children*) and Alice Cooper. All in all, it's a wild satire of American life, the kind of entertainment created just for the fun of it, right down to the optional multiple endings.

WHAT ABOUT BOB?

Touchstone
1991
99 minutes
Directed by: Frank Oz
Starring: Richard Dreyfuss,
   Bill Murray
OFRB rating: PG—Mature Theme
MPAA rating: PG

Dr. Leo Marvin is a cold-hearted, career-oriented psychiatrist who's definitely on his way to the top. He has a successful practice and a best-selling book, and he's planned a month's vacation in New Hampshire, where the *Good Morning America* crew will do a show about him. But fate plays a cruel joke on Leo when a colleague sends him a patient named Bob Wiley. Bob is so crippled with neuroses that he can barely leave his apartment and worse, he's the terror of psychiatrists everywhere. When Leo tells Bob that he's going

away for a month, Bob will have none of it. He uses all manner of subterfuge to locate Leo's isolated summer home where he finds the egomaniacal Leo, and makes his life hell. Refusing to go away, Bob befriends Leo's family, upstages him during the *Good Morning America* interview and, most astonishing of all, gets better. Leo, meantime, becomes angrier and angrier until he's positively beserk with rage and ultimately goes insane himself.

CAUTION: This film is not likely to be of interest to anyone under the age of ten. Bob, in order to prove to himself that he doesn't have Tourette Syndrome (which can cause involuntary outbursts of obscenity), swears voluntarily. Leo goes quite mad and his homicidal mania is a little unnerving.

GO: The film touches on the ways relationships can heal.

✗ WHERE THE RED FERN GROWS

Doty-Dayton Productions
1974
90 minutes
Directed by: Norman Tokar
Starring: James Whitmore,
   Beverly Garland, Stewart
   Petersen
OFRB rating: F
MPAA rating: G

Billy Coleman is a young boy growing up in the Ozarks, whose heart's desire is a pair of hounds. He asks his grandfather to explain why it is that though he's been asking God for puppies for as long as he can remember, he still has none. His grandfather replies that

God will do His share, but that Billy will have to meet Him halfway. So Billy goes out and works at every possible odd job and finally earns the money to buy the dogs. He begins training them at once and soon becomes a champion coon hunter. Then one night, Billy and his dogs accidentally surprise a cougar. The dogs save Billy's life, but one is killed and the other, crushed by grief, dies a few days later. The dogs are buried side by side, and a rare red fern, the symbol of enduring love from a native legend, grows between the graves.

✘**STOP:** The dogs die and when Billy fights with two mountain boys one of them trips, hits his head and dies.

GO: This is a terrific film about a boy with grit, determination and the will to succeed. ■ ▲

✘ WHERE THE RED FERN GROWS II

Morningstar
1992
92 minutes
Directed by: Jim McCullough
Starring: Wilford Brimley,
    Doug McKeon, Chad McQueen
OFRB rating: F
MPAA rating: G

Billy Coleman, now a bitter amputee, returns to Louisiana after a harrowing four years of service in World War II. At home, his grandfather reminds him of the deal he made with God as a child, and tells him to go out and look in the barn; there, Billy finds a pair of Redbone hound pups and his old coonskin hat. At first, Billy doesn't want the dogs, but when his sister tells him that their grandfather has only a few weeks to live, he reluctantly agrees to train them. But the weeks turn into months, and Grandpa is looking better than ever. Even so, Billy turns down a job offer in California because of his grandfather's health. Grandpa overhears this, and on the next coon hunt, when one of the hounds is killed, explains to Billy that if one surrounds oneself with living things, sooner or later, one watches them die. On the way back to the farm he dies himself and, after the funeral, Billy gives the remaining dog to a young friend and prepares to go to his new life in California.

✘**STOP:** There is much grief in this film. Billy's grandfather dies and so does one of the beloved dogs. Billy is forced to give away the other dog.

CAUTION: Billy's embittered description of battlefield surgery may leave some young viewers disturbed. Too, the concept of running down raccoons may upset some children.

GO: This film is a surprisingly profound examination of the pain and joy of life itself.

✘ WHITE FANG

Walt Disney
1991
109 minutes
Directed by: Randal Kleiser
Starring: Klaus Maria Brandauer,
    Ethan Hawke, Pius Savage
OFRB rating: PG—Frightening
    Scenes
MPAA rating: PG

At the turn of the century, Jack Conroy, a young man on his way to his father's claim in the Yukon, hooks up with Alex Larsen, a friend of his father's. Along the way, they are trailed by a wolf-pack, and during a mishap on some thin ice lose their ammunition. The wolves, as if aware of the fact that their prey is helpless, close in for the attack. One of the she-wolves is killed, and her cub, White Fang, is forced to travel the frozen wasteland alone, living by his wits. Then one day he's caught in an Indian snare and turned into a sled dog. Meanwhile, Alex and Jack reach the Klondike and travel up the Yukon River to the Indian village where, coincidentally, White Fang lives. Jack and the savage wolf strike up a tentative kinship, and each in turn saves the other from certain death — Jack from a grizzly and White Fang from an implacable pit bull in a dog fight. Jack then wins White Fang's love with his patient kindness, and in the end, White Fang repays this kindness by again saving Jack's life.

STOP: The fight between White Fang and the pit bull is in agonizing slow motion. Alex is travelling with the corpse of a friend, and at one point the coffin spills open and the blue-faced corpse tumbles out.

CAUTION: A third member of Jack's party is killed during the wolves' assault.

GO: Despite the above-mentioned cautions, this is an exciting adventure story with minimal violence.
■ ▲

✗ WHO FRAMED ROGER RABBIT?

Touchstone Home Video
1988
104 minutes
Directed by: Robert Zemeckis
Starring: Bob Hoskins,
   Christopher Lloyd
OFRB rating: PG
MPAA rating: PG

Los Angeles in 1947 is a place where humans and animated beings co-exist. The cartoons are an underclass, living mainly in an area called Toontown, where they work in low-class jobs and in show business. A few of the toons are stars, like Roger Rabbit, who's one of the box-office mainstays of media mogul R.K. Maroon. But Roger is losing his concentration and costing Maroon a fortune. The reason, allegedly, is that Roger's wife Jessica is having an affair with Marvin Acme, the novelty king who owns Toontown. So Maroon hires Eddie Valiant, a boozy, down and out human private eye, who agrees to get some dirt on Jessica. After catching Jessica's racy act at the seedy Ink and Paint Club, Eddie photographs her and Marvin playing "patty-cake" in a back room. (They really *are* playing "patty-cake.") When Roger sees the pictures he goes berserk, and the next day Marvin Acme is murdered. Though the evil Judge Doom (inventor of Dip, the only substance which can destroy a toon) is sure that Roger is guilty, Eddie is equally convinced of the rabbit's innocence and sets out to set things right. Then a terrible conspiracy is revealed: Judge Doom intends to secure ownership of Toontown and destroy it to make room for an expressway. In the end, the characters meet at the Acme Gag Factory for a final confrontation with the Judge, who is not at all what he seems to be.

✗STOP: Judge Doom is slowly run over by a steamroller and is then revealed to be a toon himself, and a real figure of terror. His eyes swirl and glow and his hand turns into a frightening buzz-saw. Roger and Jessica are bound together and are repeatedly in terrible danger of being sprayed with Dip.

CAUTION: This isn't really a kids' film. One pre-teen we know remarked, "I saw this film when I was eleven, and I had to watch it five times before I understood it." The figure of Jessica Rabbit is cut in the 1950s full-figure girl mold, and her ample charms are prominently displayed.

GO: This is simply one of the most mind-boggling achievements in film history. The combination of live-action and animation used new techniques that set a precedent for films that followed. This film won four Academy Awards including a 1988 Special Achievement Oscar.

▲

✗ WILLOW

RCA/Columbia
1988
130 minutes
Directed by: Ron Howard
Starring: Billy Barty, Warwick Davis, Val Kilmer, Jean Marsh
OFRB rating: PG—Warning: Violence and Frightening Scenes
MPAA rating: PG

Willow begins: "It is a time of dread. Seers have foretold the birth of a child who will bring about the downfall of the powerful Queen Bavmorda. Seizing all pregnant women in the realm, the evil queen vows to destroy the child when it is born." But when the baby of the prophecy is born, it's spirited out of the queen's dungeons by a midwife. With a pack of Bavmorda's wolves close on her trail, the midwife places the baby on a small raft and floats her down river wher she is taken in by Willow Ufgood, an unsuccessful and diminutive magician. He keeps the child until a pack of the queen's wolves falls upon his village, and he decides to take the baby back. On the way he is joined by a criminal named Madmartigan, a pair of Brownies and a sorceress. Together they battle trolls, a two-headed dragon and the queen's soldiers. The baby then falls into the hands of the sinister General Kael, who takes her to the evil queen. And in the film's climax, as the queen conducts the ritual which will banish the baby to everlasting night, Willow dupes her into destroying herself.

✗STOP: This film is violent. The midwife is torn to pieces by hideous wolves, which then run snarling through a village, tearing cradles apart and terrorizing the inhabitants. Combat scenes, though virtually bloodless, are fierce in the extreme. Swords cleave bodies with meaty impact, spears and arrows thud on the mark, fists crunch facial bones and the slain die with their eyes open. Magical transformations are intensely biological, depicted as agonizing and accentuated with sound.

GO: Despite the pervasive violence, the film is extremely well-made. The cinematography, editing, special effects and art direction are superb; the performances are generally strong, and the fantasy world is brought vividly to life. Here, loyalty, courage, perseverence and love allow even the smallest underdog to triumph in the end.

✗ THE WITCHES

Warner Home Video
1990
92 minutes
Directed by: Nicolas Roeg
Starring: Anjelica Huston,
    Rowan Atkinson, Bill Paterson,
    Brenda Blethyn
OFRB rating: PG—Frightening
    Scenes
MPAA rating: PG

When Luke's parents die in a car crash, he moves with his grandmother to England where they live happily enough until his grandmother develops a respiratory ailment. As part of her treatment, they plan a stay at a seaside resort. But their stay coincides with an international witches' convention, and while Luke is playing in the convention hall he overhears a dastardly plot: the witches have developed a formula to turn every child in Britain into a mouse. Luke knows from the stories his grandmother has told him that witches hate children and he watches in horror while the witches try their formula on an innocent boy. Luke is next. But even as a mouse, Luke is courageous and resourceful. And with his grandmother's help, he steals the witches' potion, sneaks into the kitchen and doctors the soup intended for their banquet. The witches thus disposed of, Luke (still a mouse) returns home with his grandmother and lives in a little model house. Only the timely arrival of a white witch restores him to human form.

✗ STOP: This film is not for young children! The witches (The Grand High Witch in particular) are hideous, scary allegories of child abductors.

CAUTION: In one of Luke's grandmother's stories, a witch steals a young girl and puts her into a painting, where her parents are forced to watch her grow old, imprisoned on the canvas. When Luke is a mouse, a cook cuts off half his tail; it bleeds. In one scene a witch tries to lure Luke out of a tree with a variety of enticements and this may disturb some children

GO: Brilliant special effects highlight Roald Dahl's tale of childhood courage in the face of terror and adversity.

■

YOUNG EINSTEIN

Warner Home Video
1988
90 minutes
Directed by: Yahoo Serious
Starring: Odile de Clezio,
    John Howard, Yahoo Serious
OFRB rating: PG
MPAA rating: PG

Albert Einstein, the twenty-year-old son of an apple farmer, isn't cut out to follow in his father's footsteps. He's an environmentalist, and a scientist. For example, when a crate of apples accidentally drops on his head, he formulates his first complete scientific principle: for every action there is an equal and opposite reaction. And he proves it, by building a catapult and launching himself sky-high. It's at this time that Albert's father reveals a well-kept family secret: his granddad was also a great inventor; he died in a mysterious accident while trying to put bubbles in beer. Well, Albert decides to continue where his grandfather left off, and bends a beer atom, setting off a miniature atomic blast that does indeed put bubbles in the brew. Armed with his new formula, $E=MC^2$, he sets off for the mainland patent office. On the way, he meets the delectable Marie Curie and the evil snob Preston Preston. Preston has Albert committed to the asylum for mad scientists, steals Albert's formula and begins the process by which carbonated beer will be mass-produced. There's just one problem: Preston Preston has inadvertently created the first atomic bomb. Now Albert must escape from the asylum, get to the award ceremonies in Paris and defuse the bomb before it goes off.

CAUTION: In one scene, the chef in the insane asylum makes a kitten pie with live kittens. There is some sexual innuendo.

GO: Albert saves the kittens. And as for the sexual innuendo, Albert's innocence is cleverly used as a foil; in other words, what he doesn't get, young viewers won't get either. This is a truly off-beat film with genuinely funny moments and something for everyone.

▲

✗ YOUNG SHERLOCK HOLMES

Paramount
1985
109 minutes
Directed by: Barry Levinson
Starring: Roger Ashton-Griffiths,
  Alan Cox, Earl Rhodes,
  Nicholas Rowe, Nigel Stock,
  Sophie Ward
OFRB rating: PG—Frightening
  Scenes
MPAA rating: PG-13

In the heart of the Victorian era, young John Watson is sent to a new school in London. There he meets young Holmes, who astounds him by deducing the details of his life from a moment's observation, and Elizabeth, Holmes's true love. The three soon learn that prominent citizens are dying of unknown causes, but only Holmes believes it's murder. He has noticed in the obituaries that victims were all in the graduating class of 1809. However, Scotland Yard will have nothing to do with his theories, and it isn't until Elizabeth's Uncle Waxplatter becomes the next victim that Holmes takes up the case with vigour. His only clues are Waxplatter's last words, and a blowpipe of exotic construction. The friends trace the pipe's origins and discover an ancient death-cult connected to the destruction of an Egyptian village, and to a high ranking faculty member of the school itself. In the end, the cult kidnaps Elizabeth to turn her into a mummy, setting in motion a climactic chain of heart-stopping events.

✗STOP: The hallucinations experienced by the drugged murder victims are extremely frightening. When the murderer fires at Holmes, Elizabeth steps in front to shield him and is shot herself. Elizabeth dies tragically in Holmes' arms.

CAUTION: The action is too intense and the mystery too complicated for most young children.

GO: An exciting action mystery in an historical setting, this film is best selected for pre-teens and up and may kick-start an interest in the Sherlock Holmes stories.

Chapter 9

VIDEO VOCABULARY:
A GLOSSARY OF TERMS

8mm — a consumer format used in camcorders.

Animation/animated — a series of drawings which are painted on transparent cels and then photographed in succession to produce the effect of motion. Commonly referred to as cartoons, there are as many different styles of animation as there are styles of painters. Animated feature films like *Beauty and the Beast* are now produced with the aid of sophisticated computer programs; instead of relying on the traditional transparent cel method the drawings are rendered directly on computer and transferred to film or video.

Beta — the first consumer VCR format. Although its actual quality is better than VHS, today this is an obscure videotape format that is difficult to find for rental.

Betacam — a high-end expensive professional format used in news productions and most corporate and industrial films. Currently the world's predominant professional standard.

Camcorder — a video camera recording device. It is very difficult to rent movies intended for home viewing on any format which is camcorder based.

Cel — a transparent sheet of plastic made specifically for animation work.

Claymation — a clay or plasticine figurine is adjusted step by step and filmed frame by frame in order to produce the illusion of movement. This technique was made famous by Willis O'Brien, the mastermind behind the original *King Kong*, and was later used by Ray Harryhausen in many movies, including the *Sinbad* series.

Commercial blacks — when a film is made for television, the story will be structured to accommodate commercials at certain points without disrupting the story's continuity. On the video, these will appear as short (one to two second) segments of black.

Director's cut — despite what you might think, directors do not always have the last say when it comes to the final decisions on how a movie will look — except in the director's cut where what you see is the director's true vision of the edited production.

Dropout — a problem on the videotape that causes black or white streaks in the picture when it is played on your television.

Dubbing/duplication — the transferring or copying of material from one video cassette to another. An audio-dub is the recording of the sound only.

Feel-good movies — a phrase used to describe movies that make you want to jump up and shout: Yes! I can do it! They are also sometimes called "stand-up-and-cheer" movies.

Four-head VCRs — most standard VCRs come equipped with two heads. A four-head machine gives you the ability to freeze frame with a clear picture and to watch slow-motion.

Format — describes types of VCRs. The predominant format throughout the world is VHS, but there are various formats in existence today. See also Beta, VHS, SVHS, 8mm, and laserdisk.

Freeze-frame — the technique of stopping on a particular frame of the film and allowing the soundtrack of the film to continue. This technique is often used at the end of films with the credits running over the frozen frame.

Generation — refers to the number of times a master tape has been duplicated between machines.

Glitch — a disturbance in the video image and/or soundtrack which could be caused by physical damage to the tape or playback heads, or by dirt or dust on the VCR heads or on the videotape.

High resolution — resolution which exceeds current North American standards of television resolution.

Iconographic films — films which use still pictures or drawings to tell a story. Sometimes the camera is used to mimic the eye of the viewer, slowly scanning page by page over a story book.

Laserdisk — an emerging format found in limited quantities at some video stores. It looks much like a silver record (or a large CD), and requires its own special player. The resolution is much higher, requiring a high-resolution television to see the true benefits.

Letterbox — a way to present a video in widescreen format, as it was shown in theatres. Because a movie screen is rectangular and a television screen is square, sometimes as much as 40% of the picture is cut off to fit the TV screen. To avoid this, movies are sometimes released with a black strip at the bottom and top portions of the screen, enabling viewers see the film the way the filmmaker intended.

Limited-time release — some videos are released for a limited period of time. (Usually no longer than one year, and sometimes as little as 50 days.) Beyond this time the video release is put in moratorium and no more copies are made until such time as the copyright holder decides to release it again. This can be as long as seven or eight years.

Live-action — film which uses actors and settings in real-life situations, as seen in most feature films. Sometimes films will have a mixture of live-action and animation as seen in *Who*

Framed Roger Rabbit?, *Mary Poppins* and *Bedknobs and Broomsticks*.

Macrovision —a process used in the production of videocassettes which makes any illegal copies of these cassettes unwatchable.

Made-for-TV — a film intended for television only and not for theatres. Productions of this kind will be written to accommodate commercials.

Montage — a series of related images, often set to music, and mostly used to denote the passage of time.

Moratorium — is a term used to describe titles that are out-of-print and for which no re-release date has been announced.

Out-of-print — means a title is no longer available either because it has gone into moratorium or because the copyright has expired.

Panning — the movement of a camera from left to right or right to left.

Partly-animated — a film that is not fully-animated but may have a fixed background with one or two moving elements, such as a hand, a mouth, or a bird flying across the screen.

Pause — to momentarily stop your videotape without losing your place in the movie. Try not to do this for too long as it can damage the videotape and cause the VCR play/record mechanisms to deteriorate.

Picture — a function commonly found beside the tracking function on a VCR. It can to used to enhance picture quality. On some machines it is labelled "sharpness."

Piracy — the illegal duplication of a copyrighted program without the permission of the copyright holder.

Pixilation — an inanimate object is photographed in a succession of positions to give the illusion that the object is in motion. This technique was made famous by Canadian Norman Maclaren and was used in the films *Fireman Sam: The Hero Next Door* and *Wind in the Willows*.

Puppetmation — the art of filming string puppets or stick marionettes so that it appears that there are no strings. This technique was used in *The Muppet Movie*.

Re-made/re-make — a movie based on a previously-filmed story which has been re-interpreted and re-filmed by a new filmmaker. The differences between the re-make and the film upon which it is based may range from subtle to obvious.

Re-released — signifies that the film or video was released in a previous year, but has not necessarily been changed or altered.

Restored/remastered — usually this means that a print made from the original has been cleaned and polished significantly, and the sound-track, improved. In some cases a remastered film is expanded with never-before seen images, mostly in the form of newly discovered stills.

Sell-thru — videos which are intended for sale at your local video store.

Splice — describes two strips of videotape held together by a joint made of *specially formulated* video adhesive tape. Attempting to do this at home with regular tape will cause serious damage to your machine!

SVHS — Super-VHS, a camcorder format with higher resolution requiring a high resolution television to see the true benefits.

Tape grade — refers to the quality of a video cassette and is a relative comparison between brands or types of cassette.

Tape mode — refers to the recording mode of the VCR. There are up to three modes on consumer models: SP (standard-play), LP (long-play) and EP/SLP (extended play or super long-play). Each refers to the amount of recording time available on a videocassette.

Tape tab — the small square tab found on the spine of the videocassette which prevents accidental erasure when removed.

Tracking — if you are having a problem with a fuzzy line of distortion running through your playback picture, try adjusting the tracking. This is a control found on your VCR which is used to balance the stability of the playback picture on your television.

Trailer — also known as a preview, this is a promotional advertisement for a film that is soon to be released. Trailers are usually seen before the feature presentation.

VCR/VTR — videocassette recorder and videotape recorder are for most purposes interchangeable terms for the machine that plays your videotape. Not all VCRs are the same, as options and performance levels differ between models.

VHS — today's standard format for videos bought or rented from your local video store. Remember that your VHS tape in North America won't necessarily play on a VHS machine abroad.

Videotaped — this means that the film or television show you are watching was recorded on videotape and not film. Videotape is the preferred medium for most television shows and news programs.

Voice-over/over-dubbed — the technique of replacing someone's spoken or singing voice with another voice. This technique is done after the film or videotape has been made. Over-dubbing is sometimes used to change the language of a film. Movies which have used this technique include the original *Pippi Longstocking, The Dog Who Stopped the War*, and most song videos for little children.

Wide-screen — see Letterbox

Chapter 10

LISTS OF FILMS

Over the years, parents, teachers, librarians and care-givers have asked us to compile lists on a variety of themes and we have included many of these here to help you select videos for special occasions (like sleep-overs and theme parties) or for kids with special interests (such as horse-lovers and mystery buffs).

These lists are in no way representative of everything available on a particular topic — there simply isn't space to go into such detail — and we have tried to include titles that are suitable for most children. However, because we have not reviewed or rated the videos in the following lists, we urge you to check the rating on the box and use your own discretion when renting these titles. Some of the titles listed are currently out-of-print but have been included because they are still available for rental at some outlets. Titles indicated with a ◆ are reviewed in the body of this book; refer to them for further information.

For more information write to us at:

The Original Kids' Video Company
P.O. Box 609
Station K
Toronto, Ontario
Canada M4P 2H1

Animals
(domesticated or trained)

150 Years of the Grand National (horses)
A Summer to Remember (orangutan)
* Baby Animals Just Want To Have Fun
* Beethoven (St. Bernard)
* Benji the Hunted (dog, baby bobcats)
Big Cats of the Big Top
Big Red (dog)
* The Black Stallion
* The Black Stallion Returns
* The Cat From Outer Space (cat)
The Courage of Rin TinTin (dog)
Flipper (dolphin)
Flipper and the Elephant (dolphin)
Flipper's New Adventure (dolphin)
Flipper's Odyssey (dolphin)
Greyfrier's Bobby (dog)
* The Incredible Journey (cat, dogs)
* Journey of Natty Gann(wolf)
* Kidsongs: Old MacDonald's Farm
   (farm animals)
* Ladyhawke (trained hawk, wolf)
* Little Heroes (dog)
* Milo and Otis (cat, dog)
* Old Yeller (dog)
Puppy Pals
* That Darn Cat
* The Three Lives Of Thomasina (cat)
* Where the Red Fern Grows (hound dogs)

Animals (wild)

Animals Are Beautiful People:
   The Secret Life of Wildlife
* Baby Animals in the Wild
* The Bear
* Born Free (lions)
Challenge to White Fang (wolf-dog)
Charlie the Lonesome Cougar
Charlie and the Talking Buzzard
Christian the Lion
Clarence the Cross-Eyed Lion
* Doctor Doolittle
Dolphin Adventure
Flight of the Grey Wolf
Goldy: The Last of the Golden Bears
Goldy 2: The Saga of the Golden Bear
* Kidsongs: A Day with the Animals
King of the Grizzlies
Koko, a Talking Gorilla

The Legend of Lobo (wolf)
Let's Go to the Zoo with Captain Kangaroo
The Life and Times of Grizzly Adams
   (grizzly bear, skunk, raccoon)
Living Free (lions)
Lorne Green's New Wilderness series
* Lost in the Barrens (caribou,bear)
* The Metro Toronto Zoo
* The Monkey Folk
Napoleon and Samantha (lion)
* National Geographic Series:
*   Cheetah
*   Creatures of the Mangrove
*   Elephant
*   The Grizzlies
*   Lions of the African Night
*   Realm of the Alligator
*   Reptiles and Amphibians
*   The Secret Leopard
*   Sharks
*   Whales
Nature: Leopard —A Darkness in the Grass
* Never Cry Wolf (wolves)
Nikki: Wild Dog of the North
* Ring of Bright Water(otter)
Sharks: The True Story
* Sharon, Lois and Bram at the Zoo
   (zoo animals)
* Tadpole and the Whale
* White Fang (wolf-dog)
Wildlife International (series of 10 videos)
The Yearling (deer)
Zoo Babies

Art

* Don't Eat the Pictures:
   Sesame Street at the Metropolitan Museum
   of Art
Draw and Color With Uncle Fred:
   A Cartoony Party
Draw and Color With Uncle Fred:
   Far Out Pets
Draw and Color With Uncle Fred:
   Your Very Own Cartoonys
Draw Squad With Capt. Mark Kistler:
   Adventure 1
Draw Squad With Capt. Mark Kistler:
   Adventure 2
Draw Squad With Capt. Mark Kistler:
   Adventure 3

The Hideaways
How to Draw Comics the Marvel Way
◆ Let's Draw!
Squiggles Dots and Lines
◆ Vincent and Me
Wow, You're a Cartoonist

 Babies
◆ Baby's First Workout
◆ Babysongs series
◆ Babyvision
Esther Williams Swim Baby Swim
Helping Your Baby Sleep Through the Night
◆ Infantastic Lullabyes
◆ Jim Henson's Peek-a-boo
Once Upon A Potty for Her
Once Upon A Potty for Him
◆ Stories to Remember series

 Balloons
Around the World in Eighty Days
Charlie and the Great Balloon Chase
Fantastic Balloon Voyage
Five Weeks in a Balloon
Lassie's Greatest Adventure
Let the Balloon Go
◆ Mysterious Island
Night Crossing
◆ The Red Balloon

 Based on books
◆ The 5,000 Fingers of Dr.T (Dr. Seuss)
◆ 20,000 Leagues Under the Sea
    (Jules Verne)
A Cry in the Wild (*Hatchet*, Gary Paulsen)
◆ A Dog of Flanders (Ouida)
◆ Abel's Island (William Steig)
Adventures of Huckleberry Finn
    (Mark Twain)
Alexander and the Terrible, Horrible, No
    Good, Very Bad Day (Judith Viorst)
◆ Alice in Wonderland (Lewis Carroll)
◆ The Angel and the Soldier-Boy
    (Peter Collington)
◆ Anne of Green Gables / Anne of Avonlea /
    Anne of the Island
    (Lucy Maud Montgomery)
Any Friend of Nicholas Nickleby Is a Friend
    of Mine (Ray Bradbury)

Arnold of the Ducks (Mordicai Gerstein)
Around the World in Eighty Days
    (Jules Verne)
◆ Babar the Little Elephant
    (Laurent de Brunhoff)
Ballet Shoes (Noel Streatfeild)
◆ Bedknobs and Broomsticks (Mary Norton)
◆ Berenstain Bears series
    (Stan and Jan Berenstain)
Big Red (Jim Kjelgaard)
The Black Arrow (Robert Louis Stevenson)
◆ Black Beauty (Anna Sewell)
◆ The Black Stallion (Walter Farley)
◆ Born Free (Joy Adamson)
◆ The Boy Who Loved Trolls
    ("ofoeti" by John Wheatcroft)
◆ Bridge to Terabithia (Katherine Patterson)
Call of the Wild (Jack London)
The Centerville Ghost (Oscar Wilde)
◆ Charlotte's Web (E.B. White)
◆ Chitty Chitty Bang Bang (Ian Fleming)
Chocolate Fever (Robert Kimmel Smith)
Clowning Around
    (*Clowning Sim*, David Martin)
◆ Curious George (Margaret and H.A. Rey)
◆ The Dragon that Wasn't, Or Was He?
    (translated from the Dutch, Marten
    Toondner)
◆ The Electric Grandmother (Ray Bradbury)
The Elephant's Child
    (*Just So Stories*, Rudyard Kipling)
◆ Emil and the Detectives (Erich Kastner)
◆ Encyclopedia Brown (Donald J. Sobol)
Fantastic Balloon Voyage (Jules Verne)
◆ Ferngully (Diana Young)
Five Lionni Classics: The Animal Fables of
    Leo Lionni (Leo Leonni)
◆ A Girl of the Limberlost
    (Gene Stratton Porter)
The Gold Bug (Edgar Allan Poe)
◆ Granpa (John Burningham)
◆ Gryphon (Charles Baxter)
Gulliver's Travels (Jonathan Swift)
Hamlet (Shakespeare)
Hans Brinker (Mary Mapes Dodge)
◆ Hardy Boys series (Franklin W. Dixon)
◆ The Haunting of Barnes Palmer
    (Margaret Mahy)
Heidi (Johanna Spyri)
The Hoboken Chicken Emergency
    (D. Manus Pinkwater)

The Hobbit (J.R.R. Tolkien)

◆ The House of Dies Drear (Virginia Hamilton)

◆ How to be a Perfect Person In Just Three
   Days (Stephen Manes)

How to Eat Fried Worms (Thomas Rockwell)

How to Raise a Street-Smart Child
   (Grace Hechinger)

◆ The Incredible Journey (Sheila Burnford)

Island of the Blue Dolphins (Scott O'Dell)

Ivanhoe (Sir Walter Scott)

Jacob Have I Loved (Katherine Patterson)

Jacob Two-Two and the Hooded Fang
   (Mordecai Richler)

Journey to the Center of the Earth
   (Jules Verne)

◆ Kidnapped (Robert Louis Stevenson)

◆ The Knights of the Round Table
   (*Le Mort eD'Arthur*, Thomas Mallory)

◆ Konrad (*Konrad ode Das Kind aus
   Konserven-buechse*
   by Christine Noestlinger)

◆ The Land of Faraway (Astrid Lindgren)

◆ Lantern Hill (*Jane of Lantern Hill*,
   Lucy Maud Montgomery)

Lassie Come Home (Eric Knight)

◆ The Last Unicorn (Peter S. Beagle)

The Light in the Forest (Conrad Richter)

The Light Princess (George MacDonald)

◆ The Lion, the Witch and the Wardrobe
   (C.S. Lewis)

◆ The Little Engine That Could (Watty Piper)

Little House on the Prairie series
   (Laura Ingalls Wilder)

Little Lord Fauntleroy
   (Frances Hodgson Burnett)

◆ The Little Mermaid
   (Hans Christian Andersen)

Little Miss Trouble & Friends
   (Roger Hargreaves)

◆ Little Women (Louisa May Alcott)

Looking For Miracles (A.E. Hochner)

◆ Lost in the Barrens (Farley Mowat)

◆ Macbeth (Shakespeare)

◆ Madeline (Ludwig Bemelmans)

◆ Mark Twain and Me
   (*Enchantment*, Dorothy Quick)

◆ Mary Poppins (P.L Travers)

A Midsummer Night's Dream (Shakespeare)

◆ Mike Mulligan and His Steam Shovel
   (Virginia Lee Burton)

◆ Miracle at Moreaux

(*Twenty and Ten* by Claire Huchet Bishop)

The Miracle Worker
   (*The Story of My Life*, Helen Keller)

Misty (*Misty of Chincoteague*,
   Marguerite Henry)

The Moonspinners (Mary Stewart)

The Mouse and His Child (Russell Hoban)

Mr. Men (Roger Hargreaves)

◆ My Friend Flicka (Mary O'Hara)

◆ Mysterious Island (Jules Verne)

◆ Nancy Drew series (Carolyn Keene)

◆ Necessary Parties (Barbara Dana)

◆ Never Cry Wolf (Farley Mowat)

◆ The Neverending Story I, II (Michael Ende)

◆ Old Yeller (Fred Gipson)

Oliver Twist (Charles Dickens)

◆ The Once and Future King (T.H. White)

Paddington Bear series (Michael Bond)

◆ Peter Pan (James Barrie)

◆ The Phantom Tollbooth (Norton Juster)

◆ Pippi Longstocking series (Astrid Lindgren)

◆ The Prince and the Pauper (Mark Twain)

◆ Prince Caspian and the Voyage of the
   Dawn Treader (C.S. Lewis)

◆ The Princess Bride (William Goldman)

◆ The Railway Children (E. Nesbit)

◆ Ramona series (Beverly Cleary)

Rebecca of Sunnybrook Farm
   (Kate Douglas Wiggin)

◆ Ring of Bright Water (Gavin Maxwell)

Robinson Crusoe
   (Robert Louis Stevenson)

Romeo and Juliet

Runaway (*Slakes Limbo* by Felice Holman)

Rupert (Alfred Bestall M.B.E.)

◆ The Secret Garden
   (Frances Hodgson Burnett)

The Secret Life of Walter Mitty
   (James Thurber)

◆ The Secret of N.I.M.H.
   (*Mrs. Frisby and the Rats of N.I.M.H.*,
   Robert C. O'Brien)

◆ The Selfish Giant (Oscar Wilde)

Seven Alone (Honore Morrow)

Shelley Duvall's Bedtime Stories series
   (13 Stories)

The Silver Chair (C.S. Lewis)

◆ The Snowman (Raymond Briggs)

◆ The Swiss Family Robinson
   (Johann David Wyss)

◆ The Sword in the Stone

(*The Once and Future King*, T.H. White)
- The Tale of Peter Rabbit and Benjamin Bunny (Beatrix Potter)
- The Tale of Samuel Whiskers (by Beatrix Potter)

A Tale of Two Cities (Charles Dickens)

The Tempest (Shakespeare)

The Three Musketeers (Alexandre Dumas)
- Thomas the Tank Engine series (The Rev. W. Awdry)
- The Time Machine (H.G. Wells)
- The Three Worlds of Gulliver (*Gulliver's Travels*, Jonathan Swift)

To Sir With Love (E. R. Braithwaite)
- Treasure Island (Robert Louis Stevenson)
- A Tree Grows in Brooklyn (Betty Smith)

Twelfth Night (Shakespeare)

Tuck Everlasting (Natalie Babbitt)
- The Velveteen Rabbit (Margery Williams)

Walking on Air (Ray Bradbury)

A Waltz Through the Hills (G.M. Glaskin)
- Watership Down (Richard Adams)
- Where the Red Fern Grows (Wilson Rawls)
- White Fang (Jack London)
- Who Has Seen the Wind? (W.O. Mitchell)
- Willy Wonka and the Chocolate Factory (*Charlie and the Chocolate Factory*, Roald Dahl)
- Wind in the Willows (Kenneth Graham)

Winds of Change (*The Illiad and the Odyssey*, Homer)
- Winnie-the-Pooh (A.A. Milne)
- The Witches (Roald Dahl)

The Yellow Winton Flyer (*The Reivers*, William Faulkner)

NOTE: The Children's Circle Video Series of 31 videocassettes contains approximately 130 stories, most of them based on books. The Rabbit Ears Series of approximately 39 videos are for the most part based on books, stories or legends.

 Battle scenes

This list was compiled at the request of a nine-year-old boy interested in the way armies make formations. Films that were considered too violent and Restricted films were not included.

- Bedknobs and Broomsticks

Heaven and Earth

Kagemusha

Khartoum
- The Incredible Mr. Limpet

Lawrence of Arabia

The Silk Road

Waterloo

 Bible stories

Bible Heroes

Children's Heroes of the Bible: The Story of Jesus Part 1

Children's Heroes of the Bible: The Story of Jesus Part 2

Great Bible Stories:
  David and Goliath
  Noah's Ark
  Abraham
  Moses
  The Apostle Paul
  The Story of Peter

Hanna-Barbera's Greatest Adventure Stories from the Bible series

One Minute Bible Stories (New Testament)

One Minute Bible Stories (Old Testament)

Our Dwelling Place: The Birth of Jesus

Our Dwelling Place: The Trial of Jesus

Rabbit Ears: The Greatest Stories Ever Told
  David and Goliath
  Jonah and the Whale
  Noah and the Ark
  The Savior is Born

 Camp

- Ernest Goes to Camp
- Kidsongs: A Day at Camp
- Looking for Miracles
- The Parent Trap
- Poison Ivy

 Canadian films/Videos

- The Challengers

Cirque du Solei: Circus of the Sun

La Magie Continues
Nouvelle Experience
We Reinvent the Circus
+ Curse of the Viking Grave
+ Lantern Hill
+ Lost In the Barrens
+ The Mystery of the Million Dollar Hockey
   Puck
+ Tales for All series
+ Toby McTeague
Tucker and the Horse Thief
+ White Fang
+ Who Has Seen the Wind?
+ The Wild Pony

 Canadian settings

+ Anne of Green Gables
+ Anne of Green Gables: The Sequel
+ Big Red
+ Curse of the Viking Grave
+ George's Island
+ Lantern Hill
+ Looking for Miracles
+ Lost in the Barrens
+ The Mystery of the Million Dollar Hockey
   Puck
+ Never Cry Wolf
+ Road to Avonlea
+ Tales for all Series
+ Toby McTeague
+ Who Has Seen the Wind?

 Christmas

Alvin and the Chipmunks:
   A Chipmunk Christmas
An American Christmas Carol
Babar and Father Christmas
+ Babes In Toyland
+ Babysongs Christmas
The Bear Who Slept Through Christmas
Bells of St. Marys
Benji's Very Own Christmas Story
Berenstain Bears Christmas Tree
Bugs Bunny's Looney Christmas Tales
Cabbage Patch Kids Christmas
Cartoon Holidays Featuring Betty Boop
+ A Charlie Brown Christmas
+ A Child's Christmas in Wales
+ A Christmas Carol

Christmas Eve on Sesame Street
+ A Christmas Sing-along
+ A Christmas Story
+ A Christmas Tree
+ A Currier and Ives Christmas
+ A Disney Christmas Gift
Dot and Santa Claus
+ Ernest Saves Christmas
+ A Family Circus Christmas
For Better or Worse: Bestest Present Ever
Frosty the Snowman
Garfield's Christmas
George and the Christmas Star
The Gift of Winter
Gumby's Holiday Special
Hanna-Barbera's Christmas Sing-a-long
Here Comes Santa Claus
+ Home Alone
The Homecoming
   (premiere episode of *The Waltons*)
A House Without A Christmas Tree
How The Flintstones Saved Christmas
How The Grinch Stole Christmas
It's a Wonderful Life
Jack Frost
+ A Jetson Christmas Carol
Jiminy Cricket's Christmas
Jingle Bell Rap
+ The Little Crooked Christmas Tree
Little Drummer Boy
The Littlest Angel
+ A Merry Mirthworm Christmas
Madeline's Christmas
MGM Cartoon Magic: Peace on Earth
Mickey's Christmas Carol
Miracle on 34th Street
The Nativity
Nutcracker: The Motion Picture
+ The Nutcracker Prince
+ One Magic Christmas
Pee Wee's Christmas Special
+ A Pink Panther Christmas
Pinocchio's Christmas
+ Prancer
Rudolph and Frosty's Christmas in July
Rudolph the Red-Nosed Reindeer
Rudolph's Shiny New Year
Santa Claus Is Coming to Town
Santa Claus: The Movie
Santabear's First Christmas
Santabear's High Flying Adventure

Scrooge
Scrooged
Shari's Christmas Concert
The Simpsons' Christmas Special
The Small One
The Snowman
'Twas the Night Before Christmas
Very Merry Christmas Songs
* A Very Merry Cricket
* A Walt Disney Christmas
Wee Sing: Best Christmas Ever
Where The Toys Come From
White Christmas
* A Year Without Santa
Yogi Bear's All-Star Comedy Christmas
   Caper

 The Circus

115th Edition of Barnum & Bailey Ringling
   Brothers Circus
116th Edition of Barnum & Bailey Ringling
   Brothers Circus (featuring the Shanghai
   Acrobats)
Big Cats of the Big Top
* Big Top Pee-Wee
Cirque de Soleil:
   Circus of the Sun
   La Magie Continues
   Nouvelle Experience
   We Reinvent the Circus
* Kidsongs: A Day at the Circus
Most Death Defying Acts of All Time
* National Geographic: The Soviet Circus

 **Combined live-action
         and animation**

* Bedknobs and Broomsticks
The Dot series (Dot and Keeto; Dot and the
   Whale; Dot Goes to Hollywood; Dot and
   the Bunny, etc.)
Dunder Klumpen
* Jack and the Beanstalk
The Light Princess
* Mary Poppins
* Pete's Dragon
* The Snow Queen
* So Dear to My Heart
* Three Caballeros
* Who Framed Roger Rabbit?

 Dance, opera and music

Amahl and the Night Visitors (opera)
An Evening With Danny Kaye:
   Danny Kaye Conducts the New York
   Philharmonic with Zubin Mehta
Backstage at the Kirov (ballet)
Ballet Class for Beginners: David Howard
Ballet Shoes
The Children of Theatre Street (ballet)
El Amor Brujo (flamenco)
A Fantasy Garden Ballet Class
Flamenco at 5:15
I Can Dance (ballet)
The Little Humpbacked Horse (ballet)
The Nutcracker with Baryshnikov and
   Kirkland (ballet)
Nutcracker: The Motion Picture (ballet)
Saint-Saen's Carnival of Animals (orchestra)
Ustinov Reads the Orchestra
Who's Afraid of Opera? with Joan
   Sutherland

 Dinosaurs and dragons

Adventures in Dinosaur City
* Baby, Secret of the Lost Legend
* Barney and the Backyard Gang Series
* Denver the Last Dinosaur series
Dinosaur! A Fun-filled Trip Back in Time!
Dinosaur! An Amazing Look at the
   Prehistoric Giants
Dinosaurs, Dinosaurs, Dinosaurs
Dinosaurus! Stone Age Monsters
   Return to Life
* The Dragon That Wasn't (or Was He?)
Dragonslayer
Flight of Dragons
The Infinite Voyage: The Great Dinosaur
   Hunt
* Jurassic Park
* The Land Before Time
The Last of the Red Hot Dragons
Mister Roger's Dinosaurs and Monsters
More Dinosaurs
PBS Dinosaur Series:
   Flesh on the Bones
   The Death of the Dinosaur
   The Monsters Emerge
   The Nature of the Beast
* Pete's Dragon
Planet of the Dinosaurs

- Polka Dot Door: Dinosaurs
  Prehistoric World
  Puff the Magic Dragon
  The Railway Dragon
  Reading Rainbow: Digging Up Dinosaurs
  The Reluctant Dragon
  Return of the Dinosaurs
- Sleeping Beauty (dragon)
  We Are the Dinosaurs
  Whatever Happened to the Dinosaurs?
  The Wonders of Earth and Space
  The World's Greatest Dinosaur Video

 Dogs

- Beethoven
  Benji
- Benji the Hunted
- Big Red
- Bingo
  Challenge to Lassie
  The Courage of Rin Tin Tin
- Digby, The Biggest Dog in the World
  The Dog Care Video Guide
  A Dog of Flanders
  Flipper's New Adventure
  For The Love of Benji
  The Great Adventure
  Homeward Bound: The Incredible Journey
- The Incredible Journey
  Lassie Come Home
  Lassie's Greatest Adventure
- Little Heroes
  The Magic of Lassie
- Milo and Otis
  Oh Heavenly Dog
- Old Yeller
  Rin Tin Tin In The Paris Conspiracy
- The Shaggy D.A.
- The Shaggy Dog
  Toby McTeague
- Where the Red Fern Grows

 Easter

The Adventures of Little Koala and Friends:
  Laura and the Mystery Egg
The Berenstain Bears' Easter Surprise
Bil Keane's A Family Circus Easter
Bobby Goldsboro's Easter Egg Mornin'
Bugs Bunny's Easter Funnies

Buttons and Rusty and the Easter Bunny
Daffy Duck's Easter Egg-citement
The Easter Bunny Is Coming to Town
Greatest Adventure Stories from the Bible:
  The Easter Story
Here Comes Peter Cottontail
It's the Easter Beagle, Charlie Brown
Peter and the Magic Egg
- Teenage Mutant Ninja Turtles:
  The Turtles' Awesome Easter
  Welcome Back Wil Cwac Cwac
  The World of David the Gnome: Rabbits,
  Rabbits, Everywhere!

 English not required (videos that explain themselves)

Most ballets and cartoons also work well with these viewers.

- The Angel and the Soldier Boy
- Disney's Singalong series
- Granpa
- Lyric Language French/English series
- Nutcracker: The Motion Picture
- The Red Balloon
  Sign Me-A-Story
- The Snowman

 Family movies (even parents will enjoy!)

- Adventures in Babysitting
- The Adventures of Baron Munchausen
  Amazing Grace and Chuck
- Back to the Future I, II, III
  batteries not included
- Better Off Dead
  Bill and Ted's Bogus Journey
  Bill and Ted's Excellent Adventure
- The Boy Who Could Fly
- Defense Play
  Dragonslayer
- E.T.
- Explorers
- Ferris Bueller's Day Off
- The Gods Must Be Crazy I, II
- The Goonies
- Harry and the Hendersons
- Home Alone I
- Home Alone II: Lost in New York
- Honey, I Blew Up the Kid
- Honey, I Shrunk the Kids
- Hook

- The Incredible Journey
- The Karate Kid I, II, III
- Labyrinth
- Lady Jane
- Ladyhawke
- Legend
- License to Drive
- Lionheart
- Looking For Miracles
- Lucas
- Maid-to-Order
- The Man From Snowy River
- Milo and Otis
  Monster Squad
- Mysterious Island
- The Neverending Story I, II
- One Magic Christmas
- Pee-Wee's Big Adventure
  Pure Luck
  Raising Arizona
- Real Genius
  The Rescue
- Russkies
- Spacecamp
- Stand and Deliver
- Star Trek I, II, III, IV,V,VI
- Star Wars trilogy
- Superman I, II, III, IV
- Swiss Family Robinson
- Three Amigos
  Three Men and a Baby
- Three Men and a Little Lady
  Top Gun
- Treasure Island
- Willow
- Willy Wonka and the Chocolate Factory
- The Wizard of Oz
- Young Einstein
- Young Sherlock Holmes

 Fitness

American Junior Workout
- Baby's First Workout
- Dance! Workout with Barbie
  Funfit: Mary Lou Retton Workout
- Funhouse Fitness: The Funhouse Funk
- Funhouse Fitness: The Swamp Stomp
  Kids In Motion
- Mousercise
  Teen Steam with Alyssa Milano

The Teen Workout
Tip Top With Suzy Prudden: Ages 3-6
Tip Top With Suzy Prudden:
  Ages 7 and Over
Workout With Daddy and Me
Workout With Mommy and Me:
  Ages 3 and Up
You and Me Kid (Vol. 4'

 Ghosts

- Blackbeard's Ghost
- The Burbs
- The Canterville Ghost
- Escape to Witch Mountain
- Frankenweenie
- George's Island
  Ghost Chase
- Ghost Dad
- Ghostbusters, Ghostbusters II
- The Legend of Sleepy Hollow
  (many versions)
  Lonesome Ghosts
- The Peanut Butter Solution
  Topper

 Halloween (scary movies)

- The Boy Who Left Home to Learn About the
  Shivers
  Bugs Bunny's Hallowe'en Special
  Buttons and Rusty and the Halloween Party
  in Which Witch is Which?
  Campfire Thrillers
- Disney's Cartoon Classics Vol. 13:
  Donald's Scary Tales
- Disney's Cartoon Classics Vol. 14:
  Halloween Haunts
- E.T.: The Extra-Terrestrial
- Ernest Scared Stupid
  Garfield's Halloween Adventure
  Ghostly Thrillers
  Grandpa's Silly Scaries
  The Great Bear Scare
  Halloween is Grinch Night
  It's the Great Pumpkin, Charlie Brown
  The Legend of Sleepy Hollow
  The Monster Squad
- Spaced Invaders
- Watcher in the Woods

Horses

150 Years of the Grand National
Black Beauty
- The Black Stallion
- Black Stallion Returns
  Dark Horse
  The Horsemasters
  International Velvet
- Legend of the White Horse
- The Man From Snowy River
  Misty
- The Moon Stallion
  My Friend Flicka
  National Velvet
  The New Adventures of Black Beauty
  Phar Lap
  Prince and the Great Race
- Return to Snowy River
  Ride A Wild Pony
  Stephanie Powers' Introduction to
    Horseback Riding and Horsecare
  Summer of the Colt
  Sylvester
  White Mane

 "How to" videos/interactive videos

Baseball the Pete Rose Way
Blockbuster Magic
Cooking With Dad
The Dog Care Video Guide
Gymnastics Fun with Bela Karolyi
Here's Howe! (Hockey with Gordie Howe)
Hey, What About Me?: A Video Guide for
  Brothers and Sisters of New Babies
Hockey for Kids and Coaches
Hockey My Way: Wayne Gretzky
How to Raise a Street-Smart Child
Karate for Kids
Ken Dryden series
Kids Get Cooking: The Egg
- Let's Get a Move On!
- Let's Build
- Let's Draw
- Look What I Found
- Look What I Grew
- Look What I Made
  My First Activity Video
  My First Cooking Video
  My First Green Video
- My First Musical Instrument

My First Nature Video
My First Science Video
Neat Stuff to Know and Do
- Shari Lewis: Lamb Chop's Play Along!
  Jokes, Riddles, Knock-Knocks and
    Funny Poems
  Betchas, Tricks and Silly Stunts
  Action Songs
  Action Stories
- Shari Lewis Presents: 101 Things To Do
  Stephanie Powers' Introduction to
    Horseback Riding and Horse Care
  Wayne Gretzky: Above and Beyond
  Wayne Gretzky: Hockey My Way

 Kids making a difference/ overcoming difficulties

Amazing Grace and Chuck
  (global social reform)
Brother Sun, Sister Moon (religious reform)
- The Challengers (sexual discrimination)
  Dark Horse (wheelchair-bound due to
    accident)
- A Girl of the Limberlost (poverty)
  Heidi (character overcomes illness)
- Lady Jane (political and social justice)
  Let the Balloon Go
    (overcoming physical handicap)
- Lost in the Barrens (racial prejudice)
  Love Leads the Way (character is blind)
- Mac and Me
    (character is wheelchair-bound)
  Mask (living with a handicap)
  The Miracle Worker
    (deafness, blindness, no speech)
  Romeo and Juliet
    (seeing beyond hatred and prejudice)
- The Secret Garden
    (character overcomes illness)
  Seven Alone
    (overcoming pioneering hardships)
- Stand and Deliver
    (culturally disadvantaged)
- A Summer to Remember (no speech)
  Walking on Air
    (character is wheelchair-bound)
  Wild Hearts Can't Be Broken
    (character is blind)

Knights/ Medieval times

The Adventures of Robin Hood
Black Arrow
Dragonslayer
Ivanhoe
◆ Knights of the Round Table
◆ Ladyhawke
◆ Lionheart
Prince Valiant
◆ Robin Hood: the Movie
The Story of Robin Hood
The Sword and the Rose

 Learning a Language

The BBC Language Course for Children
 (French, German, Italian, Spanish)
◆ Lyric Language French/English
Spanish Club: ¡ Fiesta!

The making of...

Classic Creatures: *Return of the Jedi*
From *Star Wars* to *Jedi*:
 The Making of a Saga
Great Adventurers and Their Quests:
 Indiana Jones and the Last Crusade
Great Movie Stunts and the Making of
 Raiders of the Lost Ark
◆ The Illusion of Life:
 The Wonderful World of Disney
Inside the Labyrinth:
 The making of the film *Labyrinth*
The Making of *Star Wars*/SP FX *The*
 Empire Strikes Back
The Making of *Teenage Mutant Ninja*
 Turtles: Behind the Scenes
Movie Magic
◆ The Plausible Impossible:
 The Wonderful World of Disney
Secrets of *Back to the Future* Trilogy
Work in Progress: Beauty and the Beast

 Mother's day

The Bugs Bunny Mother's Day Special

 Musicals

◆ The 5000 Fingers of Dr. T.
◆ Annie
◆ Babes in Toyland
◆ Bedknobs and Broomsticks

◆ Cannon Movietales series
◆ Chitty Chitty Bang Bang
◆ Cinderella (Rodgers and Hammerstein)
The Court Jester
◆ Disney's Singalong series
Doctor Doolittle
The Glass Slipper
◆ Grease I, II
◆ The Great Muppet Caper
The Happiest Millionaire
Jim Henson's Muppet Video series
The King and I
◆ The Little Prince
◆ Mary Poppins
The Muppet Movie
◆ The Muppets Take Manhattan
◆ The New Adventures of Pippi Longstocking
◆ Newsies
Oliver!
The One and Only Genuine Original
 Family Band
◆ Peter Pan
◆ Pete's Dragon
Popeye
◆ Sebastian's Caribbean Jamboree
◆ Sebastian's Party Gras
Singing in the Rain
◆ The Sound of Music
Summer Magic
That's Dancing
That's Entertainment I, II
◆ Willy Wonka and the Chocolate Factory

 Mysteries

Almost Partners
Benji
◆ Cloak and Dagger
◆ Condorman
◆ Crystalstone
The Double McGuffin
The Edison Twins
◆ Emil and the Detectives
◆ Encyclopedia Brown
 One Minute Mysteries
 Missing Time Capsule)
The Golden Treasure
◆ The Goonies
◆ The Hardy Boys series
◆ The Moon Stallion
◆ The Moonspinners

- The Mystery of the Million Dollar Hockey Puck
- Nancy Drew series
  Oh Heavenly Dog
- The Quest
- Sharon, Lois and Bram Elephant Show: Mysteries (Vol.1)
- The Treasure
- The Undercover Gang
  Young Detectives on Wheels

 Parties for boys

- Adventures in Dinosaur City
  Boris and Natasha
- Clash of the Titans
- Mom and Dad Save the World
  Monster Squad
- Mysterious Island
  Rad
- Real Genius
  Shark: The True Story
- Shipwrecked
- Spacecamp
- Spaceballs
- Spaced Invaders
- The Three Ninjas
  War Games

 Parties for girls

- Annie
- Beethoven
- Candleshoe
- The Challengers
- Frog
- Girls Just Want To Have Fun
- Grease I, II
- The Incredible Journey
- Labyrinth
- Maid-to-Order
- The New Adventures of Pippi Longstocking
- The Night Train to Kathmandu
- The Parent Trap
  Poison Ivy
- Rags to Riches
  Ramona
- Reach for the Sky
- Road to Avonlea
- The Three Lives of Thomasina

- The Trouble With Angels
  Three Men and a Baby
- Troop Beverly Hills
  Wild Hearts Can't Be Broken
  Who's That Girl?

 Parties for girls and boys

- 20,000 Leagues Under the Sea
- Adventures in Babysitting
- Baby, Secret of the Lost Legend
- Back to the Future I, II, III
- Beethoven
- Cloak and Dagger
- Defense Play
- The Dirt Bike Kid
- Explorers
- Godzilla movies
  The Great Whales
  In Search of the Titanic (National Geographic)
- Jason and the Argonauts
  King Kong
  The Land of Faraway
- The Love Bug
- Mac and Me
- Mysterious Island
  Rad
  Radical Moves
- The Seventh Voyage of Sinbad
  Sharks: The True Story
  Short Circuit I, II
- Sinbad and the Eye of the Tiger
- Spacecamp
- Star Wars I, II, III
  Suburban Commando
- Superman
- Wizards of the Lost Kingdom

 Pirates

- Blackbeard's Ghost
  The Crimson Pirate
- George's Island
- The Goonies
- Hook
- Kidnapped
  Long John Silver
- Peter Pan (Disney)
- Peter Pan (with Mary Martin)
  The Pirate Movie

The Pirates of Penzance
- Shipwrecked
- Treasure Island (various versions)

 Positive female role-models

- Adventures in Babysitting
  Almost Partners
- Anne of Green Gables
- Annie
- The Baby-Sitters Club
  Ballet Shoes
- Better Off Dead
  Born Free
- The Boy Who Could Fly
  Brother Sun, Sister Moon
- The Canterville Ghost
- The Challengers
  Courage Mountain
- Don't Tell Mom the Babysitter's Dead
- Far And Away
- Ferngully
- The Frog Prince (Cannon Movietales)
- Girl of the Limberlost
- Hook
- The Journey of Natty Gann
- Labyrinth
- Lady Jane
- The Man From Snowy River
  The Miracle Worker
  The Moon Stallion
  The Moonspinners
- The New Adventures of Pippi Longstocking
- Pollyanna
  Prince and the Great Race
- The Quest
  Ramona
- Reach for the Sky
- Return to Oz
- Road to Avonlea
- The Secret Garden
- Shipwrecked
- Spacecamp
- Stand and Deliver
- Star Wars trilogy
- The Tadpole and the Whale
  A Tree Grows in Brooklyn
- Vincent and Me
  Wild Hearts Can't Be Broken
- The Wizard
  Young Detectives on Wheels

- Young Einstein
- Young Sherlock Holmes

 Retrospectives (movies about adults recalling childhood)

We do not recommend these for children! Just because there are children in these films doesn't mean they are suitable for children's viewing.

Desert Bloom
Dreamchild
Empire of the Sun
Fanny and Alexander
Hope and Glory
My Life as a Dog
Radio Flyer
Stand By Me
Zelly and Me

 Robots and computers

- And You Thought Your Parents Were Weird
- D.A.R.Y.L.
- Explorers
  Forbidden Planet
  Konrad
- National Geographic:
  Miniature Miracle. The Computer Chip
- Real Genius
  Robbie the Robot
  Short Circuit I, II
  War Games
  Weird Science

 Safety

A Cannon Movietale:
  Little Red Riding Hood
Baby Alive: EmergencyTreatment/Accident
  Prevention
Berenstain Bears Learn About Strangers
Bicycle Safety Camp
Cartoon All-Stars to the Rescue
Dr. Lee Salk: Supersitters Basics
Home Alone:
  A Kids Guide to Playing It Safe
How to Raise a Street Smart Child
It's O.K. to Say No to Drugs
Kid Safe

Kids Have Rights Too
Let's Sing and Dance Music Video
Never Talk to Strangers
The Right Thing to Do
* Shelley Duvall's Faerie Tale Theatre:
   Little Red Riding Hood
Strong Kids, Safe Kids
* Too Smart for Strangers:
   Winnie-the-Pooh

 Scary sleep-over movies
The Birds
* The Canterville Ghost
Dragonslayer
* Ernest Scared Stupid
The Fly (1958)
* Frankenweenie
* Ghost Dad
* Ghostbusters I, II
* The Goonies
* Indiana Jones and the Last Crusade
* Indiana Jones and the Temple of Doom
* Ladyhawke
* The Last Starfighter
* Legend
* Little Monsters
Monster Squad
The Mummy (1958)
* My Science Project
* Mysterious Island
* Raiders of the Lost Ark
The Rescue
Scrooge
* Something Wicked This Way Comes
* Treasure Island (1990)
* Watcher in the Woods
* Willow
* Young Sherlock Holmes

 School
The Blackboard Jungle
The Children of Theatre Street
Dead Poets Society
The King and I
* Lambada
* Lean On Me
The Miracle Worker
* Stand and Deliver
To Sir With Love

 Science and ecology
* 3-2-1-Contact: Bottom of the Barrel
* 3-2-1-Contact: Down the Drain
* 3-2-1-Contact: The Rotten Truth
Carl Sagan: Cosmos
The Earth Day Special
Help Save Planet Earth
Ida Fanfanny and Three Magical Tales
The Miracle of Life
Mr. Wizard's World: Air and Water Wizardry
Mr. Wizard's World: Puzzles, Problems and
   Impossibilities
* National Geographic:
   The Incredible Human Machine
   The Incredible Invisible World
   Miniature Miracle —The Computer Chip
   Rain Forest
The Tell Me Why series
The Wonders of Earth and Space

 Sex education
Goldie and Kids
What Kids Want to Know About Sex and
   Growing Up
What's Happening to Me?:
   A Guide to Puberty
Where Did I Come From?

 Sign language
Musign
Say It By Signing
Sign Me-A-Story

 Space (fiction and non-fiction)
batteries not included
The Black Hole
Buckaroo Banzai
Close Encounters of the Third Kind
* E.T.
* The Empire Strikes Back
* Explorers
* Flight of the Navigator
* Forbidden Planet
An Incredible Odyssey
* The Last Starfighter
* Mac and Me
NASA: The First 25 Years
Nukie

352

- Return of the Jedi
- Spaceballs
- Spacecamp
- Spaced Invaders
- Star Trek I, II, III, IV, V, VI
- Star Wars
  Supergirl
- Superman I, II, III, IV
  War of the Worlds
  The Wonders of Earth and Space

 Sports (fiction and non-fiction)

- The Absent Minded Professor
  (basketball)
  Amazing Grace and Chuck (basketball)
  Bad News Bears (baseball)
  Bad News Bears Go to Japan (baseball)
  Bad News Bears in Breaking Training
  (baseball)
  Baseball the Pete Rose Way (baseball)
- Better Off Dead (skiing)
  Breaking Away (bicycling)
  The Court Jester (sword-fighting)
  Days of Thunder (car racing)
- The Dirt Bike Kid
  Herbie Goes to Monte Carlo (car racing)
  Hockey for Kids and Coaches
  Hockey My Way: Wayne Gretzky
  Hoosiers (basketball)
  The Juggler of Notre Dame (juggling)
- The Karate Kid I, II, III (martial arts)
  Ken Dryden series (hockey)
  Ladybugs (baseball)
- Mystery of the Million Dollar Hockey
  Puck (hockey)
  Popeye (boxing)
- The Princess Bride (sword-fighting)
  RAD (BMX Biking)
  Radical Moves (skateboarding)
- Reach for the Sky (gymnastics)
- Robin Hood (archery)
- Teen Wolf (basketball)
- Teen Wolf Too (boxing)
  The Three Musketeers (sword-fighting)
  Tigertown (baseball)
  Toby McTeague (dog-sledding)
  Wayne Gretzky:
    Above and Beyond (hockey)

 Thanksgiving

Bugs Bunny's Thanksgiving Diet
Garfield's Thanksgiving

 Valentine's day

Be My Valentine, Charlie Brown
Berenstain Bears: Cupid's Surprise
Big Screen Sweethearts
Bugs Bunny: Cupids Capers
Courtin' Cut-Ups
Dino and Juliet
Fred Flintstone Woos Again
Rompin' Romance

 Vehicles

- 20,000 Leagues Under the Sea (submarines)
- The Absent Minded Professor (antique car)
  Chitty Chitty Bang Bang (antique car)
  The Great Locomotive Chase (trains)
  The Great Race (antique car)
- Ivor the Engine (trains)
- Jimbo and the Jet Set
- Kidsongs: Cars, Boats, Trains and Planes
- National Geographic: Love Those Trains
- The Railway Children (trains)
- Russkies (submarines)
- Thomas the Tank Engine series (trains)
  Trains, Trucks and Boats

 Witches

A Cannon Movietale: Hansel and Gretel
A Cannon Movietale: Snow White
- East of the Sun, West of the Moon
- The Lion, the Witch and the Wardrobe
- Shelley Duvall's Faerie Tale Theatre:
    Hansel and Gretel
- Sleeping Beauty
- The Snow Queen
- The Three Lives of Thomasina
- The Witches
- The Wizard of Oz

Movies not made for children that children love

This list contains titles that are popular with children between the ages of 0 and 13. Interestingly, they all contain similar elements — either a baby or young child as the focus; a bumbling or incompetent adult or adults not in control of the situation; an animal (preferably a cute one); or a child getting the better of an adult. Please note the ratings of these films before showing them to a young child.

Arachnophobia
* Baby, Secret of the Lost Legend
* Batman
* Beetlejuice
* Better Off Dead
* Big Man On Campus
* Edward Scissorhands
* Ferris Bueller's Day Off
* Gremlins
* Home Alone I
* Home Alone II: Lost in New York
King Ralph

* License to Drive
Look Who's Talking
Look Who's Talking Too
Mr. Mom
Naked Gun
Naked Gun 2-and-a-half
* The Princess Bride
Problem Child I, II
Pure Luck
Raising Arizona
* Spaceballs
Splash
Stand By Me
* Strange Brew
* Three Amigos
Three Men and a Baby
* Three Men and a Little Lady
Time Bandits
Top Gun
* Troop Beverly Hills
* UHF
* Uncle Buck
* Vice Versa
* What About Bob?
* Who Framed Roger Rabbit?
Who's that Girl?

INDEX OF VIDEOS

A

B

E

P

Q
R

T

FOR THE BABYSITTER
Videos we are saving for your visit

_____   _____

_____   _____

_____   _____

_____   _____

_____   _____

_____   _____

_____   _____

_____   _____

_____   _____

_____   _____

_____   _____

_____   _____

_____   _____

_____   _____

_____   _____

_____   _____

_____   _____

_____   _____

_____   _____